The Collected Supernatural and Weird Fiction of Hugh Walpole Volume 1

The Collected Supernatural and Weird Fiction of Hugh Walpole Volume 1

One Novel 'The Old Ladies' and Fifteen Short Stories of the Strange and Unusual Including 'The White Cat', 'Lizzie Rand', 'Mrs. Porter and Miss Allen', 'The Tiger' and 'The Twisted Inn'

Hugh Walpole

LEONAUR

The Collected
Supernatural and Weird
Fiction of
Hugh Walpole
Volume 1
One Novel 'The Old Ladies' and Fifteen Short Stories of the Strange and Unusual
Including 'The White Cat', 'Lizzie Rand', 'Mrs. Porter and Miss Allen', 'The Tiger'
and 'The Twisted Inn'
by Hugh Walpole

FIRST EDITION

Leonaur is an imprint of Oakpast Ltd

Copyright in this form © 2018 Oakpast Ltd

ISBN: 978-1-78282-702-3 (hardcover)
ISBN: 978-1-78282-703-0 (softcover)

http://www.leonaur.com

Publisher's Notes

The views expressed in this book are not necessarily
those of the publisher.

Contents

Mrs. Porter and Miss Allen

One of the largest flats on the fourth floor of Hortons was taken in March 1919 by a Mrs. Porter, a widow. The flat was seen, and all business in connection with it was done, by a Miss Allen, her lady companion. Mr. Nix, who considered himself a sound and trenchant judge of human nature, liked Miss Allen from the first; and then when he saw Mrs. Porter he liked her too. These were just the tenants for Hortons—modest, gentle ladies with ample means and no extravagant demands on human nature. Mrs. Porter was one of those old ladies, now, alas, in our turbulent times, less and less easy to discover—"something straight out of a book," Mr. Nix called her.

She was little and fragile, dressed in silver grey, forehead puckered a little with a sort of anticipation of being a trial to others, her voice cultured, soft, a little remote like the chime of a distant clock. She moved with gestures a little deprecatory, a little resigned, extremely modest—she would not disturb anyone for the world. . . . Miss Allen was, of course, another type—a woman of perhaps forty years of age, refined, quiet, efficient, her dark hair, turning now a little grey, waved decorously from her high white forehead, pince-nez, eyes of a grave, considering brown, a woman resigned, after, it might be, abandoning young ambitions for a place of modest and decent labour in the world—one might still see, in the rather humorous smile that she bestowed once and again upon men and things, the hint of defiance at the necessity that forced abnegation.

Miss Allen had not been in Mrs. Porter's service for very long. Wearied with the exactions of a family of children whose idle and uninspiring intelligences she was attempting to governess, she answered, at the end of 1918, an advertisement in the "Agony" column of *The Times*, that led her to Mrs. Porter. She loved Mrs. Porter at first sight. ' Why, she's a dear old lady," she exclaimed to her ironic spirit—"dear old ladies" being in those days as rare as crinolines. She was of the kind for which Miss Allen had unconsciously been, looking: generous, gentle, refined, and intelligent Moreover, she had, within the last six months, been left quite alone in the world—Mr. Porter had died of apoplexy in August 1918. He had left her very wealthy, and Miss Allen discovered quickly in the old lady a rather surprising desire to see and enjoy life—surprising, because old ladies of seventy-one years of age and of Mrs. Porter's gentle appearance do not, as a rule, care for noise and bustle and the buzz of youthful energy.

"I want to be in the very middle of things, dear Miss Allen," said Mrs. Porter, "right in the very middle. We lived at Wimbledon long enough, Henry and I—it wasn't good for either of us. Find me somewhere within two minutes of all the best theatres."

Miss Allen found Hortons, which is, as everyone knows, in Duke Street, just behind Piccadilly and Fortnum and Mason's, and Hatchard's and the Hammam Turkish Baths and the Royal Academy and Scott's hat-shop and Jackson's Jams—how could you be more perfectly in the centre of London?

Then Miss Allen discovered a curious thing—namely, that Mrs. Porter did not wish to keep a single piece, fragment, or vestige of her Wimbledon effects. She insisted on an auction—everything was sold. Miss Allen attempted a remonstrance—some of the things in the Wimbledon house were very fine, handsome, solid mid-Victorian sideboards and cupboards, and chairs and tables.

"You really have no idea, Mrs. Porter," said Miss Allen, "of the cost of furniture these days. It is quite terrible; you will naturally get a wonderful price for your things, but the difficulty of buying—"

Mrs. Porter was determined. She nodded her bright bird-like head, tapped with her delicate fingers on the table and smiled at Miss Allen.

"If you don't mind, dear. I know it's tiresome for you, but I have my reasons." It was not tiresome at all for Miss Allen; she loved to buy pretty new things at someone else's expense, but it was now, for the first time, that she began to wonder how dearly Mrs. Porter had loved her husband.

Through the following weeks this became her principal preoccupation—Mr. Henry Porter. She could not have explained to herself why this was. She was not, by nature, an inquisitive and scandal-loving woman, nor was she unusually imaginative. People did not, as a rule, occur to her as existing unless she saw them physically there in front of her. Nevertheless, she spent a good deal of her time in considering

Mr. Porter.

She was able to make the Horton flat very agreeable. Mrs. Porter wanted "life and colour," so the sitting-room had curtains with pink roses and a bright yellow cage with two canaries, and several pretty water-colours, and a handsome fire-screen with golden peacocks, and a deep Turkish carpet, soft and luxurious to the feet. Not one thing from the Wimbledon house was there, not any single picture of Mr. Porter. The next thing that Miss Allen discovered was that Mrs. Porter was nervous.

Although Hortons sheltered many human beings within its boundaries, it was, owing to the thickness of its walls and the beautiful training of Mr. Nix's servants, a very quiet place. It had been even called in its day "cloistral." It simply shared with London that amazing and never-to-be-overlauded gift of being able to offer, in the very centre of the traffic of the world, little green spots of quiet and tranquillity. It seemed, after a week or two, that it was almost too quiet for Mrs. Porter.

"Open a window, Lucy dear, won't you," she said. "I like to hear the omnibuses."

It was a chill evening in early April, but Miss Allen threw up the window. They sat there listening. There was no sound, only suddenly, as though to accentuate the silence, St. James's Church clock struck the quarter. Then an omnibus rumbled, rattled, and was gone. The room was more silent than before.

"Shall I read to you?" said Miss Allen.

"Yes, dear, do." And they settled down to *Martin Chuzzlewit*.

Mrs. Porter's apprehensiveness became more and more evident. She was so dear an old lady, and had won so completely Miss Allen's heart, that that kindly woman could not bear to see her suffer. For the first time in her life she wanted to ask questions. It seemed to her that there must be some very strange reason for Mrs. Porter's silences. She was not by nature a silent old lady; she talked continually, seemed, indeed, positively to detest the urgency of silence. She especially loved to tell Miss Allen about her early days. She had grown up as a girl in Plymouth, and she could remember all the events of that time—the balls, the walks on the Hoe, the shops, the summer visits into Glebeshire, the old dark house with the high garden walls, the cuckoo clock and the pictures of the strange old ships in which her father, who was a retired sea-captain, had sailed.

She could not tell Miss Allen enough about these things, but so soon as she arrived at her engagement to Mr. Porter there was silence. London shrouded her married life with its thick, grey pall. She hated that Miss Allen should leave her. She was very generous about Miss Allen's freedom, always begging her to take an afternoon or evening and amuse herself with her own friends; but Miss Allen had very few friends, and on her return from an expedition she always found the old lady miserable, frightened, and bewildered. She found that she loved her, that she cared for her as she had cared for no human being for many years, so she stayed with her and read to her and talked to her, and saw less and less of the outside world.

The two ladies made occasionally an expedition to a theatre or a concert, but these adventures, although they were anticipated with eagerness and pleasure, were always in the event disappointing. Mrs. Porter loved the theatre; especially did she adore plays of sentiment—plays where young people were happily united, where old people sat cosily together reminiscing over a blazing fire, where surly guardians were suddenly generous, and poor orphan girls were unexpectedly given fortunes.

Mrs. Porter started her evening with eager excitement. She dressed for the occasion, putting on her best lace cap, her cameo brooch, her smartest shoes. A taxi came for them, and they always had the best stalls, near the front, so that the old lady should not miss a word. Miss Allen noticed, however, that very quickly Mrs. Porter began to be disturbed. She would glance around the theatre and soon her colour would fade, her hands begin to tremble; then, perhaps at the end of the first act, perhaps later, a little hand would press Miss Allen's arm:

"I think, dear, if you don't mind—I'm tired—shall we not go?"

After a little while Miss Allen suggested the cinema. Mrs. Porter received the idea with eagerness. They went to the West-End house, and the first occasion was a triumphant success. How Mrs. Porter loved it! Just the kind of story for her—Mary Pickford *in Daddy Long Legs*. To tell the truth, Mrs. Porter cried her eyes out. She swore that she had never in her life enjoyed anything so much. And the music! How beautiful! How restful! They would go every week. . . .

The second occasion was, unfortunately, disastrous. The story was one of modern life, a woman persecuted by her husband, driven by his brutality into the arms of her lover. The husband was the customary cinema villain—broad, stout, sneering, and over-dressed. Mrs. Porter fainted and had to be carried out by two attendants. A doctor came to see her, said that she was suffering from nervous exhaustion and must be protected from all excitement. . . . The two ladies sat now every evening in their pretty sitting-room, and Miss Allen read aloud the novels of Dickens one after the other.

More and more persistently, in spite of herself, did curiosity about the late Mr. Porter drive itself in upon Miss Allen. She told herself that curiosity was vulgar and unworthy of the philosophy that she had created for herself out of life. Nevertheless, it persisted. Soon she felt that, after all, it was justified. Were she to help this poor old lady to whom she was now most deeply attached, she must know more. She could not give her any real help unless she might gauge more accurately her trouble—but she was a shy woman, shy, especially, of forcing personal confidences. She hesitated; then she was aware that a barrier was being created between them. The evening had many silences, and Miss Allen detected many strange, surreptitious glances thrown at her by the old lady. The situation was impossible. One night she asked her a question.

"Dear Mrs. Porter," she said, her heart beating strangely as she spoke, "I do hope that you will not think me impertinent, but you have been so good to me that you have made me love you. You are suffering, and I cannot bear to see you unhappy. I want, oh, so eagerly, to help you! Is there nothing I can do?"

Mrs. Porter said nothing. Her hands quivered; then a tear stole down her cheek. Miss Allen went over to her, sat down beside her and took her hand.

"You must let me help you," she said. "Dismiss me if I am asking you questions that I should not. But I would rather leave you altogether, happy though I am with you, than see you so miserable. Tell me what I can do."

"You can do nothing, Lucy dear," said the old lady.

"But I must be able to do something. You are keeping from me some secret—"

Mrs. Porter shook her head. . . .

It was one evening in early May that Miss Allen was suddenly conscious that there was something wrong with the pretty little sitting-room, and it was shortly after her first consciousness of this that poor old Mrs. Porter revealed her secret. Miss Allen, looking up for a moment, fancied that the little white marble clock on the mantelpiece had ceased to tick.

She looked across the room, and for a strange moment fancied that she could see neither the clock nor the mantelpiece—a grey dimness filled her sight. She shook herself, glanced down at her hands, looked up for reassurance, and found Mrs. Porter, with wide, terrified eyes, staring at her, her hands trembling against the wood of the table.

"What is it, Lucy?"

"Nothing, Mrs. Porter."

"Did you see something?"

"No, dear."

"Oh, I thought . . . . I thought . . ." Suddenly the old lady, with a fierce impetuous movement, pushed the table away from her. She got up, staggered for a moment on her feet, then tumbled to the pink sofa, cowering there, huddled, her sharp fingers pressing against her face.

"Oh, I can't bear it. ... I can't bear it. . . . I can't bear it anymore! He's coming. He's coming. Oh, what shall I do? What shall I do?"

Miss Allen, feeling nothing but love and affection for her friend, but realising strangely too the dim and muted attention of the room, knelt down beside the sofa and put her strong arms around the trembling, fragile body.

"What is it? Dear, dear Mrs. Porter. What is it? Who is coming? Of whom are you afraid?"

"Henry's coming! Henry, who hated me. He's coming to carry me away!"

"But Mr. Porter's dead!"

"Yes. . . ." The little voice was now the merest whisper. "But he'll come all the same. . . . He always does what he says!"

The two women waited, listening. Miss Allen could hear the old lady's heart thumping and leaping close to her own. Through the opened windows came the sibilant rumble of the motor-buses. Then Mrs. Porter gently pushed Miss Allen away. "Sit on a chair, Lucy dear. I must tell you everything. I must share this with someone."

She seemed to have regained some of her calmness. She sat straight up upon the sofa, patting her lace cap with her hands, feeling for the cameo brooch at her breast. Miss Allen drew a chair close to the sofa: turning again towards the mantelpiece, she saw that it stood out boldly and clearly; the tick of the clock came across to her with almost startling urgency.

"Now, dear Mrs. Porter, what is it that is alarming you?" she said.

Mrs. Porter cleared her throat. "You know, Lucy, that I was married a great many years ago. I was only a very young girl at the time, very ignorant of course, and you can understand, my dear, that my father and mother influenced me very deeply. They liked Mr. Porter. They thought that he would make me a good husband and that I should be

12

very happy. . . . I was not happy, Lucy dear, never from the very first moment!"

Here Mrs. Porter put out her hand and took Miss Allen's strong one. "I am very willing to believe that much of the unhappiness was due to myself. I was a young, foolish girl; I was disturbed from the very first by the stories that Mr. Porter told me, and the pictures he showed me. I was foolish about those things. He saw that they shocked me, and I think that that amused him. From the first it delighted him to tease me. Then—soon—he tired of me. He had mistresses. He brought them to our house. He insulted me in every way possible. I had years of that misery. God only knows how I lived through it. It became a habit with him to frighten and shock me. It was a game that he loved to play. I think he wanted to see how far I would go. But I was patient through all those many years. Oh! so patient! It was weak, perhaps, but there seemed nothing else for me to be.

"The last twenty years of our married life he hated me most bitterly. He said that I had scorned him, that I had not given him children, that I had wasted his money—a thousand different things! He tortured me, frightened me, disgusted me, but it never seemed to be enough for him, for the vengeance he felt I deserved. Then one day he discovered that he had a weak heart—a doctor frightened him. He saw perhaps for a moment in my eyes my consciousness of my possible freedom. He took my arm and shook me, bent his face close to mine, and said: 'Ah, you think that after I'm dead you will be free. You are wrong. I will leave you everything that I possess, and then—just as you begin to enjoy it—I will come and fetch you!' What a thing to say, Lucy dear! He was mad, and so was I to listen to him.

"All those years of married life together had perhaps turned both our brains. Six months later he fell down in the street dead. They brought him home, and all that summer afternoon, my dear, I sat beside him in the bedroom, he all dressed in his best clothes and his patent leather shoes, and the band playing in the Square outside. Oh! he was dead, Lucy dear, he was indeed. For a week or two I thought that he was gone altogether. I was happy and free. Then—oh, I don't know—I began to imagine . . . to fancy. . . . I moved from Wimbledon. I advertised for someone, and you came. We moved here. . . . It ought to be . . . it is . . . it *must* be all right, Lucy dear; hold me, hold me tight! Don't let me go! He can't come back! He can't, he can't!"

She broke into passionate sobbing, cowering back on to the sofa as she had done before. The two women sat there, comforting one another. Miss Allen gathered the frail, trembling little body into her arms, and like a mother with her child, soothed it.

But, as she sat there, she realised with a chill shudder of alarm that moment, a quarter of an hour before, when the room had been dimmed and the clock stilled. Had that been fancy? Had some of Mrs. Porter's terror seized her in sympathy? Were they simply two lonely women whose nerves were jagged by the quiet monotony and seclusion of their lives? Why was it that from the first she, so unimaginative and definite, should have been disturbed by the thought of Mr. Porter? Why was it that even now she longed to know more surely about him, his face, his clothes, his height . . . everything.

"You must go to bed, dear. You are tired out. Your nerves have never recovered from the time of Mr. Porter's death. That's what it is. . . . . You must go to bed, dear."

Mrs. Porter went. She seemed to be relieved by her outburst. She felt perhaps now less lonely. It seemed, too, that she had less to fear now that she had betrayed her ghost into sunlight. She slept better that night than she had done for a long time past. Miss Allen sat beside the bed staring into the darkness, thinking. . . .

For a week after this they were happy. Mrs. Porter was in high spirits. They went to the Coliseum and heard Miss Florence Smithson sing "Roses of Picardy," and in the cinema, they were delighted with the charm and simplicity of Alma Taylor. Mrs. Porter lost her heart to Alma Taylor.

"That's a *sweet* girl," she said. "I would like to meet her. I'm sure she's *good*."

"I'm sure she is," said Miss Allen.

Mrs. Porter made friends in the flat. Mr. Nix met them one day at the bottom of the lift and talked to them so pleasantly. "*What* a gentleman!" said Mrs. Porter afterwards as she took off her bonnet.

Then one evening Miss Allen came into the sitting-room and stopped dead, frozen rigid on the threshold. Someone was in the room. She did not at first think of Mr. Porter. She was only sure that someone was there. Mrs. Porter was in her bedroom changing her dress.

Miss Allen said, "Who's there?" She walked forward. The dim evening saffron light powdered the walls with trembling colour. The canaries twittered, the clock ticked; no one was there. After that instant of horror, she was to know no relief. It was as though that spoken "Who's there?" had admitted her into the open acceptance of a fact

14

that she ought for ever to have denied.

She was a woman of common sense, of rational thought, scornful of superstition and sentiment. She realised now that there was something quite definite for her to fight, something as definite as disease, as pain, as poverty and hunger. She realised too that she was there to protect Mrs. Porter from everything—yes, from everything and everybody!

Her first thought was to escape from the flat, and especially from everything in the flat—from the pink sofa, the gate-legged table, the birdcage and the clock. She saw then that, if she yielded to this desire, they would be driven, the two of them, into perpetual flight, and that the very necessity of escaping would only admit the more the conviction of defeat. No, they must stay where they were; that place was their battleground.

She determined, too, that Mr. Porter's name should not be mentioned between them again. Mrs. Porter must be assured that she had forgotten his very existence.

Soon she arrived at an exact knowledge of the arrival of these "attacks" as she called them. That month of May gave them wonderful weather. The evenings were so beautiful that they sat always with the windows open behind them, and the dim colour of the night-glow softened the lamplight and brought with it scents and breezes and a happy murmurous undertone. She received again and again in these May evenings that earlier impression of someone's entrance into the room.

It came to her, as she sat with her back to the fireplace, with the conviction that a pair of eyes were staring at her. Those eyes willed her to him, and she would not; but soon she seemed to know them, cold, hard, and separated from her, she fancied, by glasses. They seemed, too, to bend down upon her from a height. She was desperately conscious at these moments of Mrs. Porter. Was the old lady also aware? She could not tell. Mrs. Porter still cast at her those odd, furtive glances, as though to see whether she suspected anything, but she never looked at the fireplace nor started as though the door was suddenly opened.

There were times when Miss Allen, relaxing her self-control, admitted without hesitation that someone was in the room. He was tall, wore spectacles behind which he scornfully peered. She challenged him to pass her guard and even felt the stiff pride of a victorious battle. They were fighting for the old lady, and she was winning. . . .

At all other moments she scorned herself for this weakness. Mrs.

Porter's nerves had affected her own. She had not believed that she could be so weak. Then, suddenly, one evening Mrs. Porter dropped her cards, crumpled down into her chair, screamed, "No, no . . . Lucy! . . . Lucy! He's here! . . ."

She was strangely, at the moment of that cry, aware of no presence in the room. It was only when she had gathered her friend into her arms, persuading her that there was nothing, loving her, petting her, that she was conscious of the dimming of the light, the stealthy withdrawal of sound. She was facing the fireplace; before the mantelpiece there seemed to her to hover a shadow, something so tenuous that it resembled a film of dust against the glow of electric light. She faced it with steady eyes and a fearless heart.

But against her will her soul admitted that confrontation. From that moment Mrs. Porter abandoned disguise. Her terror was now so persistent that soon, of itself, it would kill her. There was no remedy; doctors could not help, nor change of scene. Only if Miss Allen still saw and felt nothing could the old lady still hope. Miss Allen lied and lied again and again.

"You saw nothing, Lucy?"

"Nothing."

"Not there by the fireplace?"

"Nothing, dear. . . . Of course, nothing!"

Events from then moved quickly, and they moved for Miss Allen quite definitely in the hardening of the sinister shadow. She led now a triple existence: one life was Mrs. Porter's, devoted to her, delivered over to her, helping her, protecting her; the second life was her own, her rational, practical self, scornful of shadow and of the terror of death; the third was the struggle with Henry Porter, a struggle now as definite and concrete as though he were a blackmailer confining her liberty.

She could never tell when he would come, and with every visit that he paid he seemed to advance in her realisation of him. It appeared that he was always behind her, staring at her through those glasses that had, she was convinced, large gold rims and thin gold wires. She fancied that she had before her a dim outline of his face— pale, the chin sharp and pointed, the ears large and protuberant, the head dome-shaped and bald. It was now that, with all her life and soul in the struggle for her friend, she realised that she did not love her enough. The intense love of her life had been already in earlier years given. Mrs. Porter was a sweet old lady, and Miss Allen would give her life for her—but her soul was atrophied a little, tired a little, exhausted perhaps in the struggle so sharp and persistent for her own existence.

"Oh, if I were younger I could drive him away!" came back to her again and again. She found too that her own fear impeded her own self-sacrifice. She hated this shadow as something strong, evil, like mildew on stone, chilling breath. "I'm not brave enough. . . . I'm not good enough. . . . I'm not young enough!" Incessantly she tried to determine how real her sensations were. Was she simply influenced by Mrs. Porter's fear? Was it the blindest imagination? Was it bred simply of the close, confined life that they were leading?

She could not tell. They had resumed their conspiracy of silence, of false animation and ease of mind. They led their daily lives as though there was nothing between them. But with every day Mrs. Porter's strength was failing; the look of horrified anticipation in her eyes was now permanent. At night they slept together, and the little frail body trembled like a leaf in Miss Allen's arms.

The appearances were now regularised. Always when they were in the middle of their second game of "Patience" Miss Allen felt that impulse to turn, that singing in her ears, the force of his ironical gaze. He was now almost complete to her, standing in front of the Japanese screen, his thin legs apart, his hostile, conceited face bent towards them, his pale, thin hands extended as though to catch a warmth that was not there.

A Sunday evening came. Earlier than usual they sat down to their cards. Through the open window shivered the jangled chimes of the bells of St. James's.

"Well, he won't come yet . . ." was Miss Allen's thought. Then with that her nightly resolve: "When he comes I must not turn—I must not look. She must not know that I know."

Suddenly he was with them, and with a dominant force, a cruelty, a determination that was beyond anything that had been before.

"Four, five, six. . . ." The cards trembled in Mrs. Porter's hand. "And there's the spade, Lucy dear."

He came closer. He was nearer to her than he had ever been. She summoned all that she had—her loyalty, her love, her honesty, her self-discipline. It was not enough.

She turned. He was there as she had always known that she would see him, his cruel, evil, supercilious face, conscious of its triumph, bent toward them, his grey clothes hanging loosely about his thin body, his hands spread out. He was like an animal about to spring.

17

"God help me! God help me!" she cried. With those words she knew that she had failed. She stood as though she would protect with her body her friend. She was too late.

Mrs. Porter's agonised cry, "You see him, Lucy! . . . You see him, Lucy!" warned her.

"No, no," she answered. She felt something like a cold breath of stagnant water pass her. She turned back to see the old woman tumble across the table, scattering the little cards.

The room was emptied. They two were alone; she knew, without moving, horror and self-shame holding her there, that her poor friend was dead.

Absalom Jay

Somewhere in the early nineties was Absalom Jay's first period. He was so well-known a figure in London at that time as to be frequently caricatured in the weekly society journals, and Spy's "Absalom," that appeared in the 1894 volume of *Vanity Fair*, is one of his most successful efforts. In those days were any one so ignorant as to be compelled to ask who Jay was he would probably receive the answer: "Oh, don't you know? He's a cousin of John Beaminster's. He founded the 'Warrington' with Pemmy Stevens. He's . . . Oh, I don't know. . . . he goes everywhere. Knows more people than anyone else in London, I should imagine."

Spy's caricature of him has caught that elegant smartness that was Absalom's most marked individuality, *too* smart critics have been known to say; and certainly, if the ideal of correct dress is that no one should notice your clothes Absalom was not correct. Everyone always noticed his clothes. But here again one must be fair. It may not have been altogether his clothes that one noticed. From very early years his hair was snow-white, and he wore it brushed straight back from his pink forehead in wavy locks. He wore also a little white tufted Imperial. He had an eyeglass that hung on a thick black cord. His favourite colour was a dark blue, and with this he wore spats (in summer of a truly terrific whiteness), a white slip, black tie, and pearl pin. He wore wonderful boots and shoes and was said to have more of these than any man in London.

It was also said that his feet were the smallest (masculine) in the British Isles. He was made altogether on a very small scale. He was not, I should think, more than five-feet-six in height, but was all in perfect proportion. His enemies, of whom he had, like everyone else, a few, said that his wonderful pink complexion was not entirely Nature's work, but here his enemies lied. Even at the very last he did not give way to the use of cosmetics. He was the kindest-hearted little man in the world, and in the days of his prosperity was as happy as the day was long. He lived entirely for Society, and because this is intended to be a true portrait, I must admit that there was something of the snob in his character. He himself admitted it frankly. "I like to be with people of rank," he would say, "simply because I'm more comfortable with them. I know just what to say to Johnny Beaminster, and I'm tongue-tied with the wife of my barber. *Que voulez-vous?*"

I'm afraid, however, that it went a little further than that. In the Season his looking-glass was thronged with cards, invitations to dinner and dances and musical evenings. "I live for Society," he said, "as some men live for killing pheasants, and other men for piling up money. My fun is as good as another man's. At any rate I get good company."

It was his intention to be seen at every London function, public or private, that could be considered a first-class function; people wondered how he got about as he did. It seemed as though there must be three or four Absaloms.

His best time was during the last few years of King Edward VII.'s reign. His funny little anxious face could be frequently seen in those groups of celebrities invited to meet the king at some famous house-party. It was said that the king liked his company, but I don't know how that can have been because Absalom was never in his brightest days very amusing. He talked a good deal, but always said just what everyone else said. He was asked everywhere because he was so safe, because he was so willing to fetch and carry, and because he knew exactly what it was that ladies wanted. He entertained only a little in return, but nobody minded that because, as everyone knew, "he really hadn't a penny in the world"—which meant that he had about £1,500 a year in various safe investments.

A year before the war he was seized with a little gust of speculation. Against the advice of "Tony" Pennant, who looked after his investments for him, he ventured to buy here and sell there with rather serious results. He pulled up just in time to save disaster, but he had to give up his little house in Knightsbridge and took a flat at Hortons in Duke Street. Although this was a "service "flat he still retained his man James, who had been with him for a number of years and knew his habits to perfection.

He made his rooms at Hortons charming, and he had the dark blue curtains and the gold mirror bristling with invitations, and the old coloured prints and the big, signed photographs of Queen Alexandra and the Duchess of Wrexe in their silver frames, and the heavy silver cigarette-box that King Edward had given him, all in their accustomed places. Of course, the flat was small. His silver-topped bottles and silver-backed brushes, and rows of boots and shoes and the two big trouser-presses simply overwhelmed his bedroom.

But he was over sixty-five now (although he would have been horrified if he thought that you knew it) and he didn't need much space—moreover, he was always out.

Then came the war, and the first result of this was that James joined up! During those first August days Absalom hadn't fancied that the war would touch him at all, although he was hotly patriotic and cried out daily at the "Warrington" that he wished he were a lad again and could shoulder a gun.

James's departure frightened him; then "Tony" Pennant explained to him that his investments were not so secure as they had been and he'd be lucky if any of them brought him in anything. And of course, the whole of his social world vanished—no more parties, no more balls, no more Ascots and Goodwoods, no more shooting in Scotland, no more opera. He bustled around then in a truly remarkable manner and attacked his friends with the pertinacity of a bluebottle. The war was not a month old before Bryce-Drummond secured him a job in one of the Ministries at six hundred a year. It was not a very difficult job (it consisted for the most part in interviewing eager young men, assuring them that he would do his best for them, and then sending them along to somebody else). He had a room to himself, and a lady typist who looked after him like a mother. He was quite delighted when he discovered that she was a daughter of the Bishop of Polchester and very well connected. She was most efficient and did everything for him.

He took his work very seriously indeed, and was delighted to be "doing his bit." No one knew exactly what it was that he did at the Ministry, and he himself was very vague about it, but he hinted at great things and magnificent company. During those first years when there were so many wonderful rumours, he hinted and hinted and hinted. "Well, I mustn't mention names, of course; but you can take it from me" and people really did think he *did* know.

He had been in the closest touch with so many great people before the war that it was only natural that he should be in touch with them still. As a matter of fact, he knew nothing except what his typist told him. He led an extremely quiet life during these years, but he didn't mind that because he understood that it was the right thing to do. All the best people were absorbed in their work—even old Lady Agatha Beaminster was running a home for Serbians, and Rachel Seddon was a V.A.D. in France, and old "Plumtree" Caudle was a Special Constable. He did not therefore feel left out of things, because there was nothing really to be left out of. Moreover, he was so hard up that it was safer to be quiet. All the more would he enjoy himself when the war was over.

But as the years went on and there seemed to be no sign of the war being over, he began to be querulous. He missed James terribly, and when in the summer of 1917 he heard that James was killed in Mesopotamia it was a very serious blow. He seemed to be suddenly quite alone in the world. In Hortons now they employed only women, and the girl straight from Glebeshire who "valeted" him seemed to have but little time to listen to his special needs, being divided up between four flats and finding it all she could do, poor girl, to satisfy them all. "After the war," Mr. Nix, the manager of Hortons, assured Absalom, "we shall have men again!"

"After the war!"—those three simple little words became the very Abracadabra of Absalom's life. "After the war" everything would be as it had always been—prices would go down, Society would come up, his gold mirror would once again be stuck about with invitations, he would find a successor to James, and a little house. What would he live on? Oh, that would be all right. They would keep him at the Ministry. He was so useful there that he couldn't conceive that they would ever get on without him—there would be his work, of course, and probably they would raise his salary. He was an optimist about the future. Nothing made him so indignant as unjustified pessimism. When someone talked pessimistically it was as though he, Absalom Jay, were being personally threatened. Throughout the terrible spring of 1918 he remained optimistic. "Britain *couldn't* be beaten"—by which he meant that Absalom Jay must be assured of his future comforts.

In spite of all that had happened he was as incapable in June 1918 as he had been in June 1914 of imagining a different world, a different balance of moral and ethical values. Then the tide turned. During that summer and early autumn of 1918 Absalom was as happy as he had ever been. He simply lived for the moment when "life would begin again." He began to go out a little, to pay calls, to visit an old friend or two. He found changes, of course. His own contemporaries seemed strangely old; many of them had died, many of them had shattered nerves, many were frightened of the future.

If they were frightened it was their own fault, he declared. They *would* talk of ridiculous things like the Russian Revolution—nothing angered him more than to hear chatter about the Russian Revolution—as though that absurd affair with its cut-throats and Bolsheviks and Jews and murderers could have anything to do with a *real* country like England.

It was all the fault of our idiotic government; one regiment of British soldiers and *that* trouble would have been over. . . . No, he'd no patience. . . .

November 11th came, and with it the Armistice; he actually rode all the way down Whitehall on a lorry and waved a flag. He *was* excited, it seemed as though the whole world were crying, "Hurray! Absalom Jay! You were right, after all. You shall have your reward."

He pictured to himself what was coming: 1919 would be the year; let those dirty ruffians try and imitate Russian methods. They would see what they would get. He resumed his old haughtiness of demeanour to dependents. It was necessary in these days to show them their place. Not that he was never kind. When they behaved properly he was very kind indeed. To Fanny, the portress at Hortons—a nice girl with a ready smile and an agreeable willingness to do *anything*, however tiresome—he was delightful, asking her about her relations and once telling her that he was grateful for what she did. He was compelled, however, to speak haughtily to Rose, the "valet." He was forced often to ring twice for her, and once when she came running and out of breath and he showed her that she had put some of his waistcoats into one drawer and some into another, thereby making it very difficult for him to find them, she actually tossed her head and muttered something.

He spoke to her very kindly then, and showed her how things were done in the best houses, because, after all, poor child, she was straight up from the country. However, she did not take his kindliness in at all the right spirit, but burst out angrily that "times was different now, and one was as good as another"—a shocking thing to say, and savouring directly of Bolshevism. He was getting into the habit of calling almost everything Bolshevism.

Then the first blow fell. He found a letter on his table at the Ministry; he opened it carelessly and read therein that as the war was in process of being "wound up," changes were taking place that would compel the Ministry, most reluctantly, to do without Mr. Jay's services.

Would he mind taking a month's notice? . . .

He would mind very much indeed—Mind? It was as though a thunderbolt had struck him on the very top of his neat little head. He stood in front of the Ministerial fireplace, his little legs extended, the letter trembling in his hand, his eyes, if the truth must be spoken, flushed with tears. Dismissed! With a month's notice! He would speak . . . he would protest . . . he would abuse. . . . In the end, of course, he did nothing. Bryce-Drummond said he was so very sorry, "but really everythin' was tumblin' about one's ears these days," and offered him a cigarette. Lord John, to whom he appealed, looked distressed and said it was "a damn shame; upon his word, he didn't know what we were all coming to." . . .

Absalom Jay was left; he realised that he could do nothing; he retired into Hortons.

There was in his soul a fund of optimism, or rather, to speak more accurately, it took him time to realise the shifting sands upon which his little house was built. He made now the very most of Hortons. It is true that time began to lie heavy upon his hands. He rose very late in the morning, having his cup of tea and boiled egg at nine, his bath at ten; he read the *Morning Post* for an hour; then the barber, Merritt, from next door, came in to shave him and give him the news of the day. Merritt was a most amusing dark and dapper little man. In him was the very spirit of St. James's, and the Lord only knows how many businesses he carried on beside his ostensible hair-dressing one. He could buy anything for you, and sell anything, too! And his gossip! Well, really, Absalom had thought himself a good gossip in his day, but he had never been anything to Merritt! Of course, half-a-crown was a good deal for a shave, and Absalom was not sure whether in these days he ought to afford it—"my only luxury" he called it.

He did not see many of his friends this Christmas time. They were all out of London he supposed. He was a little surprised that the Beaumonts hadn't asked him to spend Christmas at Hautoix. In the old days that invitation had been as regular as the Waits. However, they had lost their eldest son in the Cambrai fighting. They were having no parties this Christmas, of course.

He had thought that the Seddons might ask him. He got on so well with Roddy and Rachel. They sent him a card "from Rollo," their baby. Kind of them to remember him! So, he busied himself about the flat. He was preparing for the future—for that wonderful time when the war would be really and truly over, and the world as it had been in the old days. His life was centred in Hortons and the streets that surrounded it. He could be seen every morning walking up Duke Street into Piccadilly. He knew every shop by heart, the picture shops that seemed to be little offspring of the great "Christie's" round the corner, with their coloured plates from Ackermann's "Microcosm," and Pierce Egan, and their oils of large, full-bosomed eighteenth century ladies; and the shops with the china and the cabinets and the lacquer (everything very expensive indeed); and Bottome's, the paper shop, with Mr. Bottome's humorous comments on the day's politics chalked on to a slate near the door, and the *Vie Parisienne* very large in the window; then there was the shop at the corner of Jermyn Street, with the silk dressing-gowns of dazzling colours, and the latest fashions with pink silk vests, pyjamas; and the great tobacconists and the wine-windows of Fortnum and Masons—at last the familiar broad splendours of Piccadilly itself.

Up and down the little old streets that had known all the famous men of their day, that had lodged Thackeray and Swift and Dryden, and now lodged Mr. Bottomlev and the author of *Mutt and Jeff*, the motors rolled and hooted and honked, and the messenger boys whistled, and the flower-man went up and down with his barrow, and everything was as expensive and pleasant and humorous as could be. All this Absalom Jay adopted. He was in his own mind, although he did not know it, King of St. James's, and he felt that they must all be very glad to have him there, and that rents must have gone up since it was known that he had taken his residence among them.

He even went in one day and expostulated with Mr. Bottome for having the *Daily Herald* in his window. Mr. Bottome agreed with him that it was not a "nice" paper, but he also added that sinister sentence that Absalom was getting now so tired of hearing that "these were strange times. 'E didn't know what we were coming to."

"Nonsense, my good man," said Absalom rather tartly, "England isn't Russia."

"Looks damned like it sometimes," said Mr. Bottome.

Then as the year 1919 extended Absalom began to feel terribly lonely. This fear of loneliness was rapidly becoming a concrete and definite terror, lurking behind the curtains in his flat, ready to spring out upon him at any moment. Absalom had never in all his life been alone. There had always been people around him. Where now were they all? Men now were being demobilised, houses were opening again, hospitals were closing, dances were being given, and still his gold mirror remained innocent of invitations. He fancied, too (he was becoming very sensitive to impressions), that the men in the "Warrington" were not so eager to see him as they had been. He went to the "Warrington" a great deal now "to be cheered up." He talked to men to whom five years ago he would not have condescended to say "Good-morning"—to Isaac Monteluke, for instance, and Bandy Manners. Where were all his old friends? They did not come to the club any longer, it seemed. He could never find a bridge four now with whom he was really at home. This may have been partly because he was nervous these days of losing money—he could not afford it—and he did not seem to have his old control of his temper. Then his brain was not quite so active as it had been. He could not remember the cards. . . .

One day he heard some fellow say: "Well, if I'd had my way I'd chloroform everyone over sixty. We've had enough of the old duds messing all the world up."

Chloroform all the old duds! What a terrible thing to say? Why, five years ago it had been the other way. Who cared then what a young man said? What could he know? After all, it was the older men who had had the experience, who knew life, who could tell the others. . . .

He found himself laying down the law about things—giving ultimatums like—"They ought to be strung up on lamp-posts—pandering to the ignorant lower classes—that's what it is."

If there had been one thing above all others that Absalom had hated all his life it had been rudeness—there was the unforgivable sin. As a young man he had been deferential to his elders, and so in his turn he expected young men to be to him now. But they were not. No, they were not. He had positively to give up the "Warrington" because of the things that the young men said.

There was a new trouble now—the trouble of money. His investments were paying very badly, and the income tax was absurd. He wrote to the *Times* about his income tax, and they did not print his letter—did not print it when they printed the letters of every sort of nobody. Everything was so expensive that it took all his courage to look at his weekly bill. He must eat less; one ate, he read in the paper, far more than one needed. So, he gave up his breakfast, having only a cup of coffee and a roll, as he had often done in France in the old days. He was aware suddenly that his clothes were beginning to look shabby. Bacon, the valet, informed him of this. He did not like Bacon; he found himself, indeed, sighing for the departed Rose. Bacon was austere and inhuman. He spoke as seldom as possible. He had no faults, he pressed clothes perfectly, kept drawers in absolute order, did not drink Absalom's claret nor smoke Absalom's cigarettes. No faults—but what an impossible man! Absalom was afraid of him. He drew his little body together under the bedclothes when Bacon called him in the morning because of Bacon's ironical eyes. Bacon gave him his *Times* as though he said: "How dare you take in the *Times*—spend threepence a day when you are as poor as you are?"

It was because of Bacon that Absalom gave up Merritt. He did not dare to have him when Bacon knew his poverty.

"I'm going to shave myself in the future, Merritt," he said; "it's only laziness having you." Merritt was politely sorry, but he was not very deeply grieved. Why should he be when he had the king's valet and Sir Edward Hawksbury, the famous K.C., and Borden Hunt, the dramatist, to shave every morning?

But Absalom missed him terribly. He was now indeed alone. No more gossip, no more laughter over other people's weaknesses, no more hearty agreement over the wicked selfishness of the lower orders.

Absalom gave up the *Times* because he could not bear to see the lower orders encouraged. All this talk about their not having enough to live on—wicked nonsense! It was people like Absalom who had not enough to live on. He wrote again to the *Times* and said so, and again they did not publish his letter.

Then he woke from sleep one night, heard the clock strike three, and was desperately frightened. He had had a dream. What dream? He could not remember. He only knew that in the course of it he had become very, very old; he had been in a room without fire and without light; he had been in prison—faces had glared at him, cruel faces, young, sneering, menacing faces.... He was going to die.... He awoke with a scream.

Next day he read himself a very serious lecture. He was becoming morbid; he was giving in; he was allowing himself to be afraid of things. He must pull himself up. He was quite severe to Bacon, and reprimanded him for bringing his breakfast at a quarter to nine instead of half-past eight. He made out then a list of houses that he would visit. They had forgotten him—he must admit that. But how natural it was! After all this time. Everyone had forgotten everybody. Why, he had forgotten all sorts of people! Could not remember their names!

For months now he had been saying, "After the war," and now here "after the war" was. It was May, and already Society was looking something like itself. Covent Garden was open again. Soon there would be Ascot and Henley and Goodwood; and the Peace Celebrations, perhaps, if only those idiots at Versailles moved a little more quickly! He felt the old familiar stir in his blood as he saw the red letters and the green pillars repainted, saw the early summer sun shine upon the glittering windows of Piccadilly, saw the green shadows of Hyde Park shift and tremble against the pale blue of the evening sky, saw, once again, the private cars quiver and tremble behind the policeman's hand in the Circus; saw Delysia's name over the Pavilion, and the posters of the evening papers, and the fountains splashing in Trafalgar Square.

He put on his best clothes and went out.

He called upon Mary, Countess of Gosport, the Duchess of Aisles, Lady Glenrobert, Mrs. Leo Torsch, and dear Rachel Seddon. At the Countess of Gosport's, he found a clergyman, a companion, and a chow; at the Duchess of Aisles' four young Guardsmen, two girls, and Isaac Monteluke, who had the insolence to patronise him; at Lady Glenrobert's a vast crowd of men and women rehearsing for a Peace pageant shortly to be given at the Albert Hall; at Mr. Leo Torsch's an incredible company of artists, writers, and actors, people unwashed and unbrushed, at sight of whom Absalom's very soul trembled; at dear Rachel's charming young people, all of whom looked right through him as though he were an easy and undisturbing ghost.

He came back from these visits a weary, miserable, and tired little man. Even Rachel had seemed to have no time to give him. . . . An incredible lassitude spread through all his bones. As he entered the portals of No. 2 a boy passed him with a *Pall Mall* poster. "Railwaymen issue Ultimatum." In his room he read a *Times* leader, in which it said that the lower classes were starving and had nowhere to sleep. And they called the Times a reactionary paper! The lower classes starving! What about the upper classes? With his door closed, in his own deep privacy, surrounded by his little gods, his mirror, his silver frames, and his boot-trees, he wept—bitterly, helplessly, like a child.

From that moment he had no courage. Enemies seemed to be on every side. Everywhere he was insulted. If he went out boys pushed against him, taxi-men swore at him, in the shops they were rude to him! There was never room in the omnibuses, the taxis were too expensive, and the Tubes! After an attempt to reach Russell Square by

28

Tube he vowed he would never enter a Tube door again. He was pushed, hustled, struck in the stomach, sworn at both by attendants and passengers, jammed between stout women, hurled off his feet, spoken to by a young soldier because he did not give up his seat to a lady who haughtily refused it when he offered. . . . Tubes! . . . never again—never, oh, never again!

What then to do? Walking tired him desperately. Everywhere seemed now so far away!

So, he remained in his flat; but now Hortons itself was different. Now that he was confined to it it was very small, and he was always tumbling over things. A pipe burst one morning, and his bathroom was flooded. The bathroom wall-paper began to go the strangest and most terrible colours—it was purple and pink and green, and there were splotches of white mildew that seemed to move before your eyes as you lay in your bath and watched them. Absalom went to Mr. Nix, and Mr. Nix said that it should be seen to at once, but day after day went by and nothing was done. When Mr. Nix was appealed to he said rather restively that he was very sorry but he was doing his best—labour was so difficult to get now—"You could not rely on the men."

"But they've got to come!" screamed Absalom.

Mr. Nix shrugged his shoulders; from his lips fell those fatal and now so monotonous words:

"We're living in changed times, Mr. Jay."

Changed times! Absalom should think we were. Everyone was ruder and ruder and ruder. Bills were beginning to worry him terribly—such little bills, but men would come and wait downstairs in the hall for them.

The loneliness increased and wrapped him closer and closer. His temper was becoming atrocious as he well knew. Bacon now paid no attention to his wishes, his meals were brought up at any time, his rooms were not cleaned, his silver was tarnished. All he had to do was to complain to Mr. Nix, who ruled Hortons with a rod of iron, and allowed no incivilities or slackness. But he was afraid to do that; he was afraid of the way that Bacon would treat him afterwards. Always, everywhere now he saw this increasing attention that was paid to the lower classes. Railwaymen, miners, hairdressers, dockers, bakers, waiters, they struck, got what they wanted and then struck for more.

He hated the lower classes—hated them, hated them! The very sight of a working man threw him into a frenzy. What about the upper classes and the middle classes! Did you ever see a word in the paper

29

about them? Never!

He was not well, his heart troubled him very much. Sometimes he lay on his sofa battling for breath. But he did not dare to go to a doctor. He could not afford a doctor.

But God is merciful. He put a period to poor Absalom's unhappiness. When it was plain that this world was no longer a place for Absalom's kind He gathered Absalom to His bosom.

And it was in this way. There arrived suddenly one day a card: "The Duchess of Aisles .... Dancing." His heart beat high at the sight of it. He had to lie down on his sofa to recover himself. He stuck his card into the mirror and was compelled to say something to Bacon about it. Bacon did not seem to be greatly impressed at the sight.

He dressed on the great evening with the utmost care. The sight of his bathroom affected him; it seemed to cover him with pink spots and mildew, but he shook that off from him and boldly ventured forth to Knightsbridge. He found an immense party gathered there. Many, many people.... He didn't seem to recognise any of them. The duchess herself had apparently forgotten him. He reminded her. He crept about; he felt strangely as though at any moment someone might shoot him in the back. Then he found Mrs. Charles Clinton, one of his hostesses of the old days. She was kind but preoccupied. Then he discovered Tom Wardour—old Tom Wardour, the stupidest man in London and the greediest. Nevertheless, he was glad to see him.

"By Jove, old man, you *do* look seedy," Tom said; "what have you been doing to yourself?"

Tactless of Tom, that! He felt more than ever that someone was going to shoot him in the back. He crept away and hid himself in a corner. He dozed a little, then woke to hear his own name. A woman was speaking of him. He recognised Mrs. Clinton's voice.

"Who do you think I saw just now? ... Yes, old Absalom Jay. Like a visit from the dead. Yes, and *so* old. You know how smart he used to be. He looked quite shabby, poor old thing. Oh no, of course, he was always stupid. But now—oh, dreadful! ... I assure you he gave me the creeps. Yes, of course, he belonged to that old world before the war. *Doesn't* it seem a long time ago? Centuries. What I say is that one can't believe one was alive then at all...."

Gave her the creeps! Gave Mrs. Clinton the creeps! He felt as though his premonition had been true, and someone *had* shot him in the back. He crept away, out of the house, right away.

He crept into a Tube. The trains were crowded. He had to hang on to a strap. At Hyde Park Corner two workmen got in; they had been drinking together. Very big men they were. They stood one on each side of Absalom and lurched about. Absalom was pushed hither and thither.

"Where the 'ell are you comin' to?" one said.

The other knocked Absalom's hat off as though by an accident. Then the former elaborately picked it up and offered it with a low bow, digging Absalom in the stomach as he did so.

"'Ere y'are, my lord," he said. They roared with laughter. The whole carriage laughed. At Dover Street Absalom got out. He hurried through the streets, and the tears were pouring down his cheeks. He could not stop them; he seemed to have no control over them. They were not his tears. . . . He entered Hortons, and in the lift hid his face so that Fannie should not see that he was crying.

He closed his door behind him, did not turn on the lights, found the sofa, and cowered down there as though he were hiding from someone.

The tears continued to race down his checks. Then suddenly it seemed as though the walls of the bathroom, all blotched and purple, all stained with creeping mildew, closed in the dark about him.

He heard a voice cry—a working-man's voice—he did not hear the words, but the walls towered above him and the white mildew expanded into jeering, hideous, triumphant faces.

His heart leapt and he knew no more.

★★★★★★

Bacon and the maid found him huddled thus on the floor dead next morning.

"Well now," said Bacon, "that's a lucky thing. Young Somerset next door's been wanting this flat. Make a nice suite if he knocks a door through—gives him seven rooms. He'll be properly pleased."

The Conjurer

Everyone who looks back to childhood must be aware of the strange confusion of fact and fairystory that those early memories arouse. Here there is detail so sharp and clear that its truth cannot be questioned—the screen with the pictures from the Christmas numbers, the green china saucer in which the mustard and cress was sown, the oak guarding the lawn hung with festoons of crystal snow, the murmur of the pigeons above the rose-coloured garden wall, and, with these, the oddest figures—fairies, leprechauns, wizards—and scenes of fantasy when the cuckoo flew out of the clock, the Chinese mandarin from the drawing-room mantelpiece wiped his long moustaches with a cambric handkerchief, and the spotted rocking-horse without a tail bumped down the flight of stairs from the schoolroom to the hall-door. What is reality? Where do dreams begin? What is Truth? asked jesting Pilate.

With wonder such as this I look back to an adventure of my childhood never narrated by me before because, perhaps, I have been afraid of my neighbour's incredulity. It may be that at last I perceive that the whole of life is nothing but a succession of wonders and one adventure in it no more unreal than another. Or it may be that I am old enough now not to fear my neighbour's mocking laughter. He has laughed at me too often, and, like the bluebottle in the fairy-tale, 'I have grown accustomed to my cousin bluebottle's impertinent buzzing.' In any case, however that may be, for the first time I relate this remarkable story, giving you the details exactly as I remember them.

I must have been at the time aged thirteen or so. I was a shy, nervous and self-conscious boy—the more so that my elder brother and sister had not a doubt about anything and laughed at me, when they thought of me, for my paltry spirit.

It was, I am afraid, true. I *had* a paltry spirit. It seemed to me that so very easily, with a word or a look, with the closing of a door or the opening of a window, things might go so very wrong. The day—every day—was packed with danger, whether at school or at home. I loved my father and mother, but, at that time, also feared them. I hated to see that look in my mother's eyes as though, in spite of her love for me, the thought would come to her: 'Is this child never going to have any sense? What are we to do with him?'

Sarah, my elder sister, a boisterous, happy and extremely popular child, would look at me and say, laughing: 'Well, you *are* a little fool!'—which I was, I have no doubt. But it would have been better had she not laughed. She was (as I have since told her) in those years so carelessly contemptuous of me.

However, I am not here attempting to blame anybody. That I deserved all I got I don't for a moment doubt. I was a shy, awkward, unattractive child—which only makes this adventure the more remarkable. For several years of my childhood my father, who was a doctor, had a practice in the village of Gosforth in Cumberland. Gosforth was three miles from the sea, and some six miles from Wastwater lake. The village consisted of a long, straggling street. It was famous principally for its church, and the church was famous because of the remarkable cross in the graveyard. This cross was one of the most ancient—if not *the* most ancient—in the whole of Great Britain, and was the more remarkable because it was carved with certain pagan figures. Antiquarians in large numbers used to visit the cross, and still do, I don't doubt.

Altogether, with the sea so near, with the lake (the darkest, most mysterious of all the lakes) only a bicycle-ride away, the strange cross, the beautiful outline of Black Combe on the horizon, Gosforth was the very place to nurture the illogical fancies of a romantic child.

We lived in an old rambling house, half a mile from the village. This house had a wild, unkempt garden, a thick tangled wood ran at the back of it, and for birds, for singing, chattering, gossipy, happy birds, I have never known a place to equal it! Neither my father nor mother nor Sarah and Fred—my brother and sister—lived very much in the world of the imagination. During the holidays—I went at this time to Sedbergh School—every minute was filled with practical doings.

My father's belief was that it was bad for children to be idle, and so from morning to night we were busily employed. We were encouraged to play games, and it was one of my troubles that at any and every game I was a duffer. Not so Sarah and Fred, who simply rejoiced in them and gathered other children to share in them from near and far.

Children were not in those days hard to find. It was before the times of constant universal motoring, and, therefore, also before the times of a passionate and perpetually disappointed restlessness. We took our pleasures eagerly, but had that best of all the fairy's gifts—a conscious and excited enjoyment of little things. Almost nothing was too slight for our amusement.

It happened that, although in my childish, lonely soul I was thirsting for affection, none of the children who came to our house found me attractive. There were the Bellishaws of Uffdale, the Croxtons from Moor Park, the Adderleys from Gosforth village. The Adderleys are important in my story and so I must say a word about them—without prejudice, I hope, although even at this great distance of time I can't pretend that I love them!

The Rector of Gosforth was a bachelor, and lived in rooms at the Wastwater end of the village. The Rectory was a big rambling old house, and expensive to run, so he let it to Sir John and Lady Adderley, and lived with perfect content in a frowsty study and a small stuffy bedroom. (I can see him now, following the stream beyond the village, his black clerical hat on one side of his head, a huge pipe in his mouth, and the gleam of delighted anticipation in his eye!)

So, the Adderleys took the Rectory for a year and made a considerable splash in the neighbourhood. They were, as a family, designed for a splash; noisy, happy, confident, most exceedingly self-assured. Lady Adderley, I remember, was a large, broad woman with a big, red, freckled face, and I see her always in a vast floppy hat and gardening gloves, and carrying an enormous pair of scissors. But the three children were the important thing—Ambrose, Grace and Samuel. They were, I suppose, very 'bossy' children. At any rate, as I look back upon them they always ran everything, and that instantly. I can hear Ambrose's commanding voice now as he arrived at our door—'I say! Look here, we're going to play croquet, and bags I the red ball!'

Of course, they despised me thoroughly. They teased me, mocked me, derided me, all most good-naturedly, of course. They were bursting with rude health, and had to give freedom to some of their energy. And there I was, hopeless at games and easily stirred into a temper that was an amusing game for all of them. 'Let's make Humphrey waxy,' was their jolly cry—and waxy I was very easily made!

It happened, therefore, that when the Adderley children appeared I, whenever possible, slipped away. I hid in the wood or I slunk up the road, and then, safe for the time being from persecution, allowed my imagination its freedom, telling myself stories, or, more often, inventing wonderful crises when I played the hero—fires when I saved my sister and the Adderley girl, expeditions when we would be lost in the hills and I only discover the way out, or accidents at sea when I would swim through monstrous waves to secure assistance.

It was on one of these lonely walks that I first saw Mr. Claribel.

★★★★★★

I have already said that, as I look back, I cannot be sure of what was real and what unreal. I know for certain that it was a cold winter's day, with a little, whining, lonely wind that blew a few last shrunken leaves twistedly in the air before they fell. Above the far turn of the road the hump of Black Combe—black against the grey-white chilly sky—looked frowning upon me. And down the road came Mr. Claribel. It has always been my constant belief that he was *dancing* down the road. That, too, may be fancy, but in my memory's eye I see him, oh, so clearly! with his round black hat, his umbrella ill folded, dancing along while the cold thin air trembled through the branches.

When we met he stopped. I had never seen him before (although he had been living in the village for some considerable time) and I must have stared in a very rude way. He was odd at first sight, with his little, meagre body, his brown face, his bright blue eyes, and his long, black coat-tails flapping behind him.

Our conversation (the first of many) was something like this:

'Well, little boy, what are you doing here?'

'Walking, sir.'

'What—all alone? Haven't you anyone to walk with?'

'I like to be alone, sir.' (I was at times a priggish little boy.)

'Like to be alone? Tut! Tut! That's wrong at your age! How old are you?'

'Thirteen and three months.'

'Thirteen and three months—and all by yourself. Where's your father and mother?'

'At Grange Hall, sir. My father's the doctor.'

'Your father's the doctor? And have you no brother and sister?'

'Yes, sir. One brother and one sister.'

'And what are *they* doing?'

'Playing.'

'And so, ought you to be.' It must have been about now that he came very close to me, peering into my face. 'You haven't seen a little dog anywhere?'

'No, sir.'

'It's a small brown dog, and answers to the name of Napoleon. He's disappeared. He's always disappearing. But then so's everything else.'

I remember quite clearly that he asked me then: 'Do you know what's the secret of a happy life?'

'No, sir.'

'Never to be astonished at anything. Take it all as it comes. It's no use your being astonished, because IT doesn't care if you are. IT doesn't care what you feel.'

He said IT with terrific emphasis.

'Dear, dear,' he said. 'It's very cold talking here. Have you had your tea?'

'No, sir.'

'Well, come and have it with me.'

We started along together, he walking at a great pace, sometimes muttering to himself, sometimes dropping his umbrella, which I picked up for him, and, once and again, calling out in a high, shrill treble: 'Napoleon! Napoleon!'

Then, when we were very near to the village, a little brown dog appeared from nowhere. Really from nowhere at all. It was most uncanny. There it was, in the middle of the road, a very nice little dog, with curly brown hair, wagging its tail and looking most friendly.

'Where have you been?' Mr. Claribel said severely. But the little dog didn't mind, only chased a leaf that the wind was playing with, and ran in front of us as though it hadn't a care in the world.

I remember that I wondered whether it was right to go to tea with a complete stranger. I had always been warned that I must never speak to strangers or take anything from them, but I didn't see what harm this gentleman could do me, and I fancy that I was pleased at the thought of disobeying my family for once. Little they cared, I thought, what I did!

We arrived at the little house, with a bare little garden in front of it. This garden was remarkable to me for a large, round silver ball (like a witch-ball) that was posed on a stone pedestal in the very middle of the garden bed. There was also what should have been a small fountain (although no water was playing) and a child's railway train lying dejectedly on its side in the gravel path. I remember all the details of this house as though I were walking in at the front door this very minute.

Mr. Claribel and Napoleon led the way. He helped me off with my coat and muffler, patting me on the shoulder as he did so. Then

I followed him into the very queerest room I had ever seen. It was a small room, with a bright, prattling little fire, a pot of Christmas roses in the window, and a small table laid for tea. The queer thing about it was that it was crammed with the most incongruous things. There were, I remember, two sets of chessmen, a sailing ship modelled in silver with a glass bowl covering it, a large, speckled fish stretched out against the wall, a doll's house with very bright-looking miniature furniture, one of those large glass balls containing a house painted blue which you turn upside-down and it snows (I know because I tried), a crimson drum with the gilt arms of some regiment on the crimson, an ivory elephant, a musical box painted with little country scenes (I know it was a musical box because afterwards I played it), and many, many things more, although these are the only ones that I definitely remember. I never saw a room so crowded, and yet, in some quite happy way, we fitted in exactly, I sitting on one side of the fire, and he on the other, with Napoleon stretched out at his feet.

Soon an old lady arrived with the tea, and we turned to the table.

'I always sit up to the table at tea,' he remarked (and I observed that he took his napkin and tucked it in under his sharp, little brown chin). 'One eats so much more. Don't you think so?'

We certainly ate a great deal that evening! We had thick, rich blackberry jam; thick, rich gingerbread cake, black as thunder, sweet as heaven, damp in the middle; scones and buns and sandwiches and hot buttered toast; tea out of a magnificent old teapot with patterns of leaves and roses in silver as thick as your thumb. I remember that, while I gorged, I asked myself the question: Does he have tea all by himself to this extent every day? Could he have been expecting someone? But how could he have known that he would meet me?

And then, as he so often did, he read my thoughts.

'I knew you were coming to tea,' he said. 'There were tea-leaves in my cup at breakfast this morning.' But he didn't mean that. He had had some way of knowing. I was sure of it. But how could he . . . . when I wasn't sure of it myself!

Before I left him that afternoon he asked me every sort of question, and some of them very unusual. I may, in fact, be inventing here. Isn't it incredible, for instance, that he should have asked me whether I collected acorns? I said, of course, that I did not. He shook his head and said that was a pity. He asked me whether the big toe of my left foot ever ached, and I said that, as a matter of fact, it sometimes did. He smiled, and said that that was an excellent sign, and that he was glad to hear it. He asked me whether I liked to read, and I said I did. What books did I like best? I said Stevenson, Rider Haggard and Stanley Weyman.

He said that he had a book to give me, and out of a drawer near the fireplace he produced a thin, flat book with faded red covers. Inside there were coloured pictures, pictures of remarkable animals, animals with two heads and long swords coming out of their foreheads. There were also maps of the planetary system, and there were ladies with crowns on their heads, and one picture of a large green tree crowded with birds. There were many pages covered entirely with numbers and letters of the alphabet.

'Now, if you could learn what all that means, Humphrey,' he said, 'you could turn yourself into anything you liked any time you liked.'

'Could I really?' I asked, quite fascinated.

'Indeed, you could.'

'And can you turn yourself into anything you like?' I enquired.

'Ah,' he answered, smiling. 'That's asking. But Napoleon can.'

★★★★★★

After that I went home, swollen with food and clutching the red book under my arm. I was greatly excited. I had made a friend. I knew someone that my family didn't know. After this, in the next few weeks, I saw him frequently. I had tea with him on several occasions. Very soon I loved him dearly, for I was a sentimental little boy, longing for affection. No one had ever been so kind to me. He made me, too, begin to have some belief in myself. I brushed my hair and put on a clean collar, and really began to have some opinions of my own and assert them.

Then, of course, my new friendship was discovered. I was seen walking down the street with Mr. Claribel. It was not directly disapproved of, but I was terribly teased about it. I found that Mr. Claribel was considered in the village as someone altogether off his head. No one could charge him with any crime; on the contrary, he was a kind, crazy, old man who gave sweets to the children, visited old Mrs. Mumble when she was in bed with a bad leg, and helped Mr. Somerthwaite when his cow died. But he was *queer*, and that is enough in this world to divide a man from his fellows. As though we are not, all of us, queer as queer! If we are not queer in one way, we are certainly queer in another!

The Adderley children were especially amused at my friendship.

'Let's do Mr. Claribel asking Humphrey to tea!' Ambrose would cry, and he would present an absurd imitation of Mr. Claribel with his coat-tails and badly-folded umbrella. More than that, this new interest of mine seemed to separate me from the others more than ever. Mr. Claribel was mad, and I liked him, so I must be mad too. And then I had something that *they* hadn't got. Children are cruel not because they want to be, but because they are not yet civilised. I was like a sick or injured member of the herd, and the healthy ones must make a protest.

A strange thing was that Mr. Claribel knew exactly what they were doing. I didn't have to tell him a thing. 'If they don't look out,' he said one day, 'I'll give those children the fright of their lives,' and for a moment, as he said it, he appeared quite dangerous! But no one could have been kinder to me than he was. The stories he told me, the presents he made me (I have the round ball with the snow inside it to this day!), the affection he showed me!

So, we moved on towards Christmas. A week before Christmas the snow came. It snowed steadily for three days—real hard snow that covered the ground and stayed there. This is unusual for Cumberland, for snow rarely lies on the lower ground. After the snowfall we had one brilliant blue sky after another. We woke to glittering, sparkling mornings and looked out of the window to a lawn so thick with diamonds that it hurt the eye to gaze on it, and its virgin whiteness was unbroken save for the tiny imprints of the birds. Over everything there was a marvellous hush. You could hear voices calling or dogs barking from great distances, and the shadows cast on the snow by the fir-trees were a deep and tender purple. The oak-tree on the lawn was so heavy with snow that it seemed that, strong though it was, it must bend with its burden.

Inside the house, what excitement! In those days Christmas was an event of mystery, of almost passionate anticipation, of blissful realisation! We had no outside aids. There were one or two parties, a Christmas tree for the village children, but all the realities we must spin, like silkworms, out of ourselves!

It was a fine year, I remember, for holly—the berries were thick—and soon the house was decorated from kitchen to attic. But the principal enterprise was the inventing of presents. These were secrets evolved behind locked doors, wrapped away in paper and hidden in drawers. We children had little money, and the only place for purchases was the village shop. I had, in all, about six shillings of my own, and four people must have major presents, and by major I meant something of real importance, something original, something startling. Never mind now what my presents were. I have, in fact, altogether forgotten.

But what I do remember is that, as Christmas Day approached, I began to be overwhelmed with a sense of coming failure. I wanted this time to assert myself, to show them all that I *did* matter! My presents were to be so unusual that they would be compelled to consider me. But, of course, they were not. And, as the others grew ever more busy and important and excited, I, as I always did when the whole family was excited, became less and less of anything. When they needed a messenger or a scapegoat or an 'odd boy' they made use of me— and with good-humoured contempt. So at least I thought. I have no doubt that I imagined all this, and that they were too busy, too jolly, too happy to think of me at all, or, if they did, fancied that I was jolly and happy too. But because, perhaps, my new friendship with Mr. Claribel had given me new hopes I felt all the more deeply that I was a wretched failure, and of no use to anyone.

And the worst thing of all was the Adderleys' party. This was to be on Christmas Eve—a grand affair at the Rectory; children from all the neighbourhood, supper and games and a Christmas tree. I never suffered anywhere as I did at the Adderley parties, for it was there that I was most completely disregarded. Nobody's fault but my own. I was tongue-tied in a large company, or, if I did speak, made a remark at which everyone laughed. I *wanted* to be gay, but happiness on these occasions seemed to be always just out of my reach.

As the hours passed the thought of the Adderley festivity clouded my eyes. I saw myself, in my sensitive, excited imagination, mocked and derided, the more bitterly a failure in that I could picture to myself so easily how wonderful it would be were I a success. I could see myself applauded, could hear the comments—'What a remarkable boy! A most unusual child!' Not that I thought myself remarkable or unusual, but for once how splendid it would be if I appeared so!

My unhappiness reached a climax on the morning of Christmas Eve. I was carrying something for my mother and dropped it; I could not find something for my brother; my father said 'Come, come, Humphrey—where are your wits?' In the middle of the morning—a lovely crystal-clear day it was—I slipped away and took Mr. Claribel my present. After much thought and balancing of possibilities, I had decided that I would give him a penknife. An absurd present, perhaps, but among all his possessions I had never seen a penknife, and, as it was a thing that I needed at the time very badly myself, it was obvious that

41

other people must need one, too.

The one that I bought at the village shop (with, I am afraid, quite half my available riches) was made of tortoiseshell. (Imitation? I fear so. I didn't know it then.) It had only one blade, but it *looked* bright, and it *could* cut, because I tested it. Indeed, I remember that I liked it so much that I had a moment's awful temptation to keep it for myself. I didn't know then what I know now—that when one keeps for oneself a present that one has bought for someone else it turns, inevitably, to dust and ashes. No, I loved Mr. Claribel, and by the time that I had reached his house I was delighted at the thought of his pleasure. And he *was* pleased! He kissed me very ceremoniously on the forehead. I detested to be kissed, but on this occasion, it warmed my heart, made me think suddenly of the Adderley party, created in some way a sharp picture of my clumsiness and isolation there—and I burst into tears!

The little man made all sorts of sounds of distress, brought out the black gingerbread cake, sat with his arm on my shoulder while I ate it, then gave me *his* present, which was none other than the beautiful musical box with the pictures. I was so terribly pleased about this that I threw my arms round his neck and kissed him in my turn.

He asked me then why I was unhappy, and I told him. It was the Adderley party. I didn't like the Adderleys, and their parties were *awful*. I knew that I should make a fool of myself, that I should disgrace my father and mother, that I should come home from it so miserable that Christmas would be altogether spoilt. He nodded his head a number of times. Then he said:

'Now, don't you worry. I promise that you shall enjoy the party.'

I shook my head dismally.

'Just you wait. I've never promised anything yet that I haven't brought off. Just you wait.'

In some mysterious way relieved, I ran home, clutching my musical box.

✶✶✶✶✶✶

At the appointed hour, muffled up to our noses, our hands in thick woollen gloves, my father carrying a lantern, we set out for the Rectory.

Here it may be that, because of after events, my imagination once more leads me astray, but, looking back, I seem now to recover a kind of magic in the air that night. The sky crackled with stars, our breath drove in front of the lantern in cloudy bursts, illuminated by that fitful gleam. The star-shimmering light was brilliant enough to haze the air with a kind of silver twilight, and within this the trees and hedges seemed to sail in shapes of white marble across the fields. The frost was heavy, and the snow crunched and protested under our boots. There would be a little shiver in the air, and a dust of snow would scatter over our shoulders. There was every witness to Christmas Eve. At old Miss Mark's house down the road a little group were singing carols, and their lantern seemed to greet ours in a roguish fashion, as much as to say: 'What are *you* doing leading those ridiculous mortals along the road? Why not drop them into a pond?'

All in a quite friendly way, of course!

Across the fields came the tumbling, tangled melody of the church bells. They were practising for tomorrow, and I could see Joe Church-er, who was rather a friend of mine and a very fat man, straining at the rope, and little Harry Bone, who was so short and thin, standing on tip-toe. In any case, there they were, those rich, rollicking, impetuous chimes rolling over the white, frosted fields as though they were so wildly excited by good news that they were tumbling over themselves to tell it.

As we approached the Rectory, I was moved, I remember, by two very opposite impulses. One was to run away and hide. I tramped along in the rear of our family procession with all the certainty of being forgotten and neglected that I had all day long been expect-ing. The family had, up to this evening, the most curious fashion of behaving as though I didn't exist; *after* this evening they were never unconscious of me again! I felt miserable, and socially a pariah, but at the same time I was excited with expectation. I was quite certain that Mr. Claribel would keep his promise.

How he would do it I did not of course know, but something would happen, something that would astonish everybody!

Inside the house we were borne along on the general stream. Our wraps were taken from us, we patted our hair, straightened our waist-coats, tried to look as grown-up as possible. I remember, that, in a rather miserable, doomed kind of way, watching my sister Sarah, I decided that she looked too silly for anything. She was *not* a beauty (none of us, I fear, was that), her figure was lumpy, and her stockings *would* go crooked and her nose shiny! (Dear Sarah! how I learnt to love you afterwards! What I would give to have you sitting beside me now!) I was a caustic little critic in those days, but a critic (like so many critics) who could be changed, by a kind personal word, into an appreciator.

There were, however, for me no kind words during the first part of that evening. Everything went as wrong as it could possibly go! We all tumbled into the drawing-room and stood about, looking, most of us, angry and shy.

Lady Adderley, red in the face and fastened into a too-tight costume of light-blue silk, sailed into the midst of us, shouting out cheerful remarks to break the ice. The room was very gay, with its blaze of lights and holly over all the pictures, a thick clump of mistletoe, burdened with berries, hanging from the centre illumination that shivered with a thousand silver pennies as we moved about under it.

The ice must be broken, so we started with musical chairs, and then, at the very beginning of the evening, I disgraced myself. For a long, thin lady with a tiresome train was skirting the chairs just in front of me. She was one of those middle-aged ladies who, at a children's party, are 'younger than the youngest,' for she passed along, clutching at the back of every chair, and uttering shrill cries of pleasure and excitement. I was just behind her and trod on her train. There was a rent and a cry. The lady turned, and, for a moment, I thought that she would slap me, she looked so vexed. But she pulled herself together, smiled a bitter smile, said that it didn't matter in the least, and retired to have something done to it.

Of course, everyone had seen that I was responsible. 'Just like Humphrey,' I heard someone say. I was now in that parlous state, known to all of us in nightmares, when every step is perilous. Move where I would, I should assist some catastrophe. Oddly enough, I believe that everyone else felt something of the same discomfort. It promised to be one of those parties upon which unhappy hostesses look back, with dismay, for the rest of their lives. At the end of that very first game there was trouble because a fat little boy, clinging to the seat of the last chair, protested that *he* had won and not the thin boy with the rabbit teeth who was sitting on the chair-edge as though he were Casablanca. Other people took sides. A little girl said it was a 'shame.' We then played Blind Man's Buff, a dangerous game, because it degenerates so readily into horse-play. It did so now, and a big boy pushed a little girl over, and she started loudly to cry.

Yes, things were very wrong, and I saw Lady Adderley consulting with her husband. She was asking him, I expect, whether it would not be wise to hurry things forward. I was myself so completely neglected that I might have been a little lonely ghost, invisible to all the world. I spoke to no one. No one spoke to me. There are no miseries in after life to compare with these miseries of childhood.

★★★★★★

Then the door opened. A maid stood there and I heard her say quite clearly:

'My lady—the conjurer . . . . .'

It happened that I was standing near to Lady Adderley, and I could mark very easily her expression. Startled it was! Plainly she had invited no conjurer, nor, had she had one up her sleeve, would it have been such a man as now stood waiting in the doorway. He was tall and thin, with a long pale face, a very pronounced hooked nose, and black hair that stood up stiffly on end. He was dressed entirely in black, and over his shoulders there hung a short black cape. In one hand he carried a black soft hat with a high crown, and in the other a square red leather box which he held by a bright brass handle. He stood there, very quietly, his long legs close together, not moving at all, as thin and straight and still as a mast waiting for its flag.

Lady Adderley had invited no conjurer—that was plain. She was astonished as though she had seen a witch with a broomstick. She intended, I've no doubt, to protest, to ask who it was had come thus uninvited. She took a step forward, then she stopped. Was it something in the conjurer's eyes, politely bent upon hers, his still, assured attitude, his black cloak, even his red leather box?

Or was it simply that she felt that her party was threatened with failure, that something must be done to save it? Or was it just that she could not help herself?

In any case, she suddenly turned to her husband and I heard her say: 'This is the surprise I had for you, dear.' Then she went up to the conjurer and invited him to come forward.

I cannot be sure, but I fancy that from the moment of the conjurer's entrance the spirit of the party changed. It may have been that we were all delighted to have a surprise—a conjurer was the very last thing that we had expected! It may have been that we ourselves were beginning to be frightened at the spirit of discontent and bad temper that was springing up among us.

In any case, everybody, laughing, chattering, in the very best of tempers, settled down, forming a big circle, the older people on chairs and most of the children cross-legged on the floor.

The conjurer, who seemed to be a solemn man, for he did not smile, walked forward and took his place on a long, thick, purple rug in front of the windows. Lady Adderley placed a table in front of

45

him, and on this he laid his red leather box. Then—so suddenly as to make everyone jump—from somewhere within his cloak, it seemed, he produced a long wand, coloured crimson with a silver tip at the end of it. Then he spoke to us, and his voice was soft, and every word as clear as a bell.

He told us not to be astonished at anything that we saw, that there were a great many things more wonderful in this world than we would ever suppose, that we must never say that anything wasn't possible. For, he said, smiling for the first time (I, staring at him, felt as though I had seen that smile before), things became impossible to us as we grew older only because we closed our minds up as tight as his red leather box. Of course, if we *would* shut ourselves up inside a red leather box, that was our own fault—but he hoped that *we'd* be wiser than that. We all laughed at that, and thought within ourselves that of course we would be!

Then he waved his wand and began his tricks. At first, they were quite ordinary. He brought rolls of coloured paper from his black hat, a flower in a pot from under a table, an egg out of his left ear; and a pack of cards disappeared into thin air. I heard Ambrose, who was sitting near to me, murmur: 'He's only an ordinary conjurer, after all.' Then he paused, came forward nearer to us, and looked at us all with his piercing black eyes.

'You've seen those things before, haven't you?' he said. 'Well, now you're going to see something new.'

A little shiver of excitement ran through all of us.

'But first,' he said, 'I must have a boy to help me.'

Several boys sprang up—the kind of boys who, all their lives afterwards, would be springing forward on just such occasions.

But he shook his head.

'No,' he said. 'I want the *right* kind of boy.' He looked round, searching through the company. '*That's* the boy I want!' he said, and he nodded his head in my direction.

Even then I didn't think that it was myself he wanted! I was packed away behind a fat boy and between two fat girls. The fat boy thought that it was he! With puffs of pleasure he rose to his feet.

'No,' said the conjurer. 'That's the boy I'm going to have'—and with his red wand he pointed directly at me.

How astonished everybody was! That was the first triumph of my young life. Humphrey Porter, whom no one considered anything at all; Humphrey Porter, who was quite certain to make a mess of it!

Poor conjurer! He would soon see how grave his mistake! But here was a curious thing. I, who was terrified of doing anything before others, on this occasion knew no fear. I can see myself now, climbing through the other children, and then, before their mocking derisive eyes, taking my place quietly beside the little table, waiting for my orders.

'Thank you!' said the conjurer gravely. 'That will do very nicely.'

Then for the first time he opened the red box and took from it a number of things. There were some small china saucers, a number of little coloured boxes, a tiny pistol, some children's bricks, three small coloured flags, red, white and blue, a mouse-trap, a silver bell, a toy trumpet. Over all these things he spread a very large white handkerchief. The ground of this handkerchief was white, but I saw that it was covered with pictures of little blue ships all in full sail.

'Now,' he said, 'I want you all to understand that this is a very exceptional boy. An ordinary boy wouldn't do in the least. I'm very lucky to have found such a boy.'

(At this point I should have hung my head. But I didn't. I stared in front of me and smiled at my mother, who smiled back at me.)

'What is your name, boy?' he asked me.

'Humphrey,' I answered, and for some reason or other was quite sure that he knew without my telling him.

'Now show all your friends what you can do!' he said.

And what didn't I do in the next half-hour? I was handed the toy trumpet and, quite confidently, played beautiful tunes upon it—I who had never played a tune in my life! At his command I whistled like a bird, nay, like a whole forest of birds. 'That's a thrush,' he said, nodding his head contentedly. 'Now a blackbird. And now—what about the nightingale?' I pursed my lips together and the room was filled with the song of the nightingale.

'Now take these little boxes, Humphrey,' he said, 'and throw them into the air.'

I threw them into the air, and behold, there they stayed, suspended, shining in all their colours under the glittering silver lights. ('I know how you did *that*,' Ambrose said confidently afterwards. 'There were invisible wires coming out of the red box.' Well, if *he* knew, it was more than I did.)

I took up, under his instructions, the little silver bell and it rang a perfect carillon of chimes. I took the mouse-trap and, walking backwards and forwards, holding it in front of the audience, drew out of it one small white mouse after another. They ran up my sleeve, over my shoulders, then disappeared into the mouse-trap again. I waved the coloured flags and they grew larger and larger until they seemed to reach to the ceiling.

'Now, Humphrey,' he said, putting his hand on my shoulder (why was that touch so very familiar?), 'tell that lady over there what she has in her little white bag.'

'That lady,' I said, without hesitation, 'has in her bag a small white handkerchief, a little looking-glass with a blue border, a pink needle-case, and a small bottle of smelling-salts with a crystal stopper.'

How everyone gasped, as well they might! The lady was asked to open her bag, and there were the articles I had named. (I need scarcely say that I was as greatly astonished as anyone!)

'And that boy,' he said, pointing to Ambrose, who was standing up with his mouth wide open. 'What has *he* got in his trouser-pocket? You may as well tell us in French,' he added casually.

So, in perfect French, I told Ambrose that he was carrying in his pocket a lump of toffee, a knife with a broken blade, three coppers and a half-crown, and a catapult. (Strange things to carry in your Eton suit, but then Ambrose was very acquisitive, and I didn't know until later that Ambrose had stolen the knife from his brother and had been forbidden by his father to have a catapult. My revelations disturbed Ambrose considerably.)

So, it went on, and with every moment my glory was growing greater and greater! I could feel it mounting about me! It was as though I could see into the heart of everyone and tell how proud my father and mother were, how pleased Sarah was, and how on every side they were thinking: 'Well, I never! I'd no idea the little Porter boy had so much in him!'

At last came the final splendour. The conjurer raised the handker-chief with the little blue ships and told me to lift my arm. I did so. What happened then? How do I know, at this distance of time? Is any mystery ever fully revealed?

But it seemed to me that the conjurer grew to a tremendous height, that the room was filled with delicious sounds, that I was aware that Christmas was better than any other time, and that no Christmas was as good as this Christmas, that high above our heads hung a splendid star, and that the conjurer, whispering from his great height into my ear, promised me that all my wishes should be fulfilled, that if only I were patient and quiet and unselfish enough, I should be happy for ever after. Nonsense, of course. No conjurer can bring off such tricks. But I know, from the later accounts that everyone gave, that we all, in our different ways, felt for a moment the enchantment, were confident of our happiness, knew ourselves to be transformed.

'And that, ladies and gentlemen,' he said, bowing, 'is the end of my little entertainment.'

How everyone clapped, how they laughed, how they chattered! And while they were talking he was gone. When we turned round to find him there was no sign of him—gone with his hat and his red leather box and his red wand.

I remained, of course, to enjoy my triumph. I'll say no more about that. I smiled and I laughed, and I said that it was nothing to do with me, and I ate the largest supper of my life.

'And to think,' said Mother on the way home, 'that you've taken us all in, Humphrey.'

'It's always the quiet ones,' said my father, 'who come out strong on an occasion.'

★★★★★★

A few days later I went and had tea with Mr. Claribel. I talked nineteen to the dozen, telling him every detail of that wonderful evening—and once again, as so often before, felt that he knew it all before I told him.

Then came one of the most amazing things! He sneezed, and out of his pocket took his handkerchief. It was a white handkerchief covered with little blue ships in full sail.

'But that——!' I cried.

He tweaked my ear.

'When you go home tonight, Humphrey,' he said, 'look at that red book I once gave you. If you study page seventy-three, learn it by heart and practise a little, you will become a very good conjurer. It's quite easy.'

★★★★★★

But I don't know. Many a day did I study page seventy-three. All to no purpose. I cannot even make a rabbit jump out of a hat.

It needs, I expect, more than a book.

Lizzie Rand

Lizzie Rand was just forty-six years of age when old Mrs. Roughton McKenzie died leaving her all her money. Months later she had not thoroughly realised what had happened to her.

Until that day of Mrs. McKenzie's death she had never had any money. She had spent her life, her energies, her pluck and her humour in the service of one human being after another, and generally in the service of women. It seemed to her to be really funny that the one who had during her life begrudged her most should in the end be the one who had given her everything; but no one had ever understood old Mrs. McKenzie, and as likely as not she had left her money to Lizzie Rand just to spite her numerous relations. Lizzie had expected nothing. She never did expect anything, which was as well perhaps, because no one ever gave her anything. She was not a person to whom one naturally gave things; she had a pride, a reserve, an assertion of her own private liberty that kept people away and forbade intimacy. That had not always been so. In the long ago days when she had been Adela Beaminster's secretary she had given herself. She had loved a man who had not loved her, and out of the shock of that she had won a friendship with another woman, which was still perhaps the most precious thing that she had. But that same shock had been enough for her. She guarded, with an almost bitter ferocity, the purity and liberty of her soul.

All the women whose secretaries she had afterwards been had felt this in her, and most of them had resented it. Old Mrs. McKenzie had resented it more than any of them. She was a selfish, painted, over-decorated old creature, a widow with no children and only nephews and nieces to sigh after her wealth. One of Lizzie's chief duties had been to keep these nephews and nieces from the door, and this she had done with a certain grim austerity, finding that none of them cared for the aunt and all for the money. The outraged relations decided, of course, at once that she was a plotting, despicable creature; it is doing her less than justice to say that the idea that the money would be left to her never for a single instant entered her head. Mrs. McKenzie taunted her once for expecting it.

"Of course, you're waiting," she said, "like all of them, to pick the bones of the corpse."

Lizzie Rand laughed.

"Now is that like me?" she asked. "And, more important, is it like you?"

Mrs. McKenzie sniggered her tinkling, wheezy snigger. There was a certain honesty between them. They had certain things in common.

"I don't like you," she said. "I don't see how anyone could. You're too self-sufficient—but you certainly have a sense of humour."

There had been a time once when many people liked Lizzie, and she reflected now, with a little shudder, that perhaps only one person in the world, Rachel Seddon, the woman friend before-mentioned, liked and understood her. Why had she shut herself off? Why presented so stiff, so immaculate, so cold a personality to the world? She was not stiff, not cold, not immaculate. It was, perhaps, simply that she felt that it was in that way only that she could get her work done, and to do her work thoroughly seemed to her now to be the job best worthwhile in life.

During the war she had almost broken from her secretaryship and gone forth to do Red Cross work or anything that would help. A kind of timidity that had grown upon her with the years, a sense of her age and of her loneliness, held her back. Twenty years ago, she would have gone with the first. Now she stayed with Mrs. McKenzie.

Mrs. McKenzie died on the day of the Armistice, November 11, 1918. Her illness had not been severe. Lizzie had had, at the most, only a week's nursing; it had been obvious from the first that nothing could save the old lady. Mrs. McKenzie had not looked as though she were especially anxious that anything should save her. She had lain there in scornful silence, asking for nothing, complaining of nothing, despising everything. Lizzie admitted that the old woman died game.

There had followed then that hard, bewildering period that Lizzie knew by now so well where she must pull herself, so reluctantly, so heavily towards the business of finding a new engagement. She did not, of course, expect Mrs. McKenzie to leave her a single penny. She stayed for a week or two with her friend Rachel Seddon. But Rachel, a widow with an only son, was so tumultuously glad at the return of her boy, safe and whole, from the war, that it was difficult for her just then to take any other human being into her heart. She loved Lizzie, and would do anything in the world for her; she was indeed for ever urging her to give up these sterile companionships and secretaryships and come and make her home with her. But Lizzie, this time, felt her isolation as she had never done before.

"I'm getting old," she thought. "And I'm drifting off . . . soon I shall be utterly alone." The thought sent little shivering ghosts climbing about her body. She saw in the gay, happy, careless, kindly eyes of young Tom Seddon how old she was to the new generation.

He called her "Aunt Liz," took her to the theatre, and was an angel . . . nevertheless an angel happily, almost boastfully, secure in another, warmer planet than hers.

Then came the shock. Mrs. McKenzie had left her everything— the equivalent of about eight thousand pounds a year.

At first her sense was one of an urgent need of rest. She sank back amongst the cushions and pillows of Rachel's house and refused to think . . . refused to think at all. . . . She considered for a moment the infuriated faces of the McKenzie relations. Then they, too, passed from her consciousness.

When she faced the world again, she faced it with the old common sense that had always been her most prominent characteristic. She had eight thousand a year. Well, she would do the very best with it that she could. Rachel, who had appeared to be more deeply excited than she over the event, had various suggestions to offer, but Lizzie had her own ideas. She could not remember the time when she had not planned what she would do when somebody left her money. . . .

She took one of the most charming flats in Hortons, bought beautiful things for it, etchings by D. T. Cameron, one Nevinson, and a John drawing, some Japanese prints; she had books and soft carpets and flowers and a piano; and had the prettiest spare room for a friend. Then she stopped and looked about her. There were certain charities in which she had been always deeply interested, especially one for Poor Gentlewomen. There was a home, too, for illegitimate babies. She remembered, with a happy irony, the occasion when she had tried to persuade Mrs. McKenzie to give something to these charities and had failed. . . . Well, Mrs. McKenzie was giving now all right. Lizzie hoped that she knew it.

There accumulated around her all the business that clusters about an independent woman with means. She was on committees; many people who would not have looked twice at her before like I her now and asked her to their houses.

Again, she stopped and looked about her.

Still there was something that she needed. What was it? Companionship? More than that. Affection, a centre to her life; someone who needed her, someone to whom she was of more importance than anyone else in the world. Even a dog. . . .

She was forty-six. Without being plain she was too slight, too hard-drawn, too masculine, above all too old to be attractive to men. An old maid of forty-six. She faced the truth. She gave little dinner-parties, and felt more lonely than ever. Even it seemed there was nobody who wanted to make her a confidante. People wanted her money, but herself not at all. She was not good conversationally. She said sharp sarcastic things that frightened people. People did not want the truth; they wanted things to be wrapped up first, as her mother and sister had wanted them years ago.

She was a failure socially, in spite of her money. She could not be genial, and yet her heart ached for love.

At this moment Mr. Edmund Lapsley appeared. Lizzie met him at a party given by Mrs. Philip Mark in Bryanston Square. Mrs. Mark was an old friend of Rachel's, a kindly and clever woman with an ambitious husband who would never get very far.

Her parties were always formed by a strange mixture dictated first by her kind heart and secondly her desire to have people in her house who might possibly help her husband. Edmund Lapsley originated in the former of these impulses. He was not much to look at—long, lanky, with a high bony head, a prominent Roman nose and large, cracking fingers. He was shabbily dressed, awkward in his manner, and apprehensive. It was his eyes that first attracted Lizzie's attention. They were beautiful large brown eyes, with the expression of a lost and lonely dog seated deep in their pupils. He sat with Lizzie in a corner of the crowded drawing-room to arrange his long legs so that they should not be in the way, cracked his long fingers together and endeavoured to be interested in the people whom Lizzie pointed out to him.

"That's Henry Trenchard," Lizzie said, "that wild-looking boy with the untidy hair. . . . He's very clever. Going to be our great novelist . . . . . That's his sister, Millie. Mrs. Mark's sister, too. Isn't she pretty? She's the loveliest of the family. That stout clergyman is a Trenchard cousin.

They all hang together in the most wonderful way, you know. His wife ran away and never came back again. I don't think I wonder; he looks heavy. . . ." And so on.

Lizzie wondered to herself why she bothered. It was not her habit to gossip, and Mr. Lapsley was obviously not at all interested.

"I beg your pardon," she said; "you don't want to know who these people are."

"No," he said in a strange, sudden, desperate whisper. "I don't. I lost my wife only three months ago. I'm trying to go out into the world again. I can't. It doesn't do any good." He gripped his knee with one of his large bony hands.

"I'm so sorry," Lizzie said. "I didn't know. How tiresome of me to have gone on chattering like that! You should have stopped me."

He seemed himself to be surprised at the confession that he had made. He stared at her in a bewildered fashion like an owl suddenly flashed into light. He stared, saying nothing. Suddenly in the same hurried, husky whisper he went on: "Do you mind my talking to you? I want to talk to somebody. I'd like to tell you about her."

"Please," said Lizzie, looking into his eyes, that were tender and beautiful, so unlike his ugly body, and full of unhappiness.

He talked; the words tumbled out in an urgent, tremulous confusion.

They had been married, it appeared, ten years, ten wonderful happy years. "How she can have cared for me, that's what I never understood, Miss—Miss—"

"Rand," said Lizzie.

"I beg your pardon. Difficult to catch . . . when you are introduced. . . . Never understood. I was years older than she. I'm fifty now—forty when I married her, and she was only twenty. Thirty when she—when she died. In childbirth it was. The child, a boy, was born dead. Everyone prophesied disaster. They all told her not to marry me, she was so pretty, and so young, and so brilliant. She sang, Miss Rand, just like a lark. She did, indeed. She was trained in Paris. I oughtn't to have proposed to her, I suppose. That's what I tell myself now, but I was carried off my feet, completely off my feet. I couldn't help myself at all. I loved her from the first moment that I saw her. You know how those things are, Miss Rand. And, in any case, I don't know. Ten perfect years, that's a good deal for anyone to have, isn't it? And she was as happy as I was. It may seem strange to you, looking at me, but it was really so. She thought I was so much cleverer than I was—and better too.

54

"It used to make me very nervous sometimes lest she should find me out, you know, and leave me. I always expected that to happen. But she was so charitable to everyone. Never could see the bad side of people, and they were always better with her than with anyone else. We'd always hoped for a child, and then, as the years went on, we gave it up. 'Edmund,' she said to me, 'we must make it up to one another.' And then she told me it was going to be all right. You wouldn't have believed two ordinary people could be so happy as we were when we knew about it.

"We made many plans, of course. I was a little apprehensive that I'd be rather old to bring up a child, but she was so young that made it all right—so wonderfully young. . . . Then she died. It was incredible, of course. I didn't believe it . . . I don't believe it now. She's not dead. That's absurd. You'd feel the same if you'd seen her, Miss Rand. So full of life, and then suddenly , . . nothing at all. It's impossible. Nature isn't like that. Things gradually die, don't they, and change into something else. Not suddenly. . . ."

He broke off. He was clutching his knees and staring in front of him. "I don't know why I talk to you like this, Miss Rand . . . I hope you'll forgive me. I shouldn't have bothered you."

"I'm pleased that you have, Mr. Lapsley." She got up. She felt that he would be glad now to escape. "Won't you come and see me? I have a flat in Horton's Chambers in Duke Street, No. 42. . . . Do come. Just telephone."

He looked up at her, not rising from his seat. Then he got up.

"I will," he said. "Thank you."

He was still staring at her, and she knew that he had something further to say. She could see it struggling in his eyes. But she did not want him to confess any more. He would be the kind of man to regret afterwards what he had done. She would not burden his conscience. And yet she had the knowledge that it was something very serious that he wanted to tell her, something that had been, in reality, at the back of all his earlier confession.

She refused the appeal in his eyes, said goodnight, took his hand for a moment and turned away.

Afterwards she was talking to Katherine Mark.

"I see you were kind to poor Mr. Lapsley," Katherine said.

"How sad about his wife!" Lizzie answered.

"Yes. And she really was young and beautiful. No one understood why she married him, but I've never seen anything more successful. . .

.. I didn't think he'd come tonight, but I'm fond of him. Philip doesn't care for him much, but he reminds me of a cousin of ours, John Trenchard, who was killed in Russia in the second year of the war. But John was unhappier than Mr. Lapsley. He never had his perfect years."

"Yes, that's something," Lizzie acknowledged.

It was strange to her afterwards that Edmund Lapsley should persist so vividly in her mind. She saw him with absolute clarity almost as though he were with her in her flat. She thought of him a good deal. He needed someone to comfort him, and she needed someone to comfort. She hoped he would come and see her.

He did come, one afternoon, quite unexpectedly and without telephoning first. Fortunately, she was there, alone, and wanting someone to talk to. At first, he was shy and self-conscious. They talked stiffly about London, and the weather, and the approaching Peace, and whether there would ever be a League of Nations, and how high prices were, and how impossible it was to get servants and when you got them they went. . . . Lizzie broke ruthlessly in upon this. "It isn't the least little good, Mr. Lapsley," she said, "our talking like this. It's mere waste of time. We both know plenty of people to whom we can chatter this nonsense. Either we are friends, or we are not. If we are friends we must go a little further. Are we friends?"

He seemed to be at a loss. He blinked at her.

"Yes," he said.

"Well, then," she looked at him and smiled. "I don't want to force your confidence, but there was something that you were anxious to tell me about the other night, some way in which I could help you. I stopped you then, but I don't want to stop you now. I'll be honoured indeed if there's anything I can do."

He gulped, stammered, then out it came. At the first hint of his trouble it was all that Lizzie could do to repress an impatient gesture. His trouble was—spiritualism!

Of all the tiresome things, of all the things about which she had no patience at all, of all the idiotic, money-wasting imbecilities! He poured it all out. He had read books, at last a friend had taken him. . . . . . A Dr. Orloff, a very wonderful medium, a very trustworthy man, a man about whom there could be no question.

On the first occasion the results had been poor—on the second his Margaret had spoken to him, actually spoken to him. Oh! but there could be no doubt! Her very voice. . . . His own voice shook as he spoke of it.

Since then he had been, he was forced to admit, a number of times—almost every day . . . every day . . . every afternoon. He talked to Margaret every day now for half an hour or more.

He was sure it was right, he was doing nobody any harm . . . they two together . . . it could not be wrong, but . . . He stopped. Lizzie gave him no help. She sat there looking in front of her. She despised him; she was conscious of a deep and bitter disappointment. She did not know how he could betray his weakness, his softness, his gullibility. She had thought him . . . She looked up suddenly, knowing that his voice had stopped. He was gazing at her in despair, his eyes wide with an unhappiness that struck deep to his heart.

"You despise me!" he said.

"Yes," she answered. "I do." But she was aware at the same time that she could have gone across to him and put her hand on his head and comforted him. "That's all false! You know it is. You're only deluding yourself because you want to persuade yourself—it's weak of you. Your wife can't come to you that way."

"Don't take it from me!" His voice was an agonised cry. "It's all I have. It's true. It's true. It must be true!"

They were suddenly in contact . . . she felt a warm sense of protection and pity, a longing to comfort and help so strong that she instinctively put her hand to her heart as though she would restrain it.

"Oh, I didn't mean," she cried, "that I'd take anything away from you. No, no—never that. If you thought that I meant that, you're wrong. Keep anything you've got. Perhaps I'm mistaken. The mediums I've known have been charlatans. That's prejudiced me. Then I don't think I want my friends to come back to me in quite that way. . . . If it's true, it seems to be forcing them, against their will, as it were. Oh! I know a great many people now are finding it all true and good. I don't know anything about it. I shouldn't have said what I did. And then you see I've never lost anyone whom I loved very much."

"Never?" Mr. Lapsley asked, staring at her with wide-open eyes.

"No, never, I think."

He got up and came across to her, standing near to her, looking down upon her. She saw that she had aroused his interest, that she had suddenly switched his attention upon herself.

She had aroused him in the only way that he could be aroused, by stirring his pity for her. She knew exactly how suddenly he saw her—as a lonely, unhappy, deserted old maid. She did not mind; that the attention of any one single human being should be centred upon her for herself was a very wonderful, touching thing.

Silence fell between them; the pretty room, grey and silver in the half-light, gathered intimately around them. When at last he went away it seemed that the last ten minutes had added years to their knowledge of one another.

A strange time for Lizzie followed. Edmund Lapsley had rushed into her life with a precipitate urgency that showed how empty before it had been. But there was more than their mere contact in the affair. She was fighting a battle; all her energies were in it; she was ruthless, savage, tooth-and-nail; he should be snatched from this spiritualism.

It was a silent battle. He never spoke to her again of it. He did not say whether he went or not, and she did not ask him. But soon they were meeting almost every day, and she felt with a strange almost savage pleasure that her influence over him grew with every meeting. She discovered many things about his character. He was weak, undecided, almost subservient, a man whom she would have despised perhaps had it not been for the real sweetness that lay at the roots of him. She very quickly understood how this girl, Margaret, although so young and so ignorant of the world, must have dominated him. "Any woman could!" she thought almost angrily to herself, and yet there was a kind of pride behind her anger.

She would not confess to herself that what she was really fighting was the memory of the dead girl, or, if she confessed at all, it was to console herself with the thought that it was right for him now to "cheer up a little."

Cheer up he did; it was curious to watch the rapidity with which he responded to Lizzie's energy and humour and vitality.

At last she challenged him:

"Well, what about Dr. Orloff?" she asked.

He looked at her with a sudden startled glance, then almost under his breath he said: "I don't go any more; I thought you didn't want me to."

So sudden a confession of her power took her breath away. She asked her next question.

"But Margaret?" she said. He answered that as though he were arguing some long-debated question with himself:

"I don't know," he replied slowly. "You were right. That wasn't the proper way to bring her back, even though it were genuine. I must tell you, Miss Rand," he said, suddenly flinging up his head and looking across at her, "you've shown me so many things since we first met. I

58

was getting into a very bad way, indulging myself in my grief. Margaret wouldn't have liked that either, but it wasn't until I knew you that I saw what I was doing. Thank you."

"Oh, you mustn't!" She shook her head. "You mustn't take me for Gospel like that, Mr. Lapsley. You make me frightened for my responsibility. We are friends, and we must help one another, but we must keep our independence."

He shook his head, smiling.

"There's always been somebody who's taken my independence away," he said. "And I like it."

After he had gone she had the tussle of her life. She ate dinner alone, then sat far into the night fighting. Why should she fight at all? Here was the charge given straight into her hand, the gift for which she had longed and longed, the very man for her, the man whom she could care for as she would her child. Care for and protect and guide and govern. Govern! Like a torch flaring between dark walls that word lit her soul for her. Govern! That was what she wanted; all her life she had wanted it.

She wanted to feel her power, to dominate, to command. And all for his good. She loved him, she loved his sweetness and his goodness and his simplicity. She could make him happy and contented and at ease for the rest of his days. He should never have another anxiety, never another responsibility. Why fight then? Wasn't it obviously the best thing in the world, both for him and for her? She needed him. He her. She abandoned herself then to happy, tender thoughts of their life together. What it would be! What they could do with old Mrs. McKenzie's money!

She sat there trying to lose herself in that golden future. She could not quite lose herself. Threading it was again and again the warning that something was not right with it, that she was pursuing some course that she should not. The clock struck half-past eleven. She gave a little shiver. The room was cold. She knew then, with that little shiver, of what she had been thinking. Margaret Lapsley. . . .

Why should she be thinking of her? She was dead. She could not complain. And if she were still consciously with them, surely, she would rather that he should be cared for and loved and guarded than pursue a lonely life full of regrets and melancholy. What kind of girl had she been? Had she loved him as he had loved her? How young she had died! How young and fresh and happy! . . . Lizzie shivered again. Ah! She was old. Forty-six and old—old in thoughts and hopes and dreams. Pervaded by a damp mist of unhappiness, she went to bed and lay there, looking into the dark.

With the morning her scruples had vanished. She saw Margaret Lapsley no more. She was her own sane, matter-of-fact mistress. A delightful fortnight followed. All her life afterwards Lizzie looked back to those fourteen days as the happiest of her time. They were together now every afternoon. Very often in the evening too they went to the theatre or music. He was her faithful dog. He agreed with all her suggestions, eagerly, implicitly. Mentally, he was not stupid; he knew many things that she did not, and he was not so submissive that he would not argue. He argued hotly, growing excited, calling out protests in a high treble, then suddenly laughing like a child.

For those days she abandoned herself utterly. She allowed herself to be surrounded, to be hemmed in, by the companionship, the care, the affection. . . . Oh, it was wonderful for her! Only those who had known her years and years of loneliness could appreciate what it was to her now to have this. She warmed her hands at the fire of it and let the flames fan their heat upon her cheeks.

Once she said to him:

"Isn't it strange that we should have made friends so quickly? It isn't generally my way. I'm a shy character, you know."

"So am I," he answered her. "I never would have talked to you as I have if you hadn't helped me. You have helped me. Wonderfully, marvellously. I only wish that Margaret could have known you. You would have helped her too."

He talked to her now continually of Margaret, but very happily, with great contentment.

"Margaret would have loved you," he liked to say. Lizzie was not so sure.

Then suddenly came the afternoon, for days past now inevitable, when he asked her to marry him.

They were sitting together in the Horton flat. It was a day of intense heat. All the windows were wide open, the blinds down, and into the dim, grey, shadowy air there struck shafts and lines of heat, bringing with them a smell of dust and pavements. The roses in a large yellow bowl on the centre table flung their thick scent across the dusky mote-threaded light. The hot town lay below them like a still sea basking at the foot of their rock.

"I want you to marry me, Lizzie," he said. "It may seem very soon after Margaret's death, but it's what she would have wished, I know.

Please, please don't refuse me. I don't know how I have the impertinence to ask, but I must. I can't help myself—"

At his words the happiness that had filled her heart during the last fortnight suddenly left her, as water ebbs out of a pool. She felt guilty, wicked, ashamed. She had never before been so aware of his helplessness and also of some strange, reproaching voice that blamed her. Why should she be blamed? She looked at him and longed to take his head in her hands and kiss him and keep him beside her and never let him go again.

At last she told him that she would give him her answer the next day.

When at last he left her, she was miserable, weighted with a sense of some horrible crime. And yet why? What was there against such a marriage? She was pursued that evening, that night. Next day she would not see him, but sent down word that she was unwell and would he come tomorrow? All that day, keeping alone in her flat, feeling the waves of heat beat about her, tired, exhausted, driven, the whole of her life stole past her.

"Why should I not marry him? Why *must* I not marry him?"

The consciousness that she was fighting somebody or something grew with her through the day. Towards evening, when the heat faded and dusk swallowed the colours and patterns of her room, she seemed to hear a voice: "You are not the wife for him. He will have no freedom. He will lose his character. He will become a shadow."

And her answer was almost spoken to the still and empty room. "But he will be happy. I will give him everything. Why may I not think of myself at last after all these years? I've waited and waited, and worked and worked. . . ."

And the answer came back: "You're old. You're old. You're old." She *was* old. She felt that night eighty, a hundred.

She went to bed at last; closed her eyes and slept.

She woke suddenly; the room swam in moonlight. She had forgotten to draw her blinds. The high, blue expanse of heaven flashing with fiery stars broke the grey spaces of her room with splendour.

She lay in bed watching the stars. She was suddenly aware that a figure stood there between her bed and the thin shadowy pane. She gazed at it with no fear, but rather as though she had known it before.

It was the figure of a young girl in a white dress. Her hair was black, her face very, very young, her eyes deep and innocent, full of light. Her hands were lovely, thin and pale, shell-coloured against the starry sky.

The women looked at one another. A little unspoken dialogue fell between them.

"You are Margaret?"

"Yes."

"You have come to tell me to leave him alone?"

"Yes."

"Why? "

"Oh, don't you see? He won't be happy. He won't grow. His soul won't grow with you. You are not the woman for him. Someone else—perhaps—later—but oh! let me have him a little longer just now. I love him so! Don't take him from me!"

Lizzie smiled.

"You beautiful dear! . . . How young you are! How lovely!"

"Leave him to me! Leave him to me!"

The moon fell into fleecy clouds. The room was filled with shadow.

★★★★★★

With the morning nothing had been dimmed. Lizzie was happy with a strange sense of companionship and comfort.

When Edmund came she saw at once that he was greatly troubled.

"Well?" he asked her.

"You've seen Margaret!" she cried. "Last night!" He nodded his head.

"It may have been a dream. . . ."

"You don't want to marry me. . . ."

"Oh yes! Don't think I would go back. . . ."

She put her hands on his shoulders.

"It's all right, Edmund. I'm not going to marry you. I'm too old. We're friends for always, but nothing more. Margaret was right."

"Margaret!" He stared at her. "But you didn't know her!"

"I know her now," she answered. Then, laughing, "I've got two friends instead of one husband! Who knows that I'm not the richer!"

As she spoke she seemed to feel on her cheek the soft, gentle kiss of a young girl.

A Carnation for an Old Man

Richard Herries, his sister Margaret, and their friend, Miss Felstead, arrived in Seville one February evening soon after midnight.

Their Seville adventure began unfortunately. As Margaret Herries always declared afterwards: 'We might have known that it was fated to end disastrously. It had so dismal a beginning.'

It had indeed. At each visit they expected to step out of the train into a glorious tumultuous mixture of *castanets*, bull-fighters, carnations, Carmen and Andalusian dancers. Instead of this they were received by a gentle drizzle and a Square quite silent and occupied only by some somnolent motorcars.

They needed encouragement. It had been a long and wearisome journey from Granada. Why, as Margaret said over and over again in the course of it, when Granada and Seville were so close to one another on the map they should be such an infinite distance by train only the Spanish railway authorities could explain, and they, so she was informed, never explained anything. They had been already unfortunate at Granada where it had been cold and where Miss Felstead (who was very romantic) had been unable, in spite of bribes, to persuade the custodian to allow her to see from the Alhambra Tower the sunset light up the Sierras. It would be too bad were Seville to be unfavourable also.

But it really started badly. They had engaged rooms at the Hotel Royal in the Plaza de San Fernando. This had been done only after a most vigorous and almost acrimonious discussion. The point was that the Hotel Royal was a Spanish hotel run for the Spanish and therefore cheaper than those which accommodated especially the English and American. Cheaper, yes, but, Margaret was sure, much nastier. Wasn't Spanish sanitation notorious? What about the smells they had smelt in Barcelona? And didn't the Spaniards cook everything in rancid oil?

Economically minded though Margaret always was, for once she was against economy. She changed places indeed with her brother, who was the most generous soul alive. But the bill at the English hotel in Granada had seemed to him quite beyond justice, and an English lady (a very clean and particular English lady) had told him that she always patronised the Royal when she went to Seville. An excellent hotel, she told him, clean, the servants polite and remarkably willing. A marvellously cheap Pension and the food good and plentiful. So, Richard had for once insisted.

And now behold the miserable commencement! Miss Felstead (who had eyes like gimlets) perceived at once that in the Square there were two hotel omnibuses asleep like everything else, and that on the windows of one of these were inscribed the magical words 'Hotel Royal,' so she marshalled the two young dreamy porters and steered them with the luggage in the proper direction.

On the steps of the omnibus was a hotel porter fast asleep. He was awakened, the luggage piled on the roof of the omnibus and the three travellers installed inside. Then occurred the disgraceful event! After waiting for some ten minutes and drinking in the miserable fact that Seville station at midnight in the rain was worse than Sheffield on a Sunday, it occurred to Margaret Herries that nothing at all was happening. The hotel porter, who was again dozing off, explained to Richard—who had a literary rather than practical knowledge of Spanish—that the driver of the omnibus had, some half-hour before, disappeared into the station for conversation with a friend.

'Well,' suggested Richard, 'fetch him.'

The porter, who had all the individuality, nobility and gravity of his race, walked with dignified austerity to the edge of the station, looked at it, shook his head, and returned wrapped in melancholy and thinking, apparently, of lottery tickets. After a while he pressed, very gently, the hooter of the omnibus, but with no result. Then, strongly urged, he went once more to the edge of the station but returned empty-handed.

So, half an hour was passed. By this time Margaret and her friend were frantic with railway-nerves, bodily hunger (they had had only twenty minutes at Bobadilla to snatch some food three hours earlier), weariness and disappointment. Finally, all the luggage was taken off the omnibus, after another half an hour a taxi-cab was found and they set off for the hotel. The last view they had of the porter was curled up inside the omnibus, happily reposing.

As Margaret always afterwards said, this was an Omen. She had herself never believed very much in Omens before. Miss Felstead was the one for Omens—but after the horrible week in Seville with its dreadful ending she never laughed at Omens again.

But for her everything was wrong with Seville from the beginning and, oddly, for Richard everything was right. He was an old man now—seventy-five years of age—and of course wanted his comforts. As a matter of fact, the Herries always did want their comforts and saw that they got them. But once and again there would be a 'freak' Herries who never seemed to know quite what he did want, and Richard had been rather like that. It was because he had been like that that his many sisters had always looked after him so thoroughly. First Hettie, and then, when she married, Florence, and then, when she married, Rosalind, and then, when she died, the youngest of them, Margaret. On two occasions Richard had almost married, might have been married altogether had he not been looked after so completely.

He had not, be it understood, objected to being looked after; he had rather liked it. He had felt perhaps that only so could he preserve his own secret life. And then they were immensely kind, especially Margaret.

Margaret had always adored her brother. She was not at all a sentimental person. She was a definite type of Englishwoman—a little mannish, thick-set and square, given to white collars, Scotch tweeds and brogues, rosy of complexion with strong black hair flecked now with grey, a snub nose, an obstinate mouth and a clear calm forehead. No other country could possibly produce a woman so calm, so determined, so masculine and yet feminine, so kind and so obtuse and so certain that all the things that she didn't know were unworthy of any sensible person's attention, so unsexual and yet so obviously designed for maternity.

She poured all her maternity on to Richard and yet apparently without a shadow of emotion. They never under any conditions showed emotion the one for the other, but they were devoted, self-sacrificing, and very good companions.

For seventy-five years Richard Herries had submitted to his sisters because he was both lazy and dreamy. He was the Herries type that dreams dreams and they have always either submitted and been wrapped away to nothing or rebelled and been cast out.

People described him as a 'dear little old man.' He was short and fat with snow-white hair and rosy cheeks, clean-shaven and of an immaculate shining neatness. He had a delightful chuckle, a fashion of jingling his change in his wide trousers pocket. He seemed to enjoy everything. No one would have guessed that for some while now he had been one of the loneliest souls in Christendom.

It had begun a year or two before at a concert of modern music in Berlin. Schnabel was playing and he, Richard, had suddenly realised that he was miserably unhappy, that he had wasted the whole of his life, that he had done none of the things that he ought to have done. Margaret was with him and he bought her a tie-pin. Nevertheless, for some days he still felt miserable. This feeling returned at certain intervals, once when he watched 'Punch and Judy' outside the Garrick Theatre, once when he read Madariaga's *Englishmen, Frenchmen, Spaniards,* once when he ate too much at a dinner-party, once when he saw his reflection in a looking-glass, once when he was staying in Cumberland and watched the birds fly over Derwent-water on a September evening. . . . And now again on this visit to Spain!

He connected these distresses at once, like all good Herries, with his stomach. He liked his food and his wine, but when he was unhappy he had only a biscuit for luncheon.

He rearranged his pictures in his London flat, hanging the Utrillo over the piano and the Segonzac over the bookcase, hoping that that would put things right. He had fancied at the time that it had, but here he was now in Spain with no pictures to rehang and his stomach in perfect order.

He was unhappy, rebellious and discontented, and especially he detested Miss Felstead. When a very courteous, aged English gentleman detests an amiable lady, what is he to do about it? Avoid her company? Yes, but you cannot do that if you are travelling with her in a foreign country. Say as little as possible? This he tried, but his unusual silence at once aroused suspicion. Was he ill? Was he uncomfortable? Was he (Margaret hinted) simply sulking? Whenever Margaret thought that anything was wrong she was extremely sensible and cheerful. She was as sensible as a chemist's shop and as cheerful as a fine day on the Scottish moors. She was breezy and jolly and accommodating. Miss Felstead, on the other hand, was tender and gentle and mysterious. In shape Miss Felstead was as slender as an umbrella handle, and in complexion rather blotchy, so that, quite frankly, when she was tender she was awful.

Richard had never liked her, but she was one of those English maiden ladies with no money and no relations upon whom others are always taking pity. It was rumoured, too, that she was extremely intelligent, that she would have been an authoress of note had she not possessed so critical a mind. When she was young she read Dante in Italian and belonged to a Browning Society, now that she was no longer young she raved about a Czecho-Slovakian pianist and read papers like 'Light' and 'Whence? Why? Whither?' But Richard had always suspected her intelligence and his suspicions were confirmed when in the Prado, before 'Las Hilanderas,' she had said: 'Very fine, of course, but does one *like* it?'

That evening, in order to annoy her, he had passionately defended the bull-fight and had sent her at once into a rocking wailing recitative of 'Ah, but the horses! The poor, poor horses!'

He suspected that in her heart she detested him as truly as he detested her. She was jealous, in the curious tenacious way that such maiden ladies have, of Margaret's affection for him. The thought that she perhaps detested him gave him some comfort.

In any case, and for whatever the reason, he had from the moment that he set foot in Seville the worst attack of rebellion he had ever known.

He was exceedingly fond of Spain and of the Spanish. It was by his firm wish that they were there now. Margaret did not like Spain; it seemed to her a lazy, purposeless, priest-ridden country. She could not understand what Richard saw in it, but loved him too dearly to refuse his wish.

He timidly suggested that he should come this time without her. He, seventy-five years of age and travel alone?

'But I'm perfectly fit. I've been there before. I know the language.'

Margaret smiled then, one of those smiles peculiarly the property of the Herries women, a smile self-confident, indulgent, maternal, kindly and patronising, a smile that had, on more than one earlier occasion, made murder a conceivable practice.

'Dear Richard . . . at *your* age . . . and Spain of all countries to be alone in!'

Yes. 'Spain of all countries!' That was Margaret's honest view of it. She thought that Spain was bad for everybody and especially for the Spaniards.

So, whether it were Margaret's anti-Spanish feeling or Miss Felstead's romanticism or simply the air or the disappointment over the omnibus at the station or the fact that they were at a Spanish hotel, whatever the reason, from the very first moment in Seville Richard and Margaret were at loggerheads.

'If I only had known!' Margaret said again and again afterwards. But of course, she did not know. No one, thank heaven, ever does.

Richard had never been to Seville before. His first visit, some ten years earlier, had been along the southern coast, Malaga, Algeciras and Cadiz. The second time, five years ago, had taken him into the Basque country and as far south as Madrid and Toledo. At present his favourite town in Spain was Segovia, but he had stayed there only two days because Margaret was homesick for Cumberland. He looked back on it as a lovely city of silver-grey stone, flowers and green trees. He wouldn't mind settling there, he had told Margaret, for a year or two.

He was thinking of Segovia this first morning in Seville. He had slipped out of his hotel without letting the women know and had almost the air of a guilty schoolboy as, seeing the tower of the Cathedral beckoning to him across the blue above the Spanish Bank, he turned in that direction.

After that first step his story enters into another world. How many other worlds are there? Millions, says one, none at all, says another. 'Two are all I need,' says the poet. Richard Herries had all his life known only one and longed always, like ancestors of his, for another. Margaret's account of it afterwards was: 'On that very first morning in Seville he was unwell. Of course, for one thing we were staying in a hotel for Spaniards—a most unwise thing to do, but Richard would have it. Then he went out all by himself that first morning, a most unusual thing for him to do. If I had only known that first day how ill he was!'

Luckily, she did not.

But he didn't feel ill at all. He had never felt so well in his life before.

Although the sky was blue there was a sharp nip in the air. It was eleven o'clock and everyone was beginning to wake up. At one all the shops would shut until four, the hour when everyone would *really* be awake. This was a sort of false dawn and very pleasant it was. In February Seville knows nothing of tourists save for an occasional meteoric flash of a boat-load from Cadiz or Malaga or Gibraltar. Richard might be said to be the guest of all the town.

His head was undoubtedly queer—not unpleasantly so, but as though he had taken a draught of some very potent sparkling wine. His limbs were light, made of gauze, and he seemed to have no age at all.

He was accustomed to the quiet and removed but friendly dignity of the Spaniard. That was one of the things that he liked best about Spain. They never pressed you to buy anything or go anywhere or do anything active, with the important exception, of course, of the boys who wanted to clean your boots for you. If you were a pretty young woman and alone, they might stare at you and even follow you, because pretty young women do not walk about alone in Spain, but that was the only active interest they took. And yet they were friendly, kind and beautifully polite. Richard loved good manners.

So, today as Richard passed under the lovely portal that leads into the garden where the orange trees nestle under the Cathedral walls the audacious thought came to him that he would stay in Seville for many weeks, perhaps until June even, see the Holy Week with its processions, enjoy the Feria, bask in the suns of May and, best of all, bury his nose in carnations. Now all his life long his favourite flower had been the carnation, and especially that purple one that is divinely streaked with mauve and crimson.

It had been his thought when he had first come to Spain that he would find a country buried in carnations, but it had been on every occasion too early in the year and he had been bitterly disappointed when offered a miserable bunch of these flowers, already half dead, for the exorbitant sum of four or five *pesetas*. Why, they were cheaper in Piccadilly!

But now standing in that lovely garden with its uneven and crooked flags beneath his feet, the Giralda at his left stretching to the heavens, and the Patio de los Naranjos, its stone encrusted as though with jewels, the Madonna above the great door regarding him so benignly, the birds flying from buttress to buttress, he trembled with the excitement of his new experience—he would stay here. Margaret and Miss Felstead should return without him. He had in his heart the sweet burning awe of falling once again in love. . . .

He gave some money to the old twisted beggar who, with trembling hand, lifted the black leather flap for him to enter, and passed inside.

Luncheon at the Royal was served from half-past twelve until half-past two, and at half-past two Richard had not yet returned. Margaret was a resolute, contained, sensible woman, but her distress was nevertheless acute and it was not made easier by Elsie Felstead's little wails: 'I know something has happened to him! How could we let him go out alone! He might be ill and neither of us know it for days! What about the police?'

'Oh, be quiet, Elsie!' Margaret seldom snapped at her friend, but when she did her friend knew it. 'Of course, he's all right. Richard's not a child and he knows Spanish far better than we do.' All the same she could have flung her arms around him and kissed him when he came in at last through the hotel door.

Instead of kissing him, being English, she scolded him.

Richard was very quiet. He said he was sorry, but he had been in the Cathedral. He had not noticed the time. It was a very beautiful cathedral.

Every sympathy must be felt for Margaret. Here she was in a strange country and her only brother, who was in her charge, whom she loved very dearly, was ill and refused to admit it.

That evening she attacked him about it.

'Richard, you are not well. Go to bed and I'll have some dinner sent up to you.'

'I'm perfectly well.' His voice was testy and his eyes absent-minded.

'Now I know you're not. You can't deceive me after all these years. You are sickening for something or that's what you look like. Elsie agrees with me.'

'Damn Elsie,' said Richard.

Margaret was upset and with reason. This was altogether unlike Richard. 'Will you let me take your temperature?'

'No.'

Then followed Margaret's most irritating method of persuasion, her jolly, patronising, friendly method.

'Now, old boy,' putting her hand on his shoulder, 'this is childish. What harm is there in my taking your temperature? After all, if you are going to be ill you may just as well know it.'

'But I am *not* going to be ill,' he answered with much firmness. 'As a matter of fact, I never felt better.' Then he went on, looking at her in an odd way, rather as though he were seeing her now for the first time in his life. 'The fact is, Margaret, I'm going about by myself a bit while we're here. You and Elsie might go to Malaga or Cadiz perhaps if you are bored by Seville—just for a day or two—'

He looked at her sternly as though he were giving her an order. He had never looked at her like that in all their lives together before. But she simply answered:

'Very well, Richard. Perhaps we will.' And she said nothing more about temperatures.

She was deeply alarmed. She lay for a long while awake thinking. What had happened to her brother? Something had occurred during those hours when he was alone in the town? Love? Absurd at his age . . . and yet one read in the newspapers the oddest stories about old men. A Spanish siren? They were pretty, some of these Spanish women with their combs and black shawls. But no . . . not Richard. . . . He was not like that. She resolved that she would not let him escape her in the morning. Where he went so would she.

And then in the morning an awful thing occurred. Richard lied to them both. He had never, in Margaret's belief, lied to her before. Dressed and ready, Margaret knocked at his door. He poked his head out.

'All right, my dear. Go down and wait for me. I'll be with you in a moment.'

They sat, the two of them, in the little hall of the Royal and waited. They waited for a long time, very uncomfortable because the men also seated in the hall, and having apparently all the day in front of them, stared at them so markedly. At last they sent someone up to enquire. He came back. The *señor* was not there. The *femme-de-chambre* had seen him, half an hour before, with his hat and cane. Was there another exit to the hotel? Yes, there was another exit . . . Margaret and Miss Felstead stared at one another in mutual horror.

Richard was not only unwell; he was also insane. But Richard was not insane; he was merely conscious of happiness as he had never been conscious of it before.

On making his escape he went straight to the Cathedral, passed through the Court of the Orange Trees, gave half a *peseta* to the blind beggar who lifted the black flap for him, and stepped into his true life.

That was how he now expressed it to himself, that was how he saw it. He was seventy-five years of age, had had on the whole a full, interesting and happy existence, and yet—had never been alive until yesterday! Had been asleep, mummified, blind, deaf, dumb and had not known it.

It was not, as he very well knew, that this church was of such marvellous beauty. He had seen cathedrals possibly of greater beauty, Chartres, St. Mark's in its own kind, even Ely on its slender scale. It was not that he was converted suddenly to any religious belief. Like most men he did not believe in very much but rather snatched at moments of love and beauty for confirmation of his unuttered hopes. It was not that he felt better or kinder or wiser since yesterday; it was simply that he was alive, alive to his finger-tips. It was like falling in love, but there was no one to fall in love with.

If it were not the most beautiful cathedral that he had ever seen, it was nevertheless the most alive. It gave him an impression of vastness as no other cathedral had done. But it was a vastness perfectly lighted. Although far from the darkness of a cathedral like Barcelona, it was quite without the shrill brightness that takes away mystery. The light came from many sources, now in long paths of softening colour, now in splashes of blue and purple that seemed almost to spring like fountains from the ground, now in dim misty gold from behind the shadowy pillars. In all this clarity there was no especial neatness or spruceness. What especially pleased him was that the building seemed always to continue its own natural life, crumbling here, breaking away a little there, stiffening in one place, failing in another. The magnificent colour of the highly placed windows was enrapturing. Never in his life had he seen such true deeps of rose and opal and onyx and crimson. High in air the windows sailed like magical clouds on the points of the vast pillars, and the great gates, thin like black silver or a wall of gold, like the gate before the altar, or a mist of cloud, were everywhere.

On this second day he realised that the church was like a town: here women were kneeling, there children playing, priests passed swiftly on some business, on a seat near to him a woman was suckling a child, before a neighbouring chapel two dogs were playing, two old men were sweeping with brooms, some men in a group nearby were discussing their affairs. Life, heightened by the beauty and majesty of the place, was going on everywhere around him, and to himself too something especial was about to happen.

He looked up, a smile on his lips, as though he knew what was coming, and encountered the grave, happy eyes of Santa Emilia.

Santa Emilia has been waiting (for how many years I shouldn't like to say) very patiently in the right corner of a picture that hangs in a chapel that shall be nameless, nameless because it would be a piece of the worst impertinence if, in the course of this little history, I were to reveal her exact position. I will not even assert definitely that her name is Emilia.

On one of the walls of one of these chapels, then, there is a large painting (by Murillo, perhaps, as so many of the paintings in this city are by that artist), and it is flanked on either side by some six other paintings in the shape of panels. These panels are of a lovely gentle colouring—soft rose and silver, the palest of greens and of dove grey. It was in the largest of these panels that Emilia had for so many years been so sweetly and patiently sitting. In her picture the heavens open and someone, God the Father Himself, perhaps, is delivering judgment, and several Saints seated on the grass listen in a mild surprise.

It is impossible to suppose that Santa Emilia herself was watching for any casual comer. For one thing her chapel was dark, well defended by its high iron gates, and it was but seldom that visitors penetrated that obscurity. Then she had other things to do. Her face, young, eager, ardent, was raised to the sky in an attitude of worship, her hands with their lovely slender fingers folded on her lap, a green scarf falling lightly over the white meshes of her robe. Why, after all these years, should she notice Richard Herries? The answer to that is that obviously it must have been astonishing to her that anyone should notice her at all, choose her from among so many others. She was carrying in one hand a red flower that might have been a carnation (Richard was certain that it was) and it was the agitation of this flower against her fingers that warned her that something exceptional was occurring. So, she turned and looked towards the gates and at once in that first glance exchanged they loved one another.

She had been waiting always for just such an experience as this. She had never known anything of earthly love. From her babyhood her life had been dedicated to Christ and she had wanted nothing else. When the Pestilence had struck her convent in Seville she had been only twenty-three years of age, but was even then distinguished among the others for the purity and goodness of her life.

The Pestilence was raging throughout Seville and she had gone into the town and wrought so many services there in caring for the sick and comforting the bereaved that, at her death from that same disease, she had been canonised.

She was only a very minor Saint; she had not lived long enough nor caused enough public attention (for with Sainthood as with everything else, advertisement is a great help) to be remembered very dearly by anyone. And then her position was obscure, seated there in one of the most obscure paintings in one of the darkest of the chapels. She was nevertheless most happy, for to worship God continually when you are certain of His existence is the happiest of all possible lives. .

Nevertheless, she was, and always had been, a completely human being as well as a Saint, and now, looking down into the rosy, earnest

73

face of that old man who was so very like the child that she might have had, had life been different, she loved him as she would, had it been so ordered, have loved her son.

Richard stayed there a long time. He told her many things that he had never told anyone in his life before. Then he went away. . . .

His life was at once, from that moment, so immensely heightened, intensified and ennobled that anyone, encountering him, must perceive the change. All true love must of course ennoble the possessor of it, but here was a miracle—not because Santa Emilia had turned her head and smiled at him—Saints are continually engaged in these acts of mercy—but because this experience had come to him so very late in his life when everything might have been supposed to be over for him.

Back in his hotel he wanted very badly to give some sort of explanation to the two ladies. But what could he say? He was not so rapt in his own miracle but that he could realise perfectly well that to say to Margaret: 'You must excuse me if I seem a little absent-minded. The fact is that I have fallen in love with a Saint in the Cathedral,' would be simply to invite her instantly to summon a doctor.

So he said nothing at all. But he was in fact so charming, so gentle and so happy that Margaret asked him no questions. One thing that pleased her greatly was to see that he had quite altered his attitude to Miss Felstead. He was not irritated any longer by her remarks, did not snap at her romanticism, was patient with her sentiment. He was patient with everyone and everything and his eyes shone with a happy light.

'We were quite wrong,' his sister said to her friend, 'to think him ill. Seville seems to be doing him a world of good. We may as well stay on for a while, although I can't say that I like either the hotel or the town.'

He had now, it was plain, a passion for the Cathedral, and in that, too, they allowed him to have his way. After all it did no one any harm.

In many places of worship, it would soon have attracted attention that a little elderly gentleman should stay for so long, day after day in the same position, his face close to the iron gates, staring in front of him. But in this Cathedral, nothing human was either odd or vulgar.

He told her everything, he who had never told anyone anything before. Few people realise the tomb-like silence in which most Englishmen spend their lives. Their education trains them to silence, their marriage system encourages it, their belief in physical exercise makes intellectual silence easy.

No one, standing near at hand, would have heard anything: Richard's lips indeed did not move, but Santa Emilia heard everything.

So many things that she could not have believed possible! How far from her cloistered Spanish life of four hundred years before was this strange English one; a family life, made up of gardens shadowed by old trees and guarded by rose-red walls, of sports desperately important, of sisters and sisters and sisters, of many months of rain and mist and fog, of a religion that was no religion, and, finally, what drew her heart just as four hundred years ago it would have been drawn, a sense of babyhood, a perpetual nursery with rocking cradles and the good God coming laden with gifts for good children down through the chimney—as though this little old man with the white hair were the child for whom, although she did not know it, she had always longed.

Yes, he told her everything—even that he had thought that Spain would be filled with carnations, but that, alas, he had found only some faded ones. Was that a carnation that she held in her hand? Yes, she told him that it was. It had not been one until that moment. As she spoke it became one. She spoke, but no one watching beside Richard would have seen her lips move. He alone saw and heard.

In another place and at another time he would have known that he was very unwell. His heart had been for many years weak and all the symptoms that he so greatly dreaded were now present. But he did not realise them. He was not aware of his body. He was happy as one is happy in a dream when one suddenly, after aeons of disappointment, has perfect satisfaction. Santa Emilia went with him everywhere. Margaret and Miss Felstead of course did not know this. Margaret was worried a little about his appearance. Like many good women she was especially proud of detecting the approach of illness in anyone. She was certain that Richard 'was sickening for something.' But he denied any ailment. He had never, he told her, felt so well in his life before, and that indeed was true.

Taking Santa Emilia everywhere, he found Seville most enchanting. Even the Museo, with its too *saccharine* Murillo, its pathetic air of desertion, its courtyard that echoed so sadly the weary feet of the tourists, seemed to him beautiful because of Santa Emilia's pride in it. Seville, in spite of its energy and jollity and measure of full, healthy life, is especially the city of children and old men. Nowhere in Spain—and I suspect nowhere else in the world—are there such marvellous old men with such marvellous faces, and nowhere else are the children so gay. No matter where—in the crowded Sierpes, along the banks of the brown Guadalquivir, in the quiet fountain-singing gardens of Murillo—it is the old men and the children who are everywhere.

When at last Santa Emilia knew how deeply she loved her friend, she asked Santa Isabela what she must do. Santa Isabela had always stood, a tall and gracious figure, at her side, looking up towards God coming in Judgment.

'I have been here,' Santa Emilia said, 'such a very long time. There are so many parts of Heaven that I have not visited. We should be so very happy together.'

'Perhaps,' said Santa Isabela, 'he does not want to leave the world yet. I have noticed how strongly men cling to the world.'

'I will ask him,' said Santa Emilia.

She asked him.

He said that he would go wherever she would take him. She promised that he should see gardens and gardens of carnations. He told her that he wanted only the one that she carried in her hand.

It was afternoon when she told him this and Vespers were just over. Two choir-boys were showing some tourists the carving in the Choir, and one of them swung on the foot of the great bronze lectern to show the tourists what a Spanish choir-boy dared to do. Many women were kneeling in the vast church, and their prayers rose up to the Madonna above the High Altar; she bent upon them glances of the utmost tenderness and protection.

'Yes,' said Santa Isabela. 'You are permitted to go. Santa Rosa will take your place here.'

So, they went together into Heaven.

★★★★★★

A little crowd gathered. The Englishman had fallen suddenly in a faint. No, alas, he was dead. Of heart failure, said one of the Canons who had been passing and knew something of medicine.

Behind Margaret's deep distress there were two consolations: she had known for days that he was not well although he said otherwise, and on his face, there was a look of radiant happiness.

★★★★★★

It was not until many weeks later that the Dean of the Cathedral, who was an authority on the pictures, taking some friends into the little chapel, was puzzled.

'I always had thought,' he explained, 'that Santa Emilia held a flower. I was wrong. I must have been deceived by the light.'

'And who was Santa Emilia?' asked a friend.

'A minor Saint. Nothing much is known about her. She died young, very young, in this city, of the Plague.'

Angelina

1

Angelina Braid, on the morning of her third birthday, woke very early. It would be too much to say that she knew it was her birthday, but she awoke, excited. She looked at the glimmering room, heard the sparrows beyond her windows, heard the snoring of her nurse in the large bed opposite her own, and lay very still, with her heart thumping like anything. She made no noise, however, because it was not her way to make a noise. Angelina Braid was the quietest little girl in all the Square. "You'd never meet one nigher a mouse in a week of Sundays," said her nurse, who was a "gay one" and liked life.

It was not, however, entirely Angelina's fault that she took life quietly: in 21 March Square it was exceedingly difficult to do anything else. Angelina's parents were in India, and she was not conscious, very acutely, of their existence. Every morning and evening she prayed "God bless Mother and Father in India," but then she was not very acutely conscious of God either, and so her mind was apt to wander during her prayers.

She lived with her two aunts—Miss Emily Braid and Miss Violet Braid—in one of the smallest houses in the Square. So slim was No. 21, and so ruthlessly squeezed between the opulent No. 20 and the stout, ruddy faced No. 22, that it made one quite breathless to look at it; it was exactly as though an old maid, driven by suffragette wildnesses, had been arrested by two of the finest possible policemen, and carried off into custody. Very little of any kind of wildness was there about the Misses Braid.

They were slim, neat women, whose rather yellow faces had the flat, squashed look of lawn grass after a garden roller has passed over it. They believed in God according to the Reverend Stephen Hunt, of St. Matthew-in-the-Crescent—the church round the corner—but in no other kind of God whatever. They were not rich, and they were not poor; they went once a week—Fridays—to visit the poor of St. Matthew's, and found the poor of St. Matthew's on the whole unappreciative of their efforts, but that made their task the nobler. Their house was dark and musty, and filled with little articles left them by their grandparents, their parents, and other defunct relations. They had no friendly feeling towards one another, but missed one another when they were separated. They were, both of them, as strong as horses, but very hypochondriacal, and Dr. Armstrong of Mulberry Place made a very pleasant little income out of them.

I have mentioned them at length, because they had a great deal to do with Angelina's quiet behaviour. No. 21 was not a house that welcomed a child's ringing laughter. But, in any case, the Misses Braid were not fond of children, but only took Angelina because they had a soft spot in their dry hearts for their brother Jim, and in any case, it would have been difficult to say "No."

Their attitude to children was that they could not understand why they did not instantly see things as they, their elders, saw them; but then, on the other hand, if an especially bright child did take a grown-up point of view about anything, *that* was considered "forward" and "conceited," so that it was really very difficult for Angelina.

It's a pity Jim's got such a dull child," Miss Violet would say. "You never would have expected it."

"What I like about a child," said Miss Emily, "is a little cheerfulness and natural spirit—not all this moping."

Angelina was not, on the whole, popular. . . . The aunts had very little idea of making a house cheerful for a child. The room allotted to Angelina as a nursery was at the top of the house, and had once been a servant's bedroom. It possessed two rather grimy windows, a faded brown wallpaper, an old green carpet, and some very stiff, hard chairs. On one wall was a large map of the world, and on the other an old print of Romans sacking Jerusalem, a picture which frightened Angelina every night of her life, when the dark came and the lamp illuminated the writhing limbs, the falling bodies, the tottering walls. From the windows the Square was visible, and at the windows Angelina spent a great deal of her time, but her present nurse—nurses succeeded one another with startling frequency—objected to what she called "window-gazing." "Makes a child dreamy," she said; "lowers her spirits."

Angelina was, naturally, a dreamy child, and no amount of nurses could prevent her being one. She was dreamy because her loneliness forced her to be so, and if her dreams were the most real part of her day to her, that was surely the fault of her aunts. But she was not at all a quick child; although today was her third birthday she could not talk very well, could not pronounce her r's, and lisped in what her trail of nurses told her was a ridiculous fashion for so big a girl. But, then, she was not really a big girl; her figure was short and stumpy, her features plain and pale with the pallor of her first Indian year. Her eyes were large and black and rather fine.

On this morning she lay in bed, and knew that she was excited because her Friend had come the night before and told her that today would be an important day. Angelina clung, with a desperate tenacity, to her memories of everything that happened to her before her arrival on this unpleasant planet. Those memories now were growing faint, and they came to her only in flashes, in sudden twists and turns of the scene, as though she were surrounded by curtains and, every now and then, was allowed a peep through. Her Friend had been with her continually at first, and, whilst He had been there, the old life had been real and visible enough; but on her second birthday He had told her that it was right now that she should manage by herself. Since then. He had come when she least expected Him; sometimes when she had needed Him very badly He had not appeared. . . . She never knew. At any rate. He had said that today would be important. . . . She lay in bed listening to her nurse's snores, and waited.

2

At breakfast she knew that it was her birthday. There were presents from her aunts—a picture-book and a box of pencils—there was also a mysterious parcel. Angelina could not remember that she had ever had a parcel before, and the excitement of this one must be prolonged. She would not open it, but gazed at it, with her spoon in the air and her mouth wide open.

"Come, Miss Angelina—what a name to give the poor lamb!—get on with your breakfast now, or you'll never have done. Why not open the pretty parcel?"

"No. Do you think it is a twain?"

"Say train—not twain."

"Train."

"No, of course not; not a thing that shape."

"Oh! Do you think it's a bear?"

"Maybe—maybe. Come now, get on with your bread and butter."

"Don't want any more."

"Get down from your chair, then. Say your grace now."

"Thank God nice bweakfast. Amen."

"That's right! Now open it then."

"No, not now."

"Drat the child! Well, wipe your face, then."

Angelina carried her parcel to the window, and then, after gazing at it for a long time, at last opened it. Her eyes grew wider and wider, her chubby fingers trembled. Nurse undid the wrappings of paper, slowly folded up the sheets, then produced, all naked and unashamed, a large rag doll.

"There! There's a pretty thing for you, Miss 'Lina."

She had her hand about the doll's head, and held her there, suspended.

"Give her me! Give her me!" Angelina rescued her, and, with eyes flaming, the doll laid lengthways in her arms, tottered off to the other corner of the room.

"Well, there's gratitude!" said the nurse; "and never asking so much as who it's from."

But nurse, aunts, all the troubles and disappointments of this world had vanished from Angelina's heart and soul. She had seen, at that first glimpse that her nurse had so rudely given her, that here at last, after long, long waiting, was the blessing that she had so desired. She had had other dolls—quite a number of them. Even now Lizzie (without an eye) and Rachel (rather fine in bridesmaid's attire) were leaning their disconsolate backs against the boarding beneath the window seat. There had been, besides Rachel and Lizzie, two Annies, a Mary, a May, a Blackamoor, a Jap, a Sailor, and a Baby in a Bath. They were now as though they had never been; Angelina knew with absolute certainty of soul, with that blending of will and desire, passion, self-sacrifice and absence of humour that must inevitably accompany true love, that here was her Fate.

"It's been sent you by your kind Uncle Ted," said nurse. "You'll have to write a nice letter and thank him."

But Angelina knew better. She—a name had not yet been chosen—had been sent to her by her Friend. . . . He had promised her last night that this should be a day of days.

Her aunts, appearing to receive thanks where thanks were due, darkened the doorway.

"Good-morning, mum. Good-morning, mum. Now, Miss 'Lina, thank your kind aunties for their beautiful presents."

She stood up, clutching the doll.

"T'ank you, Auntie Vi'let; t'ank you, Auntie Em'ly—your lovely pwesents."

"That's right, Angelina. I hope you'll use them sensibly. What's that she's holding, nurse?"

"It's a doll Mr. Edward has sent her, mum."

"What a hideous creature! Edward might have chosen something— Time for her to go out, nurse, I think—now, while the sun's warm."

But she did not hear. She did not know that they had gone. She sat there in a dreamy ecstasy rocking the red-cheeked creature in her arms, seeing, with her black eyes, visions and the beauty of a thousand worlds.

3

The name Rose was given to her. Rose had been kept, as a name, until someone worthy should arrive. . . . "Wosie Bwaid," a very good name. Her nakedness was clothed first in Rachel's bridesmaid's attire—alas, poor Rachel!—but the lace and finery did not suit those flaming red cheeks and beady black eyes. Rose was, there could be no question, a daughter of the soil; good red blood ran through her stout veins. Tess of the countryside, your laughing, chaffing, arms-akimbo dairymaid; no poor white product of the overcivilized cities. Angelina felt that the satin and lace were wrong; she tore them off, searched in the heaped-up cupboard for poor neglected Annie No. 1, found her, tore from her her red woollen skirt and white blouse, stretched them about Rose's portly body.

"T'ank God for nice Wose, Amen," she said, but she meant, not God, but her Friend. He, her Friend, had never sent her anything before, and now that Rose had come straight from Him, she must have a great deal to tell her about Him. Nothing puzzled her more than the distressing fact that she wondered sometimes whether her Friend was ever really coming again, whether any of the wonderful things that were happening on every side of her wouldn't suddenly one fine morning vanish altogether, and leave her to a dreary world of nurse, bread and milk, and the Romans sacking Jerusalem. She didn't, of course, put it like that; all that it meant to her was that stupid people and tiresome things were always interfering between herself and *real*

81

fun. Now it was time to go out, now to go to bed, now to eat, now to be taken downstairs into that horrid room where she couldn't move because things would tumble off the tables so . . . all this prevented her own life when she would sit and try, and try, and remember *what* it was all like once, and wonder why when once things had been so beautiful they were so ugly and disappointing now.

Now Rose had come, and she could talk to Rose about it. "What she sees in that ugly old doll!" said the nurse to the housemaid. "You can take my word, Mary, she'll sit in that window looking down at the gardens, nursing that rag and just say nothing. It fair gives you the creeps . . . left too much to herself, the poor child is. As for those old women downstairs, if I 'ad my way—but there! Living's living, and bread and butter's bread and butter!"

But of course, Angelina's heart was bursting with affection, and there had been, until Rose's arrival, no one upon whom she might bestow it. Rose might seem to the ordinary observer somewhat unresponsive. She sat there whether it were tea-time, dressing-time, bedtime always staring in front of her, her mouth closed, her arms, bowshaped, standing stiffly away from her side, taking, it might seem, but little interest in her mistress's confidences. Did one give her tea she only dribbled at the lip; did one place upon her head a straw hat with red ribbon torn from poor May—once a reigning favourite—she made no effort to keep it upon her head. Jewels and gold could rouse no appreciation from her; she was sunk in a lethargy that her rose-red cheeks most shamefully belied.

But Angelina had the key to her. Angelina understood that confiding silence, appreciated that tactful discretion, adored that complete submission to her will. It was true that her end had only come once to her now within the space of many, many weeks, but He had sent her Rose. "He's coming soon, Wose—weally soon—to tell us stowies. Bu-ootiful ones."

She sat, gazing down into the Square, and her dreams were longer and longer and longer.

4

Miss Emily Braid was a softer creature than her sister, and she had, somewhere in her heart, some sort of affection for her niece. She made, now and then, little buccaneering raids upon the nursery, with the intention of arriving at some intimate terms with that strange animal. But she had no gift of ease with children; her attempts at friendliness were viewed by Angelina with the gravest suspicion and won no return. This annoyed Miss Emily, and because she was conscious that she herself was in reality to blame, she attacked Angelina all the more fiercely. "This brooding must be stopped," she said. "Really, it's most unhealthy."

It was quite impossible for her to believe that a child of three could really be interested by golden sunsets, the colours of the fountain that was in the centre of the garden, the soft, grey haze that clothed the houses on a spring evening; and when, therefore, she saw Angelina gazing at these things, she decided that the child was morbid. Any interest, however, that Angelina may have taken in her aunts before Rose's arrival was now reduced to less than nothing at all.

"That doll that Edward gave the child," said Miss Emily to her sister, "is having a very bad effect on her. Makes her more moody than ever."

"Such a hideous thing!" said Miss Violet.

"Well, I shall take it away if I see much more of this nonsense."

It was lucky for Rose meanwhile that she was of a healthy constitution. The meals, the dressing and undressing, the perpetual demands upon her undivided attention, the sudden rousings from her sleep, the swift rockings back into slumber again, the appeals for response, the abuses for indifference, these things would have slain within a week one of her more feeble sisters. But Rose was made of stern stuff, and her rosy cheeks were as rosy, the brightness of her eyes as undimmed. We may believe—and surely many harder demands are made upon our faith—that there did arise a very special relationship between these two. The whole of Angelina's heart was now devoted to Rose's service, and how can we tell that the whole of Rose's was not devoted to Angelina ? . . . And always Angelina wondered when her Friend would return, watched for Him in the dusk, awoke in the early mornings and listened for Him, searched the Square with its trees and its fountain for His presence.

"Wosie, when did He say He'd come next?" But Rose could not tell. There *were* times when Rose's impenetrability was, to put it at its mildest, aggravating.

Meanwhile, the situation with Aunt Emily grew serious. Angelina was aware that Aunt Emily disliked Rose, and her mouth now shut very tightly and her eyes glared defiance when she thought of this, but her difference with her aunt went more deeply than this. She had known for a long, long time that both her aunts would stop her "dreaming" if they could. Did she tell them about her Friend, about the kind of pictures of which the fountain reminded her, about the vivid, lively memories that the tree with the pink flowers—the almond tree in the corner of the garden; you could just see it from the nursery window—called to her mind; she knew that she would be punished—put in the corner, or even sent to bed. She did not think these things out consecutively in her mind, but she knew that the dark room downstairs, the dark passages, the stillness and silence of it all frightened her, and that it was always out of these things that her aunts rose.

At night when she lay in bed with Rose clasped tightly to her, she whispered endlessly about the gardens, the fountain, the barrel organs, the dogs, the other children in the Square—she had names of her own for all these things and Him, who belonged, of course, to the world outside. . . . Then her whisper would sink, and she would warn Rose about the rooms downstairs, the dining-room with the black chairs, the soft carpet, and the stuffed birds in glass cases—for these things, too, she had names. Here was the land of death and destruction, the land of crooked stairs, sudden dark doors, mysterious bells and drippings of water—out of all this her aunts came. . . .

Unfortunately, it was just at this moment that Miss Emily Braid decided that it was time to take her niece in hand. "The child's three, Violet, and very backward for her age. Why, Mrs. Mancaster's little girl, who's just Angelina's age, can talk fluently, and is beginning with her letters. We don't want Jim to be disappointed in the child when he comes home next year." It would be difficult to determine how much of this was true; Miss Emily was aggravated and, although she would never have confessed to so trivial a matter, the perpetual worship of Rose—"the ugliest thing you ever saw"—was irritating her. The days followed, then, when Angelina was constantly in her aunt's company, and to neither of them was this companionship pleasant.

"You must ask me questions, child. How are you ever going to learn to talk properly if you don't ask me questions?"

"Yes, auntie."

"What's that over there?"

"Twee."

"Say 'tree,' not 'twee'."

"Tree."

"Now look at me. Put that wretched doll down. . . . Now. . . . That's right. Now tell me what you've been doing this morning."

"We had bweakfast—nurse said I—(long pause for breath)—was dood girl; Auntie Vi' let came; I dwew with my pencil."

"Say 'drew,' not 'dwew'."

"Drew."

All this was very exhausting to Aunt Emily. She was no nearer the child's heart. . . . Angelina maintained an impenetrable reserve. Old maids have much time amongst the unsatisfied and sterile monotonies of their life—this is only true of *some* old maids; there are very delightful ones—to devote to fancies and microscopic intuitions. It was astonishing now how largely in Miss Emily Braid's life loomed the figure of Rose, the rag doll.

"If it weren't for that wretched doll, I believe one could get some sense out of the child."

"I think it's a mistake, nurse, to let Miss Angelina play with that doll so much."

"Well, mum, it'd be difficult to take it from her now. She's that wrapped in it." . . . And so she was. . . . Rose stood to Angelina for so much more than Rose.

"Oh, Wosie, *when* will He come again? . . . P'r'aps never. And I'm forgetting. I can't remember at all about the funny water and the twee with the flowers, and all of it. Wosie, *you* 'member—Whisper." And Rose offered in her own mysterious taciturn way the desired comfort.

And then, of course, the crisis arrived. I am sorry about this part of the story. Of all the invasions of Aunt Emily, perhaps none was more strongly resented by Angelina than the appropriation of the afternoon hour in the garden. Nurse had been an admirable escort because, as a lady of voracious appetite for life, with, at the moment, but slender opportunities for satisfying it, she was occupied alertly with the possible vision of any male person driven by a similar desire. Her eye wandered; the hand to which Angelina clung was an abstract, imperceptive hand—Angelina and Rose were free to pursue their own train of fancy—the garden was at their service. But with Aunt Emily how different! Aunt Emily pursued relentlessly her educational tactics. Her thin, damp, black glove gripped Angelina's hand; her eyes (they had a "peering" effect, as though they were always searching for something beyond their actual vision) wandered aimlessly about the garden, looking for educational subjects. And so up and down the paths they went, Angelina trotting, with Rose clasped to her breast, walking just a little faster than she conveniently could.

Miss Emily disliked the garden, and would have greatly preferred that nurse should have been in charge, but this consciousness of trial inflamed her sense of merit. There came a lovely spring afternoon; the almond tree was in full blossom; a cloud of pink against the green hedge, clumps of daffodils rippled with little shudders of delight, even the statues of "Sir Benjamin Rundle" and "General Sir Robinson Cleaver" seemed to unbend a little from their stiff angularity. There were many babies and nurses, and children laughing and crying and shouting, and a sky of mild forget-me-not blue smiled protectingly upon them. Angelina's eyes were fixed upon the fountain, which flashed and sparkled in the air with a happy freedom that seemed to catch all the life of the garden within its heart. Angelina felt how immensely she and Rose might have enjoyed all this had they been alone. Her eyes gazed longingly at the almond tree; she wished that she might go off on a voyage of discovery, for, on this day of all days, did its shadow seem to hold some pressing, intimate invitation. "I shall get back—I shall get back. . . . He'll come and take me; I'll remember all the old things," she thought. She and Rose, what a time they might have if only She glanced up at her aunt.

"Look at that nice little boy, Angelina,"

Aunt Emily said. "See how good "But at that very instant that same playful breeze that had been ruffling the daffodils, and sending shimmers through the fountain, decided that now was the moment to catch Miss Emily's black hat at one corner, prove to her that the pin that should have fastened it to her hair was loose, and swing the whole affair to one side. Up went her hands; she gave a little cry of dismay.

Instantly, then, Angelina was determined. She did not suppose that her freedom would be for long, nor did she hope to have time to reach the almond tree; but her small, stumpy legs started off down the path almost before she was aware of it. She started, and Rose bumped against her as she ran. She heard behind her cries; she saw in front of her the almond tree, and then coming swiftly towards her a small boy with a hoop. . . . She stopped, hesitated, and then fell. The golden afternoon, with all its scents and sounds, passed on above her head. She was conscious that a hand was on her shoulder, she was lifted and shaken. Tears trickling down the side of her nose were checked by little points of gravel.

She was aware that the little boy with the hoop had stopped and said something. Above her, very large and grim, was her aunt. Some bird on a tree was making a noise like the drawing of a cork. (She had heard her nurse once draw one.) In her heart was utter misery. The gravel hurt her face, the almond tree was farther away than ever; she was captured more completely than she had ever been before.

"Oh, you naughty little girl—you *naughty* girl," she heard her aunt say; and then, after her, the bird like a cork. She stood there, her mouth tightly shut, the marks of tears drying to muddy lines on her face.

She was dragged off. Aunt Emily was furious at the child's silence; Aunt Emily was also aware that she must have looked what she would call "a pretty figure of fun" with her hat askew, her hair blown "any way," and a small child of three escaping from her charge as fast as she could go.

Angelina was dragged across the street, in through the squeezed front door, over the dark stairs, up into the nursery. Miss Violet's voice was heard calling, "Is that you, Emily? Tea's been waiting some time."

It was nurse's afternoon out, and the nursery was grimly empty; but through the open window came the evening sounds of the happy Square. Miss Emily placed Angelina in the middle of the room. "Now say you're sorry, you wicked child!" she exclaimed breathlessly.

"Sowwy," came slowly from Angelina. Then she looked down at her doll.

"Leave that doll alone. Speak as though you were sorry."

"I'm velly sowwy."

"What made you run away like that?" Angelina said nothing. "Come, now! Didn't you know it was very wicked?"

"Yes."

"Well, why did you do it, then?"

"Don't know."

"Don't say 'don't know' like that. You must have had some reason. Don't look at the doll like that. Put the doll down." But this Angelina would not do. She clung to Rose with a ferocious tenacity. I do not think that one must blame Miss Emily for her exasperation. That doll had had a large place in her mind for many weeks. It were as though she, Miss Emily Braid, had been personally, before the world, defied by a rag doll. Her temper, whose control had never been her strongest quality, at the vision of the dirty, obstinate child before her, at the thought of the dancing, mocking garden behind her, flamed into sudden, trembling rage.

She stepped forward, snatched Rose from Angelina's arms, crossed the room and pushed the doll, with a fierce, energetic action, as though there was no possible time to be lost, into the fire. She snatched the poker, and with trembling hands pressed the doll down. There was a great flare of flame; Rose lifted one stolid arm to the gods for vengeance, then a stout leg in a last writhing agony. Only then, when it was all concluded, did Aunt Emily hear behind her the little half-strangled cry which made her turn. The child was standing, motionless, with so old, so desperate a gaze of despair that it was something indecent for any human being to watch.

5

Nurse came in from her afternoon. She had heard nothing of the recent catastrophe, and, as she saw Angelina sitting quietly in front of the fire she thought that she had had her tea, and was now "dreaming "as she so often did. Once, however, as she was busy in another part of the room, she caught half the face in the light of the fire. To anyone of a more perceptive nature that glimpse must have seemed one of the most tragic things in the world. But this was a woman of "a sensible, hearty" nature; moreover, her "afternoon" had left her with happy reminiscences of her own charms and their effect on the opposite sex.

She had, however, her moment. . . . She had left the room to fetch something. Returning, she noticed that the dusk had fallen, and was about to switch on the light when, in the rise and fall of the firelight, something that she saw made her pause. She stood motionless by the door.

Angelina had turned in her chair; her eyes were gazing, with rapt attention, toward the purple dusk by the window. She was listening. Nurse, as she had often assured her friends, "was not cursed with imagination," but now fear held her so that she could not stir or move save that her hand trembled against the wallpaper. The chatter of the fire, the shouts of some boys in the Square, the ringing of the bell of St. Matthew's for evensong, all these things came into the room. Angelina, still listening, at last smiled; then, with a little sigh, sat back in her chair.

Heavens! Miss 'Lina! What were you doing there? How you frightened me!" Angelina left her chair, and went across to the window. "Auntie Emily," she said, "put Wosie into the fire, she did. But Wosie's saved. . . . He's just come and told me."

"Lord, Miss 'Lina, how you talk!" The room was right again now just as, a moment before, it had been wrong. She switched on the electric light, and, in the sudden blaze, caught the last flicker in the child's eyes of some vision, caught, held, now surrendered.

"'Tis company she's wanting, poor lamb," she thought, "all this being alone. . . . Fair gives one the creeps."

She heard with relief the opening of the door. Miss Emily came in, hesitated a moment, then walked over to her niece. In her hands she carried a beautiful doll with flaxen hair, long white robes, and the assured confidence of one who is spotless and knows it.

"There, Angelina," she said. "I oughtn't to have burnt your doll. I'm sorry. Here's a beautiful new one."

Angelina took the spotless one; then with a little thrust of her hand she pushed the half-open window wider apart. Very deliberately she dropped the doll (at whose beauty she had not glanced) out, away, down into the Square.

The doll, white in the dusk, tossed and whirled, and spun finally, a white speck far below, and struck the pavement.

Then Angelina turned, and with a little sigh of satisfaction looked at her aunt.

Hugh Seymour (A Prologue)

1

When Hugh Seymour was nine years of age he was sent from Ceylon, where his parents lived, to be educated in England. His relations having, for the most part, settled in foreign countries, he spent his holidays as a minute and pale-faced guest in various houses where other children were of more importance than he, or where children as a race were of no importance at all. It was in this way that he became during certain months of 1889 and 1890 and '91 a resident in the family of the Rev. William Lasher, Vicar of Clinton St. Mary, that large rambling village on the edge of Roche St. Mary Moor in South Glebeshire.

He spent there the two Christmases of 1890 and 1891 (when he was ten and eleven years of age), and it is with the second of these that the following incident, and indeed the whole of this book, has to do. Hugh Seymour could not, at the period of which I write, be called an attractive child; he was not even "interesting" or "unusual." He was small, with bones so brittle that it seemed that at any moment he might crack and splinter into sharp little pieces; but although he was so thin his face had a white and overhanging appearance, his cheeks being pale and puffy and his under-lip jutted forward in front of projecting teeth—he was known as "the White Rabbit" by his schoolfellows. He was not, however, so ugly as this description would apparently convey, for his large, grey eyes, soft, and even at times agreeably humorous, were pleasant and cheerful.

During these years when he knew Mr. Lasher he was undoubtedly unfortunate. He was short-sighted, but no one had, as yet, discovered this, and he was, therefore, blamed for much clumsiness that he could not prevent and for a good deal of sensitiveness that came quite simply from his eagerness to do what he was told and his inability to see his way to do it. He was not, at this time, easy with strangers and seemed to them both conceited and awkward.

Conceit was far from him—he was, in fact amazed at so feeble a creature as himself!—but awkward he was, and very often greedy, selfish, impetuous, untruthful and even cruel: he was nearly always dirty, and attributed this to the evil wishes of some malign fairy who flung mud upon him, dropped him into puddles and covered him with ink simply for the fun of the thing!

He did not, at this time, care very greatly for reading; he told himself stories—long stories with enormous families in them, trains of elephants, ropes and ropes of pearls, towers of ivory, peacocks, and strange meals of saffron buns, roast chicken, and gingerbread. His active, everyday concern, however, was to become a sportsman; he wished to be the best cricketer, the best footballer, the fastest runner of his school, and he had not—even then faintly ne knew it—the remotest chance of doing any of these things even moderately well. He was bullied at school until his appointment as his dormitory's story-teller gave him a certain status, but his efforts at cricket and football were mocked with jeers and insults. He could not throw a cricket-ball, he could not see to catch one after it was thrown to him, did he try to kick a football he missed it, and when he had run for five minutes he saw purple skies and silver stars and had cramp in his legs. He owned, however, during these years at Mr. Lasher's, one great overmastering ambition.

In his sleep, at any rate, he was a hero; in the wideawake world he was, in the opinion of almost everyone, a fool. He was exactly the type of boy whom the Rev. William Lasher could least easily understand. Mr. Lasher was tall and thin (his knees often cracked with a terrifying noise), blue-black about the cheeks, hooked as to the nose, bald and shining as to the head, genial as to the manner, and practical to the shining tips of his fingers. He had not, at Cambridge, obtained a rowing blue, but "had it not been for a most unfortunate attack of scarlet fever—" He was President of the Clinton St. Mary Cricket Club, 1890 (matches played, six; lost, five; drawn, one), knew how to slash the ball across the net at a tennis garden-party, always read the prayers in church as though he were imploring God to keep a straighter bat and improve His cut to leg, and had a passion for knocking nails into walls, screwing locks into doors, and making chicken runs.

He was, he often thanked his stars, a practical Realist, and his wife, who was fat, stupid, and in a state of perpetual wonder, used to say of him, "If Will hadn't been a clergyman he would have made *such* an engineer. If God had blessed us with a boy, I'm sure he would have been something scientific. Will's no dreamer." Mr. Lasher was kindly of heart so long as you allowed him to maintain that the world was made for one type of humanity only. He was as breezy as a west wind, loved to bathe in the garden pond on Christmas Day ("had to break the ice that morning"), and at penny readings at the village schoolroom would read extracts from *Pickwick*, and would laugh so heartily himself that he must stop and wipe his eyes.

"If you must read novels," he would say, "read Dickens. Nothing to offend the youngest among us—fine breezy stuff with an optimism that does you good and people you get to know and be fond of. By Jove! I can still cry over Little Nell and am not ashamed of it."

He had the heartiest contempt for wasters "and "failures," and he was afraid there were a great many in the world. "Give me a man who is a man," he would say, "a man who can hit a ball for six, run ten miles before breakfast, and take his knocks with the best of them. Wasn't it Browning who said:

"God's in His heaven,
All's right with the world?"

Browning was a great teacher—after Tennyson, one of our greatest. Where are such men today?"

He was, therefore, in spite of his love for outdoor pursuits, a cultured man.

It was natural, perhaps, that he should find Hugh Seymour "a pity." Nearly everything that he said about Hugh Seymour began with the words—

"It's a pity that—"

"It's a pity that you can't get some red into your cheeks, my boy."

"It's a pity you don't care about porridge. You must learn to like it."

"It's a pity you can't make a little progress with your mathematics."

"It's a pity you told me a lie because—"

"It's a pity you were rude to Mrs. Lasher. No gentleman—"

"It's a pity you weren't attending when—"

Mr. Lasher was very earnestly determined to do his best for the boy, and, as he said, "You see, Hugh, if we do our best for you, you must do your best for us. Now I can't. I'm afraid, call this your best."

Hugh would have liked to say that it *was* the best that he could do in that particular direction (very probably Euclid), but if only he might be allowed to try his hand in quite *another* direction he might do something very fine indeed. He never, of course, had a chance of saying this, nor would such a declaration have greatly benefited him, because, for Mr. Lasher, there was only one way for everyone and the sooner (if you were a small boy) you followed it the better.

"Don't dream, Hugh," said Mr. Lasher; "remember that no man ever did good work by dreaming. The goal is to the strong. Remember that."

Hugh did remember it and would have liked very much to be as strong as possible, but whenever he tried feats of strength he failed and looked foolish.

"My dear boy, *that's* not the way to do it," said Mr. Lasher, "it's a pity that you don't listen to what I tell you."

2

A very remarkable fact about Mr. Lasher was this—that he paid no attention whatever to the county in which he lived. Now there are certain counties in England where it is possible to say "I am in England," and to leave it at that; their quality is simply English with no more individual personality. But Glebeshire has such an individuality, whether for good or evil, that it forces comment from the most sluggish and inattentive of human beings. Mr. Lasher was perhaps the only soul, living or dead, who succeeded in living in it during forty years (he is still there, he is a Canon now in Polchester) and never saying anything about it. When on his visits to London people inquired his opinion of Glebeshire, he would say: "Ah well! ... I'm afraid Methodism and intemperance are very strong ... all the same, we're fighting 'em, fighting 'em!"

This was the more remarkable in that Mr. Lasher lived upon the very edge of Roche St. Mary Moor, a stretch of moor and sand. Roche St. Mary Moor, that runs to the sea, contains the ruins of St. Arthe Church ("buried until lately in the sand, but recently excavated through the kind generosity of Sir John Porthcullis, of Borhaze, and shown to visitors, 6*d.* a head, Wednesday and Saturday afternoons free"), and is one of the most romantic, mist-laden, moon-silvered, tempest-driven spots in the whole of Great Britain.

The road that ran from Clinton St. Mary to Borhaze across the moor was certainly a wild rambling, beautiful affair, and when the sea-mists swept across it and the wind carried the cry of the Bell of

Trezent Rock in and out above and below, you had a strange and moving experience. Mr. Lasher was compelled to ride on his bicycle from Clinton St. Mary to Borhaze and back again, and never thought it either strange or moving. "Only ten at the Bible tonight. Borhaze wants waking up. We'll see what open-air services can do." What the moor thought about Mr. Lasher it is impossible to know!

Hugh Seymour thought about the moor continually, but he was afraid to mention his ideas of it in public. There was a legend in the village that several hundred years ago some pirates, driven by storm into Borhaze, found their way on to the moor and, caught by the mist, perished there; they are to be seen, says the village, in powdered wigs, red coats, gold lace and swords, haunting the sand-dunes. God help the poor soul who may fall into their hands! This was a very pleasant story, and Hugh Seymour's thoughts often crept round and about it. he would like to find a pirate, to bring him to the vicarage, and present him to Mr. Lasher. He knew that Mrs. Lasher would say, "Fancy, a pirate! Well! Now, fancy! Well, here's a pirate!" And that Mr. Lasher would say, "It's a pity, Hugh, that you don't choose your company more carefully. Look at the man's nose!"

Hugh, although he was only eleven, knew this. Hugh did on one occasion mention the pirates. "Dreaming again, Hugh! Pity they fill your head with such nonsense! If they read their Bibles more!"

Nevertheless, Hugh continued his dreaming. He dreamt of the Moor, of the pirates, of the cobbled street in Borhaze, of the cry of the Trezent Bell, of the deep lanes and the smell of the flowers in them, of making five hundred not out at cricket, of doing a problem in Euclid to Mr. Lasher's satisfaction, of having a collar at the end of the day as clean as it had been at the beginning, of discovering the way to make a straight parting in the hair of not wriggling in bed when Mrs. Lasher kissed him at night, of many, many other things.

He was at this time a very lonely boy. Until Mr. Pidgen paid his visit he was most remarkably lonely. After that visit he was never lonely again.

3

Mr. Pidgen came on a visit to the vicarage three days before Christmas. Hugh Seymour saw him first from the garden. Mr. Pidgen was standing at the window of Mr. Lasher's study; he was staring in front of him at the sheets of light that flashed and darkened and flashed again across the lawn, at the green cluster of holly-berries by the drive-gate, at the few flakes of snow that fell, lazily, carelessly, as though they were trying to decide whether they would make a grand affair of it or not, and perhaps at the small, grubby boy who was looking at him with one eye and trying to learn the Collect for the day (it was Sunday) with the other. Hugh had never before seen anyone in the least like Mr. Pidgen. He was short and round, and his head was covered with tight little curls. His cheeks were chubby and red and his nose small, his mouth also very small. He had no chin. He was wearing a bright blue velvet waistcoat with brass buttons, and over his black shoes there shone white spats.

Hugh had never seen white spats before. Mr. Pidgen glowed with cleanliness, and he had supremely the air of having been exactly as he was, all in one piece, years ago. He was like one of the china ornaments in Mrs. Lasher's drawing-room that the housemaid was told to be so careful about, and concerning whose destruction Hugh heard her on at least one occasion declaring, in a voice half-tears, half-defiance, Please, ma'am, it wasn't me. It just slipped of itself!" Mr. Pidgen would break very completely were he dropped.

The first thing about him that struck Hugh was his amazing difference from Mr. Lasher. It seemed strange that any two people so different could be in the same house. Mr. Lasher never gleamed or shone, he would not break with however violent an action you dropped him, he would certainly never wear white spats. Hugh liked Mr. Pidgen at once. They spoke for the first time at the midday meal when Mr Lasher said, "More Yorkshire pudding, Pidgen?" and Mr. Pidgen said "I adore it."

Yorkshire pudding happened to be one of Hugh's special passions just then, particularly when it was very brown and crinkly, so he said quite spontaneously and without taking thought, as he was always told to do:

"So, do I!"

"My *dear* Hugh!" said Mrs. Lasher; "how very greedy! Fancy! After all you've been told! Well, well! Manners, manners!"

"I don't know," said Mr. Pidgen (his mouth was full), "I said it first, and I'm older than he is. I should know better. . . . I like boys to be greedy, it's a good sign—a good sign. Besides, Sunday—after a sermon—one naturally feels a bit peckish. Good enough sermon, Lasher, but a bit long."

Mr. Lasher, of course, did not like this, and, indeed, it was evident to anyone (even to a small boy) that the two gentlemen would have different opinions upon every possible subject. However, Hugh loved Mr. Pidgen there and then, and decided that he would put him into the story then running (appearing in nightly numbers from the moment of his departure to bed to the instant of slumber—say ten minutes); he would also, in the imaginary cricket matches that he worked out on paper, give Mr. Pidgen an innings of two hundred not out and make him captain of Kent. He now observed the vision very carefully and discovered several strange items in his general behaviour. Mr. Pidgen was fond of whistling and humming to himself; he was restless and would walk up and down a room with his head in the air and his hands behind his broad back, humming (out of tune) "Sally in our Alley," or "Drink to me only." Of course, this amazed Mr. Lasher.

He would quite suddenly stop, stand like a top spinning, balanced on his toes, and cry, "Ah! Now I've got it! No, I haven't! Yes, I have. By God, it's gone again!"

To this also Mr. Lasher strongly objected, and Hugh heard him say, "Really, Pidgen, think of the boy! Think of the boy!" and Mr. Pidgen exclaimed, "By God, so I should! . . . Beg pardon. Lasher! Won't do it again! Lord save me, I'm a careless old drunkard!"

He had any number of strange phrases that were new and brilliant and exciting to the boy who listened to him. He would say "by the martyrs of Ephesus!" or "Sunshine and thunder!" or "God stir your slumbers!" when he thought anyone very stupid. He said this last one day to Mrs. Lasher, and, of course, she was very much astonished. She did not from the first like him at all. Mr. Pidgen and Mr. Lasher had been friends at Cambridge and had not met one another since, and everyone knows that that is a dangerous basis for the renewal of friendship. They had a little dispute on the very afternoon of Mr. Pidgen's arrival, when Mr. Lasher asked his guest whether he played golf.

"God preserve my soul! No!" said Mr. Pidgen. Mr. Lasher than explained that playing golf made one thin, hungry and self-restrained. Mr. Pidgen said that he did not wish to be the first or last of these, and that he was always the second, and that golf was turning the fair places of England into troughs for the moneyed pigs of the Stock Exchange to swill in.

"My dear Pidgen!" cried Mr. Lasher, "I'm afraid no one could call me a moneyed pig with any justice—more's the pity—and a game of golf to me is—"

"Ah! you're a parson, Lasher," said his guest.

In fact, by the evening of the second day of the visit it was obvious that Clinton St. Mary Vicarage might, very possibly, witness a disturbed Christmas. It was all very tiresome for poor Mrs. Lasher. On the late afternoon of Christmas Eve, Hugh heard the stormy conversation that follows—a conversation that altered the colour and texture of his after-life, as such things may when one is still a child.

4

Christmas Eve was always, to Hugh, a day with glamour. He did not any longer hang up his stocking (although he would greatly have liked to do so), but, all day, his heart beat thickly at the thought of the morrow, at the thought of something more than the giving and receiving of presents, something more than the eating of food, something more than singing hymns that were delightfully familiar, something more than putting holly over the pictures and hanging mistletoe on to the lamp in the hall. Something there was in the day like going home, like meeting people again whom one had loved once and not seen for many years, something as warm and romantic and lightly coloured *and* as comforting as the most inspired and impossible story that one could ever, lying in bed and waiting for sleep, invent.

Today there was no snow but a frost and there was a long bar of saffron below the cold sky and a round red ball of a sun. Hugh was sitting in a corner of Mr. Lasher's study, looking at Doré's *Don Quixote* when the two gentlemen came in. He was sitting in a dark corner and they, because they were angry with one another, did not recognise anyone except themselves. Mr. Lasher pulled furiously at his pipe and Mr Pidgen stood up by the fire with his short fat legs spread wide and his mouth smiling, but his eyes vexed and rather indignant.

"My dear Pidgen," said Mr. Lasher, "you misunderstand me, you do indeed! It may be (I would be the first to admit that, like most men, I have my weakness) that I lay too much stress upon the healthy, physical, normal life, upon seeing things as they are and not as one would like them to be. I don't believe that dreaming ever did any good to any man!"

"It's only produced some of the finest literature the world has ever known," said Mr. Pidgen.

"Ah! Genius! If you or I were geniuses, Pidgen, that would be another affair. But we're not; we're plain, commonplace, humdrum human beings with souls to be saved and work to do—work to do!"

There was a little pause after that, and Hugh, looking at Mr. Pidgen, saw the hurt look in his eyes deepen.

"Come, now. Lasher," he said at last.

"Let's be honest one with another; that's your line, and you say it ought to be mine. Come now, as man to man, you think me a damnable failure now—beg pardon—complete failure—don't you? Don't be afraid of hurting me. I want to know!"

Mr. Lasher was really a kindly man, and when his eyes beheld things—there were, of course, many things that they never beheld—he would do his best to help anybody. He wanted to help Mr. Pidgen now; but he was also a truthful man.

"My dear Pidgen! Ha, ha! What a question I'm sure many, many people enjoy your books immensely. I'm sure they do; oh, yes!"

"Come now, Lasher, the truth. You won't hurt my feelings. If you were discussing me with a third person you'd say, wouldn't you; 'Ah, poor Pidgen, might have done something if he hadn't let his fancy run away with him. I was with him at Cambridge. He promised well, but I'm afraid one must admit that he's failed—he would never stick to anything'?"

Now this was so exactly what Mr. Lasher had on several occasions, said about his friend that he was really for the moment at a loss. He pulled at his pipe, looked very grave, and then said:

"My dear Pidgen, you must remember our lives have followed such different courses. I can only give you my point of view. I don't myself care greatly for romances—fairy tales and so on. It seems to me that for a grown-up man. . . . However, I don't pretend to be a literary fellow; I have other work, other duties, picturesque, but nevertheless necessary."

"Ah!" exclaimed Mr. Pidgen, who, considering that he had invited his host's honest opinion, should not have become irritated because he had obtained it; "that's just it. You people all think only *you* know what is necessary. Why shouldn't a fairy story be as necessary as a sermon? A lot more necessary, I dare say. You think you're the only people who can know anything about it. You people never use your imaginations."

"Nevertheless," said Mr. Lasher, very bitterly (for he had always said, "If one does not bring one's imagination into one's work one's work is of no value"), "writers of idle tales are not the only people who use their imaginations. And, if you will allow me, without offence, to say so, Pidgen, your books, even amongst other things of the same sort, have not been the most successful."

This remark seemed to pour water upon all the anger in Mr. Pidgen's heart. His eyes expressed scorn, but not now for Mr. Lasher—for himself. His whole figure drooped and was bowed like a robin in a thunderstorm.

"That's true enough. Bless my soul. Lasher, that's true enough. They hardly sell at all. I've written a dozen of them now, *The Blue Pouncet Box, The Three-tailed Griffin, The Tree without any Branches*, but you won't want to be bothered with the names of them. *The Griffin* went into two editions, but it was only because the pictures were rather sentimental. I've often said to myself, 'If a thing doesn't sell in these days it must be good,' but I've not really convinced myself. I'd like, them to have sold. Always, until now, I've had hopes of the next one, and thought that it would turn out better, like a woman with her babies. I seem to have given up expecting that now. It isn't, you know, being always hard-up that I mind so much, although that, mind you, isn't pleasant, no, by Jehoshaphat, it isn't. But one would like now and again to find that people have enjoyed what one hoped they *would* enjoy. But I don't know, they always seem too old for children and too young for grown-ups—my stories, I mean."

It was one of the hardest traits in Mr. Lasher's character, as Hugh well realised, "to rub it in" over a fallen foe. He considered this his duty; it was also, I am afraid, a pleasure. "It's a pity," he said, "that things should not have gone better; but there are so many writers today that I wonder anyone writes at all. We live in a practical, realistic age. The leaders amongst us have decided that every man must gird his loins and go out to fight his battles with real weapons in a real cause, not sit dreaming at his windows looking down upon the busy market-place." (Mr. Lasher loved what he called "images." There were many in his sermons.) "But, my dear Pidgen, it is in no way too late. Give up your fairy stories now that they have been proved a failure."

Here Mr. Pidgen, in the most astonishing way, was suddenly in a terrible temper. "They're not!" he almost screamed. "Not at all. Failures, from the worldly point of view, yes; but there are some who understand. I would not have done anything else if I could. You, Lasher, with your soup-tickets and your choir-treats, think there's no room for me and my fairy stories. I tell you, you may find yourself jolly well mistaken one of these days. Yes, by Caesar, you may. How do you know what's best worth doing? If you'd listened a little more to the things you were told when you were a baby, you'd be a more intelligent man now."

"When I was a baby?" said Mr. Lasher, incredulously, as though that were a thing that he never possibly could have been, "My *dear* Pidgen!"

"Ah, you think it absurd," said the other, a little cooler again. "But how do you know who watched over your early years and wanted you to be a dreamy, fairytale kind of person instead of the cayenne pepper sort of man you are. There's always someone there, I tell you and you can have your choice, whether you'll believe more than you see all your life or less than you see. Every baby knows about it; then, as they grow older it fades and, with many people goes altogether. He's never left *me*—St. Christopher, you know. Of course, the ideal thing is somewhere between the two; recognise St. Christopher and see the real world as well. I'm afraid neither you nor I is the ideal man Lasher. Why, I tell you, any baby of three knows more than you do! You're proud of never seeing beyond your nose. I'm proud of never seeing my nose at all; we're both wrong. But I *am* ready to admit *your* uses. You *never* will admit mine; and it isn't any use your denying my Friend. He stayed with you a bit when you first arrived, but I expect He soon left you. You're jolly glad He did."

My *dear* Pidgen," said Mr. Lasher, "I haven't understood a word."

Pidgen shook his head. "You're right. That's just what's the matter with me. I can't even put what I see plainly." He sighed deeply. "I've failed. There's no doubt about it. But, although I know that, I've had a happy life. That's the funny part of it. I've enjoyed life more than you ever will, Lasher. At least, I'm never lonely. I like my food, too, and one's head's always full of jolly ideas, if only they seemed jolly to other people."

Upon my word, Pidgen," said Mr. Lasher. At this moment Mrs. Lasher opened the door.

"Well, well. Fancy! Sitting over the fire talking! Oh, you men! Tea! Tea! Tea, Will! Fancy talking all the afternoon! Well!"

No one had noticed Hugh. He, however, had understood Mr. Pidgen better than Mr. Lasher did.

5

This conversation aroused in Hugh, for various reasons, the greatest possible excitement. He would have liked to have asked Mr. Pidgen many questions.

Christmas Day came, and beauty enthroned it: a pale blue sky, faint and clear, was a background to misty little clouds that hovered, then fled and disappeared, and, from these, flakes of snow fell now and then across the shining sunlight. Early in the winter afternoon a moon like an orange feather sailed into the sky as the lower stretches of blue changed into saffron and gold. Trees and hills and woods were crystal-clear, and shone with an intensity of outline as though their shapes had been cut by some giant knife against the background.

Although there was no wind the air was so expectant that the ringing of church bells and the echo of voices came as though across still water. The colour of the sunlight was caught in the cups and run-nels of the stiff frozen roads, and a horse's hoofs echoed, sharp and ringing, over fields and hedges. The ponds were silvered into a sheet of ice, so thin that the water showed dark beneath it. All the trees were rimmed with hoar-frost.

On Christmas afternoon, when three o'clock had just struck from the church tower, Hugh and Mr. Pidgen met, as though by some con-spirator's agreement, by the garden gate. They had said nothing to one another and yet there they were; they both glanced anxiously back at the house and then Mr. Pidgen said:

"Suppose we take a walk."

"Thank you very much," said Hugh. "Tea isn't till half-past four."

"Very well, then, suppose you lead the way."

They walked a little, and then Hugh said: "I was there yesterday, in the study, when you talked all that about your books, and everything." The words came from him in little breathless gusts because he was excited.

Mr. Pidgen stopped and looked upon him. "Thunder and sun-shine! You don't say so! What under heaven were you doing?"

"I was reading, and you came in and then I was interested."

"Well?"

Hugh dropped his voice.

"I understood all that you meant. I'd like to read your books if I may. We haven't any in the house."

"Bless my soul! Here's someone wants to read my books!" Mr. Pidgen was undoubtedly pleased. "I'll send you some. I'll send you them all!"

Hugh gasped with pleasure. "I'll read them all, however many there are!" he said excitedly. "Every word."

"Well," said Mr. Pidgen, "that's more than anyone else has ever done."

"I'd rather be with you," said the boy very confidently, "than Mr. Lasher. I'd rather write stories than preach sermons that no one wants to listen to." Then more timidly he continued: 'I know what you meant about the Man who comes when you're a baby. I remember Him quite well, but I never can say anything because they'd say I was silly. Sometimes I think He's still hanging round only He doesn't come to the vicarage much. He doesn't like Mr. Lasher much, I expect. But I *do* remember Him. He had a beard and I used to think it funny the nurse didn't see Him. That was before we went to Ceylon, you know; we used to live in Polchester then.

"When it was nearly dark and not quite He'd be there. I forgot about Him in Ceylon, but since I've been here I've wondered . . . it's sometimes like someone whispering to you and you know if you turn round He won't be there, but He *is* there all the same. I made twenty-five last summer against Porthington Grammar; they're not much good *really*, and it was our second eleven, and I was nearly out second ball; anyway, I made twenty-five, and afterwards as I was ragging about I suddenly thought of Him. I *know* He was pleased. If it had been a little darker I believe I'd have seen Him. And then last night, after I was in bed and was thinking about what you'd said I *know* He was near the window, only I didn't look lest He should go away. But, of course, Mr. Lasher would say that's all rot, like the pirates, only I *know* it isn't."

Hugh broke off for lack of breath, nothing else would have stopped him. When he was encouraged he was a terrible talker. He suddenly added in a sharp little voice like the report from a pistol: "So one can't be lonely or anything, can one, if there's always someone about?"

Mr. Pidgen was greatly touched. He put his hand upon Hugh's shoulder. "My dear boy," he said, "my dear boy—dear me, dear me. I'm afraid you're going to have a dreadful time when you grow up. I really mustn't encourage you. And yet, who can help himself?"

"But you said yourself that you'd seen Him, that you knew Him quite well?"

"And so, I do—and so I do. But you'll find, as you grow older, there are many people who won't believe you. And there's this, too. The more you live in your head, dreaming and seeing things that aren't there, the less you'll see the things that *are* there. You'll always be tumbling over things. You'll never get on. You'll never be a success."

"Never mind," said Hugh, "it doesn't matter much what you say now; you're only talking 'for my good' like Mr. Lasher. I don't care, I heard what you said yesterday, and it's made all the difference. I'll come and stay with you."

"Well, so you shall," said Mr. Pidgen, "I can't help it. You shall come as often as you like. Upon my soul, I'm younger today than I've felt for a long time. We'll go to the pantomime together if you aren't too old for it. I'll manage to ruin you all right. What's that shining?" He pointed in front of him.

They had come to a rise in the Polwint Road. To their right, running to the very foot of their path, was the moor. It stretched away, like a cloud, vague and indeterminate to the horizon. To their left a dark brown field rose in an ascending wave to a ridge that cut the sky, now crocus-coloured. The field was it with the soft light of the setting sun. On the ridge of the field something, suspended, it seemed in mid-air, was shining like a golden fire.

What's that?" said Mr. Pidgen again. "It's hanging. What the devil!"

They stopped for a moment, then started across the field. When they had gone a little way Mr. Pidgen paused again.

"It's like a man with a golden helmet. He's got legs; he's coming to us."

They walked on again. Then Hugh cried, "Why, it's only an old scarecrow. We might have guessed."

The sun, at that instant, sank behind the hills and the world was grey.

The scarecrow, perched on the high ridge, waved its tattered sleeves in the air. It was an old tin can that had caught the light; the can hanging over the stake that supported it in drunken fashion seemed to wink at them. The shadows came streaming up from the sea and the dark woods below in the hollow drew closer to them.

The scarecrow seemed to lament the departure of the light. "Here, mind," he said to the two of them, "you saw me in my glory just now, and don't you forget it. I may be a knight in shining armour after all. It only depends upon the point of view."

"So, it does," said Mr. Pidgen, taking his hat off; "you were very fine—I shan't forget."

6

They stood there in silence for a time. . . .

7

At last they turned back and walked slowly home, the intimacy of their new friendship growing with their silence. Hugh was happier than he had ever been before. Behind the quiet evening light, he saw wonderful prospects a new life in which he might dream as he pleased, a new friend to whom he might tell these dreams, a new confidence in his own power. . . .

But it was not to be.

That very night Mr. Pidgen died, very peacefully, in his sleep, from heart failure. He had had, as he had himself said, a happy life.

8

Years passed, and Hugh Seymour grew up. I do not wish here to say much more about him. It happened that when he was twenty-four his work compelled him to live in that Square in London known as March Square. Here he lived for five years, and during that time he was happy enough to gain the intimacy and confidence of some of the children who played in the garden there. They trusted him and told him more than they told many people. He had never forgotten Mr. Pidgen; that walk, that vision of the scarecrow, stood, as such childish things will, for a landmark in his history. He came to believe that those experiences that he knew, in his own life, to be true, were true also for some others. That's as it may be. I can only say that Barbara and Angelina, Bim and even Sarah Trefusis were his friends. I dare say his theory is all wrong.

I can only say that I *know* they were his friends; perhaps, after all, the scarecrow *is* shining somewhere in golden armour. Perhaps, after all, one need not be so lonely as one often fancies that one is.

Epilogue
Hugh Seymour

1

It happened that Hugh Seymour, in the month of December, 1911, found himself in the dreamy orchard-bound cathedral city of Polchester. Polchester, as all its inhabitants well know, is famous for its cathedral, its buns, and its river, the cathedral being one of the oldest, the buns being among the sweetest, and the Pol being amongst the most beautiful of the cathedrals, buns and rivers of Great Britain.

Seymour had known Polchester since he was five years old, when he first lived there with his father and mother, but he had only once during the last ten years been able to visit Glebeshire, and then he had been to Rafiel, a fishing village on the south coast. He had, therefore, not seen Polchester since his childhood, and now it seemed to him to have shrivelled from a world of infinite space and mystery into a toy town that would be soon packed away in a box and hidden in a cupboard. As he walked up and down the cobbled streets he was moved by a great affection and sentiment for it.

As he climbed the hill to the cathedral, as he stood inside the Close, with its lawns, its elm trees, its crooked cobbled walks, its gardens, its houses with old bow-windows and deep overhanging doors, he was again a very small boy with soap in his eyes, a shining white collar tight about his neck, and his Eton jacket stiff and unfriendly. He was walking up the aisle with his mother, his boots creaked, the bell's note was dropping, dropping, the fat verger with his staff was undoing the cord of their seat, the boys of the choir-school were looking at him and he was blushing, he was on his knees and the edge of the kneeler was cutting into his trousers, the precentor's voice, as remote from things human as the cathedral bell itself, was crying "Dearly beloved brethren."

He would stop there and wonder whether there could be any connexion between that time and this, whether those things had really happened to him, whether he might now be dreaming and would wake up presently to find that it would be soon time to start for the cathedral, that if he and his sisters were good they would have a chapter of the *Pillars of the House* read to them after tea, with one chocolate each at the end of every two pages. No, he was real, March Square was real, Polchester and London were real together—nothing died, nothing passed away.

On the second afternoon of his stay he was standing in the Close, bathed now in yellow sunlight, when he saw coming towards him a familiar figure. One glance was enough to assure him that this was the Rev. William Lasher, once Vicar of Clinton St. Mary, now Canon of Polchester Cathedral. Mr. Lasher it was, and Mr. Lasher the same as he had ever been. He was walking with his old energetic stride, his head up, his black overcoat flapping behind him, his eyes sharply investigating in and out and all around him. He saw Seymour, but did not recognize him, and would have passed on.

"You don't know me?" said Seymour, holding out his hand.

"I beg your pardon I—" said Canon Lasher.

"Seymour—Hugh Seymour—whom you were once kind enough to look after at Clinton St. Mary."

"Why! Fancy! Indeed! My dear boy! My dear boy!" Mr. Lasher was immensely cordial in exactly his old, healthy, direct manner. He insisted that Seymour should come with him and drink a cup of tea. Mrs. Lasher would be delighted. They had often wondered. . . . Only the other day Mrs. Lasher was saying. . . . And you're one of our novelists, I hear," said Canon Lasher in exactly the tone that he would have used had Seymour taken to tight-rope walking at the Halls.

"Oh, no!" said Seymour, laughing, "that's another man of my name. I'm at the Bar."

"Ah," said the Canon, greatly relieved, "that's good! That's good! Very good indeed!"

Mrs. Lasher was, of course, immensely surprised. "Why! Fancy! And it was only yesterday! Whoever would have expected! I never was more astonished! And tea just ready! How fortunate! Just fancy you meeting the Canon!"

The Canon seemed, to Seymour, greatly mellowed by comfort and prosperity; there was even the possibility of corpulence in the not distant future. He was, indeed, a proper Canon.

"And who," said Seymour, "has Clinton St. Mary now?"

"One of the Trenchards," said Mr. Lasher.

"As you know, a very famous old Glebeshire family. There are some younger cousins of the Garth Trenchards, I believe. You know the Trenchards of Garth? No? Ah, very delightful people. You should know them. Yes, Jim Trenchard, the man at Clinton, is a few years senior to myself. He was priest when I was deacon in—let me see—dear me, how the years fly—in—'pon my word, how time goes!"

All of which gave Seymour to understand that the Rev. James Trenchard was a failure in life, although a good enough fellow. Then it was that suddenly, in the heart of that warm and cosy drawing-room, Hugh Seymour was, sharply, as though by a douche of cold water, awakened to the fact that he must see Clinton St. Mary again. It appeared to him, now, with its lanes, its hedges, the village green, the moor, the Borhaze Road, the pirates, yes, and the Scarecrow. It came there, across the Canon's sumptuous Turkey carpet, and demanded his presence.

"I must go," Seymour said, getting up and speaking in a strange, bewildered voice as though he were just awakening from a dream. He left, at last, promising to come and see them again.

He heard the Canon's voice in his ears: "Always a knife and fork, my boy . . . any time if you let us know." He stepped down into the little lighted streets, into the town with its cosy security and some scent, even then in the heart of winter, perhaps, from the fruit of its many orchards. The moon, once again an orange feather in the sky, reminded him of those early days that seemed now to be streaming in upon him from every side.

Early next morning he caught the ten o'clock train to Clinton.

2

"Why," in the train he continued to say to himself, "have I let all these years pass without returning? Why have I never returned? . . . Why have I never returned?"

The slow, sleepy train (the London express never stops at Clinton) jerked through the deep valleys heavy with woods, golden brown at their heart, the low hills carrying, on their horizons, white drifting clouds that Hung long grey shadows. Seymour felt suddenly as though he could never return to London again exactly as he had returned to it before.

"That period of my life is over, quite over. . . . Someone is taking me down here now—I know that I am being compelled to go. But I want to go. I am happier than I have ever been in my life before."

Often, in Glebeshire, December days are warm and mellow like the early days of September. It was so now; the country was wrapped in with happy content, birds rose and hung, like telegraph wires, beyond the windows. On a slanting brown field gulls from the sea, white and shining, were hovering, wheeling, sinking into the soil. And yet, as he went, he was not leaving March Square behind, but rather taking it with him. He was taking the children too—Bim, Angelina, John, even Sarah (against her will), and it was not he who was in charge of the party. He felt as though the railway carriages were full and he ought to say continually, "Now, Bim, be quiet. Sit still and look at the picture-book I gave you. Sarah, I shall leave you at the next station if you aren't careful," and that she replied, giving him one of her dark, sarcastic looks, "I don't care if you do. I know how to get home all right without your help."

He wished that he hadn't brought her, and yet he couldn't help himself. They all had to come. Then, as he looked about the empty carriage, he laughed at himself. Only a fat farmer reading *The Glebeshire Times.*

"Marnin', sir," said the farmer. "Warm Christmas we'll be havin', I reckon. Yes, indeed. I see the Bishop's dying—poor old soul, too."

When they arrived at Clinton he caught himself turning round as though to collect his charges; he thought that the farmer looked at him curiously.

"Coming back again has turned my wits.

"Now, Angelina, hurry up, can't wait all day." He stopped then abruptly, to pull himself together. "Look here, you're alone, and if you think you're not, you're mad. Remember that you're at the Bar and not even a novelist, so that you have no excuse."

The little platform—usually swept by all the winds of the sea, but now as warm as a toasted bun—flooded him with memory. It was a platform especially connected with school, with departure and return—departures when money in one's pocket and cake in one's play-box did not compensate for the hot pain in one's throat and the cold marble feeling of one's legs; but when every feeling of every sort was swallowed by the great overwhelming desire that the train would go so that one need not any longer be agonized by the efforts of replying to Mr. Lasher's continued last words: "Well, goodbye, my boy. A good time, both at work and play"—the train was off.

"Ticket, please, sir! "said the long-legged young man at the little wooden gate. Seymour plunged down into the deep, high-hedged lane that even now, in winter, seemed to cover him with a fragrant odour of green leaves, of flowers, of wet soil, of sea spray. He was now so conscious of his company that the knowledge of it could not be avoided. It seemed to him that he heard them chattering together, knew that behind his back Sarah was trying to whisper horrid things in Bim's ear, and that he was laughing at her, which made her furious.

"It's the strangest feeling I've ever had," he thought. "I just won't take any notice of them. I'll go on as though they weren't there." But the strangest thing of all was that he felt as though he himself were being taken. He had the most comfortable feeling that there was no need for him to give any thought or any kind of trouble. "You just leave it all to me," someone said to him. "I've made all the arrangements."

The lane was hot, and the midday winter sun covered the paths with pools and splashes of colour. He came out on to the common and saw the village, the long straggling street with the whitewashed cottages and the hideous grey slate roofs; the church tower, rising out of the elms, and the pond, running to the common's; edge, its water chequered with the reflection of the white clouds above it.

The main street of Clinton is not a lovely street; the inland villages and towns of Glebeshire are, unless you love them, amongst the ugliest things in England, but every step caught at Seymour's heart.

There was Mr. Roscoe's shop which was also the post-office, and in its window, was the same collection of liquorice sticks, saffron buns, reels of cotton, a coloured picture of the royal family, views of Trezent Head, Borhaze Beach, St. Arthe Church, cotton blouses made apparently for dolls, so minute were they, three books, Ben Hur," "The Wide, Wide World," and "St. Elmo," two bottles of sweets, some eau-de-Cologne, and a large white card with bone buttons on it. So, moving was this collection to Seymour that he stared at the window as though he were in a trance.

The arrangement of the articles was exactly the same as it had been in the earlier days—the royal family in the middle, supported by the jars of sweets; the three books, dusty and faded, in the very front; and the bootlaces and liquorice sticks all mixed together as though Mr. Roscoe had forgotten which was which.

"Look here, Bim," he said aloud, "I'll lift you up— I really am going off my head!" he thought. He hurried away. "If I am mad I'm awfully happy," he said.

The white vicarage gate closed behind him with precisely the old-remembered sound—the whiz, the sudden startled pause, the satisfied click. Seymour stood on the sunbathed lawn, glittering now like green glass, and stared at the house. Its square front of faded red brick preserved a tranquil silence; the only sound in the place was the movement of some birds, his old friend the robin perhaps in the laurel bushes behind him.

Although the sun was so warm there was in the air a foreshadowing of a frosty night; and some Christmas roses, smiling at him from the flower beds to right and left of the hall door, seemed to him that they remembered him; but, indeed, the whole house seemed to tell him that. There it waited for him, so silent, laid ready for his acceptance under the blue sky and with no breath of wind stirring. So beautiful was the silence, that he made a movement with his hand as though to tell his companions to be quiet. He felt that they were crowded in an interested, amused group behind him waiting to see what he would do. Then a little bell rang somewhere in the house, a voice cried "Martha!"

He moved forward and pulled the wire of the bell; there was a wheezy jangle, a pause, and then a sharp irritated sound far away in the heart of the house, as though he had hit it in the wind and it protested. An old woman, very neat (she was certainly a Glebeshire woman), told him that Mr. Trenchard was at home. She took him through the dark passages into the study that he knew so well, and said that Mr. Trenchard would be with him in a moment.

It was the same study, and yet how different! Many of the old pieces of furniture were there—the deep, worn leather armchair in which Mr. Lasher had been sitting when he had his famous discussion with Mr. Pidgen, the same bookshelves, the same tiles in the fireplace with Bible pictures painted on them, the same huge black coal-scuttle, the same long, dark writing-table. But instead of the old order and discipline there was now a confusion that gave the room the air of a wastepaper basket. Books were piled, up and down, in the shelves, they dribbled on to the floor and lay in little trickling streams across the carpet; old bundles of papers, yellow with age, tied with string and faded blue tape, were in heaps upon the windowsill, and in tumbling cascades in the very middle of the floor; the writing-table itself was so hopelessly littered with books, sermon papers, old letters and new letters, bottles of ink, bottles of glue, three huge volumes of a Bible

Concordance, photographs, and sticks of sealing-wax, that the man who could be happy amid such confusion must surely be a kindly and benevolent creature. flow orderly had been Mr. Lasher's table, with all the pens in rows, and little sharp drawers that clicked, marked A, B, and C, to put papers into.

Mr. Trenchard entered.

He was what the room had prophesied—fat, red-faced, bald, extremely untidy, with stains on his waistcoat and tobacco on his coat, that was turning a little green, and chalk on his trousers. His eyes shone with pleased friendliness, but there was a little pucker in his forehead, as though his life had not always been pleasant. He rubbed his nose, as he talked, with the back of his hand, and made sudden little darts at the chalk on his trousers, as though he would brush it off. He had the face of an innocent baby, and when he spoke he looked at his companion with exactly the gaze of trusting confidence that a child bestows upon its elders.

"I hope you will forgive me," said Seymour, smiling; "I've come, too, at such an awkward time, but the truth is I simply couldn't help myself. I ought, besides, to catch the four o'clock train back to Polchester."

"Yes, indeed," said Mr. Trenchard, smiling, rubbing his hands together, and altogether in the dark as to what his visitor might be wanting.

"Ah, but I haven't explained; how stupid of me! My name is Seymour. I was here during several years, as a small boy, with Canon Lasher—in my holidays, you know. It's years ago, and I've never been back. I was at Polchester this morning and suddenly felt that I must come over. I wondered whether you'd be so good as to let me look a little at the house and garden."

There was nothing that Mr. Trenchard would like better. How was Canon Lasher? Well? Good. They met sometimes at meetings at Polchester. Canon Lasher, Mr. Trenchard believed, liked it better at Polchester than at Clinton. Honestly, it would break Mr. Trenchard's heart if *he* had to leave the place. But there was no danger of that now. Would Mr. Seymour—his wife would be delighted would he stay to luncheon?

"Why, that is too kind of you," said Seymour, hesitating, "but there are so many of us, such a lot—I mean," he said hurriedly, at Mr. Trenchard's innocent stare of surprise, "that it's too hard on Mrs. Trenchard, with so little notice."

111

He broke off confusedly.

"We shall only be too delighted," said Mr. Trenchard. "And if you have friends . . ."

"No, no," said Seymour, "I'm quite alone."

When, afterwards, he was introduced to Mrs. Trenchard in the drawing-room, he liked her at once. She was a little woman, very neat, with grey hair brushed back from her forehead. She was like some fresh, mild-coloured fruit, and an old-fashioned dress of rather faded green silk, and a large locket that she wore gave her a settled, tranquil air as though she had always been the same, and would continue so for many years. She had a high, fresh colour, a beautiful complexion and her hands had the delicacy of fragile egg-shell china. She was cheerful and friendly, but was, nevertheless, a sad woman; her eyes were dark and her voice was a little forced as though she had accustomed herself to be in good spirits. The love between herself and her husband was very pleasant to see.

Like all simple people, they immediately trusted Seymour with their confidence. During luncheon they told him many things, of Rasselas, where Mr. Trenchard had been a curate, of their joy at getting the Clinton living, and of their happiness at being there, of the kindness of the people, of the beauty of the country, of their neighbours, of their relations, the George Trenchards, at Garth, of Glebeshire generally, and what it meant to be a Trenchard.

"There've been Trenchards in Glebeshire," said the Vicar, greatly excited, "since the beginning of time. If Adam and Eve were here, and Glebeshire was the Garden of Eden, as I dare say it was, why, then Adam was a Trenchard. "

Afterwards, when they were smoking in the confused study, Seymour learnt why Mrs. Trenchard was a sad woman.

"We've had one trial, under God's grace," said Mr. Trenchard. "There were a boy and a girl—Francis and Jessamy. They died, both, in a bad epidemic of typhoid here, five years ago. Francis was five, Jessamy four. 'The Lord giveth and the Lord taketh away.' It was hard losing both of them. They got ill together and died on the same day."

He puffed furiously at his pipe. "Mrs. Trenchard keeps the nursery just the same as it used to be. She'll show it to you, I dare say."

Later, when Mrs. Trenchard took him over the house, his sight of the nursery was more moving to him than any of his old memories. She unlocked the door with a sharp turn of the wrist and showed him the wide sunlit room, still with fresh curtains, with a wallpaper of robins and cherries, with the toys—dolls, soldiers, a big dolls' house, a rocking-horse, boxes of bricks.

"Our two children, who died five years ago," she said in her quiet, calm voice, "this was their room. These were their things. I haven't been able to change it as yet. Mr. Lasher," she said, smiling up at him, "had no children, and you were too old for a nursery, I suppose."

It was then, as he stood in the doorway, bathed in a shaft of sunlight, that he was again, with absolute physical consciousness, aware of the children's presence. He could tell that they were pressing behind him, staring past him into the room, he could almost hear their whispered exclamations of delight.

He turned to Mrs. Trenchard as though she must have perceived that he was not alone. But she had noticed nothing; with another sharp turn of the wrist she had locked the door.

4

Tomorrow was Christmas Eve: he had promised to spend Christmas with friends in Somerset. Now he went to the little village post-office and telegraphed that he was detained; he felt at that moment as though he would like never to leave Clinton again.

The inn, the "Hearty Cow," was kept by people who were new to him—"foreigners, from upcountry." The fat landlord complained to Seymour of the slowness of the Clinton people, that they never could be induced to see things to their own proper advantage. "A dead-alive place *I* call it," he said; "but still, mind you," he added, "it's got a sort of a 'old on one."

From the diamond-paned windows of his bedroom next morning he surveyed a glorious day, the very sky seemed to glitter with frost, and when his window was opened he could hear quite plainly the bell on Trezent Rock, so crystal was the air. He walked that morning for miles; he covered all his old ground, picking up memories as though he were building a pleasure-house. Here was his dream, there his disappointment, here that flaming discovery, there this sudden terror—nothing had changed for him, the Moor, St. Arthe Church, St. Dreot Woods, the high white gates and mysterious hidden park of Porthcullis House—all were as though it had been yesterday that he had last seen them. Polchester had dwindled before his giant growth. Here the moor, the woods, the roads had grown, and it was he that had shrunken.

At last he stood on the sand-dunes that bounded the moor, and looked down upon the marbled sand, blue and gold after the retreating tide. The faint lisp and curdle of the sea sang to him. A row of sea-gulls, one and then another quivering in the light, stood at the water's edge; the stiff grass that pushed its way fiercely from the sand of the dunes was white with hoar-frost, and the moon, silver now, and sharply curved, came climbing behind the hill.

He turned back and went home. He had promised to have tea at the Vicarage, and he found Mrs. Trenchard putting holly over the pictures in the little dark square hall. She looked as though she had always been there, and as though, in some curious way, the holly, with its bright red berries, especially belonged to her.

She asked him to help her, and Seymour thought that he must have known her all his life. She had a tranquil, restful air, but, now and then, hummed a little tune. She was very tidy as she moved about, picking up little scraps of holly. A row of pins shone in her green dress. After a while they went upstairs and hung holly in the passages.

Seymour had turned his back to her and was balanced on a little ladder, when he heard her utter a sharp little cry.

"The nursery door's open," she said. He turned, and saw very clearly, against the half-light, her startled eyes. Her hands were pressed against her dress and holly had fallen at her feet. He saw, too, that the nursery door was ajar.

"I locked it myself, yesterday; you saw me."

She gasped as though she had been running, and he saw that her face was white.

He moved forward quickly and pushed open the door. The room itself was lightened by the gleam from the passage and also by the moonlight that came dimly through the window. The shadow of some great tree was flung upon the floor. He saw, at once, that the room was changed. The rocking-horse that had been yesterday against the wall had now been dragged far across the floor. The white front of the dolls' house had swung open and the furniture was disturbed as though some child had been interrupted in his play. Four large dolls sat solemnly round a dolls' tea-table, and a dolls' tea-service was arranged in front of them. In the very centre of the room a fine castle of bricks had been rising, a perfect Tower of Babel in its frustrated ambition.

The shadow of the great tree shook and quivered above these things.

Seymour saw Mrs. Trenchard's face, he heard her whisper:

114

"Who is it? What is it?"

Then she fell upon her knees, near the tower of bricks. She gazed at them, stared round the rest of the room, then looked up at him, saying very quietly:

"I knew that they would come back one day. I always waited. It must have been they. Only Francis ever built the bricks like that, with the red ones in the middle. He always said they *must* be . . ."

She broke off and then, with her hands pressed to her face, cried, so softly and so gently that she made scarcely any sound. Seymour left her.

5

He passed through the house without anyone seeing him, crossed the common, and went up to his bedroom at the inn. He sat down before his window with his back to the room. He flung the rattling panes wide.

The room looked out across on to the moor, and he could see, in the moonlight, the faint thread of the beginning of the Borhaze Road. To the left of this there was some sharp point of light, some cottage perhaps. It flashed at him as though it were trying to attract his attention. The night was so magical, the world so wonderful, so without bound or limit, that he was prepared now to wait, passively, for his experience. That point of light was where the Scarecrow used to be, just where the brown fields rise up against the horizon. In all his walks today, he had deliberately avoided that direction. The Scarecrow would not be there now; he had always in his heart fancied it there, and he would not change the picture that he had of it. But now the light flashed at him. As he stared at it he knew that today he had completed the adventure that had begun for him many years ago, on that Christmas Eve when he had met Mr. Pidgen.

They were whispering in his ear. We've had a lovely day. It was the most beautiful nursery. . . . Two other children came too. They were *their* things. . .

"What, after all," said his Friend's voice, "does it mean but that if you love enough we are with you everywhere—forever?"

And then the children's voices again:

"She thought they'd come back, but they'd never gone away—really, you know."

He gazed once more at the point of light, and then turned round and faced the dark room.

The White Cat

Very strange things happen to very ordinary people. This is an account of one of them. It would have been difficult, perhaps, to find in the whole of America a more ordinary man than Mr. Thornton Busk. He did not himself think that he was anything at all unusual, and yet he had always had a very pretty pride in himself and considered, as most of us do, that it was quite essential for the happy continuance of the history of the world that he should live and be well fed and have a happy and prosperous time.

He came to Hollywood from New York partly because of the climate, partly because he thought he might do a little writing for the films, partly because a very lovely girl whom he knew had gone to try her own fortune there. He'd been in Hollywood five years and it may be said of him that during that time he was happy rather than successful. He had a very cheerful nature. He was good-looking in a quite ordinary way, dark and slim and always correctly dressed. He was useful to women who did not know what to do with their time, and he never had an original idea about anything.

He discovered to his mild surprise that he was not needed by anybody to write for the films, and soon had, as everyone has in Hollywood, a personal story about how near he'd come to achieving this, and by what an unlucky chance he'd just missed that, and how So-and-so, the director of one of the best films of the decade, was his very best friend, and would have given him so much to do if it hadn't happened that there were so many people already engaged in doing it.

He did not really feel himself ill-used. There are so many parties of so many kinds in Hollywood that you can go out somewhere all the time wherever you are. And there is always a chance that someone quite world-famous will be sitting next to you at the Vendome or dancing quite close to you at the Trocadero. His five years were entertaining and even exciting, and it seemed to him that he had plenty of friends. At the end of the five years what he hadn't got was plenty of money. He discovered with a shock that his capital was almost gone and that although millions of dollars were rolling about the Hollywood streets, none of them seemed to roll in his direction.

It was then that he began to think seriously of a charming English lady, Mrs. Grace Ferguson. Mrs. Ferguson was a rich widow who had a pretty house on Rodeo Drive, and entertained a great deal in a quiet, ladylike fashion. She was one of the English who, coming to California on a short visit, are entrapped by the sun and never again escape. Her husband, a kind elderly man, who was on the London Stock Exchange, had been dead some ten years. She was quite alone in the world. Except for her large white cat, Penelope, she had apparently no near friends. She had, of course, plenty of acquaintances, and as it is the practice of every American to be charming at the actual moment of contact, all her acquaintances seemed to her to be friends.

It is quite possible for an English man or woman to make very real and beautiful friendships in America, lasting ones and sincere, but it is often very difficult for the English to distinguish clearly between friendships and acquaintances. The dividing line is so very clear in their own more cautious country.

There were horrible times when Mrs. Ferguson felt very lonely indeed, and wondered if she had any friends. At such horrible moments she would feel a great wave of homesickness for the long white moors of Northumberland, the rocky bays of Cornwall, and the deep violet-scented lanes of Devonshire. She found that it was then that she wrote long letters to friends in England, saying that she would very shortly be home, recalling the many happy days they'd spent together, and hoping a little wistfully that they had not all entirely forgotten her.

Then quickly again would come the delightful excitements of her social world. A concert in the Bowl under the stars (the seats were very damp and it was necessary to wear quite heavy Arctic clothing), an eventful premiere at Grauman's Chinese Theatre, a lovely trip in somebody's yacht to Catalina, a most interesting lecture given by a *yogi* from India. It seemed to her on such occasions that she was surrounded by friends, warm-hearted, enchanted to see her, hating to be parted from her, ready to do anything in the world to make her happy.

Thornton Busk was one of these. A very, very charming man, always smiling, always at your service, full of jokes, a little flirtatious (but not to any dangerous extent), good-hearted and unselfish. She liked him very much indeed. She told him that he would always be welcome at any of her parties. When Thornton began to consider her seriously, he was surprised at himself for not having considered her seriously before. She had, he understood, so much money that she really did not know what to do with it all, and in these days, that was most unusual. Moreover, she was not like so many ladies with money, vulgar and prepossessing. She had the rather aesthetic charm of the delicate English lady. Someone with whom you'd never consider being passionate. Someone with whom you would never be bored.

But when he began to consider her more seriously, he found that passion was not so difficult to conceive. It was unquestioned that she had never been awakened. He knew, he had been told it often enough, how stolid and unimaginative were most elderly English husbands. There had been no scandal about her in Hollywood. She liked men, but kept them at a distance. It would be amusing to awaken her. He flattered himself that it would not really be difficult. Here, indeed, was a splendid way out of all his troubles. He began to pay her very definite court. He noticed that as soon as he began to take a deeper interest in Grace Ferguson, her house and its surroundings also became more personally alive to him.

It was a pretty place in the English style, with cosy rooms and a charming garden at the back with a small pool, a badminton court, some large banana trees and fine mimosa bushes. Her drawing-room and dining-room were in white with some good etchings. Everything was in admirable taste, but a little like herself, quietly aesthetic, rather without personality, gently hospitable. On a certain afternoon he found himself sitting at the end of the dark-blue sofa, very close to her, as she asked him whether he would have tea or a highball. When he said a highball, she asked whether he preferred Scotch or Bourbon. It was all very restful, very friendly, almost intimate.

'Say, do you know what I've been thinking?' And he leaned over the end of the sofa and with one hand touched her arm.

'No, what?'

'Wouldn't it be a grand idea to go down to San Diego for a night or two? There's the fair, and we'd get one or two more—Barney, the Thwaites and Lucille. We'd have a grand time.'

'Yes, I think I should like that,' she said in her quiet English way. 'The fair ought to be amusing. I loved them at home when I was a child.'

He looked on her face so steadily that she glanced up and looked back at him, questioningly, as though she would say: 'Aren't you a little different today? What's happened?' And he felt different. He thought for the first time since he had known her that he would like to take her in his arms and kiss her. He wondered why he had never wanted to do this before. He did not know that once a plan begins to work in your brain, it gathers about it aid, assistance. It amuses itself with cheating you a little.

'We've been grand friends,' he said, 'a long time now. I heard an Englishman say the other day that Americans were superficial, but I don't think so, do you?' And he touched her hand for a brief instant; almost stroked it, and then sat back on the sofa, turning away from her a little.

She looked at him with her mild blue eyes, smiling gently, a little maternally. She was thinking: 'He's a nice boy. I like him better today than ever before.' She said, 'Yes, I think you are superficial, most of you. English people take friendship very seriously. When they have a friend it's for life.'

'That's the matter with the English,' he answered. 'They're altogether too serious. They can't have a good time and then forget about it.' He turned and looked at her very gravely indeed. 'But you're not like that with me, Grace. You mean a hell of a lot to me, you do, indeed. I like you being quiet, cautious. American girls aren't quiet anymore.'

'I'm glad our friendship means something to you,' she said gently. 'I've never quite known.'

'Well, you know now,' he answered. 'You're just about the best friend I've got.'

He finished his highball reflectively. What would she do if he should kiss her? English women are so strange. They lead you on and then pretend that they know nothing about it. And the trouble is that they really are surprised. They complain bitterly that you've ruined a beautiful friendship, and very often they really do value the friendship more than the passion.

What would Grace be like if she should surrender? And would he be feeling the same about her if she hadn't a penny? Yes, he believed he would. He felt quite a holy feeling stealing over him, and he asked for another highball. All the same, it was pleasant to think that she was so wonderfully wealthy. And then he noticed the cat. He had never really thought of it before, except that it had occurred to him once and again that women without husbands, lovers or children were apt

119

to waste a great deal of emotion on animals. If he had thought about the cat at all, he'd have been aware of its odd devotion to Grace. Odd, he thought, because cats are always aloof. They lived their own lives and despised human beings.

But this cat, a very large and pure white Persian (or was it a Persian? He'd never seen a Persian so large and so white. He must ask her, some time, its breed)—this cat, Penelope, seemed really to be devoted to Grace. He had noticed that, when Grace left the room, the cat sank into a kind of cold neutrality. He had sometimes attempted to win it over, not because he liked cats, but because he believed in that old adage that animals and children were fond of only good men. Any little proof that he was good, he eagerly accepted. But Penelope would never have anything to do with him at all. It wasn't that she disliked him, it was rather that he did not exist. And he had felt on one or two occasions, when he was waiting in the drawing-room for Grace, that under the icy grey stare Penelope caused him to sink into nothing.

This afternoon, however, was the first occasion on which he was aware that the cat quite definitely regarded him. As he touched Grace's hand for that brief instant, the cat, that had been lying in a great white mass near the window, raised itself ever so slightly. The big handsome head turned in his direction.

'That's the best-looking cat I've ever seen,' he said. 'How old is it.? Have you had it always?'

'Yes, from a tiny kitten. How old is it? Oh, I don't know—eight or nine years, perhaps.'

'Seems damn fond of you.'

'Yes, it is.'

'That's strange. One gets to thinking that cats have no feelings for anyone but themselves.'

Grace Ferguson smiled. 'Oh, that's quite untrue. Come here, Penelope.'

The cat raised itself at once, and, with great delicacy for so large an animal, softly crossed the floor. It stood with its back arched a little against Grace's leg. It purred very gently. Then for a moment the purr ceased. It raised its head and looked at Thornton.

'You know,' he said, laughing, 'I don't think that cat likes me.'

'Perhaps it doesn't,' she replied. 'Penelope can be jealous.'

'Jealous?' This was altogether a new idea to him. 'I don't think,' he said, 'that cats care that much. They think only of themselves.'

'It's very easy,' she answered, 'to explain affection by love of personal comfort. I suppose cats are selfish, but Penelope isn't an ordinary cat.'

It was after this little conversation that Thornton began to be involved in strange personal experiences. We all know what it is to enter on a certain day into a new atmosphere. We pass into a world where everything seems to go perversely. Letters that we need do not arrive, appointments are broken, a fog, especially on this Californian coast, comes up and obscures the sun, the ground seems to quiver right beneath our feet. It was so now with Thornton. In the first place he had a strange sense of urgency—as though someone whispered to him, 'Lose no time over this or it will be too late.'

Hollywood is a nervous, hysterical place. Nothing is sure from day to day for anyone. Even the principal stars, who are supposed to live in such settled glory, do not know from picture to picture how their reputation may be affected. And this uncertainty spreads outside the actual studios into the surrounding world. While Thornton had money in the bank he could defy the sudden unexpected demands on his purse. There is a kind of careless extravagance in the air and with it forgetfulness, so that one is constantly exposed to expenses that one cannot pay. And because everyone else is suffering from the same economic uncertainty, emotional explosions are quite common. The air seems thinner here and nerves more frequently exasperated.

Thornton's rooms were the upper part of a strange, rather desolate little wooden building on Sunset Boulevard, the lower half of which was occupied by a lady who evidenced each night in brilliant electric lights that she gave psychic readings. These rooms had seemed smart and elegant when he first occupied them, but everything becomes easily shabby and worn in Hollywood because of the brilliant sunshine, unless it is carefully looked after. He had decorated his rooms in Mexican fashion . . . Mexican rugs and hangings of very bright colours, and then, contrary to these, a roll-top desk at which he had hoped to write for the films, a modern armchair that swirled round when you sat on it in a surprisingly disconcerting fashion, a settee of brown plush, which clung to you as though in a bad temper when you wanted to leave it.

He had photographs of filmstars in silver frames and hoped that his friends would consider them intimate gifts. But he did not care for the silver. The sudden sense that his surroundings were shabby and ominous was one thing that made him want to hasten into Mrs. Ferguson's arms. The sooner that he was in her beautiful house the better.

He developed a kind of obsession, not so much for herself as for her possessions. And yet, he thought himself that he loved her; that he couldn't have conceived such tenderness for her simply because she was wealthy. This was in all probability true. He looked forward to seeing her, and when he saw her he at once imagined her in his arms, and a sense of comfort and affection stole about him. For the first time he began to pity himself and to wonder why it was that, with such good brains, he had not gone further. Some guys have all the breaks, he told himself. But now perhaps, with her at his side always encouraging him, showing him what it was that he could do best, he would astonish the world with his gifts.

So the afternoon came, a foggy, cold afternoon, with a mist that seemed gloomily alive; to have arms and tentacles and a sort of weeping dreariness like a tiresome friend who must always insist on being comforted. Her drawing-room was cheerful, a log fire was blazing, and he noticed again, as of late he had so often done, how brilliant and fresh her pictures and curtains and furniture were. When he entered the room, the white cat was asleep in front of the fire. The Chinese manservant said that his mistress would be down in a few minutes. He was alone with Penelope.

He sat down, picked up a copy of *Time*, wondered how those boys could be so brilliant week after week and also so unkind to practically everybody, tried to think of world politics and to believe himself a man of affairs, but was aware that his heart was beating with such an agitation that he was unable to think of anything but himself.

That was because within another half-hour he would propose to Grace Ferguson, and would, in all probability, be as good as married before he left that room. He had no doubt but that she would accept him.

But was it only that?

Looking about him, he felt that something in the room was discomforting, and then was conscious, to his own extreme surprise, that he hated to be alone with the cat. The animal had not moved, and then quite suddenly it stretched out a lazy paw and scratched the carpet. The sound made him shiver.

'Don't do that!' he said aloud, as though he were speaking to a living person. The cat very slowly turned its head. He noticed then for the first time how intense were its large grey eyes. And even as he looked at them, the heavy lids obscured them. It was as though the cat were looking at him with twice the intensity through that blinded vision. Nothing in the room moved, and yet it seemed to him that the cat had come closer and grown larger. The whole room was filled with a sort of warm furry odour, almost as though he would soon be stifled with it.

Grace came in and he gave a little sigh of relief. He had his highball and she had her tea. Then he said, his voice shaking a little: 'Grace, I want to tell you . . . I've been wanting to for weeks. I'm in love with you.' She turned and looked at him with so kindly a maternal expression that he felt for a moment like a little boy who had asked to be taken to the circus.

'That's very sweet of you,' she said softly, 'dear Thornton. But you can't be in love with an old woman like me.'

'Old!' he laughed. 'Why, Grace, you're wonderful! You're no age— you're every age. You're the woman I love and I want you to marry me.' At the same time, he put out his hand and caught hers. She said nothing and he began to be uneasy.

'We are neither of us children,' he said. 'I'm not much. I haven't anything to offer, except devotion and loyalty. I'll be as good to you as I know how.' (He had a ridiculous notion that he was quoting something from a story in a magazine.) She did not take her hand away, she even pressed his a little.

'I've been married once, you know,' she said. She laughed. 'There are two kinds of widows: those who believe in marriage and those who don't. It depends, I suppose, on what their experience has been.'

'Well?' he asked, drawing his chair a little nearer to hers.

'Well—I don't know. I was very happy with Egbert. The only thing I had against him really was his name. I like you very much, Thornton. I think we would get on very well together. I'll confess to you that I'm often very lonely. I can't think of anyone I'd be better friends with, but—'

'But?' he said eagerly.

'I've got accustomed to my life as it is. It isn't perfect. Nobody's life is. But on the whole, it's safe. And I'm not quite alone. There's Penelope.'

'Penelope!' he said mockingly.

'Oh, you don't know. You'd be surprised if you did.'

'Now come.' He put his arm around her gently, but he spoke with a sudden masterful decision. 'You can't pretend you won't marry me because of a cat. I could do more for you than a cat can. I love you, and that's what you haven't got in your life.'

'Yes.' He noticed that she didn't move away from him, that she came, if possible, a little closer.

'I know.' She looked at him. 'I like you so much.'

He thought that the moment had come. He drew her to him and kissed her, as he hoped, passionately. Still she did not withdraw'. She returned his kiss, but a little as though he were her boy who had just told her that he had won a prize at school. Well, after all, did he want passion He thought that on the whole he did not.

'Marry me, marry me!' he said urgently, kissing her eyes. 'You'll be so happy, Grace. I'll see that you are. I can't live without you.' He coughed suddenly. He felt as though his mouth were full of fur. He choked. 'I'm so sorry. Wait a moment.' He drank a little of his highball. 'Something in my throat.'

Then he turned to her, his whole being urgent with the necessity of her submitting. 'Listen, say yes. I don't know what I should do without you now. You can save me—make something of me. I'll serve you so faithfully.'

He actually fell on his knees beside her, put his arms round her just as he had so often seen people do in the theatre. He felt her response. For a moment it was as though she were going to yield to him completely. Then she drew back.

'Let me think it over, Thornton, Leave me to myself for a day or two.' She looked at him again, curiously, anxiously. 'Do you think Anglo-American marriages ever work? Isn't there something both so friendly and antagonistic between the two countries that we can never really be comfortable together? And I'm not very interesting. I'm terribly ordinary. One of the millions of middle-aged Englishwomen who have to content themselves with the little things. I'm afraid you might find me very dull.'

'You dull!' he cried. And now he was entirely sincere. 'Why, we've never had a dull moment together; you know that's true. It's because we've been such companions. We like so many of the same things, and I want to guard you, protect you I feel that you're so defenceless.'

It was then that he saw the cat rise very slowly from its place in front of the fire and walk across the room. It was a strange thing, but both of them turned and stared at it. It walked as though it saw neither of them, and yet Thornton felt that it enclosed him; tightened the air about his nose and throat and mouth. All that Thornton knew was that, for this moment at least, the scene was ended. He got up.

'All right, I'll give you your day or two, but don't refuse me. For

God's sake be kind.' And with a splendid masterful action, he strode from the room.

Three days later she said that she would marry him. 'After all,' she admitted, her cheek pressed against his, 'it's only Penelope who'll object.'

'That damn cat,' he said, drawing away from her ever so little; 'you're always mentioning it.'

'Well, you see, it's been the important thing in my life for so long. She's not an ordinary cat. She's done such strange things. There was Mr. Mangan, for instance—' She hesitated.

'Well!" asked Thornton, feeling, from he knew not where, a strange tremor down his spine.

'Percy Mangan. It wasn't anything really, only he flirted a little, you know—and next morning he wrote me such a strange letter. He was going back to New York, because of a nightmare, he said. I never saw him again, but I know it was something to do with Penelope.'

'Listen, darling.' He took her face firmly between his hands and was a little annoyed with himself that he should be thinking of her money rather than of her proximity. 'You're not to have exaggerated notions about this cat. That's one of the things I'm going to stop when we're married.'

Grace shook her head. 'Yes, I know. All the same, Penelope can't bear that anyone should be fond of me. She scratched Benjie Cooper's face once so that he couldn't go about in public for weeks.'

Thornton felt a chill in the room. He looked about him, but the cat was not there. 'This is all nonsense,' he said. 'Rather than have that cat make our lives miserable, I'll have it chloroformed.'

She gave him then such a strange, clear look. 'I don't think you could,' she said. 'Penelope's an extraordinary cat. If she didn't want to be chloroformed, she wouldn't be, whatever you might do.'

In fact, he went away from the house that evening less happy than he should be. He did not know what was the matter with him. He ought to be radiant. He was not in love with Grace, but he was very fond of her. They were excellent companions. Financially, he was safe for life.

It was one of those lovely evenings when the sunlit air bathes all the strange little bungalows and untidy lots and oil-pumps and new petrol stations and temporary homes of the ventriloquists or psychic readers, psychology interpreters and soul-healers, and transmutes them all into a lovely filmlike iridescence. So much more unreal, so much more exhilarating and depressing at the same time, than true sunlight. He went home. He opened his door, entered his sitting-room. There, staring at him, was the white cat. He looked again. It was not there. 'Now this is absurd,' he told himself. 'That cat is beginning to get on my nerves. There is no cat there.' But he felt in his nostrils a warm, furry, stifling sensation. He went and had a shower and changed his clothes.

He telephoned Grace. 'Just to know whether you're happy, darling.'

'Of course, I'm happy.'

'Thinking about me?'

'Yes, of course.'

'Is Penelope there sitting in front of the fire?'

'Yes. As a matter of fact, she's on my lap.'

He had an absurd instinct to scream through the telephone: 'Put her down! Put her down! Don't touch her!' But he wished Grace a loving goodnight, turned from the telephone and saw the cat walking from his sitting-room into his bedroom. He went into his bedroom. There was no cat there. That night he had a dream. Somebody warned him, he couldn't in the morning remember who, that he'd better not marry Grace Ferguson. Suspended on a little cloud between heaven and earth, he enquired why. 'It's not safe,' said the angel or the devil or whoever it might be. On about the third day from this, driving Grace up to one of the Bowl concerts, he said to her, 'Darling, I haven't been drinking. I don't know what's the matter with me.'

'Why?' she asked him, laying her little hand on his.

'I'm always seeing your cat. At least, I don't know whether I see it or don't. It seems to be there; and then it isn't.'

She pressed his hand. 'Penelope has been rather strange the last few days,' she said. 'I felt a little frightened of her myself, as though I were doing something wrong. You do love me, Thornton, don't you?'

'Love you,' he breathed.

'Because if you didn't, if you were marrying me for some other reason, I can imagine Penelope doing something terrible. She isn't an ordinary cat. You say you fancy you've seen her. Well, so did I once. I was at Palm Springs for a week or two and I left her at home with the servants. You'll think me ridiculous. I know, but she came every evening just as the sun was fading behind the mountains. She would be there, she would rub herself against my leg.'

For the first time since his friendship with her, Thornton was irritable.

'Oh, don't, Grace! This is ridiculous. We're both ridiculous.'

They got out, gave the car to a parking attendant and walked slowly up the hill without speaking.

Two nights later, he awoke suddenly and thought that he was choking to death. He sat up gasping, beating the air with his hands. As he sat there, his heart hammering, his whole body trembling, staring into the darkness, something again whispered to him: 'Give this marriage up. You're in danger.'

Next day he felt so unwell that he consulted a doctor. There was, it seemed, nothing actually the matter with him, but his friends all noticed the change. He was pale and he looked as though he hadn't slept. His manner was nervous and irritable. For three days he did not see Grace, and during that time quite seriously considered whether he would not run away. Something was driving him. He would write to her when he got to New York. He would borrow some money from someone there and go to Europe. He would fly to New York. He nearly did.

And then his pride and his real affection for Grace, his thought, too, of the economic comforts waiting for him, these were all too much for him. He stayed. He spent the long afternoon in Grace's drawing-room, tempting her to comfort him. When she knew that he suffered, she was distraught and distressed; her affection for him grew into love, because the real basis of her nature was maternal. She loved him that afternoon. Penelope sat without moving in a square of sunlight and never looked at either of them.

On that same evening, he went to bed early. He had no appetite. His whole body was weary, as though he were beginning some kind of attack. Was it influenza? He took several aspirins and a strong highball.

He awoke quite suddenly with a start of apprehension. He switched on the electric light and saw from his clock that it was a quarter to three in the morning. Then he looked around the room and saw the white cat lying up against the wall opposite the bed. He knew then such fear as he had never before experienced. The cat this time did not vanish as he looked at it. It seemed to grow larger, and there was something quite horrible about its watching, emotionless impassivity. While he sat there and stared, he told himself of his own foolishness. All that he had to do was to get out of bed and walk out of the door.

He moved and felt that he was caught, as one sometimes is, by the bedclothes. He pushed against them and got one bare foot to the floor. At the same moment the cat moved, not its head, but rather its back, which seemed to arch and shiver very slightly as though it were shaking itself.

He got the other foot to the floor, and then, his hands gripping the bedclothes, he watched the animal. It slowly rose, stretched first one leg, then the other, then very softly came towards him. When it was half-way across the floor it crouched, watching him with its large grey eyes; the great white body seemed to be instinct with power. It looked as though it might spring with a tiger's action.

He screamed hysterically, 'Get out! Get out!' and then, drawing himself back into bed again, let himself drop on the other side away from the door.

The cat moved towards the bed, and now it was so close to him that he could feel the hot foetid jungle air of its breath, and in its deep grey eyes he saw an intensity of malevolence. But the stupor of a few moments ago had left him. He felt now all activity. Could he but reach the door and escape, all would be well. But as he turned his head, the cat gave a soundless leap and to his horror was crouching there on the top of the bed quite close to him.

He made a movement and the cat, drawing itself on its belly, came to the very edge of the bed, its eyes with a steady burning intensity fixed on him.

He fell on his knees. The air, now close against his eyes, nostrils and mouth, was of so sickening a stench that he could not breathe.

He looked up. His mouth opened for a scream of terror, but no sound came.

The cat leapt. He felt its claws on his cheek. He was stifled with the press of warm fur. . . .

When next morning Grace Ferguson read that Mr. Thornton Busk was found in his apartment, clad in his pyjamas, on the floor of his bedroom, dead, she burst into a storm of tears. It seemed that he had died of heart failure. Feeling unwell, he had crawled out of bed to get assistance and had died there on the floor. On each check there was a tiny scratch for which there was no accounting.

She cried her heart out. She had been so very fond of Thornton. She felt at the same time a strange relief. She had been free for so long, and now she was free again. Poor Thornton! The excitement of these last few days had been too much for him. The Chinese boy brought in the saucer of milk that Penelope enjoyed always at a settled time. Grace Ferguson blew her nose, dried her eyes, and, her voice a little broken with her crying, said:

'Come, Penelope. Here's your milk, darling.' The cat got up, walked across to the saucer, began happily to lap. It purred its hearty contentment.

The Tiger

Little Homer Brown had one night, after too luxurious a supper, a nasty dream. He dreamed that he was in a jungle. He was lost in a thick dark mass of bush that seemed to rise like a forest with green spikes on every side of him. He walked with naked feet on pointed grass sharp as razor blades, and then he saw shining at him out of the dark mass two burning eyes. Petrified with something more than terror, as one is in dreams, he stood there waiting for the tiger to spring. As the tiger sprang he woke up.

The only thing about this dream was that in the morning he remembered it. He never remembered his dreams, which was a pity, because they were in general pleasant ones, and he had not much romance in his actual waking life. It seemed that he forgot the pleasant ones and remembered the nightmares, which was perhaps characteristic of him because he was of the sort that worries over little troubles and forgets too quickly the larger delights.

He remembered his tiger for three days at least. He told his sister, who kept house for him, and several of his more intimate friends about it. They wisely cautioned him against eating steak just before going to bed. The trouble with him was, as he thought about it, that he was convinced in his heart that there was more in the tiger than steak. He had all his life been afraid of the future, that something would spring out at him one day and eat him up.

He was a man small of stature, sentimental of nature, and likely to catch colds. But, like many another Englishman, he was brave enough before the things which he could see. He had so little imagination in general that the things which he could see were the only things about which he did worry. But again, like many Englishmen, he had one thin stream of imagination running underground deep in his subconscious life. He had been aware of the dark steady flow of it on certain

occasions—once when as a child he had been taken to the pantomime and all the houses in Dick Whittington's London had rocked
before the inebriated cook; once in an animal shop in Edgware Road
when he had seen a sad monkey stare at him from behind the window; once when he had proposed marriage to a lady friend and had
been rejected, and once when a motorcar in which he was riding had
killed a black Cocker spaniel.

On such occasions he had seen visions. It was as though the earth
had opened up beneath his feet and he had realised that he was walking on a kind of hot pie crust over an underworld of energetic little demons. But for the most part he forgot these revelations and
lived quietly enough with his tall, bony sister in a neat little house in
Wimbledon, pursuing every morning his successful little insurance
job somewhere in the bowels of the city.

And he forgot the tiger.

★★★★★★

It was this insurance business that sent him one day to New York.
Quite an adventure for him. Phoebe, his sister, who was as kind as she
was tiresome, and, though he didn't know it, absolutely necessary to
his existence, was disturbed at his going alone. She would have liked
greatly to accompany him and hinted at this; but he sniffed at his
coming freedom and would not have had her with him for anything.
Nevertheless, when he found himself quite alone on the gigantic liner
his heart failed him. He discovered that he had lived so long with his
particular cronies that he had quite forgotten how to make new acquaintances. He was afraid to play cards lest he should lose his money,
he couldn't dance, and for reading he had a kind of shyness as though
by giving himself away to a book he was endangering some mysterious part of his morality. So, he walked up and down the deck a great
deal, very proudly holding his head up and daring any stranger to
speak to him, but secretly hoping that some stranger might.

In New York, however, he was not lonely. That warmth and eagerness of hospitality which always astonishes every Englishman and
sends him racing through strangely conflicting moods of suspicion,
pride and, although he tries not to show it, sentimentality—these
caught little Homer Brown by the throat and caused him to think
that after all he must be a very fine fellow indeed.

He started with a room at the Brevoort, but this was a little remote
for his business, and in a very short while he was staying with a Mr.
and Mrs. Moody in West Sixty-Ninth Street.

Mr. and Mrs. Moody were very quiet Americans. Mrs. Moody was so quiet that you had to listen very carefully if you wanted to hear what she had to say. Mr. Moody was stout and broad-shouldered, but oddly timorous for a Mid-Westerner. You would think, to look at him, that he would defy the world, but as a matter of simple fact he couldn't defy a living thing. Englishmen are much more sentimental than Americans, but they are not, of course, so demonstrative. Little Homer conceived slowly a passion for the large, hearty and gentle Mr. Moody, and Mr. Moody, having been brought up in the usual American creed that ten American men were worth only one American woman, was surprised that anybody should pay him much attention. And before Homer Brown returned to England these two had formed a greater friendship than they knew.

Homer Brown was delighted with New York. He loved to feel that every minute of the day was important and it didn't matter to what you were hurrying so long as you hurried. The noise around him excited him as a small rather lonely child is excited at a large children's party where everyone shouts and sings for no especial reason.

At home in Wimbledon he always went to bed at ten o'clock. In New York he found that he could be up till three or four in the morning and not feel at all tired the next day. At least, this was so for the three weeks that his business kept him in New York. It is true that he slept on the boat returning to England for three days and nights almost without a break. The sad thing was that, back in London again, he found himself unsettled. He missed the noise, the hurry, the cold sharp air, the sense of rise and fall as though he were sailing on an invigorating sea of waves and buildings, and he missed very much indeed the warmth of pleasure with which people had treated him.

No one in London said that they were delighted to meet you, but only, 'Hello, old man. Haven't seen you about lately.' No lady in London told him to his face that he was too amusing for anything or that it had been just lovely being with him. And then, oddly, he missed the large Mr. Moody. He had never missed a man's company before. He wrote him a rather affectionate letter, but received no answer. American men have time only for business letters.

And so, it happened that he was very quick in manoeuvring to send himself back to New York again. He was amazed at his own eagerness when one fine spring day he found himself once more plunging through the Atlantic, straining his eyes towards the Statue of Liberty. His first acute disappointment on arrival this time was to find that the Moodys were in Colorado. Mrs. Moody had not been well, and, as Homer knew, the slightest wish on her part was immediate law to Mr. Moody. He had a sentimental feeling that he would like to be near their street, so he found two rooms in one of the West Sixties, rather high up, and out of his window he could see on the left a huge building crashing to the ground and on the right another structure slowly climbing to the sky. Although the Moodys were away, he was not, of course, alone in New York. He had a whole circle of acquaintances, and almost every evening he went to a party, bathed in the splendid glamour like a tired business man having a holiday at the seaside. The summer came and he did not return to England, and he did not leave New York. The Moodys were still away, and quite suddenly one hot summer's night he discovered himself to be alone. He sat in front of his open window looking at the pale purple-misted sky, listening to the hooting of the taxis, to the clanging electric hammer, to the wriggling, rasping clatter of the Elevated, and to the flashing of strange adventurous discovery; he had no invitation for that evening and nearly all his friends were away. What should he do? He would just walk out and take the air and let adventure have its own way.

★★★★★★

When he had walked for a while he discovered that it is a very strange thing to be alone in New York. He had never been alone there before. He was standing in Fifth Avenue somewhere about Forty-Fourth Street when he realised that he couldn't make up his mind to cross the street. He looked down the shining length of that wonderful avenue, saw the packs of motor-cars and omnibuses held like animals in leash, knew that he must cross now if ever, and his legs refused to move. The lights changed and the cars swept down, and as they passed him they seemed to him to toss their heads and lick their lips as though they would say, 'We should like to find you in our path— toss you in the air and then ride over you. One day we shall lure you forward.'

I have already said that in the main he had very little imagination, but once and again something stirred it, and it was the gleaming mass of those fiery eyes that held him now prisoner to the pavement. He pretended to himself that he was lingering there admiring the beautiful evening and watching the stars come out along the river of sky which ran between the high cliffs of the buildings.

But it was not so. He was frightened. He didn't move because he didn't dare to move. New York was suddenly hostile and dangerous. Guarded by his friends, he had felt until now that the City was benignant and especially gratified that he should be there. The City was benignant no longer. He turned away, his heart beating, and after a while found himself in Broadway. Here was a lovely land—like the fairy play of one's childhood, scattered with silver and golden fruit.

He admired the lighted signs, the cascade of silver that poured out of the purple fountain, the great flowers of amethyst and rose that unfolded in the middle of the sky and then faded tremblingly away, the strange figures of dancing men that hung on ropes of crimson fire, turned somersaults, and vanished into thin air. And he loved with a strange trembling passion the building that soared into peaks of silver light far, far above the town. The only fairy palace ever seen by him in actual truth.

He stood staring at these things and was pushed about by the hurrying crowds. He bore them no malice. They, too, were the sharers of this marvellous fairyland. And then, withdrawing his eyes from the heights, it seemed to him for the first time that the faces on every side of him were pale and unhappy and apprehensive. The laughter appeared to him loud and false. The haste had something of panic in it. Shrill bells rang through the air. Everyone scattered and pressed against everyone else. The fire-engines came clanging down the street, and it was as though he felt the ground rock under his feet.

He thought that he would go into some show, and after a while he pushed through some doors, paid his money at the box-office for he knew not what, and was conducted by a girl, who looked at him with a sad and weary indifference, into his place. He had been to the theatre on many occasions before with his friends and they had always been jolly together, or he had fancied that they had. He had never noticed before that many of the American theatres have no music in the intervals between the acts, nor had he realised how sadly American audiences sit, as though they were waiting for some calamity to occur.

He looked on the row of faces that stretched out beyond him to the wall, and they all seemed to him grave, preoccupied, and weary. Again, apprehensive. He had often abused in London the chattering, foolish chocolate-munching sibilants of the theatre crowd, but he would have liked them to be with him tonight. The play was strange and odd, and for his Wimbledon propriety extremely indecent. It was concerned with ladies of easy virtue in China who were imprisoned in small gilt cages, and there was a woman with a white Chinese face who terrified him.

134

As the play proceeded it became for him more and more a bad dream, as though it were his dream and all the people watching it were all his creation. So strange a hold did this gain upon him that during the third act he was largely occupied with wondering what would happen to the audience when he woke up; what would become of them when he stretched his arms and, yawning, found them all vanishing into smoke as he looked around on the familiar things in his Wimbledon bedroom. The last act of the play presented an exotic situation in which a mother finds that she has unwittingly killed her own daughter. This seemed to little Homer the climax of his bad dream, and, just as one always wakes up from a nightmare when the final crash arrives, so now Homer got up and walked out although the play was not quite finished.

He hoped that his bad dream was over, but it was not. It seemed to continue with him as he walked through the plunging lights and shadows that played over Broadway. The faces now on every side of him were white and strained; everyone was feeling the heat of the night, and a large silver fountain in the middle of the sky that was for ever spilling its water among the stars which it stridently outshone accentuated Homer's thirst so desperately that he went into a drug store and drank a strange sickly concoction of pineapple, ice-cream, and soda water.

★★★★★★

After that afternoon he never seemed quite to wake from his dream again. He received a letter from his sister urging him to come home. It appeared that for once they were enjoying a beautiful summer in England. It was neither too hot nor too cold. But as he read her letter he had a strange, aching vision of the dark cool lanes, the lap of the sea heard very faintly from across the fields, the sudden dip of the hills and the cottages, of the small villages nestling to the stream, roses and carnations everywhere. Of course, he ought to go home. There was nothing to keep him here now. There had been nothing really to keep him this time at all. None of his friends was in New York, the weather would soon be appalling. It was not very comfortable in his lodgings, and he had always a strange little headache that ran like an odd tune, a little distorted, always through his head. Of course, he ought to go home. But he could not. And he could not because he was held in this odd dreaming condition. Could he but wake up he would take the next boat back. Perhaps he would wake up tomorrow.

A few nights later the weather was desperately hot. There was no

135

air, and after a brief sleep he woke to feel his heart pounding in his chest like a hammer. His windows were wide open, but there was no coolness. He lay there on his bed, his pyjama jacket open, and the sweat pouring from his body. He threw off his pyjamas, plunged into a cold bath, and then lay a little comforted, quite naked, on the top of his bed. As he lay there he heard, beneath the sharp staccato cry of an occasional car, a kind of purr as though someone were gently sleeping nearby. *Purr, purr, purr.* . . . . It was not, he assured himself, the breathing of an individual, but simply the night sound of the City.

He had never heard it quite like that before; and between the breathing there came short restless sounds as though someone were turning over or brushing something aside as he moved. The sound had a little of the rhythm of a train when in a sleeping-car you wake in the middle of the night. Rhythm translating itself into a little tune, but this was not so much a tune as a measure that advanced and then receded and then advanced again. He had the idea that it was almost as though someone were walking in his sleep, padding stealthily along the quiet streets beyond his window, and, so thinking, at last he fell asleep.

Everyone who has lived in New York during hot weather must have noticed that the town seems to change completely its inhabitants. Those who can afford it leave the City. But many of the inhabitants, Southerners, negroes, South Americans who are accustomed to great heat, pervade the streets with a kind of new ownership. They have a sort of pride as though this were their weather and they alone know how to deal with it. They walk about as though they owned the town. Homer, coming one morning out of his door, noticed passing him a large, stout, honey-coloured negro. Rather a handsome fellow with the free disengaged movements of an animal. His big heavy body was clothed in dark, quiet garments, and he passed with lithe, springy gestures. Homer did not know why he noticed him. The negro did not look at him, but passed on with his strange determined ease down the street. That evening Homer met him again. 'He must live near here,' Homer thought. Then he had a curious idea. 'If he were naked and in a dark forest you would think that he was an animal.'

That night once again Homer dreamed of the Tiger. It was not so hot a night, but damp and humid. Homer was once again walking with naked feet on sharp spiky grass. And once again he was held with sudden terror, and once again saw the gleaming eyes and smelled the thick foetid breath of an animal. He woke in a panic of terror, and was at first delighted to find that he was in his plain simple little room, and then he was horrified to discover that the smell of an animal's breath seemed still to linger with him in the room. It was so strong that he could not possibly be imagining it. He got up, walked about the room, sniffing. He went to the window and leaned out and saw the town lying under a dazzling sheet of stars.

There was a little breeze, and when he turned back into the room again he found the smell was gone. In the morning it was as though he had had actual contact with some animal, and he had hard work to convince himself that some large dark-coloured beast had not padded round his room while he slept. He seriously examined himself. 'This won't do,' he said to himself. 'This hot weather is getting on your nerves. You must leave for England at once.'

He went that very morning to some shipping office, booked a passage for himself for the next week, and sent a cable to his sister. He felt now as though at last he had awaked from his dream, and England seemed to come very close to him with its cool breezes and long, gently undulating moors and sudden little woods with scattered anemones. But while he was sitting in his little Italian restaurant eating his luncheon he heard again through the open door a purr as if it were of someone breathing close beside him, and as he heard it his body trembled as though someone said to him, 'You are not going home. You will never go home.' That afternoon he sat in Central Park and watched the blue motionless water and felt a desperate longing for Moody's return.

'I am not very well,' he said to himself. 'It is as though I am only half awake. Must be this hot weather,' and he did a strange thing, because he went up to some children who were playing at the edge of the water and put his hand on the arm of one of them and spoke to it about something. The child answered him gravely, not at all alarmed, and pointed to some boat that it was sailing on the water. The child was a real thing. But was it not part of his dream? If he woke suddenly in his Wimbledon bedroom where would the child be? So, he hurried home in a panic, and then, just outside his door, passed again the large, heavy negro, who did not look at him, but went on padding steadily forward. He hurried into his house.

When the time for the actual sailing came he did not go. He sent a cable to his sister saying, 'Important business prevents leaving. Sailing later.' But there *was* no important business. The weather grew ever more hot, but he was accustomed to it now and, although it depressed him, he liked it. He liked, too, the slightly acrid, rather foetid smell that seemed now to accompany him everywhere. For a while he was puzzled as to where he had known this smell before and then he thought of the monkey rooms and the snake rooms in the London zoo. It had been just that warmth, damp and pungent.

On a very hot afternoon, sitting in his room, he suddenly thought, 'There must be animals somewhere. Animals that like this heat.' It was, he imagined, what a jungle smell would be; and the light beyond his windows beating down from the blazing blue sky on to the roofs and pavements had a glossy shimmer as though he were looking at a scene through very thin sheets of opalescent metal. Then, once he had this idea that there were animals about, he began to wonder where they would be. He had the odd fancy to picture to himself this vast city, honey-combed with underground cells and passages, like the dark shadowy cells behind the Roman amphitheatres where they kept their beasts for feast days and holidays.

It would be a strange thing were the whole of New York built about these dark stone cellars and the wild beasts for ever prowling there. Sitting at his window in his pyjamas, he fancied how these hordes of animals would slink about, padding their way from passage to passage, and the only things seen in that grey dusk were thousands and thousands of fiery eyes, and then it might happen one day that some of them would escape and appear in the streets. Lions and tigers and leopards and panthers, dazzled at first by the bright staring light and then accustomed to it, plunging into the middle of the multitudes. A great lion with tawny head finding its way through the entrance of one of those vast skyscrapers, padding up the stairs, and then confronting a group of clerks and stenographers.

Yes, that would be fine, and how the people would rush from the building to the street! He'd heard it said that if all the human beings ran at the same moment from the skyscrapers into the street, they would be piled one upon the other five deep, and he could see them heaped up in this hot dry weather struggling in masses, and from the windows of the building the lions and tigers peering down at them and waiting with slow licking lips for the splendid meal that was coming to them.

Moving from this still further, he came to his own especial tiger—the animal about which he had dreamed so many years ago, waiting now for him somewhere in the underground beneath the street. At this thought a pleasant warm shiver ran through his body. He put his hand in front of his eyes as though he would shut out from them some picture, and the familiar animal smell seemed to increase in the room.

★★★★★★

It was just then, at the end of August, that the Moodys returned to New York. Homer was very glad to see them, but not as glad as he would have been a month ago, because he had now something else to think about. They didn't know about all these animals, all these beasts prowling under the streets in the shadowy dark. And they must not know, because they would think him foolish and wouldn't understand. So, because he had a secret from them, he was very mysterious and preoccupied and not so frank with them as he had been. They noticed, of course, the change and commented on it to each other.

Moody had a real affection for this little Englishman, largely because he had been noticed by him and made to suppose that he was somebody; partly because he had a truly kind heart and wanted people to be happy; so, he was distressed and asked Mrs. Moody, for whose opinion and judgement he had the profoundest respect, if she knew what the matter could be. 'He seems preoccupied with something,' he said to her. 'He always thinks of something else. He doesn't look well at all. Perhaps it's the heat that's got on his nerves. Englishmen can't stand it. When I was in his room last night he asked me whether I noticed a smell. I noticed nothing. But he said that I should in time. He seems to have a terror of the subway. He implored me yesterday not to use it. His eyes were terrified as he spoke to me about it. I don't like the look of things at all. I think he'd better go home.'

But Homer now saw the Moodys through a dark glass. He wondered how it could be that all the inhabitants of New York were not aware of their great danger. He thought it might be his duty to write to one of the papers about it. But, after all, the animals had been there so long the people must all know. He supposed that they were so confident of their control that it didn't worry them. But suppose you had, as he had, one particular animal who was watching and waiting for you. He knew now exactly where his tiger must be. Somewhere underground between Fortieth and Forty-Fourth Street, where the traffic and the press of people are thickest, and he began to be fascinated by that part of New York.

He found that if he went down to the Grand Central Station and stood on that great shining floor he could almost hear the animals moving beneath his feet, and he fancied that if he went lower down through the gates to the trains and stood there in absolute silence when no trains were passing he would be able to hear very clearly soft feet moving and the heavy bodies brushing the one against the other.

So, one day he got permission from the station-master to go and meet a train, and he went through and for five minutes was alone there, save for the coloured porters, and through the silence he heard quite clearly the whispering footfalls. There must be many beasts there, thousands perhaps, and you can imagine how one would push ahead of the others and wait, his eyes eagerly fixed for the black gate to open. And one day it might be that the negroes who brought them their food, great red lumps of bleeding meat, would be a little careless, and some of the beasts would slip past and moving noiselessly would be up on the sunlit street before anyone knew that they were there. His own especial tiger would be waiting more eagerly than any of them. He must be a great strong beast with a huge head and gigantic muscles. One scratch of his paw and your cheek would be torn open, and then, at the sight of the blood, the tiger would tremble all over and his eyes would shine until they were like great lamps, and then he would spring.

Then one night Homer told Moody about it. He had not intended to tell him, but it irritated him that that great heavy man should be sitting so calmly in his room and not notice the acrid smell. He told him first about the big honey-coloured negro who was always passing down his street, and Moody thought there was nothing odd in that; so that Homer, thoroughly exasperated, burst out with, 'He is one of the keepers. Although he hasn't told me I know it and he knows that I know it.'

'One of the keepers?' asked Moody. 'Keeper of what?'

'Why, of the beasts, of course. Can't you smell them everywhere?' He went on then and said that he couldn't understand why people were not frightened. 'It would be so easy some day for one of the animals to steal out while the keeper wasn't looking. Or suppose they went for the keepers one day and broke out—hundreds of them— into the streets. That would be a nice thing. You would see people run for their lives then all right.'

Moody became greatly alarmed, but, as always when one's friends are odd or queer, adopted a tone of quiet reassurance as though he were speaking to a sick child. He consulted with Mrs. Moody, and the result of this was that he invited Homer to go with him one day to call upon a friend of his. Homer went with him most readily and had with this kind gentleman two hours of most interesting conversation. The interesting, quiet man who talked to him and asked him questions was surprised at nothing which Homer had to tell him. When Homer spoke about the animals he nodded his head and said, 'I know. When did you first notice it?'

Homer, delighted to discover that he had found a sensible person at last, told him everything. 'You see,' he said, 'I shouldn't really mind, myself, a bit, but of course I am a little uneasy because of my own tiger. You can quite understand that it isn't pleasant to feel that he can escape at any time. Then he would come straight for me. He knows just where I am.'

'Why not,' said the quiet little man, 'go home for a while? Your tiger won't follow you to England.'

'Ah,' said Homer, mysteriously, 'I am not so sure. Besides, don't you think it would be cowardly? And then, there's something exciting in defying him. I am not going to show him I am afraid,' and a little warm tremor ran all over his body.

His kind friend asked him many questions about his childhood. When he was very young, had he been taken to the zoo and had he looked at the tigers there? Homer nodded his head. Of course, he had. Had he when he was very young been shown pictures of tigers? Yes, of course he had, but what had that to do with it? His little friend agreed that, of course, it had nothing to do with it, but it was just interesting. It was suggested to him that he should come and see his little friend quite often, and Homer said that he would, but, nevertheless, he had no intention of doing so. This man took it all too quietly. He would wake up one day and find out his mistake.

★★★★★★

Early in September there came those warm days, close days that are perhaps the most trying moments of all the American climate. If you took a walk you were at once bathed in perspiration. The town had indeed, for even less active imaginations than Homer's, a jungle air. The traffic now was terrific. Down on Fifth Avenue the cars would stand packed in serried ranks. Then, on the changing of the lights, they would slide furiously forward for a brief space, then sit back on their haunches again.

It happened one evening that, hurrying home in the dusk, Homer, looking up the street, saw these hundreds of gleaming eyes and thought with a furious beating of his heart that the moment had arrived at last and that the animals had escaped. He realised at once, of course, that it was the traffic; and yet, was it? Were not these things alive and acting from their own volition? It might be that they were in union with the beasts and were acting under command, and one day at a given order they would suddenly take the thing into their own hands. In great armies of shining metal, they would drive the trembling thousands of tiny human beings into panic-stricken mobs and the animals would be released.

This was fanciful perhaps, but when he returned to his room, he knew with a sudden certainty that his Tiger was free. Homer did not know how he was aware of it, but he was certain. What must he do? He wanted to escape. He was trembling with fear, but at the same time he wanted to face the animal. Some horrid fascination held him. He could imagine himself walking down some dark side street, lit only by some scattered lights, shaking slightly with the reverberation of the overhead railway, and then, turning a corner, there the Tiger would be. He sat there all night not sleeping, sitting on his bed, wondering what he must do.

At about three in the morning obeying some curious impulse, he barricaded his door, putting two chairs in front of it and pushing his bed toward it. When day came he must buy a gun; but of what use would that be? He didn't know one end of a gun from another, and, besides, it was hopeless. No gun that he could buy would injure the Tiger. His fate was certain. He could not escape it.

That morning Moody came to see him. He entered very cheerfully. 'Now, my friend,' he said, 'what's this, you're not dressed? Come on, take a bath and come have a meal with Mrs. Moody and myself. You are not well, you know. Mrs. Moody wants you to come and stay with us for a bit. Cheerful company, that's what you want.'

Homer thanked him, shook his head. It was very kind of him, but he was very busy just then and would come and see them in a day or two. Moody talked to him for a little, and then apparently alarmed at Homer's expression, went away.

When the evening came Homer dressed and went out. First, he walked on Fifth Avenue and as the traffic rushed by him felt an oppressive bewildering excitement. He knew beyond doubt that now the Tiger had come very close to him. He must be very near any one of these side streets. There were so many animals that the keepers had probably not yet discovered the loss of one of them. The Tiger was waiting in some dark alley or court, crouched against the wall in the shadow. At every step that he took he was being drawn irresistibly nearer. He was no longer afraid, but only strung up to some great pitch of emotion as though the supreme moment of his life had at last come. He was oddly hungry (he had eaten scarcely anything for days) and he went into a little Italian restaurant.

He sat down in a corner and saw that there was a very good meal for a dollar. You could have antipasto, *minestrina*, spaghetti, broccoli, and all for a dollar. At a large table near him some twenty people were having a feast, and were laughing and joking very loudly. In the far corner a violin and a piano were playing gay tunes. The *minestrina* was very good—hot and thick. He talked to the waiter and asked him if he liked New York. The waiter liked it very much. 'Now here was a real town. Something was going on all the time and there was money about. Lots of money. You could pick it up in all sorts of ways.'

Homer was about to say, 'Yes, but suppose the animals get loose one day, where will you be then?' But he didn't say it, stopped by a kind of sense that it would be bad form to mention it. He sat there staring at the gay supper party. They didn't seem to care. What would they do if he went over to them and told them that just up the street a great Tiger with huge velvety haunches was waiting? They might not believe it, and then he would look foolish, and in any case, this was the one thing that in New York nobody mentioned.

After a while he paid his bill and went out. He was now in one of those streets that seem in the evening to be the very borderland of madness. Overhead the trains rattled, on the right the street was 'up' showing black cabins of darkness and then a blaze of burning light. The trains came clattering up, issuing from forests of armed girders and tangled masonry, people hurried by as though they knew that this was a dangerous place and that they must not pause there for a moment.

Homer took a deep breath, stepped forward into the middle of the street, stared past the bright lights of a drug store, and then, with a whirl of concentrated knowledge as though everything in his past life had suddenly leaped to meet him, in one swift instant knew that the time had come. Facing him, as he stood there at the very issue of the dark side street opposite him, crouched the Tiger. Although the street was so dark, Homer could see every detail of his body. He was very like a huge cat streaked with his beautiful colours. His eyes burning just as Homer knew that they would do. His head moving very slightly from side to side. With that vision, terror leaped upon Homer. He turned, screaming there in the middle of the street, and even as he turned, the Tiger jumped. The huge body was upon him. He felt the agonising blow and then sank deep into pits of darkness.

★★★★★★

A crowd collected. His body was dragged out from under the taxi-cab. The driver began an eloquent explanation. It had not been his fault. The man had seemed bewildered by the lights, had run straight into the cab. There was no time for the driver to do anything. The policeman took notes, an ambulance was summoned.

The Moodys heard of the accident that night. It appeared that it was nobody's fault. Homer had been crossing the street, and becoming bewildered, turned back, and was struck by the taxi.

About three the next morning, Moody woke up quietly trembling, and at last roused his wife. He talked to her about the poor little Eng-lishman. 'I suppose,' he said, 'staying here in the heat was too much for him. Odd thing that, his imagining that some animal was after him.' He lay there, greatly discomforted. 'New York's getting a queer place,' he said. 'You can imagine anything if you let yourself. All this traffic, for instance. They look like animals at night sometimes.' He turned and took his wife's hand in his. 'A bit close in here,' he said. 'You don't smell anything, do you? Sort of animal smell.'

'Why, no, dear, of course not,' said Mrs. Moody.

'Imagination, I suppose,' said Moody. 'Funny thing if this town went wild one day.'

But Mrs. Moody was a sensible woman, not given to silly fancies. She patted her husband's shoulder and so fell asleep. But Mr. Moody lay there looking into the darkness.

The Twisted Inn

Mr Bannister chose his carriage with some care. He was always careful in the train because if you had work to do it was obviously necessary to have the place to yourself—when people were talking nothing could be done,

It was a dark, windy day in late November. The platform, at King's Cross was nearly deserted, and it was all very cold and gloomy. The bookstall stared vacantly across the empty lines and its books and papers fluttered discontentedly as though they protested indignantly against their unhappy neglect—a porter pushed a load of luggage vacantly down the platform and ran into Mr Bannister: he apologised still vacantly and passed on, dreaming.

Mr Bannister chose his carriage—a dirty, unappetising third furnished with six highly coloured representations of 'The Spa Longton', 'The Beach', 'Hicheton-on-Sea', 'The Station Hotel, Trament', 'The High Street, Wotton'—illustrations that were neither truthful nor entrancing.

Mr Bannister was thin and wore glasses; he had high cheekbones and sandy hair—his eyes were pale grey, watery and red at the edges; his greatcoat was threadbare and shiny, his collar was a little frayed and his trousers had never been intended to turn up. Mr Bannister was a journalist.

Times were hard just then, and, to be strictly truthful, his meals had, of late, been desperately uncertain, On Monday there had been breakfast, on Tuesday lunch, on Wednesday an excellent supper, owing to the happy discovery of a new friend; but today there had, as yet, been nothing—he sat in the corner of his carriage and thought of sausages.

During a year and a half, he had worked on the *Daily Post* and pay had been, on the whole, regular. He was a bachelor and claims on his purse were few, so things had gone well with him,

But the *Daily Post* had found the world a cold and unfeeling place and had passed silently away, leaving very few to regret its departure. Mr Bannister missed it very sincerely, and he discovered how hard life could be. Everything that he handled seemed to be a lost cause, and one paper after another faded away at his eager touch—he depended, eventually, for his living, on the crimes and misfortunes of his fellow men—the world seemed to his tired brain a procession of thieves and murderers with the divorce courts for a background.

Today he was hurrying down to a little village in a remote part of Wiltshire to investigate a crime of the night before. It was an affair of the usual kind—a woman had been murdered and there were suspicions of a lover. Mr Bannister went to it as he would to his bath or morning cigarette—to his heated brain murder was the game that everybody played: and he must be back again by the evening to report on a religious revival meeting in Clapham. The clouds were lifting—it was long since he had had two jobs in one day. and the *Telegraph* had given him both of them. The *Telegraph* was an excellent paper.

They had told him that he must be prepared, if necessary, to sleep there during the night—it would be annoying if that were to happen—he would miss the revival. He determined, therefore, to be as speedy as possible, and he would, he hoped, be able to catch the four-thirty train back to town.

It was dark and stormy and the wind whistled outside the carriage—the scudding clouds seemed to catch the top of the trees and drag them in their own hurrying direction—but the roots clung to the grey earth and the furious heavens tossed the trees back again to their original abiding-place.

Mr Bannister's coat was thin and he shivered in his corner—it was too dark to see, and the train shook so that it was impossible to write; he flung his notebook down and stared moodily out of the window. He was very hungry and was inclined to regard the world as an evil place; his mind flew back to his younger days when his ambition had challenged heaven and his poverty had seemed certain proof of genius. He had breakfasted on Swinburne, lunched on Pater, and dined on Meredith—now his library had been sold to pay his debts and his debts were still unpaid; he was very hungry,

At a small wayside station there came an old woman—a very massive old woman with a bright print skirt of blue and an immense bosom; she had a large basket, a bundle of sticks and a little boy. The basket and the sticks she placed carefully at her side; the boy she flung behind her—he fell into the corner and crouched there, against the cushions, softly sobbing.

From her treatment of the boy Mr Bannister concluded that she was cruel, and he hated her cruelty—so he looked at her sternly and frowned. She sat staring straight in front of her, her hands planted firmly on her knees—she was an enormous woman.

It growing very dark and horribly cold—it was curiously dark for that time of day, Mr Bannister thought—moreover, the pangs of hunger came crowding upon him, and, to forsake their company, he plunged into conversation.

'It is strangely dark for the hour,' he said, and he coughed nervously. But the woman made no reply: only the little boy ceased his sobbing and sat up to his corner to stare amazedly at Mr Bannister.

'It is a dreary day,' he said with a little sigh—but perhaps the wind and the noise of the train had drowned his words, for she gave *no* answer and sat there without, movement.

She was rude as well as cruel, he thought, and he leaned back in his corner and desolately thought of murders and religious meetings and the profitable emotions of highly strung people.

He sat thus for a *very* considerable time. The train rushed furiously forward, and the landscape grew darker and darker.

'There must be a terrible storm coming,' thought Mr Bannister— he watched the ebony blackness of the sky, the dark wavering outlines of fantastic trees, the sudden whites and greys of spaces of cloud and the clear shining of sudden pools.

Within the carriage there was silence, and obscurity gathered, to the corners and hid the coloured views mercifully in its arms: the outline of the enormous woman was black against the window and the curve of her great basket stood out hooplike in front of her.

Every now and again the train stopped, but no one ever seemed to get in or out, and the desolate little stations with their pathetically neat gardens stared at the train, forlornly as though they would have liked to stay and talk, for a little time.

Mr Bannister felt quite sorry for the little gardens—he was arriving at that state of worldwide sympathy consequent on an empty stomach. He was growing vaguely uneasy—he should surely have arrived at his destination some time before. He was afraid lest he should have passed his station, and so he spoke again to the woman.

'Can you tell me,' he said politely, "whether we have passed Little

Dutton? I am afraid that I must have missed it.'

But she did not answer him, and her silence frightened him so that he dared not speak to her again. The consequences of missing his stations would be very serious indeed at such a crisis in his affairs. There were plenty of other persons ready to take his place and the *Telegraph* could scarcely afford to pay men who missed their trains.

He could not understand the darkness. He had left King's Cross in the morning and, slow though the train had been, it could not be more than lunchtime now. But the carriage was most horribly dark, and only vaguely from beyond the window he caught distant outlines of trees and sombre houses.

Then suddenly he saw a star. There could be no mistake, Vividly, brilliantly, it sparkled at him through the carriage windows. A star! Then the darkness was no pretence, no sudden and furious storm as he had supposed. It was night.

But it couldn't be. He was to have arrived at Little Dutton before one, and now it was dark. Then there came to him the horrible certainty that he had slept—there could be no other possible explanation. He *must* have slept for hours, and Little Dutton *must* have been left, far, far behind. The horrible discovery left him breathless. He would have to pay for all those miles that he had travelled, and he nothing to give for them, He had ten shillings; it had been in his eyes a treasure trove on which he would have many meals in the future, and now it must go to pay for a fruitless journey, and even then, it would not be enough. He began to speak excitedly to the woman.

'I have slept—I must have been sleeping for *hours*. Look, there's a star—and I only left King's Cross an hour ago and it was morning. I must have passed Little Dutton hours ago. It is really dreadfully unfortunate—I can't think how it happened. I've never done anything like that before. But where are we going to now? Shall I be able to get out somewhere and change and be back in Little Dutton tonight? It's really most dreadfully important—I haven't the least idea—'

And then suddenly the train stopped. Through the carriage window a station lamp gleamed mistily. The large woman collected hurriedly her basket, her sticks and her little boy and vanished through the door. Mr Bannister hurriedly followed her.

He leaned out over the platform. It was a tiny wayside station with two lamps and a wild porter with a long beard. He cried discordantly: 'All change! All change!' and rushed furiously up and down and looked into every carriage.

'All change!' he cried at Mr Bannister and hurried on.

So, Mr Bannister got out and faced the situation. His watch, he found, had stopped; it was bitterly cold and the wind drove furiously down the platform. Above his head the stars and a round-faced jesting moon watched him coldly and without feeling.

He grasped the porter by the arm and tried to explain the situation. 'I want to get back to Little Dutton tonight—I must get back—it's very important.'

'Little Dutton!' The porter looked at him and laughed in the depths of his beard. 'Never heard of it. But you can't, anyhow. You can't get anywhere tonight. Six in the morning—'

'There are no trains!' Mr Bannister stared at him miserably. 'Oh, but is most unfortunate. Then I must sleep here!' He thought dismally of his ten shillings and all the noble plans that had been nipped in the bud. There is an inn?'

'Oh, yes,' said the porter, and again he laughed. 'Yes, there is an inn,' and he passed off down the platform.

Mr Bannister pulled his poor cloak more tightly about him and searched for a road. It was visible enough, stretching whitely for a time in front of him and then of a sudden fearfully black where the trees closed darkly in on it. Down this went Mr Bannister and cursed himself for a fool. By an unnecessary and ill-judged sleep, he had, perhaps, missed the turning point of his career, and how he was to get back in the morning he no idea. It occurred to him as strange that the porter had never asked him for his ticket—it was indeed a most fortunate chance and, at the thought of it, his spirits went up a great many degrees and he felt a warmer.

He disliked the blackness of the road and fancied that he was followed. For a moment he stopped and listened to make sure, and it seemed to him that the footsteps also stopped. Then suddenly there flashed across the road in the moonlight a rabbit. His heart beat furiously and he almost screamed. Then the silence and the perplexing moonlight were too much for him, and he took to his heels and ran, panting, down the dark road,

The wind whistled as he ran—it caught his coat and wrapped it, confused, round his leg—it slapped him on the face and brought water to his eyes.

Then, at a turn of the road, he came upon the inn. It stood out very plainly in the moonlight, and he wondered whether it was the brilliant white spaces and the dark caverns of shadows that gave it its strange appearance. For that it was strange there could be no question. It stood there on the edge of a wide and moonlit moor. There seemed to be no other houses near it. It was a thing of gables and overhanging eaves and large diamond-paned windows—it was strangely crooked in shape, and, looked at from, the road, seemed to lean curiously to one side, There were lights in the lower windows and the door stood ajar. He passed through it into the dim, uneven hall.

It was dark and musty, with a close, unpleasant feeling of closed windows—on his right the door was open and he turned into a small room, dusty, with the desolate air of a place long forsaken by human beings. Prim chairs of a faded pink chintz and hard little wooden legs, a round and shiny table, bare for a little green worsted mat in the middle, and a stiff horsehair sofa were the only furniture of the room. On the walls there was nothing to hide the faded green of the wallpaper with the single exception of a large photograph hanging by the door. Onto this the quivering light of a cracked light shining from the windowsill flung an uncertain light, Mr Bannister started at it with horror. It was the photograph of the large-bosomed woman in the train. She glared down at him as she had stared before into space—cold, menacing, horrible.

Then he found at his side a little man whom he knew to be the innkeeper—a man round as a ball, with a chubby face and bright brown buttons on his waistcoat.

'I should like a bed,' explained Mr Bannister, 'I have most unfortunately missed my train, and I cannot leave until five tomorrow morning. What are your charges?'

'The room will be three shillings—breakfast extra,' said the little landlord—he had a voice like a chaffinch.

'And I will have some bread and cheese and beer,' said Mr Bannister. 'Could you tell me the time?'

The landlord looked at him—his eyes dilated, his cheeks grew white and his hand shook. Then he leaned forward as though he would whisper in Mr Bannister s ear; then, as suddenly, he stepped back again, and vanished through the door out into the passage.

Mr Bannister chose one of the hard pink chintz chairs and waited for the bread and cheese. The room was a room of a thousand ghosts, and the lamp on the table created a shifting curtain of shadow that crept from corner to corner and stole, like the fingers of a gigantic hand, over the dark green wall. Through the little diamond-paned window glimmered the white expanse of the moor under the moon—a magic lake of frosted silver.

He felt very sleepy and hungry. He had no thought now of the expenses of tomorrow and of the letting slip of so great an opportunity. His one wish was for food and a splendid bed into which he might sink down, down, down, with the sheets billowing great waves about him, and so sail on a sea of dreams to a land where journalists were kings and hunger was for those who deserved it.

The eyes of the photograph followed him round the room and he moved from one hard little chair to another in a hopeless attempt to avoid their gaze, but he gave it up and slipped back into his corner and closed his eyes. Soon his head was nodding and he thought that he slept—but it was a very confused sleep, for people came creeping into the room and out again, and he thought that they were bringing his bread and cheese, but they only looked at him and then crept away, silent as they had come.

Then at last he awoke with a start, for someone was in the room—he sat up in his chair and rubbed his eyes; at the table were seated two men, bending over the lamp, their heads nodding as they talked and flinging giant shadows on the wall behind them.

They wore curious huge black hats that fell, villainously, with most sinister effect, over one ear; they wore, moreover, black cloaks that hung in sombre folds behind them over the backs of the pink chintz chairs—he could not see their faces. At their side were large glasses filled with ale, and they glittered in the light of the lamp. Then Mr Bannister, sitting silently in his dark corner, overheard their conversation.

'They are all asleep. There is no one here.'

'No—the man is alone—we are the only travellers.'

'The box is under the bed. You know your directions. I will be waiting for you at the bottom of the passage—'

'One blow will be sufficient. When I strike *I* strike hard."

These muttered sentences struck terror into Mr Bannister's heart, his hands gripped the sides of his chair and his legs shook so that they knocked against each other.

Against whom could their plot be intended? Supposing it should be meant for himself? At the thought he nearly screamed aloud. But it could not be for him. They did not know that he was there; he was a traveller and there was no box beneath his bed—at any rate no box of which he had any knowledge. The woman looked down at him from the wall and: he shuddered. She was in it, you might be sure.

The men were silent, but their great hats still nodded against the wall. He had seen a play once at the Kensington and the villain had worn a hat like that. He had been a horrible man, that villain, and Mr Bannister had hissed from the upper circle. Then it came to him in a flash that it must be the landlord of whom they had been speaking; he had wanted to speak to him before and he had been horribly afraid—it was the little rosy-cheeked landlord with a voice like a canary whom these men were plotting to murder.

The men were no longer silent, for one of them was snoring—his head had sunk down onto the table and his arms sprawled in front of him; the other also was asleep—only his head was flung back and his hands were clenched—and, even now, his face was hidden under the shadow of his hat.

Mr Bannister thought it strange that such villains should fall asleep so speedily, but now was the moment for escape. He would go and warn the landlord. He rose, trembling, from his chair and crept softly round the table, his eyes fixed on the sleepers.

One of them moved, and Mr Bannister stood transfixed with terror, his hands clasping the edge of the table, his breath coming in short gasps, his eyes round as saucers—but nothing followed. They were, both of them, sound asleep, and he turned to the door.

The handle creaked in his grasp, and he thought that this must certainly waken them, but there was still no movement, and he escaped.

The passage was as dark as the grave. There was, he thought, no time to be lost and he groped his way by the wall. The passage was heavy with the smell of decaying things, Mr Bannister thought of cabbage and a damp church in winter-time.

He knew that he must hasten, but progress was very slow and the passage seemed to have no end. He had a confused feeling that people were on all sides of him, and he imagined white faces in the dark and the soft steps of hidden pursuers. He could not understand why the passage was so long. The inn had not seemed a very large place—but this was interminable. The air grew thicker and thicker around him and he wondered whether he was descending into the heart of the earth. The thought of a living grave terrified him, and he leaned against the damp wall, his poor coat flapping against his trembling knees, and his hands stretched in front of his fact as though to guard it from unseen horrors into which he might at any moment plunge.

Then, with a sigh of relief, he saw light ahead, and, to his surprise, found himself back in the little entrance hall through which he had passed on his first arrival. But had he? As he glanced around him it seemed strangely familiar, and yet he had thought that he had come straight from the door into the narrow passage. On his he saw an ancient and trembling staircase that vanished into a higher floor. It was perhaps up this that the landlord had gone—at any rate he must warn him., and then he would escape out of this place as soon as might be.

The stairs led him on to a dim passage and he could not see the end of it, but opposite to him there was a door. There might be other doors to right and left, but he could not face the darkness that stretched on either side, and so he turned the handle and entered the room.

It was an enormous bedroom and through the open window streamed the light of the moon. There was very little furniture in the room. A large oak cupboard stood to the right of the window, and in the centre, there was an enormous bed—an ancient four-poster with faded red curtains and little wooden lions carved on the posts.

From one of these posts a body was hanging. At the sight of it his throat became horribly dry; his eyes burnt in his head like fire; suddenly frozen into stone, he stood there, choking with horror. It was the body of a little man, and it hung with its limbs swaying a little from side to side. The head lolled forward and was strangely grey in the light of the moon. It was the little landlord with a voice like a chaffinch. Mr Bannister could see his brown buttons shining with the swaying of the body,

'I am too late. Oh, dear, I am too late,' he cried, and then he turned to flee. But, as he turned with the handle of the door in his grasp, he heard steps on the stair. Someone was coming stealthily with muffled feet. 'Stockings!' thought Mr Bannister, He turned back into the room. He knew that the steps would not pass the door. He looked at the moon and then he looked at the body swaying in front of him and then he looked at the oak cupboard. 'They will find me here; he thought; 'they will think that I have done—that.'

He rushed wildly to the window, but there was no escape there. There was a hideous drop that he dared not face. Then he saw the cupboard and he flew into it, closing the door behind him.

It seemed to be full of spiders' webs—they clung about his face and his hands and were thick about his hair, but he knelt there with his back against the wall, watching for the door to open,

It opened slowly, and into the light of the moon they stepped softly, their dark cloaks trailing behind them and the shadow of their black hats hiding their faces.

'I knew who it would be,' thought Mr Bannister. He sank down in a heap on the floor of the cupboard and his teeth chattered in his head. He knew there no escape.

They did not to notice the body that swayed to and fro from the bedpost. They stepped slowly across the room, flung back the door of the cupboard and dragged out Mr Bannister.

He fell in a heap at their feet.

'I didn't do it,' he cried, 'I didn't, really. You know I didn't—I never saw him before tonight I had only asked him for a bed and some bread and cheese, I have from London. I have missed my train, I was going to Little Dutton.'

They dragged him across the floor, one on each side of him, in a moment the room seemed to be full of people. They poured in through the door and stood, in an excited crowd round him, and they all talked at the same time.

They wore, for the most part, large white cotton nightcaps, and many of them held little candlesticks with little candles burning brightly—the flames guttered a little in the breeze from the open window.

'I told you so—I knew he'd done it—he must die at once—in the middle of the night, too.'

But he could only cry helplessly: 'I didn't do it, I tell you. I was going to Little Dutton and night came on so quickly—' but he couldn't get any further because he couldn't remember what came next.

And then the door opened and the crowd made way respectfully. It was the woman of the train. She came toward him smiling grimly, and he knew that his doom was sealed.

'You tell them!' he cried, crawling toward her. 'You know that I was in the train. I was in the same carriage. Tell them I didn't do it—you know I couldn't!'

But she smiled grimly and motioned with her hand. Someone brought forward a rope, and in a moment, it was about his neck,

'No—no—not that!' he cried. 'I am a journalist. It is murder.' But they raised him in their arms, and he knew that they were going to hang him from the bedpost by the of the little landlord. The nightcaps closed round him; the candles flickered in the breeze; the woman watched him with quiet eyes, 'This is Little Dutton,' she said to him, and she touched him on the arm, I hope you will forgive my waking you, sir, but this is Little Dutton, and you would have passed it.'

He thanked her as he rubbed his eyes. She was sitting soberly opposite him, the basket on her knees, and the little boy watched him silently from the corner.

'Oh, thank you.' He gathered his gloves and his stick. 'I have been sleeping, I am afraid—thank you very much.'

As he stepped out onto the platform he looked at his watch. It was a quarter to one—lunch-time; and he was very hungry.

And so, it was a dream. He was conscious of a feeling of intense regret. The wind passed howling down the platform; the porter frowned at him as he gave up his ticket—the main street of Little Dutton stretched drearily in front of him.

For a moment he had touched Romance. For a moment he had *been* the centre of a crowd—he had lived. Now he was back again—a journalist in quest of a sordid murder case.

He wrapped his shabby coat around him and sighed. Was it, after all, a dream? Perhaps for a moment he had wakened—for a moment he had been Bannister the Romantic—Bannister the centre of life and death.

He turned into a shabby restaurant and ordered a chop. Opposite him there sat a commercial traveller, a little run to seed.

'Cold,' said Mr Bannister.

'Very,' said the traveller—and then, added, as he watched the dust whirl past the window; 'It's a dull world.'

'Not so dull,' said Mr Bannister, and he winked as one who has been through a great experience. 'I could tell you things—' he said—and he laughed.

The Oldest Talland

Mrs. Comber explained to Miss Salter that, although she had been living in Cornwall all these years, she was only now, during this stay at Rafiel, beginning truly to appreciate it.

'You see, my dear, a school's a school, and it does somehow rather take the edge off an appreciation of beauty having to keep the little boys clean and ordering the mutton, although I must say that our matron is a thoroughly capable woman—she comes from Marlborough, where she was for a term, but couldn't endure it because—Well, I'm wandering from the subject—what I mean is that one *does* see things on a holiday that one hasn't quite time for perhaps during term-time.'

Rafiel was all the more beautiful for the five days' rain that had but now submerged and obscured it. It was incredible after the dirty grey that it had so recently presented that it could now, so transcendently, glitter and shine. Mrs. Comber had watched it first from the heights of Sea View Villa. From that point it lay huddled, packed together between the hills, with its boats drawn up in rows together inside its square little harbour. Seen thus on a fine day, it caught blue from the sea and green from the hills, and wrapped its slates and stones in reflected lights. From a height it was something that might at any moment be overwhelmed by the sea—something pretty but insignificant.

How different in the heart of it! Mrs. Comber, as she picked her way along the tiny cobbled streets, exclaimed at every step that she took. At first the place offered you a straight and somewhat dingy street, with nothing very different from other streets in other Cornish towns. One or two little shops suggested to the hungry visitor saffron buns, apples and peppermints, and for the untidy inhabitant there were bootlaces, buttons and pins. There was also a Methodist chapel.

But it was when the village had tumbled so far as the post office that it suddenly made up its mind that it would, from that moment, be as incredible, as haphazard, as beautiful as water, bricks and Nature would allow it to be. Three little streets went dancing into the sea, little streets with shapeless roofs, steps leading up to green-painted doorways that hung in mid-air, streets with cobbles and dark, mysterious caverns and bursting, bulging windows, and across these three little streets a river ran for no reason at all, except that it gave an opportunity for more hanging balconies and green-and-blue reflections of painted doors and shutters. And then the streets and the river were, in an instant, pulled up by the little harbour—a square, shimmering space of blue water—with all the brown and blue-masted boats riding upon it like hounds in leash, and the grey stone pier blocking it from the sea.

The whole village hangs over this blue square and is reflected in it; the sky is painted there, and also the hills. Every mood, every glory, every temper of the place is to be found there. Beyond the stone wall there is the Atlantic, with sharp, jagged rocks (they are called the Peaks) as gateways on either side. All of this is within the compass of five minutes; it is as ancient as it can be, as crooked and unexpected and childish. There are wilder seas here than anywhere on the English coast, save, perhaps, on the Land's End, and the saffron buns, the buttons and the peppermints are very often in danger of being swept away altogether.

And meanwhile on the face of that little square harbour every mood of earth and sky is reflected.

Mrs. Comber took it, on her first vision of it, into the arms of her most extravagant enthusiasm. Her enthusiasms were always perfectly genuine affairs, for, although she always liked to have someone with whom they might be shared, she demanded no audience for their exhibition.

She nearly filled one of the three merry little streets, her cheeks blazing with excitement, a hard black hat slipping, it seemed, from her head, her hair threatening descent, her green skirt, short and showing thick square-toed shoes, her large, good-natured mouth and black, laughing eyes.

Full of health, good temper and colour she was, and she seemed to push back the street from her on both sides with her strong arms.

The natives looked at her, as they looked at all tourists, with a friendly indifference that was ready at any moment to develop into friendly attention if pounds, shillings and pence were in the air. The Rafiel citizens are not mercenary, but as most of them are supporting families on something approaching forty pounds a year, 'tourists' may often make considerable difference to personal comfort. Friendliness, moreover, is invited, and as, again, most of the aforesaid citizens have never in their lives penetrated farther into the heart of the world than St. Tryst, a town seven miles away (many of them have never seen a train), conversation with visitors is instructive and entertaining.

At the same time, be it understood, there is never intimacy.

Of these things Mrs. Comber knew nothing. You may be the wife of a schoolmaster in Cornwall for a number of years without knowing anything about Cornwall. The school had always swallowed up all possible backgrounds. This was the first time that Cornwall was considered for itself, and Mrs. Comber, in the burning joy of her enthusiasm, determined to take the inhabitants of Rafiel entirely to her heart.

Here she was, staying at a dull *pension,* and her husband away on the golf links all day—why, of course, the only thing to do was to get to know the place and the people. Anything more attractive than the people were, too! How readily they all said 'Good day,' how pleasantly they smiled, how amiably they chattered with one another on their bright little doorsteps! As the sun shone and the cobbles glittered, and the sky was blue upon blue and then blue upon that again, Mrs. Comber could have kissed the old fishermen one by one, and the old ladies one after another.

As a matter of fact, the thing that she did do, in the heat of her enthusiasm, was to trample with one of her square-toed shoes upon a small and dirty girl, to send the little thing sprawling, to pick her up with a thousand exclamations, to kiss her dirty mouth, and to carry her, after explanations, back to her family.

Her family, as Fate would have it, was the Talland family.

The Tallands and the Tresennens divide Rafiel between them. They have so divided it ever since that legendary day when the first of the Tallands stood on one of the Peaks and flung rocks at the first of the Tresennens, who stood on the other of the Peaks and did his best to respond in kind.

Relations are outwardly friendly enough between the two families (there is very little bad temper in Rafiel), but through all the centuries there has been no intermarriage between them, and the rivalry is unremitting, never forgotten, never allowed to lapse.

At the head of the Tallands at this time there ruled an old lady of mythical age. She was so old that the next oldest inhabitant in Rafiel (and he was over ninety) was supposed to be a child to her. Nobody knew how old she was, and she was popularly supposed to have had no beginning; and it was expected that death would never succeed in catching her. As far as appearance went, there was nothing of her face to be seen except a sharp nose, a sharper chin, and two eyes sharper still. The nose and the chin met, and the eyes blazed. These blazing eyes stared at you from the blackness of a dark and low-roofed kitchen. Huddled amongst cushions she faced the world from her corner by the fireplace—faced the world and cursed the Tresennens.

The Talland stronghold was a crooked and uneasy house perched behind the post office, a little way up the hill, and resting there, as it seemed, on one foot, and leering down at the post office and the harbour with a wink and a snigger; with every wind it threatened collapse. The Tallands had lived there now for a very long time, and it had the advantage of being higher in position than the chief castle of the Tresennens, although the Tresennens, from their windows, could see everyone who went in and out of the Talland doorway.

Here in her dark corner old Mrs. Talland, like the most sinister and patient of spiders, had been sitting for years and years and years.

A long time ago—ten or fifteen years back, it might be—something had happened to the old lady's throat, and her voice disappeared.

The family had at first looked on this event as an unmixed blessing, and some of the younger branches had suggested that the occasion ought to mark the end of the old lady's rule. Little these youngsters knew. After the accident Mrs. Talland's power was redoubled. Now that she could speak no more, her eyes, always fierce enough, had twice their former power. She attained a kind of mystical splendour that had been absent before, and, with the exception of her hard-faced youngest daughter, a maiden lady of some sixty years, who washed and fed her, the family trembled before her glance. Her eldest son, the greatest bully in Rafiel, quailed when she looked at him, and during these years of her rule the Tresennen family did not dare set their feet within a stone's throw of the Talland house.

And it was of the Tresennen family that Mrs. Talland was always thinking. In the days of her youth—and the number of years ago that was only Mrs. Talland knew—she had been concerned in strange happenings up on the windy hill with old Mother Perith, happenings that were connected with broomsticks and wax dolls and fires and skulls and strange weeds from the hedges.

She had not forgotten anything that she had learnt then. Brooding there in her fireplace, she knew the things that she could do to the Tresennens, if she needed. But it was a long time now since she had called those powers to her aid. . . . Scornfully she thought to herself that the Tresennens could be kept in their proper place without any need for such assistance.

Fiercely, with furious determination, she bent her will to keeping herself free, independent from any assistance in this world or the next. Clergymen, visitors, doctors had forced upon her, from time to time, their officious presences. . . . She had sent them all packing. They had fled before her glance.

Let her once, her old heart fiercely determined, give in to anyone, and her power would be gone and the Tresennens triumph.

There in her stronghold she kept back the world. Then into the kitchen, noisily, with friendship shining about her and in and out of her, Mrs. Comber burst.

The Tresennens, from their windows, marked her entry.

Mrs. Comber stood, smiling, in the doorway, holding tightly by the hand the youngest of the Tallands. Gathered in a little group by the fireplace were other Tallands, a number of them, and huddled amongst her cushions, with her hands shaking a little on her lap and her eyes flaming, was the oldest of them all. Behind her chair stood the gaunt, bony Janet Talland, whose duty it was to keep her mother clean and fed.

The room was very close, as it had every reason to be, because the street door was generally shut, and the little diamond-paned window never opened. The air was heavy with the odour of fish, dying geraniums, saffron buns and tobacco.

Mrs. Comber addressed herself to Miss Janet Talland.

'I do hope I'm not in any way interrupting or interfering, but I was silly enough—careless, perhaps I ought to say—to knock over your little girl; at least, they tell me this is her home. And how I came to do it I can't think, except that I was admiring your beautiful town and didn't really notice where I was going, which is a silly trick that I really must try—' She broke off and patted the head of the youngest of the Tallands. 'I don't think I hurt you, dear, did I? She cried just a little at first, but it was more fright than anything else, being knocked down suddenly—'

The Tallands had had strange tourists within their castle before, but never any tourist like this tourist. Mrs. Comber, so glowing with colour, so voluble, so eager, froze them into silence. Old Mrs. Talland leaned forward in her chair, and her dry fingers rattled together on her lap.

'Come 'ere, Annie,' said Miss Janet Talland. 'What be 'ee at, gettin' in the lady's way?'

Annie disengaged herself from Mrs. Comber's grasp and shuffled across the floor, whimpering.

'I do hope—' began Mrs. Comber. She stopped because she was bewildered by the sudden, sweeping disappearance of most of the Talland family through the street-door. Only the old lady and her grim-faced daughter remained. 'I do hope,' went on Mrs. Comber, more cheerfully than ever, 'that you won't visit the accident on poor little Annie. It wasn't in the least poor Annie's fault. If I'd only looked where I was going—'

It was then that Mrs. Comber noticed old Mrs. Talland. Nobody could have looked, to the outside observer, more helpless and ready for charity. 'Here,' said Mrs. Comber at once to herself, 'is a person to do good to. Here is the very interest that I have been wanting.'

'I hope you don't mind,' said Mrs. Comber gaily, 'my just stopping a moment or two. I'm not interrupting you in anything, am I? Because just tell me if I am, and go on doing just the things that you'd do if I weren't here. Make me at home, you know.' She sat down in a chair by the fire quite close to Mrs. Talland.

The old woman leant forward still farther and stared at her. It was many months now since any visitor had braved her presence, but no visitor within her memory had braved her as this one did. The flaunting, highly coloured, bold-faced thing! Mrs. Talland always disliked seeing youth and vigour and energy—it made her feel old—but this noise and heartiness in one who was no longer young simply disgusted her. She would have liked to slap Mrs. Comber's red cheeks. She looked up at her daughter. Why was Janet not sending the woman to the right-about, as she generally did? She was actually allowing her to sit there.

Janet had at first been taken aback by Mrs. Comber's energy, and then, as the minutes passed, her slow brain began to move. She knew well enough the things that her mother was thinking. She knew how she must hate the impertinence of this woman. But also, she knew that for many, many years now she had served the old woman and received no return for it, had served her faithfully and obeyed her in everything. In the woman's heart, although she had not known it until now, for many years resentment had been growing. Supposing that she should disobey her now? A fierce, hot pleasure was in her breast at the thought of getting some revenge at last. Moreover, this woman, were she treated gently, would bring things into the house—jellies and fruits and custards. And oh, how the old tyrant would hate it!

'Sit you down, ma'am,' Janet said slowly. 'You aren't disturbing us, I assure 'ee. Mother can't tark—'er speech is gone this many a year.'

'Poor old woman! Poor old woman!' said Mrs. Comber, her voice full of compassion.

'But she ain't deaf, all the same,' said Miss Talland, fearful lest the tourist should drive her mother to some sudden frenzy. ''Er 'earing's arl right.'

Mrs. Comber was filled with the most genuine feelings of pity and tenderness. She hated anyone to be as feeble and desolate as this poor old lady. The room seemed to her dirty and uncared-for. And how terrible to be unable to speak and to be in the hands of that cruel-looking woman. Mrs. Comber felt that she would never sleep again did she not relieve in some way Mrs. Talland's condition.

'Oh, but I *am* sorry!' she cried, and her large black eyes were full of tenderness. 'How dreadful not to be able to talk! I don't know what I should do if such a thing were to happen to me. Although, perhaps,' she went on, laughing gaily, 'some people would say it was a good thing, because, you know, I do talk so much, too much; and it's a trick I've tried to break myself of ever since I was a girl, and I've never been able to.'

Mrs. Talland's hands rapped against each other in an agony. What was this horrible thing, and what, above all, was Janet about? It was then that, flinging a sharp glance at her daughter, she caught a first glimpse of the thoughts that were passing behind those cold eyes. Janet stood, gaunt and severe, with her hands folded in front of her, and about her mouth there lingered the suspicion of a grim smile.

'Yes,' she said, 'it do be 'ard for mother, for she was always one to love a good tark, and now she must sit there and listen, as you might say.'

'Oh, dear, dear, I *am* sorry,' said Mrs. Comber. She found it so difficult to force herself to remember that Mrs. Talland was not deaf as well as dumb. 'But, really, Mrs. Talland, I want to do everything I can to help you.' Here Mrs. Talland's hands were more frantic than ever. 'Yes, I will, indeed. If there's anything I can do. Perhaps, Miss Talland, you can suggest—'

'Well,' said Miss Talland slowly, 'mother du have a likin' to jellies and them soup squares, as you *are* so kindly askin'. The doctor 'asn't been in for a long time, but the last day 'e *was* 'ere I remember 'is sayin' that a drop o' soup *and* a little jelly—'

Surely about Mrs. Talland's ears the world must have seemed, at that moment, to be tumbling. In her breast there was a fierce, dogged determination to fight to the bitter end, but it was the first rebellion that she had had to meet for many a long year. . . . And then from Janet—Janet, the most faithful of servants.

She did what she could with her face, striving to fling into her eyes all the hatred and loathing and disgust that was in her heart. Oh, if she could have spoken what things she would have said!

'Well,' continued Mrs. Comber amiably, 'that's very good of you, Miss Talland, to tell me the kind of thing. But do you really mean to tell me that the doctor hasn't been here for a long time?'

'No, that 'e 'asn't.' Miss Talland did not add that, owing to the plain speaking of the Talland family on his last visit, he had uttered a solemn vow never to cross their threshold again.

'And he looks such a nice, kind man,' said Mrs. Comber. 'I really must speak to him, because a doctor can be such a help sometimes. I remember once when a little boy of mine was ill that I was in such trouble about him because he'd got a rash, but it might have been just from overeating himself in the hot weather. But our doctor was so clever about him. Really, if he hadn't been there—well,' she continued brightly, getting up from her chair, 'I mustn't trouble you any longer, Miss Talland. I'm sure you must have heaps to do, and I must be getting along. But I *have* enjoyed this talk so much. It *is* so nice getting to know you all. Goodbye, Mrs. Talland. Be assured that I will do everything for you that's possible, and I'll speak to the doctor about coming to see you. I'll look in myself again in a little time. I'm *so* glad we've made one another's acquaintance. Goodbye.'

Mrs. Comber shook hands with the unresponsive Janet, and was gone.

It must be confessed that, for a moment, as the two women faced one another, Janet's courage forsook her. Mrs. Talland had not established her rule during all these years for nothing. The old woman's eyes were living flames. As she sat up amongst her cushions her whole body was tense with hatred, horror, surprise, vindictive longing to get at someone and tear limb from limb.

Certainly, at that instant, those things that had belonged to Mother Perith many years ago might now have found themselves once more a home. Janet had often seen her mother look angry before, but she had never seen her anything like this. She faced her mother's eyes—drew fire from them during a long moment, and then, slowly stealing back her gaze, she smiled. Mrs. Talland knew then that the moment had come that she had dreaded ever since she had lost her voice. Her rule was threatened.

But, worse than that, from the Tresennen windows, eyes—eager, mocking eyes—were watching. They had seen that woman come. They would see her come again.

It was well, at that moment, for Mrs. Comber that she was not within reach of Mrs. Talland's long and grasping fingers.

Very shortly after this, Mrs. Comber, up at Sea View Villa, met the doctor, who had been invited in to bridge. She talked to him a great deal, and amongst other things she mentioned the Tallands.

'Of course, it's really no business of mine, doctor, but that poor old woman did look so uncared-for there, with only that grim, ugly woman to look after her. She looked as though she needed company so badly, and I thought, perhaps, if you were to go in and just give her a bright word—'

'I'm afraid bright words, Mrs. Comber,' said the doctor, 'are not things that the Talland family care for very much. Last time I was there they were so rude to me that I vowed I'd never go again. But still—I promise you—I'll try once more.'

'Of course,' said Mrs. Comber, 'they're difficult.'

'Just as though,' the doctor said to his wife afterwards, 'she'd been visiting Cornish fishermen all her days.'

In her own mind Mrs. Comber concluded that the doctor had been rough with the poor people, and, of course, they didn't like that.

Nevertheless, the doctor kept his word and went, and, to his great surprise, was allowed by Janet to examine the old lady and to suggest medicines. Janet did not, indeed, say much to him during the visit; for the most part she remained, with her hands folded, grimly watching her mother, but the doctor was permitted to do what he would.

'Really, Mrs. Comber,' he said after his visit, 'you're a wonderful person. I don't know what you've done to them, but a month ago it was as much as my life was worth to go inside their door.'

And Mrs. Comber was pleased. She now paid a visit every afternoon, and sat there sometimes for half an hour talking to Mrs. Talland. She did not in the least mind the fact that Mrs. Talland was unable to answer her. She liked to have someone to whom she might talk without interruption.

Then she brought the vicar's wife, who brought tracts and left them on Mrs. Talland's table. And from their windows the Tresennens watched it all. . . .

And Mrs. Comber was really happy, and spent much more than she could afford on jellies and soups and chickens.

The younger Tallands had watched these things with dumb, gasping amazement. They had always left the treatment of the head of the family in Janet's capable hands. Janet had invariably good reasons for everything that she did, and it was to be supposed, therefore, that she had good reasons for what she did now. Slowly some inkling of the truth stole in upon them. Very, very slowly they understood.

Meanwhile, what old Mrs. Talland suffered no human being will ever know. She wrote desperately words on the slate that she was given for expressing her desires. But her old fingers were very shaky now.

'Burn,' 'Woman,' 'Hate,' 'Hell,' could be deciphered.

If eyes could have slain, Janet would long ago have been dead. When the washing, dressing and undressing periods arrived, Mrs. Talland would have bitten or strangled or torn her daughter had she been able, but Janet was a very strong woman.

Had only a week passed since this horrible creature's first arrival? Already the other Tallands, the sons, the daughters-in-law, paid less attention to her. No longer did they come in with soft step 'lest Granny should be sleepin'.' They pretended not to hear her when she rattled her slate-pencil at them.

They did not often come to her now and amuse her with the gossip of the town.

She could do nothing—she could do nothing.

Her doom had come upon her.

At last the definite moment of defeat came. Little Annie, who had always, until now, been in the utmost terror of her great-grandmother, was left in charge whilst Janet was busily employed with shopping.

The girl looked at the old woman and then defiantly, if just a little timidly, began to whistle between her teeth in a way that she had always understood was abominable to an older person.

Mrs. Talland rattled her pencil against her slate.

Annie continued to whistle.

Mrs. Talland stamped with her foot (it was a very feeble tap); she clapped her hands together, gnashed her two teeth.

Annie paused a moment, her legs apart, facing the chair.

'Shan't!' she said, and then, appalled by her daring, ran from the room.

The old woman was alone. Shaking from head to foot, she did what she had not done for many years: she got up from her chair. Leaning on her stick, she tottered to a drawer that was near. From this she extracted something, then tottered back to her place.

With her cap off her head, the cushions tumbling about her, muttering, she began to turn and twist the thing that she had in her hands. It was a piece of old, soiled, grimy wax.

Her brain was fiery with thoughts of that red-faced woman who had ruined her life.

She turned the wax, muttering.

But it would not twist; it was so hard and old. It fell from her nerveless fingers and lay amongst the ashes in the hearth. Her last resort was gone. The old world had faded, the old gods and devils had fled. There was a new order now, a new world.

The end of her life had come. Tired, thin tears trickled slowly down the dried furrows of her cheeks.

Twenty-four hours later she was dead.

'Poor thing,' said Mrs. Comber when she heard of the funeral. 'But I'm glad that I did a little something to brighten her last hours.'

Bim Rochester

This is the story of Bim Rochester's first Odyssey. It is a story that has Bim himself for the only proof of its veracity, but he has never, by a shadow of a word, faltered in his account of it, and has remained so unamazed at some of the strange aspects in it that it seems almost an impertinence that we ourselves should show any wonder. Benjamin (Bim) Rochester was probably the happiest little boy in March Square, and he was happy in spite of quite a number of disadvantages.

A word about the Rochester family is here necessary. They inhabited the largest house in March Square—the large grey one at the corner by Lent Street—and yet it could not be said to be large enough for them. Mrs Rochester was a black-haired woman with flaming cheeks and a most untidy appearance. Her mother had been a Spaniard, and her father an English artist, and she was very much the child of both of them. Her hair was always coming down, her dress unfastened, her shoes untied, her boots unbuttoned. She rushed through life with an amazing, shattering vigour, bearing children, flinging them into an already overcrowded nursery, rushing out to parties, filling the house with crowds of friends, acquaintances, strangers, laughing, chattering, singing, never out of temper, never serious, never, for a moment, to be depended on.

Her husband, a grave, bull-faced man, spent most of his days in the City and at his club, but was fond of his wife, and admired what he called her "energy." "My wife's splendid," he would say to his friends, "knows the whole of London, I believe. The *people* we have in our house!" He would watch, sometimes, the strange, noisy parties, and then would retire to bridge at his club with a little sigh of pride.

Meanwhile, upstairs in the nursery there were children of all ages, and two nurses did their best to grapple with them. The nurses came and went, and always, after the first day or two, the new nurse would give in to the conditions, and would lead, at first with amusement and a rather excited sense of adventure, afterwards with a growing feeling of dirt and discomfort, a tangled and helter-skelter existence. Some of the children were now at school, but Lucy, a girl, ten years of age, was a supercilious child who rebelled against the conditions of her life but was too idle and superior to attempt any alteration of them. After her there were Roger, Dorothy, and Robert. Then came Bim, four years of age a fortnight ago, and, last of all, Timothy, an infant of nine months.

With the exception of Lucy and Bim they were exceedingly noisy children. Lucy should have passed her days in the schoolroom under the care of Miss Agg, a melancholy and hope-abandoned spinster, and, during lesson hours, there indeed she was. But in the schoolroom, she had no one to impress with her amazing wisdom and dignity. "Poor Mummy, as she always thought of her mother, was quite unaware of her habits or movements, and Miss Agg was unable to restrain either the one or the other, so Lucy spent most of her time in the nursery, where she sat, calm and collected, in the midst of confusion that could have "given old Babel points and won easy." She was reverenced by all the younger children for her sedate security, but by none of them so surely and so magnificently as Bim. Bim, because he was quieter than the other children, claimed for his opinions and movements the stronger interest.

His nurses called him "deep," "although for a deep child I must say he's 'appy."

Both his depth and his happiness were at Lucy's complete disposal. The people who saw him in the Square called him "a jolly little boy," and, indeed, his appearance of gravity was undermined by the curl of his upper lip and a dimple in the middle of his left cheek, so that he seemed to be always at the crisis of a prolonged chuckle. One very rarely heard him laugh out loud, and his sturdy, rather fat body was carried gravely, and he walked contemplatively as though he were thinking something out. He would look at you, too, very earnestly when you spoke to him, and would wait a little before he answered you, and then would speak slowly as though he were choosing his words with care. And yet he was, in spite of these things, really a "jolly little boy." His "jolliness" was there in his point of view, in the astounding interest he found in anything and everything, in his refusal to be upset by any sort of thing whatever.

But his really unusual quality was his mixture of stolid English matter-of-fact with an absolutely unbridled imagination. He would pursue, day by day, week after week, games, invented games of his own, that owed nothing, either for their inception or their execution, to anyone else. They had their origin for the most part in stray sentences that he had overheard from his elders, but they also arose from his own private and personal experiences—experiences which were as real to him as going to the dentist or the pantomime were to his brothers and sisters.

There was, for instance, a gentleman of whom he always spoke as "Mr. Jack. This friend no one had ever seen, but Bim quoted him frequently. He did not, apparently, see him very often now, but at one time when he had been quite a baby Mr. Jack had been always there. Bim explained, to anyone who cared to listen, that Mr. Jack belonged to all the Other Time which he was now in very serious danger of forgetting, and when, at that point, he was asked with condescending indulgence, "I suppose you mean fairies, dear?" he always shook his head scornfully and said he meant nothing of the kind. Mr. Jack was as real as Mother, and, indeed, a great deal "realer," because Mrs. Rochester was, in course of her energetic career, able to devote only "whirlwind" visits to her "dear, darling" children.

When the afternoon was spent in the garden in the middle of the Square, Bim would detach himself from his family and would be found absorbed in some business of his own which he generally described as "waiting for Mr. Jack."

"Not the sort of child," said Miss Agg, who had strong views about children being educated according to practical and common-sense ideas, "not the sort of child that one would expect nonsense from." It may be quite safely asserted that never, in her very earliest years, had Miss Agg been guilty of any nonsense of the sort.

But it was not Miss Agg's contempt for his experiences that worried Bim. He always regarded that lady with an amused indifference. "She *bothers* so," he said once to Lucy. "Do you think she's happy with us, Lucy?"

"P'r'aps. I'm sure it doesn't matter."

"I suppose she'd go away if she wasn't," he concluded, and thought no more about her.

No, the real grief in his heart was that Lucy, the adored, the wonderful Lucy, treated his assertions with contempt.

"But, Bim, don't be such a silly baby. You know you can't have seen him. Nurse was there and a lot of us, and *we* didn't."

"I did though."

"But, Bim—"

"Can't help it. He used to come lots and lots."

"You *are* a silly! You're getting too old now—"

"I'm *not* a silly!"

"Yes, you are."

"I'm not!"

"Oh, well, of course, if you're going to be a naughty baby—"

Bim was nearer tears on these occasions than on any other in all his mortal life. His adoration of Lucy was the foundation-stone of his existence, and she accepted it with a lofty assumption of indifference, but very sharply would she have missed it had it been taken from her, and in long after years she was to look back upon that love of his and wonder that she could have accepted it so lightly; Bim found in her gravity and assurance all that he demanded of his elders. Lucy was never at a loss for an answer to any question, and Bim believed all that she told him.

"Where's China, Lucy?"

"Oh, don't bother, Bim."

"No, but *where* is it?"

"What a nuisance you are! It's near Africa."

"Where Uncle Alfred is?"

"Yes, just there."

"But *is* Uncle Alfred in—China?"

"No, silly, of course not."

"Well, then—"

"I didn't say China was in Africa. I said it was near."

"Oh! I see. Uncle Alfred could just go in the train?"

"Yes, of course."

"Oh! I see. P'r'aps he will."

But, for the most part, Bim, realising that Lucy "didn't want to be bothered," pursued his life alone. Through all the turmoil and disorder of that tempestuous nursery he gravely went his way, at one moment fighting lions and tigers, at another being nurse on her afternoon out (this was a truly astonishing adventure composed of scraps flung to him from nurse's conversational table and including many incidents that were far indeed from any nurse's experience), or again, he would be his mother giving a party, and, in the course of this, a great deal of food would be eaten, his favourite dishes, treacle pudding and cottage pie, being always included.

With the exception of his enthusiasm for Lucy he was no sentimentalist. He hated being kissed, he did not care very greatly for Roger and Dorothy and Robert and regarded them as nothing but nuisances when they interfered with his games or compelled him to join in theirs.

And now this is the story of his Odyssey.

2

It happened on a wet April afternoon. The morning had been fine, a golden morning with the scent in the air of the showers that had fallen during the night. Then, suddenly, after midday the rain came down splashing on to the shining pavements as it fell, beating on to the windows and then running, in little lines, on to the ledges and falling from there in slow, heavy drops. The sky was black, the statues in the garden dejected, the almond tree beaten; all the little paths running with water, and on the garden seats the rain danced like a live thing.

The children—Lucy, Roger, Dorothy, Robert, Bim, and Timothy—were, of course in the nursery. The nurse was toasting her toes on the fender and enjoying immensely that story by Mrs. Henry Wood, entitled *The Shadow of Ashlydyat*. It is entirely impossible to present any adequate idea of the confusion and bizarrerie of that nursery. One must think of the most confused aspect of human life that one has ever known—say, a Suffrage attack upon the Houses of Parliament, or a Channel steamer on a Thursday morning, and then of the next most confused aspect. Then one must place them together and confess defeat.

Mrs. Rochester was not, as I have said, very frequently to be found in her children's nursery, but she managed, nevertheless, to pervade the house, from cellar to garret, with her spirit. Toys were everywhere—dolls and trains and soldiers, bricks and puzzles and animals, cardboard boxes, articles of feminine attire, a zinc bath, two cats, a cage with white mice, a pile of books resting in a dazzling pyramid on the very edge of the table, two glass jars containing minute creatures of the newt variety, and a bowl with goldfish. There were many other things, forgotten by me.

Lucy, her pigtails neatly arranged, sat near the window and pretended to be reading that fascinating story, *The Pillars of the House*. I say pretending, because Lucy did not care about reading at any time, and especially disliked the works of Charlotte Mary Yonge, but she thought that it looked well that she and nurse should be engaged upon literature whilst the rest of the world rioted and gambolled their time away. There was no one who at the moment could watch and admire her fine spirit, but you never knew who might come in.

The rioting and gambolling consisted in the attempts of Robert, Dorothy, and Roger, to give a realistic presentation to an audience of one, namely, the infant Timothy, of the life of the Red Indians and their squaws. Underneath the nursery table, with a tablecloth, some chairs and a concertina, they were presenting an admirable and entirely engrossing performance.

Bim, under the window and quite close to Lucy, was giving a party. He had possessed himself of some of Dorothy's dolls' tea things, he had begged a sponge cake from nurse, and could be heard breaking from time to time into such sentences as, "Do have a little more tweacle pudding, Mrs. Smith. It's the best tweacle," and, "It's a nice day, isn't it?" but he was sorely interrupted by the noisy festivities of the Indians, who broke frequently into realistic cries of "Oh, Roger, you're pulling my hair!" or "I won't play if you don't look out!"

It may be that these interruptions disturbed the actuality of Bim's festivities, or it may be that the rattling of the rain upon the window panes diverted his attention. Once he broke into a chuckle. "Isn't they banging on the window, Lucy?" he said, but she was, it appeared, too deeply engaged to answer him. He found that, in a moment of abstraction, he had eaten the whole of the sponge cake, so that it was obvious that the party was over. "Goodbye, Mrs. Smith. It was really nice of you to come. Goodbye, dear Mrs.—— I think the wain almost isn't coming now."

He said farewell to them all and climbed upon the window seat. Here, gazing down into the Square, he saw that the rain was stopping, and, on the farther side, above the roofs of the houses, a little splash of gold had crept into the grey. He watched the gold, heard the rain coming more slowly; at first "spatter-spatter-spatter," then "spatter—spatter." Then one drop very slowly after another drop. Then he saw that the sun from somewhere far away had found out the wet paths in the garden, and was now stealing, very secretly, along them. Soon it would strike the seat, and then the statue of the funny fat man in all his clothes, and then, perhaps, the fountain.

He was unhappy a little, and he did not know why: he was conscious, perhaps, of the untidy, noisy room behind him, of his sister Dorothy who, now a squaw of a quite genuine and realistic kind, was crying at the top of her voice: "I don't care. I will have it if I want to.

You're *not* to, Roger," and of Timothy, his baby brother, who, moved by his sister's cries, howled monotonously, persistently, hopelessly.

"Oh, give over, do, Miss Dorothy!" said the nurse, raising her eye for a moment from her book. "Why can't you be quiet?"

Outside the world was beginning to shine and glitter, inside it was all horrid and noisy. He sighed a little, he wanted to express in some way his feelings. He looked at Lucy and drew closer to her. She had beside her a painted china mug which one of her uncles had brought her from Russia; she had stolen some daffodils from her mother's room downstairs and now was arranging them. This painted mug was one of her most valued possessions, and Bim himself thought it, with its strange red and brown figures running round it, the finest thing in all the world.

"Lucy," he said. "Do you s'pose if you was going to jump all the way down to the street and wasn't afraid that p'r'aps your legs wouldn't get broken?"

He was not, in reality, greatly interested in the answer to his question, but the important thing always with Lucy was first to enchain her attention. He had learnt, long ago, that to tell her that he loved her, to invite tenderness from her in return, was to ask for certain rebuff—he always began his advances, then, in this roundabout manner.

"*What do* you think, Lucy?"

"Oh, I don't know. How can I tell? Don't bother."

It was then that Bim felt what was, for him, a very rare sensation. He was irritated.

"I don't bovver," he said, with a cross look in the direction of his brother and sister Rochesters. "No, but, Lucy, s'pose someone nurse, s'pose—*did* fall down into the street and broke all her legs and arms, she wouldn't be dead, would she?"

"You silly little boy, of course not."

He looked at Lucy, saw the frown upon her forehead, and felt suddenly that all his devotion to her was wasted, that she didn't want him that nobody wanted him—now when the sun was making the garden glitter like a jewel and the fountain to shine like a sword.

He felt in his throat a hard, choking lump. He came closer to his sister.

"You might pay 'tention, Lucy," he said plaintively.

Lucy broke a daffodil stalk viciously. "Go and talk to the others," she said, "I haven't time for you."

The tears were hot in his eyes and anger was in his heart—anger

173

bred of the rain, of the noise, of the confusion.

"You *are* howwid," he said slowly.

"Well, go away, then, if I'm horrid," she pushed with her hand at his knee. "I didn't ask you to come here."

Her touch infuriated him; he kicked and caught a tender part of her calf.

"Oh! You little beast!" She came to him, leant for a moment across him, then slapped his cheek.

The pain, the indignity, and, above all, a strange confused love for his sister that was near to passionate rage, let loose all the devils that owned Bim for their habitation.

He did three things: he screamed aloud, he bent forward and bit Lucy's hand hard, he seized Lucy's wonderful Russian mug and dashed it to the ground. He then stood staring at the shattered fragments.

3

There followed, of course, confusion. Nurse started up. *The Shadow of Ashlydyat* descended into the ashes, the children rushed eagerly from beneath the table to the centre of hostilities.

But there were no hostilities. Lucy and Bim were, both of them, utterly astonished, Lucy, as she looked at the scattered mug, was, indeed, sobbing, but absent-mindedly—her thoughts were elsewhere. Her thoughts, in fact, were with Bim. She realised suddenly that never before had he lost his temper with her; she was aware that his affection had been all this time of value to her, of much more value, indeed, than the stupid old mug. She bent down—still absent-mindedly sobbing—and began to pick up the pieces. She was really astonished—being a dry and rather hard little girl—at her affection for Bim.

The nurse seized on the unresisting villain of the piece and shook him. "You naughty little boy! To go and break your sister's beautiful mug. It's your horrid temper that'll be the ruin of you, mark my words, as I'm always telling you." (Bim had never been known to lose his temper before.) "Yes, it will. You see, you naughty boy. And all the other children as good as gold and quiet as lambs, and you've got to go and do this. You shall stand in the corner all tea-time, and not a bite shall you have."

Here Bim began, in a breathless, frightened way, to sob. "Yes, well you may. Never mind. Miss Lucy, I dare say your uncle will bring you another." Here she became conscious of an attentive and deeply interested audience. "Now, children, time to get ready for tea. Run along,

Miss Dorothy, now. What a nuisance you all are, to be sure."

They were removed from the scene. Bim was placed in the corner with his face to the wall. He was aghast; no words can give, at all, any idea of how dumbly aghast he was. What possessed him? What, in an instant of time, had leapt down from the clouds, had sprung up from the Square and seized him? Between his amazed thoughts came little surprised sobs. But he had not abandoned himself to grief—he was too sternly set upon the problem of reparation. Something must be done, and that quickly.

The great thought in his mind was that he must replace the mug. He had not been very often in the streets beyond the Square, but upon certain occasions he had seen their glories, and he knew that there had been shops and shops and shops. Quite close to him, upon a shelf, was his money-box, a squat, ugly affair of red tin, into whose large mouth he had been compelled to force those gifts that kind relations had bestowed. There must be now quite a fortune there—enough to buy many mugs. He could not himself open it, but he did not doubt that the man in the shop would do that for him.

For not many more moments would he be left alone. His hat was lying on the table; he seized that and his money-box and was out on the landing.

The rest is *his* story. I cannot, as I have already said, vouch for the truth of it. At first, fortune was on his side. There seemed to be no one about the house. He went down the wide staircase without making any sound; in the hall he stopped for a moment because he heard voices, but no one came. Then with both hands, and standing on tiptoe, he turned the lock of the door, and was outside.

The Square was bathed in golden sun, a sun, the stronger for his concealment, but tempered, too, with the fine gleam that the rain had left. Never before had Bim been outside that door alone. The sky was a washed and delicate purple, and behold! on the high railings, a row of sparrows were chattering. Voices were cold and clear, echoing, as it seemed, against the straight, grey walls of the houses, and all the trees in the garden glistened with their wet leaves shining with gold; there seemed to be, too, a dim veil of smoke that was homely and comfortable.

It is not usual to see a small boy of four alone in a London square, but Bim met, at first, no one except a messenger boy, who stopped and looked after him. At the corner of the Square—just out of the Square so that it might not shame its grandeur—was a fruit and flower shop, and this shop was the entrance to a street that had much life and bustle about it. Here Bim paused with his money-box clasped very tightly to him. Then he made a step or two and was instantly engulfed, it seemed, in a perfect whirl of men and women, of carts and bicycles, of voices and cries and screams; there were lights of every colour, and especially one far above his head that came and disappeared and came again with terrifying wizardry.

He was, quite suddenly, and as it were by the agency of some out-side person, desperately frightened. It was a new terror, different from anything that he had known before. It was as though a huge giant had suddenly lifted him up by the seat of his breeches, or a witch had transplanted him on to her broomstick and carried him off. It was as unusual as that.

His under lip began to quiver, and he knew that presently he would be crying. Then, as he always did when something unusual oc-curred to him, he thought of "Mr. Jack." At this point, when you ask him what happened, always says: "Oh! He came, you know—came walking along—like He always did."

"Was he just like other people, Bim?"

"Yes, just—just like He always was."

"Yes, but what sort of things did he wear?"

"Oh, just ord'nary things like you."

There was no sense of excitement or wonder to be got out of him. It was true that "Mr. Jack" hadn't shown Himself for quite a long time, but that, Bim felt, was natural enough.

"He'll come less and seldomer and seldomer as you get big, you know. It was just at first, when one was very little and didn't know one's way about—just to help babies not to be frightened. Timothy would tell you, only he won't. Then He comes only a little—just at special times like this was."

Bim told you this with a slightly bored air, as though it were silly of you not to know, and really his air of certainty made an incredulous challenge a difficult thing. On the present occasion "Mr. Jack" was just there, in the middle of the crowd, smiling and friendly. He took Bim's hand, and, "Of course," Bim said, there didn't have to be any 'splaining. *He* knew what I wanted."

True or not, I like to think of them, in the evening air, serenely safe and comfortable, and in any case, it was surely strange that if, as one's common sense compels one to suppose, Bim were all alone in that crowd, no one wondered or stopped him or asked him where his home was. At any rate, I have no opinions on the subject. Bim says that, at once, they found themselves out of the crowd in a quiet, little "dinky" street, as he called it, a street that, in his description of it, answered to nothing that I can remember in this part of the world. His account of it seems to present a dark, rather narrow place, with overhanging roofs and swinging signs, and nobody, he says, at all about, but a church with a bell, and outside one shop a row of bright-coloured clothes hanging.

At any rate, here Bim found the place that he wanted. There was a little shop with steps down into it and a tinkling bell which made a tremendous noise when you pushed the old oak door. Inside there was every sort of thing. Bim lost himself here in the ecstasy of his description, lacking also names for many of the things that he saw. But there was a whole suit of shining armour, and there were jewels, and old brass trays, and carpets, and a crocodile, which Bim called a "crodocile." There was also a friendly old man with a white beard, and over everything a lovely smell, which Bim said was like "roast potatoes" and "the stuff Mother has in a bottle in her bedwoom."

Bim could, of course, have stayed there forever, but "Mr. Jack" reminded him of a possibly anxious family. "There, is that what you re after?" he said, and, sure enough, there on a shelf, smiling and eager to be bought, was a mug exactly like the one that Bim had broken.

There was then the business of paying for it, the money-box was produced and opened by the old man with "a shining knife," and Bim was gravely informed that the money found in the box was exactly the right amount. Bim had been, for a moment, in an agony of agitation lest he should have too little, but as he told us, "There was all Uncle Alfred's Christmas money, and what Mother gave me for the tooth, and that silly lady with the green dress who *would* kiss me."

Then they went, Bim clasping his moneybox in one hand and the mug in the other. The mug was wrapped in beautiful blue paper that smelt, as we were all afterwards to testify, of dates and spices. The crocodile flapped against the wall, the bell tinkled, and the shop was left behind them. "Most at once," Bim said they were by the fruit shop again; he knew that "Mr. Jack" was going, and he had a sudden most urgent longing to go with Him, to stay with Him, to be with Him always. He wanted to cry; he felt dreadfully unhappy, but all of his thanks, his strange desires, that he could bring out was, in a quavering voice, trying hard, you understand, not to cry, "Mr. Jack. Oh! Mr. —" and his friend was gone.

177

4

He trotted home; with every step his pride increased. What would Lucy say? And dim, unrealized, but forming, nevertheless, the basis for the whole of his triumph, was his consciousness that she who had scoffed, derided, at his "Mr. Jack," should now so absolutely benefit by Him. This was bringing together, at last, the two of them.

His nurse, in a fine frenzy of agitation, met him. Her relief at his safety swallowed her anger. She could only gasp at him: "Well, Master Bim, and a nice state Oh, dear! to think; wherever—"

On the doorstep he forced his nurse to pause, and, turning, looked at the garden now in shadow of spun gold, with the fountain blue as the sky. He nodded his head with satisfaction. It had been a splendid time. It would be a very long while, he knew, before he was allowed out again like that. Yes. He clasped the mug tightly, and the door closed behind them.

I don't know that there is anything more to say. There were the empty money-box and the mug. There was Bim's unhesitating and unchangeable story. There *is* a shop, just behind the Square, where they have some Russian crockery. But Bim alone?

I don't know.

The Fear of Death

I will acknowledge that I was disgusted when I heard that William Rollin was in the hotel. That seemed to me, at the moment, the very worst piece of bad luck. I had come to Sark to escape from everyone, to have a real holiday, and here in this same small hotel, on this same small island, was one of the human beings whom I deeply, with all my soul, disliked. One dislikes, I fancy, very few people with one's soul. Only once or twice in a lifetime does one encounter a man who affects one so strongly on a very slight acquaintance.

I had met Rollin once or twice, in London, and a good many years ago. He was a man of very considerable reputation, and all of that reputation bad. The human race, I have found, is almost universally fond of gossip and at the same time charitable. When one or two are gathered together they will tear anyone you please to shreds, but in all kindness of heart, simply because they want to pass a pleasant hour and be thought, by their fellows, amusing, interesting and broadminded. Once and again, however, someone appears whom society agrees to consider dangerous and beyond the pale. This dislike (which is also fear) does not come, especially in these days, from any horror at act or even crime. I have known men and women whose lives were publicly notorious, but there has been about them some quality of kindness or stupidity that has, on the whole, exonerated them.

Rollin's moral reputation was bad, but no moral reputation worries anyone any more, unless it is emphasised by the newspapers. No, it was the man himself, an atmosphere that accompanied him, that people could not endure. He had, of course, his own cronies, and the man was so intelligent that he was often excellent company, but he was an animal whose brilliance was dangerous. He was, for no very clear reason, an enemy to society, always involved in squabbles, disputes . . . . . . and yet there was also something pathetic about him. He was of the

179

jungle, but always alone there—and he knew it.

There was no reason, except his intelligence, for his position of importance (for he had undoubtedly a *kind* of importance). He was ugly, a bounder, a sycophant, a snob, a bully. His financial affairs were always on the edge of desperation. He had for many years been in and out of the hands of moneylenders; he had debts everywhere, and it was one of his specially charming characteristics that he never either attempted to repay, nor did he forgive anyone who was fool enough to lend him money.

Nevertheless, his intelligence was remarkable. Had his character and personality not betrayed him, he could have done anything. He was many-sided, cared about games and played them well, was an excellent linguist, read voluminously, had an interest in everything except, oddly, horses. He used to say that he had never been to a race-meeting in his life. I say 'oddly' because to look at him you would think that he had spent his life in and around stables.

His supreme passion was for pictures. Had he had money he would have been one of the finest collectors of our time; having less than none he yet managed to pick up, for almost nothing, some lovely things. He possessed a beautiful little Canaletto, a lovely Renoir still-life, a Matisse that he had bought for nothing at all in his younger days in Paris, and an Italian Primitive which in its freshness of colour and sincerity of feeling was one of the most enchanting things I have ever seen. His knowledge of and taste for pictures was extremely catholic, his judgment superb, and when he talked of them a different soul seemed to peep out from his mean little eyes. . . . .

His one genius, however, did not cover the unpleasantness of the rest of him, and it may be imagined with what disgust I saw him, when on the day after arrival I went into breakfast, seated at a table near me with a woman who was, I knew, his second wife. There was no avoiding him. I stood at his table for a moment and he introduced me to his wife. He always met one like an animal on the defensive, as though he expected an attack. An uglier man I have seldom encountered. He was short, thick-set, and wore, generally, clothes of a light colour, rather 'horsy.' He was almost bald, had small, suspicious eyes and a cruel and greedy mouth, but it was his complexion which was his real trouble.

He drank a good deal, I imagine, but he had not exactly the colour of a drunkard. He was like a piece of undercooked beef, white and red and streaky. His hand was flabby to the touch, and he always withdrew it quickly as though he were afraid that you would hold it firmly and lead him off to gaol. I know that I seem here to be describing a real Surrey-side villain. But Rollin was not a villain. He was simply a bad, nasty man, one bad man in a million kindly, weak and well-intentioned ones. Bad men are extremely rare. I have known, in fact, only two others beside Rollin.

The really curious thing was that before two days were passed I felt so strongly the pathos of the man that I almost liked him. I have always been greatly touched by men victims to the two powers of Fear and Jealousy. I have known them so well in my own nature and the misery and loneliness that these possessive demons inflict on their victims; indeed, with regard to the second of them there is no profession so harried and riven by it as that of Letters. . . . .

I very soon discovered that these two held Rollin in thrall. His jealousy was of a peculiar kind. Once he was assured that my attitude to him was friendly, words poured from him, all in that sharp, ugly assertive voice of his. Assertive he was, but never with convincing authority except in the matter of pictures. There he allowed no personal fears or jealousies to influence him, and had his worst enemy (and, by Jupiter, he had a few!) painted a good picture, he would have said that it was a good picture.

But with regard to every other occupation possible to mankind, jealousy raged in him. It did not matter in the least—politics, the Arts, the Services, religion, Society, whosoever it might be, anyone of prominence was damned, accused of dreadful offences against Society and the State, dismissed to perdition. 'Mind you, Westcott,' he said with that faint touch of Midland accent that he so greatly disliked in himself, 'I'm not jealous. Last thing I am is jealous. Nobody could call me that. Only it makes me sick to see men like Webster getting away with it. Why, do you know. . . . .'

By the second day I was both sorry for him and tired of him, so I tried to break away.

'Look here, Rollin,' I said. 'People aren't as bad as you say. We all have our little weaknesses, you know. We all live in glass houses. Why throw stones?'

Then I saw fear in his eyes, the fear that after this conversation never again, I think, left him.

'What do you mean, Westcott? I hate this hinting. . . . .'

'I don't mean anything except that we *are* all in the same boat, and abusing one another seems a futile business. I came up to London about nineteen-hundred. I'm getting on for sixty. I've been writing and publishing novels for more than thirty years. During that time I've been abused times without number, and very often with reason, but in all that time I've experienced only one piece of real dirty meanness.'

'Oh, well. . . . .' He looked at me with patronage. He would have liked to say something rude: I could hear him back in London: 'Oh yes, we went to Sark for our holiday. Peter Westcott, the novelist, was there, all geniality and speaking well of his fellows. Finds it pays. . . . .'

But he was afraid. He broke abruptly into another topic:

'Well, that's as may be. But, look here! Have you ever thought about death?'

'Death?' I asked lazily. We were lying on Dixcart beach, stretched out full-length watching the blue-green breakers, shining in the sunlight, break into foam on the pebbles. 'Of course, I have. Everyone has.'

'Doesn't it seem awful to you that one's got to die? The inevitability of it——'

'No, I can't say that it does. If I'm depressed it seems a dreary business like everything else. But in general, no. In the war death became so ordinary, part of the day's work. . . . .'

'Oh yes, I know.' His hand touched my arm. 'But if one only knew the way it was going to be. God, to die in one's bed like Armstrong the other day! What luck! Not to realise that it's coming! It's that moment of realisation that's so awful to me, Westcott. The moment when you say to yourself: "My God! I'm going to die! It's coming! It's nearly here!"'

His hand shook on my arm.

'Life's merciful,' I answered. 'Most sick people pass into some kind of coma long before they die. And, anyway, haven't you often had nightmares when you have that moment of realisation? You must have died in your dreams a thousand times over. Actual death is no worse than that.'

'I should think I have,' he said, shuddering. 'There's a dream I have——'

Just then his wife joined us.

She was a small, compact, pretty woman with unusually light-blue eyes. I had seen little of her as yet, but she struck me as one of the quietest women I had ever encountered. It was not only that she said very little, but her whole personality struck me as a waiting, listening, determining one. I had heard in London that Rollin behaved to her abominably, that she had once run away from him, but had returned and had told a friend that she had come back because she had to. She couldn't help herself. But now, as she came towards us, neat, square-shouldered, walking with quiet resolution as though she knew precisely what she intended to do and that nothing would stop her, I couldn't exactly see her committing any act 'because she couldn't help herself.' She was as controlled, as superior to fears, superstitions, gusts of temper and violence as he was inferior.

He did not want her just then, and showed it. I disliked his manner to her so much that soon I got up and left him. I might be sorry for him, but indeed and indeed he was a nasty specimen!

The little hotel where we were was a very primitive and simple place. You had to fuss for a day if you wanted a hot bath, the sanitation was more than primitive, and there was no electric light. All the same, I liked it. The proprietor, the servants, were kind and obliging. Everyone was friendly. But Rollin, of course, had soon a thousand complaints. The food, he said, was scanty and monotonous, the lack of water a disgrace, the beds hard, and so on. He complained to everyone, and everyone disliked him as much as they liked his wife. This, I should imagine, was a common experience wherever they went, and it did not make him love his wife any the better.

Sark is the ideal island for anyone who wants absolute seclusion: indeed, in these harried and public days I should think there is no island in the world quite so secluded. The South Seas are, I understand, as crowded as Piccadilly! It is not an easy island to escape from. If you wish to pay a visit to Jersey you must go for a night at least, and even the trip to Guernsey must be taken in so small a boat that the mildest of rough seas can be alarming. Moreover, the island itself likes to make you feel that it is difficult. There are few beaches and the paths to them are precipitous and unruly. The island is so small that you are always finding yourself unexpectedly at the end of it. It has no middle, so to speak—only ends!

This difficulty and apartness can be either enchanting or exasperating. The place has undoubtedly a magic; in the spring and summer it is covered with flowers, threaded with leafy lanes, and the rocky coast is superb. The air, on the warm days, seems scented with honey, and on the wild ones, is splendidly vigorous. There is still the mantle of old history hanging over it, and the old Norman dialect is stronger and more vigorous among the people than English. No motor vehicles are allowed there. There are more dogs and cats, happily domesticated, than in any place that I know. All these things give it uniqueness, and when you have been there for a day or two, you will, if you have any imagination, begin to fancy things. I am not here speaking of the supernatural, although I believe that dead pirates are as ordinary as blackberries, and smugglers, a hundred years in their graves, common company along the lanes of an evening. But that is the kind of imagination stirred by a hundred places. Where Sark is unique is that, being shut in, imprisoned if you like, you very quickly begin to have odd fancies about your fellow-captives.

I should, in any event, have been greatly interested in Rollin and his wife. Bad men, as I have already said, are rare birds, and are food for the novelist when he encounters one. Rollin, for instance—I could speculate about him endlessly. Were his cruelties, greedinesses, fears, private nastinesses the result simply of the lack of a gland or the pressure of bone on the brain? Could a little simple operation transform him into an angel? If so, why did he not have one? Was any of it his own fault? Could he help himself or did he, indeed, want to help himself? I decided very soon that he did not. He thought himself, I very soon saw, an excellent fellow: amusing, good company, vastly more brilliant than most men, broad-minded and enterprising. He had, of course, been unjustly treated, he carried a thousand grudges about with him, and his criticism of everyone was continual. But one thing he could not deny—his fear. Many men had the advantage of him there. He could not understand their serenity, and hated them for it.

Very quickly, however, Mrs. Rollin became to me more interesting than her husband. I would not say that she liked me. She appeared to have learnt, through stress of circumstances, to guard herself against any conceivable emotion. Her restraint was almost terrifying—the restraint and watchfulness of someone on a tight-rope to whom one false step meant death. Not that she was afraid of death. She was afraid, I am convinced, of nothing, having been through all the worst experiences that life has to offer. This restraint of hers soon became to me obsessing, but the odd fact was that she was the one thing in the world of which Rollin appeared to have no fear at all. He was proud of her in a kind of contemptuous fashion—proud of her looks, her composure (out of which no taunts of his ever seemed to drive her), her *savoir-faire*. But while he was proud of her she exasperated him. She had beaten him in their relationship. She despised him from the bottom of her heart.

Why, feeling about him as she did, she had not long ago left him was one thing that puzzled me. One day, when we were alone, we had a queer little conversation.

'You don't like my husband very much, do you, Mr. Westcott?' she asked me. We were sitting on a spur of Little Sark just above the *Coupée*, and the sea heaved below us, a moving floor of green and purple silk.

'No,' I said, 'I don't.'

'He's not really very likeable,' she went on calmly. 'I know him very well, and the only decent emotion anyone could ever have for him is a kind of pity. He's a very lonely man.'

'Yes,' I said, 'I suppose he is.'

'And I've lost even that emotion about him now. I've had some bad times with him, you know.' She looked at me very quietly out of her pale-blue eyes. 'It isn't decent to talk about one's husband to a stranger—not that you are altogether a stranger. I don't talk about him, you know. . . . .'

'As you're frank, I'll be frank too,' I said. 'I wonder that you haven't left him years ago.'

'Do you? I did once. But I came back. I was still in love with him, I think. For a long time, he had a physical fascination for me. Now I hate him to touch me—or should if I hated anything. . . . .All the same, I think I've had about enough of it at last—at last!' she repeated, looking out to sea.

'I'm years older than you are, Mrs. Rollin,' I said after a long pause. 'It isn't very wise of me to give advice—always a silly thing to do. But leave him. You are young, strong, attractive—if you won't think me impertinent. You have plenty of time to make a new life and a fine one.'

'Yes, I think you're right,' she said, getting up and brushing the grass off her dress.

And it was then, at that moment, that I had for a moment a sense of apprehension. Had Rollin been with us I could almost have called: 'Look out!'

Mrs. Rollin was *very* calm and resolute!

★★★★★★

The next thing that occurred was that Rollin developed an almost passionate liking for me. He was a neurotic, and, like all neurotics, saw himself as the centre of a shaking, quivering world and its only nerve-centre himself! This perpetual apprehension meant that he must have perpetual reassurance, whether he found it in whisky, women, or in a character or two safer than himself. It was his sense of my safeness, I think, that made him cling to me.

'Poor old Westcott,' I could hear him saying to himself. 'He's one of those commonplace fellows too ordinary for fate to bother to attack.'

I was like a tree under whose branches he might shelter until the storm was over, but a tree forgotten the moment that the sun was out again. He had also something extremely feminine in his personality. That was one reason why he was not at all to be trusted. Men with feminine souls are often kind, generous, self-sacrificing and even noble—but trustworthy, never!

I cannot say how greatly I disliked this sudden affection of Rollin's. Like Mrs. Rollin, I hated him to touch me, and he began to develop a habit of laying his hand on my arm and pressing into the flesh. At the first excuse I would move, and at the first move I would see that startled look of suspicion flash into his eye.

It was the Misses Mailley who advanced all unwittingly our relationship a little further. The Misses Mailley were bright, bony and athletic. They swam, they played tennis, wore the minimum of clothing, talked incessantly and laughed a great deal. They were frightened of Rollin, and so, when he was there, they talked and laughed the more.

One morning, after breakfast, we were all of us—the Rollins, the Mailleys and myself—sitting on the veranda looking down the grassy slope towards a magnificent copper beech, under which an old white horse was whisking his ear at the flies and watching out of one eye for a possible lump of sugar.

'The Silver Mines,' said one of the Miss Mailleys. 'That's the place!'

'The place for what?' asked Mrs. Rollin.

'Oh, for an easy murder! Gladys has been reading some silly book in which a man was murdered and buried in a haystack—a ridiculous place! But the Silver Mines—they're grand! No one would ever discover it.'

Rollin's hand touched my shoulder.

'The Silver Mines?' he asked.

'Yes. They're down towards the sea—near Venus' Bath. You ought to go and see them. They haven't been worked, of course, for ages, but there they are, quite unprotected, not a fence or anything! All you have to do is to take your beloved for a walk, push him down, and then, next morning, say he's left by the early boat. No one would know.'

'No. But you'd be haunted,' said the younger Miss Mailley. 'It wouldn't be worth it.'

'It might be,' said Mrs. Rollin. 'No ghost is so bad as some living people. One could deal with a ghost.'

That evening Rollin said to me:

'Stroll out to the Point, Westcott? It's a lovely evening.'

I did not want to go, but I went. We walked across the field, down the little path, climbed the hill and looked down at the sea.

'Awful girls those Mailleys,' he said. 'I can't stand them.'

'They're all right.'

'Oh, you like everyone! It's a type I hate, all cheerful and bony. Do them good to be pushed down that mine they were joking about.' He pressed his hand into my arm. 'Why have you never married, West-cott?'

'I'm a widower,' I said shortly. I had no desire to discuss my private affairs with Rollin.

'Oh, sorry. I didn't know.'

'That's all right. I was very happy.'

'Oh, marriage is all right.' He stood closer to me as though for protection. 'I've been married twice, you know. Grace'—his present lady—'has learnt my ways by this time. She took a bit of teaching, though. She's devoted to me, and to tell you the truth, Westcott, it makes a man feel safe to have someone he can trust around. I can depend on her absolutely.'

'Yes,' I said.

He came still closer, pressing his body up against mine.

'I haven't been well lately. Get all sorts of ideas in my head. Afraid of my own shadow. Upon my soul, I believe my wife's the one person in the world I'm *not* afraid of! It's nerves, of course. I'm highly-strung and not so young as I was. I don't sleep very well, and I'm a bit of a crank about my health. After all, you catch a cold and before you know where you are it's pneumonia and in a day or two you're gone.' He shivered. 'It's getting cold. Let's turn back.'

Before we reached the hotel, he said:

'Thanks for the walk. I think I shall sleep now.'

Next day we went, the three of us, to the pool in the rocks known as Venus' Bath, and had our tea there. Mrs. Rollin and I bathed off the rocks. She was a magnificent swimmer, the day was a glorious one, and just as we reached the rocks Mrs. Rollin said to me:

'I'm glad you were staying here, Mr. Westcott. It's made a difference.'

'Thanks,' I said. 'I'm glad too.'

'Oh, are you? You can't be. We're not an attractive pair.'

On the way back, we passed the Silver Mines. There was a ruined tower about whose base flowers—crimson, yellow and blue—clustered. There was the black mouth of a shaft.

'I wonder how deep that is,' Mrs. Rollin said.

'Deep as hell,' Rollin answered.

There comes for me now, as I approach the crisis of my relationship with these two, the difficulty of truth—truth in my story. I mean the truth of facts, as well as the truth of imagination. How soon in this affair did I begin myself to feel an apprehension that, after a time, began to obsess me, so that I was constantly aware of it, constantly shadowed by a sense of my own responsibility? Looking back now, I ask myself what I ought to have done: for it is one of my humiliations to remember that from beginning to end I did exactly nothing. *Could I have done anything?*

Should I have tried to persuade Rollin to leave the island by the next morning's boat? Should I have frankly asked Mrs. Rollin certain questions? But, indeed, how could I ask her anything unless she gave me her confidence? That, she never gave me. Or did she? And did she invite me to take a step, or to force her to take a step, that would have saved both herself and him? Would it have been better if such a step had been taken? I don't know. I shall never know. I give you the facts as honestly as I can remember them.

A day or two after our visit to Venus' Bath the weather broke and rain swept the island. Standing, one afternoon, in my room wondering whether I should read, write, play bridge with the Mailley girls, or sleep till dinner, I heard my door open and, looking up, saw Mrs. Rollin standing there. She was as composed, as quiet, as assured as she ever was. She came in, closing the door behind her.

'I'm not going to stop,' she said. 'If I did the scandal would be, I suppose, terrific. But the trouble of this place is that you can't be alone. I want to ask your advice, Mr. Westcott.'

She sat down in a chair near the bed.

'Tell me——' She looked up at me, smiling. 'How far is anyone justified in breaking a natural law?'

'What do you mean by a natural law?' I asked her.

'Well. . . . .after thousands of years of living together men have decided that certain laws must be obeyed if society is to keep sane. On the whole the decisions they've come to have been wise ones. But once and again it is better that a law should be broken rather than kept.'

'Yes,' I said, feeling stupid under her quiet gaze.

'Perhaps I am myself insane,' she went on. 'I don't think so—but oneself one can never tell. I feel it right to take action in a certain direction—action that you, everyone, would absolutely condemn. I want, in fact, to take the law in my own hands. Is one ever justified in doing that?'

'Yes,' I answered. 'If you are ready to face the consequences.'

'For myself you mean?'

'Yes.'

'Oh, the consequences for myself—they're nothing. I don't care in the least what happens to *me*. I died long ago. But my ghost—or the ghost of my ghost—has a fragment of hesitation. An odd remnant of religious superstition, I suppose. I don't mind breaking men's laws, you know, but is there another law, something deeper, more permanent?'

I thought then, looking at her, that she *was* insane. Her composure, the thin shadow that lurked in her pale-blue eyes, something marked her for me as a woman who had ceased to reason, because she had been driven beyond the bounds of reasoning.

She got up as abruptly as she entered.

'I wanted to ask you,' she said. 'Do you believe in God?'

'Yes,' I answered. 'I believe in a spiritual world.'

'So, do I.' She nodded her head as though pursuing her own thoughts. 'But not in eternal punishment, you know. That's altogether too crude. Never mind—I'll take what comes.' And she went out.

★★★★★★

I have said already that Sark is dangerous for the imaginative. One sees so much more than is really there. Every rock in Sark has a double meaning, and even the flowers know too well what they are about. The weather was bad and we were shut in upon ourselves. Rollin would not leave me alone. He cursed everything, the island, the hotel, the visitors, the natives and, behind my back, I do not doubt, myself.

'Well, why don't you go?' I asked him. 'There are two boats a day.'

'I can't make up my mind,' he said. He looked ill. He said that he wasn't sleeping. 'I keep seeing things in this beastly place. It's as though someone was always following one.' He broke down all his reticences. He told me that he hated his wife, but that she was the only person in the world he could trust. 'When I'm with her I'm safe,' he said. 'She's like a wall at my back.'

I think it was true that he hated her, and he became quite intolerable in her company. He bullied her, snapped at her, ordered her about like a servant, was insufferably rude to her. Once, when he had been especially intolerable, I left him. He came after me to my room.

'What did you go for?' he asked. 'You said you were coming for a walk.'

So, given the opportunity, I told him what I thought of him.

But he scarcely listened. 'Oh, you don't know,' he said. 'You've no idea how aggravating she can be. This weather gets on my nerves. I've got an idea I'm never going to leave this damned island. I shall die here, rot to pieces all amongst the ferns and stones.'

That same night I woke with a sudden start to be aware that someone was in the room. I struck a match, lit a candle (there was no electric light in the hotel), and woke up to find Rollin standing by my bed in his pyjamas, shaking from crown to heel. He sat down on the edge of the bed and caught my arm.

'What's up?' I asked.

'Let me stay here five minutes. I've had a fright.'

How I hated his pressure on my arm, his whole physical self with his pyjama-jacket open, his mottled complexion, the very colour of his red bedroom-slippers! And yet, even as I hated him, I was sorry for him. How could I be otherwise? He was a haunted man. He told me an incoherent story. He couldn't sleep, then he dropped into deep slumber and dreamt—a horrible dream in which he was lying at the bottom of a deep, black pit in a pool of sluggish water. Scaly fishes swam across his eyeballs. His body was broken and his arms waggled in the water.

'You've been eating something,' I said.

'I was dead—I was alive—I suffered. Good God, Westcott, what I suffered! But the worst moment was before I fell. I knew I was going to fall and I cried out to you, Westcott, to save me! I knew I was going to die—then—then—that moment!'

He lay down beside me on the outside of the bed. I said what I could, told him he'd been drinking too much (which he had).

'I know you think I'm a fool,' I said. 'But I'll give you some good advice. Go back to London. Try to take a decent view of things. Don't curse everybody, and behave better to your wife.'

'Oh, it's all very well for you to talk, Westcott. You're one of those damned optimists and well you may be. Everything's always gone well with you.'

'Well, it hasn't,' I answered shortly. 'When I was a boy in Cornwall, there was an old fisherman had a motto—a sloppy, sentimental motto that men like you would laugh yourselves sick over. "*It isn't life that matters, but the courage you bring to it.*" That will be a sort of maiden's prayer to you,' I added, yawning (for I was extremely sleepy), 'but it meets your case all the same. You're a coward, Rollin, frightened of your own shadow.'

He thought the motto very comic, and that did him good.

'You ought to take Sunday-school class, Westcott. Was your father a clergyman?'

'My father,' I answered, 'was the rottenest, most drunken old swine ever a son had. That's why I found that motto useful.'

He was calmer, and at last, thank God, he left me.

But that night was enough for him. He told me, next morning, that they were leaving for London on the following day.

What a morning that was! Shall I ever forget it? The whole island was veiled in a wet, creeping mist. You couldn't see a yard in front of you, and a tree jumped out at you as though it were an American gangster bidding you hold your hands up. I'm not a nervous man—or no more than most—but I woke in a state of fear and consternation. Those are the only words that I can use. I must do something—but what? I couldn't leave Rollin out of my sight. All afternoon I played bridge with him and the Mailley girls.

'What a day for a murder,' one of them said brightly. 'Three hearts. . . . .'

I looked up and saw Mrs. Rollin standing at the window watching the wet mist as it coiled like a snake against the pane. I was dummy, and I got up and went over to her.

'You're leaving tomorrow, I hear,' I said.

'Yes,' she said, turning round and smiling at me.

She stood there, motionless, scarcely breathing, but her eyes stared into mine. It was as though she said: 'Well—what are you going to do about it?'

Then she did an odd thing. She pushed with her bare palms at the window-pane as though she would break it. I was sure then that she was not sane. . . . . .

At about half-past six that evening I came on to the veranda and saw the two Rollins in mackintoshes.

'Hallo!' I cried. 'Where are you two off to?' It was odd, but it was as though I had known that they would be there.

'We are going for a walk,' said Mrs. Rollin.

191

'A walk—in this weather?'

'Yes. It's been so stuffy all day. We want a little exercise, don't we, Will?'

'I'll come too,' I said.

'No. Don't,' she answered. 'You'd hate it.'

Rollin said not a word.

'Where are you going?' I asked.

'Oh, I don't know. Over the *Coupée* to Little Sark. Down by Venus' Bath, perhaps.'

'Don't fall into the Silver Mines,' I said.

She did not answer. We none of us spoke. I shall never forget Rollin. He was like a hypnotised man, like a man in a dream. Her eyes never left his face.

I longed to cry out: 'Rollin, don't go! Don't go!' But it was as though I were hypnotised too. I only stood and stared at them. They moved off into the mist, he following her like a dog.

They were not in their places at dinner. I watched and watched the door to see them enter. At about nine o'clock I thought I heard Rollin's voice calling just outside the window: 'Westcott! Westcott!' I ran out, but the wet mist was so thick that I could see nothing. I ran a little way down the road calling: 'Rollin! Rollin!'

But, of course, there was no answer, only the distant murmur of the sea. I slept brokenly, waking again and again. . . . .

And at breakfast Mrs. Rollin was there, eating very quietly her bacon and eggs.

I went over to her.

'Good morning,' I said. 'I'm afraid you must have got very wet last night.'

'Yes, we did.'

'Where's Rollin?' I asked.

'Oh, he went by the seven-thirty boat. He had some business in Guernsey. I'm following by the ten o'clock.' Then she held out her hand, smiling. 'Goodbye,' she said.

'Goodbye,' I answered.

Young John Scarlett

That fatal September—the September that was to see young John take his adventurous way to his first private school—surely, steadily approached.

Mrs. Scarlett, an emotional and sentimental little woman, vibrating and taut like a telegraph wire, told herself repeatedly that she would make no sign. The preparations proceeded, the date—September 23rd—was constantly evoked, a dreadful ghost, by the careless, light-hearted family. Mrs. Scarlett made no sign.

From the hour of John's birth—nearly ten years ago—Mrs. Scarlett had never known a day when she had not been compelled to control her sentimental affections. From the first John had been an adorable baby, from the first he had followed his father in the rejection of all sentiment as un-English, and if larger questions are involved, unpatriotic, but also from the first he had hinted, in surprising, furtive, agitating moments, at poetry, imagination, hidden, romantic secrets. Tom, May, Clare, the older children, had never been known to hint at anything—hints were not at all in their line, and of imagination they had not, between them, enough to fill a silver thimble; they were good, sturdy, honest children, with healthy stomachs and an excellent determination to do exactly the things that their class and generation were bent upon doing. Mrs. Scarlett was fond of them, of course, and because she was a sentimental woman she was sometimes quite needlessly emotional about them, but John—no, John was of another world.

The other children felt, beyond question, this difference. They deferred to John about everything and regarded him as leader of the family, and in their deference, there was more than simply a recognition of his sturdy independence. Even John's father, Mr. Reginald

193

Scarlett, a K.C., and a man of a most decisive and emphatic bearing, felt John's difference.

John's appearance was engaging rather than handsome—a snub nose, grey eyes, rather large ears, a square, stocky body and short, stout legs. He was certainly the most independent small boy in England, and very obstinate; when any proposal that seemed on the face of it absurd was made to him, he shut up like a box. His mouth would close, his eyes disappear, all light and colour would die from his face, and it was as though he said: "Well, if you are stupid enough to persist in this thing you can compel me, of course—you are physically stronger than I—but you will only get me like this, quite dead and useless, and a lot of good may it do you!"

There were times, of course, when he could be most engagingly pleasant. He was courteous, on occasion, with all the beautiful manners that, we are told, are yielding so sadly before the spread of education and the speed of motor-cars, but you never could foretell the guest that he would prefer, and it was nothing to him that here was an aunt, ah uncle, or a grandfather who must be placated, and there an uninvited, undesired caller who mattered nothing at all. Mr. Scarlett's father he offended mortally by expressing, in front of him, dislike for the hair that grew in bushy profusion out of that old gentleman's ears.

"But you could cut it off," he argued, in a voice thick with surprised disgust. His grandfather, who was a baronet, and very wealthy, predicted a dismal career for his grandchild.

All the family realised quite definitely that nothing could be done with John. It was fortunate, indeed, that he was, on the whole, of a happy and friendly disposition. He liked the world and things that he found in it. He liked games, and food, and adventure—he liked quite tolerably his family—he liked immensely the prospect of going to school.

There were other things—strange, uncertain things—that lay like the dim, uncertain pattern of some tapestry in the back of his mind. He gave *them*, as the months passed, less and less heed. Only sometimes when he was asleep. . . .

Meanwhile, his mother, with the heroism worthy of Boadicea, that great and savage warrior, kept his impulses of devotion, of sacrifice, of adoration, in her heart. John had no need of them; very long ago, Reginald Scarlett, then no K.C., with all the K.C. manner, had told her that *he* did not need them either. She gave her dinner parties, her receptions, her political gatherings—tremulous and smiling she faced

194

a world that thought her a wise, capable little woman, who would see her husband a judge and peer one of these days.

"Mrs. Scarlett—a woman of great social
ambition," was their definition of her.

"Mrs. Scarlett—the mother of John," was her own.

2

On a certain night, early in the month of September, young John dreamt again—but for the first time for many months—the dream that had, in the old days, come to him so often. In those days, perhaps, he had not called it a dream. He had not given it a name, and in the quiet early days he had simply greeted, first a protector, then a friend. But that was all very long ago, when one was a baby and allowed oneself to imagine anything. He had, of course, grown ashamed of such confiding fancies, and as he had become more confident, had shoved away, with stout, determined fingers, those dim memories, poignancies, regrets. How childish one had been at four, and five, and six! How independent and strong now, on the very edge of the world of school! It perturbed him, therefore, that at this moment of crisis this old dream should recur, and it perturbed him the more, as he lay in bed next morning and thought it over, that it should have seemed to him at the time no dream at all, but simply a natural and actual occurrence.

He had been asleep, and then he had been awake. He had seen, sitting on his bed and looking at him with mild, kind eyes, his old Friend. His Friend was always the same, conveying so absolutely kindness and protection, and His hands, the appealing humour of His gaze recalled to John the early years, with a swift, imperative urgency. John, so independent and assured, felt, nevertheless, again that old alarm of a strange, unreal world, and the necessity of an appeal for protection from the only one of them all who understood.

"Hallo!" said John.

"Well? "said his Friend. "It's many months since I've been to see you, isn't it?"

"That's not my fault," said John.

"In a way, it is. You haven't wanted me, have you? Haven't given me a thought?"

"There's been so much to do. I'm going to school, you know."

"Of course. That's why I have come now."

Beside the window a dark curtain blew forward a little, bulged as though someone were behind it, thinned again in the pale dim shadows of a moon that, beyond the window, fought with driving clouds. That curtain would—how many ages ago?—have tightened young John's heart with terror, and the contrast made by his present stout indifference drew him, in some warm, confiding fashion, closer to his visitor.

"Anyway, I'm jolly glad you've come now. I haven't really forgotten you, ever. Only in the daytime"

"Oh, yes, you have," his Friend said, smiling. "It's natural enough and right that you should. But if only you will believe always that I once was here, if only you'll not be persuaded into thinking me impossible, silly, absurd, sentimental—with ever so many other things—that's all I've come now to ask you."

"Why, how should I ever?" John demanded indignantly.

"After all, I *was* a help—for a long time when things were difficult and you had so much to learn—all that time you wanted me, and I was here."

"Of course," said John politely, but feeling within him that warning of approaching sentiment that he had learnt by now so fundamentally to dread.

Very well; his Friend understood his apprehension.

"That's all. I've only come to you now to ask you to make me a promise—a very easy one."

"Yes?" said John.

"It's only that when you go off to school—before you leave this house—you will just, for a moment, remember me, and say goodbye to me. We've been a lot here in these rooms, in these passages, up and down together, and if only, as you go, you'll think of me, I'll be there. . . . Every year you've thought of me less—that doesn't matter—but it matters more than you know that you should remember me just for an instant, just to say goodbye. Will you promise me?"

"Why, of course," said John.

"Don't forget! Don't forget! Don't forget!" And the kindly shadow had faded, the voice lingering about the room, mingling with the faint silver moonlight, passing out into the wider spaciousness of the rolling clouds.

3

With the dear light of morning came the confident certainty that it had all been the merest dream, and yet that certainty did not sweep the affair, as it should have done, from young John's brain and heart.

He was puzzled, perplexed, disturbed, unhappy. The "twenty-third" was approaching with terrible rapidity, and it was essential now that he should summon to aid all his forces of manly self-control and common sense. And yet, just at this time, of all others, came that disturbing dream, and, in its train, absurd memories and fancies, burdened, too, with an urgent prompting of gratitude to someone or something. He shook it off, he obstinately rebelled, but he dreaded the night, and, with a sigh of relief, hailed the morning that followed a dreamless sleep.

Worst of all, he caught himself yielding to thoughts like these: "But He was kind to me—awfully decent" (a phrase caught from his elder brother). "I remember how He . . ." And then he would shake himself. "It was only a silly old dream. He wasn't real a bit. I'm not a rotten kid now that thinks fairies and all that true."

He was bothered, too, by the affectionate sentiment (still disguised, but ever, as the days proceeded, more thinly) of his mother and sisters. The girls, May and Clare, adored young John. His elder brother was away with a school friend. John, therefore, was left to feminine attention, and very tiresome he found it. May and Clare, girls of no imagination, saw only the drama that they might extract for themselves out of the affair. They knew what school was like, especially at first—John was going to be utterly wretched, miserably homesick, bullied, kept in over horrible sums and impossible Latin exercises, ill-fed, and trodden upon at games.

They did not really believe these things—they knew that their brother Tom had always had a most pleasant time, and John was precisely the type of boy who would prosper at school, but they indulged, just for this fortnight, their romantic sentiment, never alluded in speech to school and its terrors, but by their pitying avoidance of the subject filled the atmosphere with their agitation. They were working things for John—May handkerchiefs, and Clare a comforter; their voices were soft and charged with omens, their eyes were bright with the drama of the event, as though they had been supporting some young Christian relation before his encounter with the lions. John hated them more and more and more.

But more terrible to him than his sisters was his mother. He was too young to understand what his departure meant to her, but he knew that there was something real here that needed comforting. He wanted to comfort her, and yet hated the atmosphere of emotion that he felt in himself as well as in her. They ought to know, he argued, that the least little thing would make him break down like an ass and behave as no man should, and yet they were doing everything.... Oh, if only Tom were here! Then, at any rate, there would be brutal common sense. There were special meals for him during this fortnight, and an eager inviting of his opinion as to how the days should be spent. On the last night of all they were to go to the theatre—a real play this time, none of your pantomimes!

There was, moreover, all the business of clothes—fine, rich, stiff new garments—a new Eton jacket, a round black coat, a shining bowler hat, new boots. He watched this stir with a brave assumption that he had been surveying it all his life, but a horrible tight pain in the bottom of his throat told him that he was a bravado, almost a liar.

He found himself, now that the "twenty-third" was gaping right there in front of him, with its fiery throat wide and flaming, doing the strangest things. He was frightened of the dusk, he would run through the passage and up the stairs at breathless speed, he would look for a moment at the lamp-lit Square with the lights of the opposite houses like tigers' eyes, and the trees filmy like smoke, then would hastily draw the curtains and greet the warm inhabited room with a little gasp of reassurance. Strangest of all, he found himself often in the old nursery at the top of the house. Very seldom did anyone come there now, and it had the pathos of a room grown cold and comfortless. Most of the toys were put away or given to hospitals, but the rocking-horse with his Christmas-tree tail was there, and the dolls' house, and a railway with trains and stations.

He was here. He was saying to himself: "Yes, it was just over there, by the window, that He came that time. He talked to me there. That other time it was when I was down by the dolls' house. He showed me the smoke coming up from the chimneys when the sun struck through, and the moon was all red one night, and the stars."

He found himself gazing out over the Square, over the twisted chimneys, that seemed to be laughing at him, over the shining wires and glittering roofs, out to the mist that wrapped the city beyond his vision—so vast, so huge, so many people—March Square was nothing. *He* was nothing—John Scarlett nothing at all.

Then, with a sigh, he turned back. His Friend, the other night, had been real enough. Fairies, ghosts, goblins and dragons—everything was real. Everything. It was all terrible, terrible to think of, but, above and beyond all else, he must not forget, on the day of his departure, that farewell; something disastrous would surely come upon him were he so ungrateful.

And then he would go downstairs again, down to newspapers and fires, toast and tea, the large print of Frith's "Railway Station," and the coloured supplement of Greiffenhagen's "Idyll," and the tattered numbers of the *Windsor* and the *Strand* magazines, and behold, all these things were real and all the things in the nursery unreal. Could it be that both worlds were real? Even now, at his tender years, that old business of connecting the Dream and the Business was at his throat.

"Tea! Tea! Tea!" Frantic screams from May. "There's some new jam, and, John, Mother says she wants you to try on some underclothes afterwards. Those others didn't do, she said. . . ."

There came then the disastrous hour—an hour that John was never, in all his after-life, to forget. On a wild stormy evening he found himself in the nursery. A week remained now—today fortnight he would be in another world, an alarming, fierce, tremendous world. He looked at the rocking-horse with its absurd tail and the patch on its back that had been worn away by its faithful riders, and suddenly he was crying. This was a thing that he never did, that he had strenuously, persistently refrained from doing all these weeks, but now, in the strangest way, it was the conviction that the world into which he was going wouldn't care in the least for the dolls' house, and would mock brutally, derisively at the rocking-horse, that defeated him. It was even the knowledge that, in a very short time, he himself would be mocking.

He sat down on the floor and cried. The door opened; before he could resist or make any movement, his mother's arms were about him, his mother's cheek against his, and she was whispering: "Oh, my darling, my darling!"

The horrible thing then occurred. He was savage, with a wild, fierce, protesting rage. His cheeks flamed. His tears were instantly dried. That he should have been caught thus ! That, when he had been presenting so brave and callous a front to the world, at the one weak and shameful moment he should have been discovered! He scarcely realized that this was his mother; he did not care who it was. It was as though he had been delivered into the most horrible and shameful of traps. He pushed her from him; he struggled fiercely on his feet. He regarded her with fiery eyes.

"It isn't—I wasn't—you oughtn't to have come in. You needn't think—"

He burst from the room. A shameful, horrible experience.

But it cannot be denied that he was ashamed afterwards. He loved his mother, whereas he merely liked the rest of the family. He would not hurt her for worlds, and yet, why *must* she—

And strangely, mysteriously, her attitude was confused in his mind with his dreams, and his Friend, and the red moon, and the comic chimneys.

He knew, however, that during this last week he must be especially nice to his mother, and, with an elaborate courtesy and strained attention, he did his best.

The last night arrived, and, very smart and excited, they went to the theatre. His boxes had been packed and stood in a shining and self-conscious trio in his bedroom. The new play-box was there, with its stolid freshness and the black bands at the corners; inside, there was a multitude of riches, and it was, of course, a symbol of absolute independence and maturity. John was wearing the new Eton jacket, also a new white waistcoat; the parting in his hair was straighter than it had ever been before, his ears were pink. The world seemed a confused mixture of soap and starch and lights. Piccadilly Circus was a cauldron of bubbling colour.

His breath came in little gasps, but his face, with its snub nose and large mouth, was grave and composed; up and down his back little shivers were running. When the car stopped outside the theatre he gave a little gulp. His father, who was, for once, moved by the occasion, said an idiotic thing:

"Excited, my son?"

With his head high, he walked ahead of them, trod on a lady's dress, blushed, heard his father say: "Look where you're going, my boy," heard May giggle, frowned indignantly, and was conscious of the horrid pressure of his collar-stud against his throat; arrived, hot, confused, and very proud, in the dark splendour of the box.

The first play of his life, and how magnificent a play it was! It might have been a rotten affair with endless conversations—luckily there were no discussions at all. All the characters either loved or hated one another too deeply to waste time in talk. They were Roundheads and Cavaliers, and a splendid hero, who had once been a bad fellow, but was now sorry, fought nine Roundheads at once, and was tortured "off" with red lights and his lady waiting for results before a sympathetic audience.

During the torture scene John's heart stopped entirely, his brow was damp, his hand sought his mother's, found it, and held it very hard.

She, as she felt his hot fingers pressing against hers, began to see the stage through a mist of tears. She had behaved very well during the past weeks, but the soul that she adored was, tomorrow morning, to be hurled out, wildly, helter-skelter, to receive such tarnishing as it might please Fate to think good.

"I *can't* let him go! I *can't* let him go!" The curtain came down.

John turned, his eyes wide, his cheeks pale with a pink spot on the middle of each.

"I say, pass those chocolates along!" he whispered hoarsely. Then, recovering himself a little: "I wonder what they did to him? They *must* have done something to his legs, because they were all crooked when he came out."

4

Afterwards, he was lying in bed, watching the firelight, his brain filled with that same fire, so that the dancing colour on the white walls seemed to him a reflection of his brain—as though it were he that were flinging that light.

He was most terribly excited; those bright, expectant boxes facing him urged him to start off now, immediately, to begin to live even before the time for tomorrow's train. His heart was beating like a gong against the bedclothes, and he did not suppose that he could ever sleep again.

Then his mother came in. He had been, dimly, expecting her, yes, and hoping she would not come. She came in a kind of dressing-gown and sat down nervously on the edge of his bed.

"Well, dear, is everything all right?"

"Yes, Mother."

He knew that she wanted to take his hand, and was determined that she should not, holding it very hot and tightly clenched under the bedclothes.

"You'll sleep, dear, won't you, because you've got a hard day in front of you?"

"Oh, I'll sleep all right, Mother."

"Everything's packed all right?"

"Yes, Mother."

"You enjoyed the play, didn't you?"

"Awfully."

A terrible pause, whilst his brain was filled, ever, with more and more fire, and he was torn between the impulse to fling himself into his mother's arms and let everything go, and the impulse to become stiffer and stiffer, to repel her as brutally and effectively as he could.

Her eyes were upon him; she put her hand on his neck and stroked his hair.

"John, dear, you'll be a good boy, won't you? Never do what your father and I wouldn't like. You're going into the world now. There'll be temptations. Remember that you're a gentleman—always—never do anything that you'd be ashamed of. I want you to grow up a fine man to help people. You'll say your prayers, dear, won't you?"

"Yes, Mother."

"I've put that new prayer-book at the top of the play-box where you can easily get it."

"Yes, Mother."

"Goodnight, darling. God bless you."

She put her arms round him. He kissed her and felt that she was crying.

"It'll be great fun. Mother," he said, struggling to say the right thing. "It'll be all right. Mother. Wasn't the play lovely? I don't know how that man can do it every night, do you? I'll write every Sunday, I expect. All the boys do, Tom says."

She kissed him again, and went, very quietly, away.

It was only when she had gone, and he was alone with the firelight and the boxes again, that he had the conviction that someone had been in the room listening. He sat up in bed.

"My word, of course," he thought, "I must remember to say good-bye to Him tomorrow." He called out, very softly: "I say—I say, are you there?"

There was no one there. In a moment he was fast asleep.

The morning came, and with it a tremendous bustle. Reginald Scarlett, K.C., would see his son off at the station; there was a special breakfast. Young John had more money in his pocket than he had ever dreamed that he would possess. Moreover, the day was glittering after a night of rain; a blue haze was over the Square, the fountain in the garden kicked the air with ecstasy, and its falling waters hummed in the heart of the garden trees.

There was awaiting him, he knew, a ghastly shadow of depression; it hovered behind him, but with all the energy of his new-found manliness he withstood it. He laughed, joked, strutted, pretended to eat his breakfast, stood at last in the hall, kissing his sisters, watching out of the corner of his eye his mother, dreading, a little, the quarter of an hour with his father in the car, and beseeching heaven that no more paternal advice would be given him.

He kissed his mother, and, very hot and confused, shook hands with Horrocks, the butler, who choked a little over his farewell. Then he was in the car, his father beside him.

But no, he had not said farewell to Ellen, the cook. He was out again, had rushed down to the kitchen, kissed Ellen, shaken hands with Mary, whose grasp was damp and steamy, was through the hall and in the car once more. He had one final vision of his mother's white face, of Horrocks, and May, and Clare, of the dappled gold and green of the plane-trees, of the final flashing eye of the fountain, and they were away.

During the drive his father said: "I'd like you to be decent at cricket; I'll give you a sovereign for every fifty you make." And that, thank heaven, was all.

He was alone in the train. The lump that had been in his chest was rising now in his throat. Behind each eye was a hot tear.

He was enveloped by the shadow.

It was then that, struggling even now to defeat his enemy, he knew that he had forgotten something. He counted his possessions—his new umbrella, his other coat, his cap—everything was there.

He had forgotten something—or somebody. He struggled with his memory. He ran over in his mind the morning's events. He summoned his friends and relations before him.

He had forgotten somebody. Somebody? Something?

He gave it up. When he remembered the person, him or her, he'd send a postcard from school. He felt the money in his pocket and was a little cheered. He opened a picture paper with the air of a man of the world, but even as he read he knew that "someone or other" had been forgotten. . . .

The Old Ladies

Chapter 1: Mrs. Amorest Pays a Visit

Quite a number of years ago there was an old rickety building on the rock above Seatown in Polchester, and it was one of a number in an old grass-grown square known as Pontippy Square.

In this house at one time or another lived three old ladies, Mrs. Amorest, Miss May Beringer, and Mrs. Agatha Payne. They were really old ladies, because at the time of these events Mrs. Amorest was seventy-one, Miss Beringer seventy-three, and Mrs. Payne seventy. Mrs. Amorest and Mrs. Payne were wonderfully strong women for their age, but Miss Beringer felt her back a good deal.

It was a windy, creaky, rain-bitten dwelling-place for three old ladies. Mrs. Payne lived in it always; although she had fine health her legs were weak and would suddenly desert her. What she hated above anything else in life was that she should be ludicrous to people, and the thought that one day she might tumble down in Polchester High Street, there in front of everybody, determined her seclusion. She was a proud and severe woman was Mrs. Payne.

Mrs. Amorest and Mrs. Payne had lived in these rooms for some time. Miss Beringer was quite a newcomer—so new a comer in fact that the other two ladies had not as yet seen her. The lodgers on that top floor of the house had the same charwoman, Mrs. Bloxam, and she came in at eight in the morning, cooked the three breakfasts, stayed until ten and tidied the rooms. After ten o'clock the three old ladies were alone on their floor of the house, very nearly alone indeed in the whole building, because the second floor had been a store for furniture but was now deserted, and the ground floor was the offices of a strange religious sect known as the "Fortified Christians." The only "Fortified Christian" ever seen was a pale dirty young man with a blue chin who sometimes unlocked a grimy door, sat down at a grimier table, and wrote letters. Mrs. Amorest had once met him in the ground-floor passage, and it had been like meeting a ghost.

Mrs. Amorest herself stayed indoors a good deal, because three pair of stairs were a great number for an old lady, however strong she might be.

She looked an old lady of course with her snow-white hair, her charming wrinkled face, and her neat compact little body. She had also eyes as bright as the sea with the sun on it, and a smile both radiant and confiding. But she was like many other English old ladies, I suppose. I suppose so, because she never attracted the least attention in Polchester when she walked about. Nobody said, "Why, there goes a charming old lady!"

She had never known a day's illness in her life. When she had borne her son, Brand, she had been up and about within a week of his birth. And yet she had none of that aggressive good health that is so customary with physically triumphant people. She never thought about it as indeed she very seldom thought about herself at all.

Another thing that one must tell about Mrs. Amorest is that she was very poor. Very poor indeed, and of course she would not have lived in that draughty uncomfortable room at the top of the old house had it not been so.

She liked comfort and pretty things, and she had been well acquainted with both when her husband had been alive. Her husband, Ambrose Amorest, had been a poet, a poet-dramatist (*Tintagel*, A Drama in Five Acts, Elden Foster, 1880; and *The Slandered Queen*, A Drama in Five Acts, Elden Foster, 1883, were his two best-known plays). For a while things had gone well with them. Amorest had inherited from his father. Then quite suddenly he had died from double pneumonia, and it had been found that he had left nothing at all behind him save manuscripts and debts. A common affair. Every novel dealing with poets tells the same story. Brand, the only child, had at the age of eighteen gone off to seek his fortune in America. For a while things had gone well with him, then silence. It was now three years since Mrs. Amorest had heard from him.

Indeed, the old lady was now very thoroughly alone in the world. Her only relation living was her cousin Francis Bulling, who also lived in Polchester. It was because of him, in the first place, that she had come to Polchester; she thought that it would be like home to be near a relation, the only one she had. But it had not been very much like home. Mrs. Bulling had not liked her; and even after Mrs. Bulling's death, when Cousin Francis had been a grim old man, sixty-eight years of age, tortured with gout and all alone in his grim old house, he had not wanted to see her.

He was rich, but he had never given her a penny; and then, one day, when she came to see him (she never thought of the money but felt it her duty occasionally to do so), he had laughed and asked her what she would do with twenty thousand pounds a year.

She had said that she did not know what she would do, and he had said that he might as well leave it to her as to anyone else. She had tried not to think of this, but money was the one power that forced her sometimes to think of herself. She had so very little, and it was dwindling and dwindling because, kind Mr. Agnew her solicitor explained to her, her investments weren't paying as well as they did. She knew very little about investments. Her view of money in general was that one must never get into debt. She paid for everything as she got it, and if she couldn't afford something there and then, she didn't get it. From quarter to quarter the sum had to stretch itself out, and kind Mr. Neilson at the bank wanted it to stretch, she was sure, as far as it could, but, powerful man though he was, he couldn't work miracles.

Although she thought everyone kind and most people nice she was not a fool. She was not blind to people's faults, but she selected their virtues instead. She felt that she was an old woman with nothing interesting, amusing, or unusual about her, and therefore did feel it very obliging of any one to take an interest in her. It could not truthfully be said that many people did. She had her pride, and she did not like her friends to see her poverty, and so she did not ask them to her room. On the other hand, she did not wish to accept hospitality without returning it.

Then, even though you are very strong, if you are over seventy and a woman, you have only a limited store of energy. Mrs. Amorest was often weary, and sometimes felt that she could not face those stairs!

In her dreams at night the stairs figured, long-toothed, dragon-scaled, fiery to the foot—her demons!

But when she had reached her room, then all was well. In these years she had grown fond of that room. Once, when investments had behaved more nobly and she could ask her friends to visit her, it had been a very gay room indeed. She had always liked pretty things, and had inherited from her earlier, more prosperous married life certain fine pieces of furniture. In the right-hand corner of the room was her bed, and in front of the bed a screen of old rose-coloured silk. There were three old chairs also fashioned in rose colour, a rug of a rich red-brown, a little gate-legged table, and on her wash-hand stand her jug and basin were of glass, and the little water jug had around it a wreath of briar-rose. She had, too, a bookcase with twelve volumes of *Macmillan's Magazine*, some stories by Grace Aguilar and Mrs. Craik, and Tennyson's complete works in eight volumes; also, the four books published by her husband, one of poems and three of plays.

Her chiefest treasures were on her mantelpiece, a faded photograph of Brand aged twelve in football clothes—"such a sturdy little chap" was the phrase she had used in the old days when there had been visitors—and a drawing of her husband, a thin figure with hair flowing, a cape flung over his right shoulder and a book held prominently in the hand. "A rather weak face" that same visitor might have thought, but to Mrs. Amorest, rich in intimate memories, perfection; perfect in physical beauty, in spiritual significance, in human sympathy.

The room was a large one and might seem to the superficial observer chill and spare. The chest of drawers and the cupboard where Mrs. Amorest kept her clothes could not cover sufficiently the farther wall space. The windows were not large. Mrs. Payne had the view right over the Pol and the country beyond. Mrs. Amorest had chimney-pots and not a glimpse of the cathedral. Miss Beringer had the cathedral, but her room was a pound a year more than Mrs. Amorest's.

Mrs. Amorest would not have a fire until the winter had really quite closed in, and the difficult days were such as these in November when it could be so cold and so wet and so wild and yet it was not truly winter. Today was not a bad day; a pale ghostly light was over the world, the sky was scattered with tatters of white cloud as though for a celestial paper-chase, and the smoke from all the chimneys blew wildly in the wind.

Mrs. Amorest noticed these things as she prepared to go out. The cathedral had struck (very faintly heard from here) two o'clock, the sun suddenly made a struggle and threw a faint primrose glow upon the remains of Mrs. Amorest's little luncheon—a coffee cup, a tumbler, a plate with crumbled biscuit, and a half-empty sardine tin. Three water biscuits, one sardine, and a cup of coffee, and Mrs. Amorest felt fortified for the rather difficult visit to her Cousin Francis that she was about to pay.

As she arranged her bonnet over her beautiful white hair in front of the misted looking-glass she was suddenly aware that she was going to like this visit to her cousin less than any that she had ever paid him.

She would like it less for two reasons; one that he was very ill, and that she would therefore be in the hands of his housekeeper, Miss Greenacre, who both disliked and despised her; the other that kind Mr. Neilson had written to her to tell her that there were only ten pounds four shillings and fivepence to her credit in the bank, and Quarter Day was yet far distant, and that therefore the thought of Cousin Francis's money was more dominant in her brain than it had ever been before.

She didn't wish it to be so. As she stood there, twisting the purple strings of her bonnet in her thin beautiful fingers, she thought how wicked she must be to have this in her mind!

But as you grew older you seemed to have less and less power to keep things out of your mind. You were being punished perhaps for looseness of thought in your earlier days. You had been too happy and careless then and must pay now. It was the one remnant of Mrs. Amorest's strict puritan upbringing that she felt that God did not intend His servants to be too consciously happy. And yet with her, all her life, happiness would keep breaking in. Probably she must pay for that now.

She gave a little sigh as she turned away from the window. She was still wickedly hungry. That was the punishment for being physically so blooming, that you had always so healthy an appetite. She looked for a moment covetously at the sardine tin. One more sardine, one more biscuit? Then resolutely shook her head, and as was her way often when she was alone her face broke into smiles. How ridiculous to have such an appetite with her small body! Now if she had been Mrs. Payne . . . !

And perhaps if she were in a kindly mood Miss Greenacre would offer her some tea with some of those nice sponge fingers that Cousin Francis had. She was not really greedy, but she liked sponge fingers.

Before she went out she listened for a moment, her head cocked on one side like an enquiring bird. How silent the house was! Like a dead-house. The wind was playing through it like a musician plucking a note from a board there, a stair here, an ill-fitting window somewhere else. But the house itself gave no sound.

Mrs. Payne too—how silent she was! There in her room day after day, thinking, thinking—of what? Of her past, one must suppose. After seventy the past was of so much more importance than the present. And the new tenant, Miss Beringer, how quiet she was! She had been there for three days now and Mrs. Amorest had not yet seen her. "A nice-spoken lady," Mrs. Bloxam had said, "and fond of talking." Tall and thin and dressed in pale green, a strange costume for one of her years. And having decided this with a thought of cheerful approbation for her own grey silk, Mrs. Amorest started down the stairs.

Cousin Francis lived in a large stone house on the other side of the river. It was shortest if you dropped down into Seatown, crossed the wooden bridge by the mill and walked through the fields, but Mrs. Amorest avoided Seatown when she could. She hated to see the distress and poverty that she could do nothing to improve; and although a stout optimistic lady had once told her confidently that "the poor were always happy. They had none of the troubles that weighed on the rich" she couldn't altogether believe it. They had none of the *same* troubles certainly, but she herself had known for too long what it was to worry about every penny, and deny yourself everything comfortable and easy, to believe eagerly in poverty.

So, to avoid Seatown she crossed the Market-place and the bottom of the High Street and turned to the left over Tontine Bridge, skirted the river for a little way and then climbed the wooded path to Cousin Francis's large white gates.

She was tired and weary and anxious today. Do what she would she could not beat down her anxiety. Passing through the streets as unobtrusively as possible, she would nevertheless have rejoiced had there been only somebody to raise a hat or smile a smile. There was nobody at all; she mattered to nobody. In that whole town there was not a soul who cared whether she lived or died and realising that in the sharp November wind she gave a little shiver. Her legs ached today and her brain ached. That particular ache in the brain came directly from her effort to keep her thoughts in order and to bring them into some sort of consecutive discipline. Her thoughts today were like mice behind the wainscoting—*tap tap, scratch scratch*—there for a moment and then gone. Some stockings that must be mended; a discoloration of Mrs. Bloxam's eye that, said Mrs. Bloxam, had been caused by tripping over a coal-scuttle, but was derived, Mrs. Amorest feared, straight from Mr. Bloxam's fist; strange Mrs. Payne with her old discoloured purple velvet and her bushy eyebrows; and there go Mrs. Combermere and Miss Ellen Stiles! How strong and self-confident they look!

Mrs. Amorest had not been always a shy woman. In those days in Cheltenham when Mr. Harland and Mr. Crackanthorpe had come to stay over Sunday, she had acted hostess bravely, although she could never like the things that they liked, thought the books that they read and wrote quite horrible if the truth be known. Her husband had never been able to change her artistic tastes. But she had not shrunk from Mr. Harland, had indeed chaffed him a little, but now were Mrs.

Combermere to stay and speak to her she would tremble all over and stammer most-like, and have no words of her own! And yet how happy she would have been! What an event in her day! Once, at a party at the Dean's, she had been introduced to Mrs. Combermere. But that seemed long ago. The time for parties at the Dean's was past and gone; for one thing she had no clothes, for another someone might one day call on her and spy out the nakedness of the land, for another. . . .

She shivered again as she crossed the Tontine Bridge.

Then she beat up her spirits. What was happening to her? How unlike her to lose her courage! It must be that tiresome Ten Pounds Four Shillings and Fivepence that was worrying her. Never mind that. She had been in worse troubles than that ere now and God the Father had always come to her aid. He would come to her aid again. As she looked up to the cloud-streaked sky, a sky into which a faint orange glow was slowly stealing, she felt, as on so many thousands of occasions she had felt before, the presence of a large protecting friend Who put His arm out towards her and drew her up, and smiling said, "How could you ever have doubted . . . ?"

Nevertheless, she doubted once again as she walked up Cousin Francis's grim and desolate drive. Cousin Francis had that property, peculiar to certain natures, of bestowing the colour of his personality on everything and everybody close to him. His garden, the rooms of his house, his housekeeper, his secretary, his Irish terrier, his two gardeners, all of them were wind-bitten and desolate. With all his money he did not know what comfort was, nor colour, nor gentleness, nor the "laughter and the love of friends." His own gaunt and rocky body with its high cold forehead, its naked eyes and projecting teeth, its long legs and iron-grey hands held no comfort for any human soul. Even his dog did not care for him.

The house was like a gaol with its barricaded windows and cold ugly walls. Mrs. Amorest pealed the iron bell and then waited, her heart beating beneath her thin grey silk. There was a fine view of Polchester from here, the cathedral riding triumphantly on high, the houses and fields piled up at its feet, and now suddenly the sun burst its bonds and great swaths of golden glory enwrapped the scene. Mrs. Amorest stood entranced and did not hear the door open and the voice of the maid.

She turned and, blushing, said, "Oh, I beg your pardon. How is Mr. Bulling today?"

"A little better, mum."

"Oh, I'm glad of that! I wonder if I might see him for a moment?"

"If you'll step in, mum, I'll enquire."

Mrs. Amorest stepped in and was left alone in the large stone hall with its empty fireplace, its grim portrait of Mr. Bulling as Mayor of Drymouth, and its shining wooden chairs.

She looked very small in that high cold place, and Miss Greenacre, Mr. Bulling's housekeeper, might be forgiven perhaps for looking all about her for quite a while before she saw that there was anybody there. Miss Greenacre was long and thin and white and ribbed like a stick of asparagus. She had the air of one who has so many important things in mind that personal contact with her must be always three times removed. And especially for Mrs. Amorest she was removed into almost disappearing distance.

Having found her, she only said "Good afternoon," biting her words as she offered them as though to see whether they rang true or no.

"I came to enquire after Mr. Bulling," said Mrs. Amorest. She was often timid with Miss Greenacre. How fervently she wished that she was not, and the more fervently she wished it the more timid she was.

"I wonder whether I might see him for a moment?"

"Well now, that depends," said Miss Greenacre, looking down upon Mrs. Amorest with a considering air as though she were a colour waiting to be matched.

"He wasn't so well this morning, but since he's had his dinner—well, he's brightened up considerable."

Mrs. Amorest might be timid, but she refused to be patronised by any one.

"I wonder whether you would mind," she said quite sharply, "letting him know that I am here?"

Miss Greenacre entered into the game with steely zest.

"Do you know, I believe he's just dropped off—about five minutes back. It wouldn't be well to wake him, would it?"

"I think he would like to see me," said Mrs. Amorest. "If you wouldn't mind making sure whether he's asleep or not."

"Well now . . . I wonder. . . ."

She stood there biting her finger and considering. Mrs. Amorest had a sudden burning ambition to pick up a large bronze of Neptune near the door and hurl it at her. Would she then snap in two or bend? The thought of her surprise made a little smile hover about Mrs. Amorest's lips. She got up.

"Would you mind," she said very firmly indeed, "asking whether Mr. Bulling will see me?"

And to her great surprise Miss Greenacre suddenly turned and went.

Alone once more, Mrs. Amorest abruptly sat down again. She was more weary than she had known. Her legs now really were *not* strong. That walk had exhausted her more than it had ever done before, and a sudden fear, confronting her not for the first time, whispered to her that the day was coming when she would be like Mrs. Payne—alone up there at the top of that silent house forgotten by all the world, slowly more helpless, more lonely, more——

She bit her lip because her chin trembled. Her chin was always giving her away. It seemed the least stable part of all her anatomy.

"Miss Greenacre shan't see that I'm worried," was her thought, and Miss Greenacre did not, returning just then to say that Mr. Bulling was awake and would see Mrs. Amorest.

Up the heavy oak staircase, the two women went, through passages that glimmered under the guttering gas with bad oil paintings of heavy seas and buttercup meadows, and so into the long high bedroom, dark and close and smelling of medicine.

Mrs. Amorest had often visited her cousin in bed before, and was accustomed to the shining forehead, the long cold nose, the pale bony hands. Propped up against his pillows, he peered out at her like a large malevolent bird. His bed was canopied with heavy dark red curtains. On the table beside the bed was a lamp with a green shade and a row of medicine bottles. Mrs. Amorest, coming forward, noticed none of these things in her sudden discovery that he had changed terribly for the worse since her last sight of him.

Her heart was touched: the maternal was roused in her. He was suffering, and there was no one really to care for him. That horrible Miss Greenacre could not be called anything. How uncomfortable he looked! She longed to turn the pillows, to smooth the sheets, to turn the shade so that the light was not in his eyes! But even with that impulse she realised that Miss Greenacre, watching her, would say to herself, "Ah, there goes another after his money!" And was it not true? Only on her way to this house . . . So the impulse was checked and she stood there in her purple bonnet and grey silk, smiling a little, and at last timidly saying:

"And how are you, Cousin Francis, today?"

"Worse; that's the way I am," he growled from the bed; then raising his voice, "All right, Greenacre. You can leave us. I know you'd like to overhear every word we're going to say, but you can listen behind the keyhole and you won't hear a thing."

How terrible, thought Mrs. Amorest, to treat anyone like that and to call her "Greenacre." Could I ever endure it, she wondered, if I were in that position? No, indeed, I could not. But the lady did not appear discomforted. She gave Mrs. Amorest one haughty glance and departed.

"Sit down, sit down, Cousin Lucy. And take off your bonnet. I like to see your hair." This last remark was in a softer tone. It encouraged Mrs. Amorest, who took off her bonnet and laid it on the table near the medicine bottles, then brought a chair and sat down close to the bed.

"Come to see how the poor old man's getting along? To see how fast he's dying and when his money's going to be divided?"

Mrs. Amorest's pale cheeks flushed. "It wouldn't be true, Cousin Francis," she said, "to say that I haven't thought about your money, because I have, and reproached myself for doing so. But I haven't thought greatly about it, and I would have come to visit you if you hadn't a penny in the world. I would have come indeed more often than I have done."

"Well, that's honest," he answered. "More honest than most of them. I'm glad you've come today. It's probably the last time you'll see me."

"I hope indeed not."

"But indeed, it is. I'm dying, and I'm frightened of it. I've been a man all my life that's never needed anybody. I never needed a woman or a friend. My mind was given to the making of money and I made it, and now it seems a shame that I can't take any of it with me. Sometimes, when the pain's bad, I want it all to end as quickly as may be, but when the pain goes, there I am again thinking of the money and wondering how I can make the most of it in the little time that's left. But I'm lonely, Cousin Lucy, mighty lonely. All my life I never thought to be, but that is the truth now I'm here. I'm lonely and naked at the last."

Mrs. Amorest said what she could, but her mind was fixed on the desire to arrange his pillow, to smooth his hair from his forehead, to do something that would make him comfortable. His long cold fingers kept plucking at the sheets, his eyes were never still. But she would not do anything lest he should think that she wanted his money.

"What would you say to it if I were to leave you a thousand pounds a year?" he asked her.

"I should be thankful to you," she answered him. "I have not many years to live, but I would find out my boy and we could live together again."

"Where is your boy?"

"I don't know." Against her will tears gathered in her eyes. "I haven't heard now for a considerable time."

"Aye, he's forgotten you, I've no doubt. So, you're all alone?"

"Yes, I'm quite alone."

"It must have tired you coming up here to see me?"

"Yes, it was tiring."

"How old are you now?"

"I was seventy-one last March."

"Were you now? We're both old dodderers. Are you afraid of death?"

"No, Cousin Francis."

"And why not?"

"My Heavenly Father will care for me in that as He has cared for me in everything else."

"Cared for you, you say, when He has left you all alone in your old age?"

"I am not alone while He is with me."

"Well, I don't understand all that religious nonsense. But what if it should be true, after all? Who can tell? Nobody knows."

There was a silence between them, a long silence. Then the man said:

"You're a good woman, Cousin Lucy—the best of all of them that come here. I'll give you a thousand pounds a year. On my oath, I will. I'll see Agnew about it tomorrow."

Mrs. Amorest turned very pale. Then she said faintly: "Thank you, Cousin Francis."

"Is that all you've got to say? I like that too. You're not a false one like the others. Let me feel your hair."

She came closer to the bed, and he put his hand on her white hair and very slowly stroked it. They sat for a long time, he stroking her hair. Then suddenly his hand fell away and she saw that he was asleep.

She gently put on her bonnet and stole out of the room.

Chapter 2: Evening in the House—Agatha Payne

Darkness gathers swiftly in November, and below the rock the lights of the Seatown slum gaily flickered. There came up to the black walls of the houses some shadow of the last pale afterglow of the sunset, and motion was sent spinning through the evening air by the shrill, discordant notes of a cornet that someone in Seatown was enjoying.

In Pontippy Square there was no life. The tides of Polchester had passed it by. The old houses once, in eighteenth-century years, fashionable and alive, had sunk their chins into their breasts and so slept. Used largely once for warehouses, they were now, like No. 19, where lived the old ladies, let out in pieces to occasional lodgers. It was the shabbiest inch of all the genteel districts of the town.

In the Square there were only two lamps, and these at opposite corners, so that the space before No. 19 was unlighted. The pavement here, too, was broken and grass-grown, so that it made a splendid trap for the unwary. After dusk, to navigate the holes and broken stones, then to find the door, to turn the round iron knob, to discover the stair-rail, and then successfully to start upwards into the forbidding dark, was no mean feat of seamanship, and, for an old lady, it was dangerous indeed.

Some years before an old lodger had been discovered by the milkman in the morning at the bottom of the stairs with her neck and many bones broken. She had fallen a full flight. She haunted, poor old wispy-haired crumpled lady, the Square after dusk. She always had with her a little sniffing dog. You could feel him sniffing at your trousers or skirts.

The silence of Pontippy Square was another matter of note. The sniffing of a ghostly little dog could indeed be heard miles away if you chose to listen for the sound. But silent though the Square might be, once within the house with the heavy old door closed behind you, and you sank deep, deep into a well of oblivion. You might climb the stair with the hope perhaps of discovering it livelier if you went higher. But the silence follows you. When, out of breath, on the third floor now, you pause and listen, it is only the hammering of your heart that you hear. Silence everywhere.

Mrs. Payne's room was the first on the right of the stairs. If you opened the door and looked in after dusk (a liberty very rarely taken by anyone), the first things that you noticed were the two big red candlesticks and a large piece of faded orange silk hanging over a cupboard opposite the door. It was a large room and curiously jumbled with odds and ends. On the round table there was a sewing basket of pink silk, a china dish with oranges, a black-haired doll in a green dress, and two packs of cards scattered on the shabby red tablecloth. The candles in the red candlesticks gave but a faint light, and you must look well before you saw in addition to a bed a chest of drawers and the cupboard with the orange silk across it, a large black rocking-chair, a cuckoo clock, and a big oil painting of an aquarium scene—a very large picture this, with green shining water and large fish with open mouths. There was also a stuffed bird with crimson wings in a glass case.

After these things, your eyes now accustomed to the uncertain light, you perceived their mistress. Mrs. Payne was a large, stout, and shapeless woman. She had hair of a deep black and her cheeks were highly coloured. She had fine dark eyes. She looked an old gipsy woman, and perhaps she had gipsy blood in her—foreign blood, for sure. She would be rocking herself in her chair, lying back in it wearing her soiled red wrapper and her shabby crimson shoes. She was not a cleanly old woman. Her splendid hair, as black now as forty years ago, was tumbled about her head carelessly, and stuck into it, askew, was a cheap black comb studded with glass diamonds.

Her colour was swarthy, brown under the deep red of her cheeks, and there was a faint moustache on her upper lip. But she must have been handsome once, a fine bold girl in those years long ago. Quite shapeless now, her fat dirty arms naked under the wrapper, her body as it lolled back in the chair boneless. Once and again she yawned, then felt in a dirty paper bag on the table near to her for a thick slab of nougat that she crumbled idly in the bag, then ate fragments, licking slowly her fingers. Her face was expressionless. Her large black eyes stared out into the room vacantly.

As she licked her fingers she kicked one foot idly in the air. But she was not vacant. She knew what she was about. When the cuckoo burst his little door and cried that it was seven o'clock she would rise, totter across to the cupboard, produce a plate, a cup, a loaf of bread, butter, jam. She would make herself a cup of thick rich cocoa (the kettle had been long on the fire), and she would eat many pieces of thick bread and raspberry jam, and then a hunk of black dark plum-cake.

She would eat sitting up at the table, staring in front of her, her lips making a large smacking sound of satisfaction. Then once again she would lick her fingers slowly, elaborately. Then once again totter back to her chair, lie on it and rock, tossing her shabby red shoes in air.

Totter! Yes, because the only sign of age was in those legs of hers. They alone had deserted her. They would betray her in a moment, the knees failing, and she must cling to the table to save herself from falling. She hated her legs—they had betrayed her—and in the dark recesses of her mind she would imagine how she might punish them, punish them without hurting herself, just as though they were separate personalities.

But on the whole, she was not ill-contented, nor did she bear humanity a grudge. She did not dislike this life of hers. She had always been lazy, taking what came nonchalantly. She had taken Wilfred Payne and his miserable mother; she had taken a lover and his brutal desertion of her; she had taken a child that had not been her husband's (and he had never known); she had taken its death; she had taken the Roman Catholic religion for the lights and the incense; she had taken her husband's death and her own subsequent poverty; she had taken the job of companion to an old fool widow of a Polchester merchant; she had taken the widow's decease (without leaving her a farthing) and her own subsequent penury; she had taken Pontippy Square and the cold and silent room there; she had taken her absolute loneliness and isolation—everything she had taken with a luxurious sensual indifference. Her two passions—and they were in their basis one—were for food and bright colours.

For food her longing was both active and indolent. Active because she would take trouble that Mrs. Bloxam should keep her well supplied in cake and jam and nougat. She spent all that she had on these foods, and in her slothful brain there was a kind of wonder that she could purchase so much of this for so little. Her digestion did not apparently suffer.

Her passion for bright colours was a deeper longing. It had always been so. As a tiny child she had cried after a reel of coloured thread and had begged for a shining marble. And this had gathered strength perhaps because her husband and mother-in-law had sternly forbidden it. Theirs was the Nonconformist mind and vision: grey stone, drab clothes, uncoloured minds. She had hated her husband for many reasons, but chiefly because he had thrown a gay hat of hers into the fire. She would lie in bed beside him devising tortures for his soft and rounded limbs. But that was many years ago. She had long forgotten him. The past appeared to her a succession of bright and shining images. Her husband was not one of these. She did not think connectedly of her past at all. Old people do not. To the old the past comes in a series of pictures, not of necessity connected, here intensely vivid, there dim and blurred—a green field, a quiet evening, an angry quarrel, some loving face, some sharp disappointment—and all, vivid or blurred, dispassionately removed. No call for action any more. Quiescence. And then a strange wonder that to those about them these scenes so real, so actual, mean nothing, stir no reaction.

But Mrs. Payne did not wonder. She had no audience for her memories; only Mrs. Amorest who seemed to her a silly old thing, incredibly old, stupidly active, an egoist in her sense of her importance.

With this matter of activity Agatha Payne was always intending to be "on the move" one day soon. Nothing forced her to stir. Her monthly allowance was paid to her by a lawyer in Birmingham. He paid her rental for her room. The rest was in Mrs. Bloxam's hands, and Mrs. Bloxam might cheat her if she willed, so long as she brought her what she desired.

But Mrs. Bloxam did not cheat her. She had a strange tenderness towards her two old ladies. When, before the arrival of Miss Beringer, there had been two old ladies and one old gentleman, she had been yet more tender towards the old gentleman, and were there now three old gentlemen her tenderness would have known no bounds. She *did* prefer the other sex and always had. But, as she said to Mr. Bloxam, you couldn't help but be sorry for the two old things. She liked Mrs. Amorest the better of the two; there was something in Mrs. Payne's lazy indifference that frightened her, and then "her liking sweet things the way she did." Like a child. But then if it hadn't been sweet things it would have been drink, and *that*, as Mrs. Bloxam only too absolutely knew, was "another kettle of fish." Mrs. Bloxam, too, was honoured by Mrs. Payne's trust in her, and would take real trouble over the commissions she gave her, going "quite a way" up the High Street to find the raspberry jam that she preferred. But whereas Mrs. Amorest was a "real sweet old lady," and should have been "a Duchess in her own right if all had their proper due," Mrs. Payne was "not quite. . . . Well, you know. Shouldn't wonder if she went queer in the 'ead any day."

Mr. Bloxam, when he was sober enough to realise things, couldn't see what Mrs. Bloxam was about wasting her time with those old women. It wasn't as though she got anything for it—but Mrs. Bloxam felt like a mother to them, twenty years younger though she was. She felt, too, a certain power. She liked to see Mrs. Amorest's eager smile when she called her in the morning, and to feel Mrs. Payne's dependence on her. "If they 'adn't got me surely to goodness I don't know who they would 'ave and that's the truth. Poor old dears."

About Miss Beringer she had not as yet made up her mind. Miss Beringer had been there but a week. And then there was the fox-terrier. "Pip." A silly name for a dog.

It was not to be expected that Mrs. Payne considered Mrs. Bloxam as a separate identity. Had Mrs. Bloxam been a stick of nougat or a piece of brightly coloured silk then Mrs. Payne would have desired to possess her, and her sluggish brain would have suddenly awakened to the *intention* of possessing her, and from that, coil after coil unwinding, she would have entered on the campaign of possessing her with the pertinacity and determination of Napoleon advancing upon Russia.

It was fortunate indeed for her that she did not leave her room. The sight of a gay vase or a jewelled trinket in a shop window might have drawn her into committal of some crime.

I have said that physically she was still a strong woman, and the weakness in her knees was more imagined than real. But she did occasionally suffer from a strange pain in the head. This was not exactly a headache; it was rather a kind of limiting of her consciousness, a constriction of the brain, as though cords were tightening over her brows and forbidding her to think. When this came upon her she was scarcely aware of what she did, moving, apparently, under the orders of some commanding personality.

It was as though someone whispered to her "Go and do this," and she then moved hypnotically. It must be repeated that she was not essentially an unkindly woman. Now that she was old and alone strange thoughts and desires possessed her. She wished ill to no one, but she moved in a world that had been largely created out of her own lingering and possessing imagination.

The picture of the fish in the green tank of water that had been her father's, that she had known ever since, as a little child, she had gazed up at it hanging in the Birmingham dining-room, had become part of her real and active world. She moved inside it as truly as she moved about the room, and the fish, especially the large one with the silver scales and the long swinging tail, left their watery confines and swam about her room slowly opening and shutting their jaws lazily swerving in their upward or downward course.

So, too, the black-haired doll with the green dress, Miranda. Miranda had three dresses—this green one, one of ruby colour, and one of dark purple. Mrs. Payne would change the dresses from time to time and, with the change, the whole room would seem to alter. When the ruby dress was worn sunlight seemed to strike the room. The very fish were glad, and Miranda, perched up against the red candlesticks, smirked her satisfaction.

There were also the cards. With these Mrs. Payne played a game of her own, a kind of Patience maybe, but also a kind of fortune-telling, so that as she gazed at the king and queen of hearts and then lying beside them found the black, rich, thick ten of clubs, her heart beat strongly and awful destinies seemed to close about the room, and her eyes would stare far beyond those confining walls, and dynasties would rock, and the very stars would shake and quiver.

Then she would smile darkly to herself, knowing so much more of fate than the people about her.

On the evening of Mrs. Amorest's visit to her cousin she was thus playing at her cards when the door opened and the old lady entered. Mrs. Amorest had had her evening meal and had felt then an irresistible desire to talk to someone. Endeavour to control it as she might, the promise of her cousin that afternoon excited her so deeply that she was shaken through and through. One thousand pounds a year! To find her boy again, to spend the little time on this earth remaining to her with him! To see him with her own eyes happy! And it was only with this sudden wonderful promise that she realised how hard things had of late been and how, deep in her subconsciousness, the fear of some tragedy, the cessation of her money, or the running into debt and the consequent disgrace, had played upon her. But now! One thousand pounds a year! And he had meant it! she could still feel the touch of his hand upon her hair. How good he was, how kind! How many people had misjudged him!

She did not want to bother poor old Agatha Payne—she always thought of her as at least twenty years older than herself—with all her private affairs, but she must see somebody, be kind to somebody too, because tonight she wished well to all the world.

She knocked on the door, then timidly stepped forward. The cards had just come out badly, meaning nothing, pretending nothing, and Agatha Payne was therefore glad to see a friend.

In a way she liked Lucy Amorest although she despised her. Poor old thing, so lonely and deserted!

She gazed up confusedly, staring through the dim light and seeing a large green fish swerve just above Mrs. Amorest's head and disappear.

"Ah, my dear! Come along!" she said.

Her voice was bass and masculine. She rose very slowly from the table, leaving the cards upon the cloth. She moved to the rocking-chair, slowly sinking down into it. A very small fire flickered in the grate. On the other side of this there was a shabby red armchair from which the stuffing burst, now here, now there, like a pale disease.

Mrs. Amorest sat down in this as on many occasions she had done before. She seemed very small and very slight beside the large fat woman, rocking, one heel in air, opposite to her.

Agatha Payne gazed at her with sombre eyes.

"You have not been out, I suppose?" said Mrs. Amorest. This was a genteel fiction always maintained between them, that today it was true that Mrs. Payne had not gone out, that yesterday also she had remained within, but that tomorrow, all being well, would certainly see her in the open air.

"No," said Mrs. Payne, "I have not been out. It was in no way the kind of day for me. Cold and dark. Mrs. Bloxam has kindly done my shopping for me."

"I went and paid a visit to my cousin," said Mrs. Amorest, smiling, as though she would intimate that there was far more in that visit than she could expressly say.

But Agatha Payne was a bad one for secrets. She was occupied too deeply in pursuing the strange perplexing windings of her own brain to follow closely the possibilities of another.

One thing she always did—she overlooked Mrs. Amorest and was discontented that she refused to have anywhere about her a bright spot of colour. That grey dress and plain hair and quiet little face irritated her. Poor little old thing, she would think, how old and shrivelled up she is. *She's* not long for this world!

And the sense tonight that Lucy Amorest was pleased about something—it mattered not what—irritated her still more. What right had *she* to be pleased with her poverty and mean way of dressing? So, very soon, she was in an irritable temper, muttering to herself and kicking in air her red-heeled shoe.

"And so you've begun a fire!" said Mrs. Amorest brightly. "Well, I'm sure it's time, and yet I can't make up my mind to it. I said to Mrs. Bloxam this morning that I thought tomorrow I really would start one. And yet I don't know. The winter hasn't truly come, has it? And we may get quite a number of warm days yet."

Mrs. Payne, lying back shapeless in her chair, began:

"I'm sorry for you, Lucy. There's that cousin of yours, rich as he is, does nothing for you, and your boy been gone for years, no one knows where. I'm glad my child died. She would only have been a grief to me."

"He'll come back, Brand, I mean." Mrs. Amorest spoke confidently. "I feel tonight as though everything is going to turn out well. Don't you feel that way sometimes?"

"Brand? Is that your boy's name? Queer name."

"It was my husband who wished it. I think it's a nice name."

"Well, I don't think much of your Brand. Why doesn't he write and tell you what he is doing? Perhaps he's dead."

Mrs. Amorest knew well that Agatha Payne was doing her best to be provoking. She had on many occasions been through just this same conversation before, and when she had been tired, hungry, and lonely it had been difficult not to burst into tears. But she was accustomed now, and tonight she was too truly happy to care.

"I know that he's not dead," she answered. "Brand was the kind of boy who would never own that he was beaten. It was always the same, in cricket and in football. He'll tell me where he is when he's made his fortune. I'm expecting to hear any day now."

"You've been expecting to hear any day ever since I've known you," said Agatha Payne. "You're a patient woman."

Slowly, from the sluggish levels of her mind curiosity was arising. What was making Lucy Amorest so happy tonight? What news had she received? Had some fortune come to her?

The fish swam slowly back into their deep green tank; she sat up in her chair, and with her hands on the arms and her heavy breast bulging beneath her wrapper she looked attentively at her companion.

"What's the matter with you, Lucy?" she asked. "You've had some good news."

"Well, in a way I have," Mrs. Amorest confessed. "And yet it's not news exactly. My cousin spoke to me in a very kindly way this afternoon."

"Did he say he'd leave you something in his will?" asked Mrs. Payne, her interest growing very sharply.

"He did say something," answered Mrs. Amorest, smiling a little. "Of course, he may have meant nothing by it. I certainly mustn't rely on it."

"Nonsense!" said Mrs. Payne, leaning now eagerly forward. "What did he say he'd leave you?"

"Well, he *said* a thousand pounds a year!"

Mrs. Payne sank back into the chair.

"A thousand pounds! A thousand pounds a year!" Her large black eyes widened and extended. "Why, Lucy, that's a fortune!"

"Yes," said Mrs. Amorest faintly, "it is. And that's why I don't want to rely on it. It's only what he *said*, of course."

"And was there anyone else there when he said it?"

"No, there wasn't. We were quite alone, and he was very kind indeed. I have never known him so nice."

Agatha Payne stared. A thousand pounds a year! And to be given to that poor little mouse who had only a few years to live at the best. What would *she* do with a thousand pounds a year? whereas the things that Agatha Payne might do . . . the gay, glorious, coloured, glittering things that she might buy! And there suddenly came into her head the idea that she herself would have some of this money that was coming to Lucy Amorest. She was a weak, good-natured, little creature was Lucy Amorest. She would give anything away. She would do anything for anybody.

Her heart beat. It was strange, perhaps, that with her passion for gay things she had not, long ago, spent more than she had and encumbered herself with debt. But an odd laziness held her captive, and perhaps also the old house had thrown some spell over her. It had forbidden her perhaps to leave it. Old houses can do such things. They can impregnate human souls with their own subtle poison and with bricks and beams of wood and flakes of mortar wall in the human body as surely as in the cruel past errant wives and sinning nuns were confined.

Here was something beneath her hand. She smiled, and a grim forbidding smile it was.

"That's right, Lucy. Don't you count on it. You come to me and we'll talk it over. There's nothing like a little plan. Nothing."

Mrs. Amorest was frightened. She did not know why. It had been foolish of her to say anything at all about the money. It had been, in a way, betraying the confidence of her cousin.

She was tired and needed the security of her own room.

"I think I'll go to bed now," she said. "It's late."

Mrs. Payne smiled once more. "You come in again and we'll talk it over," she said.

Mrs. Amorest said goodnight and went.

She hurried into her room, lit her lamp, and began to undress. She took the photograph of her boy from the mantelpiece and kissed it. Then she knelt down and said her prayers.

Chapter 3: Life of May Beringer

Miss May Beringer was poorer than either Mrs. Amorest or Mrs. Payne. She was not only very poor, but she had to confront the possibility of having, in some six months or so, no money whatever. Literally no money. Nothing.

She was as absolutely alone in the world as it was possible for anyone to be—at least she would have been so had it not been for her dog Pip.

People talk of poverty and they talk of loneliness, and in a majority of cases do not understand the true meaning of either word. People also talk of "the working classes" and *their* hardships. Very seldom do you hear anything about the "poor gentlewoman classes" and their hardships. The poor gentlewomen of this world do, in every civilised country, by their unselfish and heroic lives, constitute a large proportion of the future citizens of the Kingdom of Heaven. Verily, they need that Paradisal promise.

Miss Beringer was one of those unfortunate women who have never been wanted by anybody. Neither her father nor mother, none of her numerous brothers and sisters, no relation near or distant—none of these wanted her.

She was the daughter of a doctor of Exeter City. She had been always, with her heavy hooked nose, faint eyebrows, pale pasty complexion and long lanky body, very homely. Nor were the defects of her person excused by the brilliance of her accomplishments. She was born and bred into a period when the daughters of Great Britain were expected neither to spin nor to sew but only to wait, in patient eagerness, for the day when a gentleman would ask them in marriage.

It was obvious from the very first that it was unlikely that anyone would beg for May's hand, because she was plain and awkward and also because she had three sisters older than herself. Her unfortunate father and mother killed themselves in the attempt to win that unceasing battle that great progeny and small incomes force upon so many virtuous and upright citizens. Two of May's sisters married, one died, two brothers went to the Colonies, one was killed in China and one, vanished into the depths of America. May, at the age of forty, found herself with an income of one hundred and fifty pounds a year, alone in the world. That was thirty years ago—thirty years of being wanted by nobody, thirty years of finding that ends were never quite meeting, thirty years of absurdities, hopes, enthusiasms, disappointments, confusions. Confusions most of all.

May Beringer was unfortunately a stupid woman. A stupid woman with a kind and generous heart, than that there is nothing more aggravating, exasperating, touching, and pathetic to be found in the human kingdom. Her stupidity was not altogether her own fault. In the first place she had never had any education. Her mother and father had not wished that "their girls" should go to a rough day-school where they would assuredly learn rude habits from rough day-girls. A governess had therefore been supplied, and because finances were so low only the poorest kind of governess could be afforded, and because the family was so large even the finest kind of governess would have been unable to deal with the situation adequately. May Beringer, therefore, had learnt nothing save that Oliver Cromwell executed Charles I. and that the Amazon was a river in America, and of these two facts she was not very certain. Moreover, she was quite unaware that she was ill-educated. Facts in the days when she was a girl were divided into divisions of the Improper, the Masculine, and the Unnecessary. With the first of these she must, of course, have nothing to do, the second she left to the men, the third were waste of time. She was therefore never challenged as to her ignorance. She was not in the least a modern girl of her time. She read only the idlest fictions, played all games very badly, and when she found that her ideas refused to clarify sufficiently for coherent conversation, took refuge in giggling silence.

Beneath all this her heart was warm, eager, and sentimental. She longed to be good and kind and generous. She did not care whether people liked her or no, all that she wished was to be allowed to like them. She adored her father and mother, loved her brothers and sisters indiscriminately, and felt romantic passions for every man who came to their house. She did not expect a proposal of marriage. She had been told very often by her frank and careless brothers and sisters that she was plain, awkward, and stupid. She had from the very earliest age developed a terror of almost everything and everybody. Her very shyness and gaucherie made her timid, and then as she was conscious of her mistakes her shyness increased.

She felt that she might be very brilliant and amusing could she only arrange her ideas in order, but always something unfortunate came in the way—she sat down when she ought to stand up, spoke when she should be silent, smiled when she should have frowned.

Then her body was clumsy, untidy. Do what she would her clothes were for ever in disorder.

She lived alone in Exeter from the years of forty to sixty. She occupied the upper part of a little house near the cathedral, and it was there that she spent the happiest part of her life. She managed on her tiny income because her father's solicitor saw that she received it in moderation, a little at a time; he paid her rent; he also let it be understood in the principal shops of the town that she was not to be permitted to run up accounts. She had at first a gay and fanciful fashion of going into a shop, looking around her happily, and then saying, "Oh, I'll have that! Would you kindly send it this afternoon?" The shopmen kindly agreed, but it was not sent, and by the following day she had quite forgotten that she had ever ordered it.

She was happy during this time in her two rooms, in her few friends, and, latterly, in the friend whom she adored, Jane Betts. It was essential to her nature that she should adore someone, and if there was no one positively close at hand then she would choose someone out of the illustrated papers or one of the Royal Family.

Jane Betts was younger than she, daughter of a retired colonel, a bright jolly woman of thirty or so, to whom life was a joke and everything a cause for wonder. She accepted the affection of May Beringer with amused acquiescence, and then suddenly, on a day, perceived something touching and even beautiful in this plain elderly woman's devotion. Where another would have been wearied or bored Jane was moved and grateful. Something serious entered into her life that had never been there before.

There followed for May Beringer the six glorious months of her life, the only truly happy time that she was ever to know. It is for ever marvellous what happy love can do for the divine soul and the awkward human body. Had fate willed it and the friendship lasted, May Beringer might have known transformation. Already, guided by the gentle hints of her friend, awkwardness was leaving her, comeliness was approaching her, a novel orderliness was mastering her poor confused brains, happiness shone from her eyes, people were beginning to say that "she wasn't so bad after all."

It was during the Christmas of that happy six months that Jane gave her friend that piece of red amber that was afterwards to play so important a part in May's life. It became, of course, her most cherished possession.

Then, alas, a large red-faced colonel arrived from India on leave, saw Jane, fell instantly in love with her in spite of her thirty years, proposed and was accepted. That was a terrible day when Jane told her friend of what had occurred, and May Beringer showed in the fashion with which she received the news the stuff of which she was beginning to be made. She said that all that she wished was that Jane should be happy: she was sorry indeed that Jane was going so far, but that, of course, neither seas nor the passing of the years should ever divide them. Unfortunately, seas and long absences are more powerful separators than friends and lovers in the full flood of their romantic ideals will honestly realise. Moreover, the red-faced colonel did not appreciate his darling Jane's friend. It was the one thing in his darling Jane that he could not understand, that she should care for that "old giggling scarecrow." And then, unfortunately, May perceived that he did not like her, and forgetting her hard-won control only a few nights before Jane's departure lost her temper and called the Colonel names. After that followed floods of tears, urgent agonising demands for forgiveness, touching reconciliations. But it may be that Jane left Exeter feeling that her good old May might in the passing of the years have become something of a good old nuisance.

It was after Jane's departure that May Beringer "took to dogs." She suddenly discovered, as many other human beings have discovered both before and since, that dogs are marvellously unaware of faults and deficiencies only too obvious to all one's friends and acquaintances, that they bear one no grudges, that when you have lost your temper and behaved abominably they take your sins upon them and ask for your forgiveness, that they have no irony nor cynicism, that they are not pessimistic, and the sight of a bone or a cat or a pat on the head is enough to make them believe that all is well with the world, and that do you but treat them kindly they will prefer you to all other human beings whatever and will exhibit that same preference in a most flattering and self-justifying manner.

To a woman of May Beringer's sentiment a dog was the perfect solution. She was not, however, by nature adapted to look after dogs successfully. For some years dogs inevitably died under her hand, and she passed through a series of soul-searching griefs swearing that she would never have another, that Gyp or Tray or Fido was surely the very last. But dog succeeded dog, and apartment succeeded apartment, landladies invariably liking the Fido or the Gyp of the moment less than did their adoring mistress.

Then, finding Exeter difficult, expensive, and the perpetual echo of Jane's dear voice, she moved into the country. She went to St. Lennan, a small seaside resort on the coast of North Glebeshire. At first it seemed that here she had met good fortune. She was now sixty years of age but was strong and healthy. She took two rooms on the sea-front from a kindly widow who had no objections at all to dogs and indeed preferred them. The winter months in North Glebeshire are bleak and wild indeed, but May Beringer threw herself into the clerical work of the parish with eager enthusiasm. She adored the clergyman and slaved for him. The clergyman was at first grateful, but soon it became apparent that Miss Beringer was a breeder of disputes and a begetter of quarrels. She wanted things her own way, and, in spite of her timidity, was touchy and sensitive to a fault. Moreover, she could not be relied on to carry anything forward to completeness. Her eagerness was not balanced by forethought nor her devotion by clear thinking.

So, after a year or two, May Beringer found herself isolated once more, and abandoned to the company of a few old maids like herself, her landlady, and her dog. She did not complain. She was always only too ready to admit that everything was her own fault.

She had acquired a passion for St. Lennan. There was something about its wind-swept sandy shore, about the fashion in which the hard green breakers split suddenly into jade and foam, slipping down into silky splendour, something in the naked line of houses, the low bare hill, the circling arm of the dim white shore that won her heart. It was cold, it was chill, but it was her own.

In the summer it was not hers. Never at any time a popular resort, there were nevertheless during the summer months families sufficient for her to feel that she was old and ugly and unwanted. Then the dog of the moment was always in trouble at that time, lured by little girls, tempted by little boys, above all excited and bemused by the presence of other dogs.

Every morning about mid-day, weather foul or fair, May Beringer might be seen robed in a long green jacket and wearing a large hard hat stuck through with a large sharp pin, striding along the shore, a small dog tethered to her with a chain. She liked small dogs, but not too small, and fox terriers were her favourites. She had, ere this, by sheer force of necessity learnt something of their proper care. They were not, as a rule, very healthy animals, and wore a strange air of bewilderment, fostered, one may imagine, by the puzzling moods to which their mistress was subject, slapping them one moment and hugging them the next.

It was when she was sixty-five and had been at St. Lennan some five years that she received the dog, Pip. She received him as a puppy from the landlady, who felt that she had not been, in the past, altogether kind to the queer and lonely old woman. Pip seemed from the beginning to understand better than any of his predecessors the purposes for which he was born into this world. He was not a handsome dog, and one coal-black ear, the rest of his body being white, gave him rather a ludicrous appearance. Nor was he intelligent. His mind was, strangely like his mistress's, compact of fear and confusion. They say that animals resemble very frequently their masters, or, maybe, masters their animals. There was, as Pip developed into maturer years, a quite ludicrous resemblance to his mistress. His body was lanky and ill-controlled like hers, his mind, as I have said, confused and panic-stricken, and he had exactly the same loving and eager heart. He was more fortunate than his mistress in this, that there was no question as to the true altar of his devotion. He loved one and one alone, he saw in her no absurdities, no oddities, no stupidities. It is true that he must often have been puzzled by her moods, but just as Mrs. Amorest was always assured that God's actions, whatever they might be, were for the best, so felt Pip about his mistress.

He was, during the years at St. Lennan, a happy dog. Except for those few weeks in the summer he might run riotously along that un-ending beach pursuing imaginary cats, sticks, and bones, barking at the breakers as they rolled towards him, confident in his own fine security, returning to those warm rooms where his beloved mistress awaited him, where there was food and warmth and unfailing affection.

In her sixty-eighth year May Beringer met upon the sands a wise old gentleman with silvery hair and a benevolent cape who talked with her in the kindest fashion. They spoke together day after day. He was, it appeared, a professor of Oxford University. He liked her very much and discovered her to be most intelligent and far-seeing. It was the month of June and the days were warm.

She told him everything of her life, speaking even to him of her beloved Jane. He became, after a short interval, so warm a friend that he begged to know whether her money were properly invested. The old solicitor friend of her family was dead. The son, who had succeed-ed to his father's position, took in the old lady less personal an inter-est, and it was not long before the kind old professor with the silvery hair had invested her money so carefully for her that she was never to see any of it again. Most of it—luckily not all. There remained to her some hundred and fifty pounds.

The shock to her when she discovered what had occurred added to the confusion of her already confused brain. She could not un-derstand how so charming an old man could have done anything so cruel. She wrote to him again and again, but, of course, received no reply. The thing that hurt her the most was not the loss of her money,

but that she had confided to him so many intimacies about her friendship with dear Jane.

She cried about that in the dark silences of the over-long night.

Something had to be done. She collected what remained of her
fortune and had the confused idea of going to Polchester and finding
there some work. What work? Governess, perhaps. It was true that she
was now seventy, but she was strong and active. At least in St. Lennan
there was no work to be found. Her heart failed her did she positively
visualise to herself what work, any work at her age, would mean, so
she did not visualise it; she simply ordered her few pieces of furniture
to be packed and sent to a Polchester depository, said farewell to her
kind landlady, and departed, Pip chained to her side.

Arrived in Polchester she stayed for a while in rooms at the top
of Orange Street, but these were expensive; she had her own bits of
furniture; where was the cheapest place?

The cheapest place was Pontippy Square.

The first vision of the bare room at the top of that old tumbling
house frightened her, but the rent was so small that she felt that it
would be wicked to refuse it. She would be here, too, her own mistress—no one could interfere with her. She was told that two other
ladies were tenants on this same floor. She would have company if she
wished. Real ladies like herself.

Only she said nothing about dogs. Were dogs allowed? She did
not enquire. Here surely no one would interfere with her, but on the
whole, it was safer not to enquire. So, she settled in. The depository
sent up her possessions—her old dark blue carpet with the large ink
spot in one corner and showing the threads in another corner where
a youthful Pip had gnawed it, her bed, her round mahogany table, her
four mahogany chairs, her two dark blue armchairs, her bookcase, her
two oil paintings "after Cuyp," and her chest of drawers. She had also
her photographs of her father, her mother, a family group, Jane Betts,
and Pip. She had her two Venetian vases—*and* her piece of red amber.

This was a very fine piece. It stood in the middle of the mantelpiece, shining and gleaming. Jane Betts had seen it, that famous
Christmas, in the shop windows of an Exeter antiquarian and, feeling
very tender towards her "dear silly old May," had gone in and bought
it. "It will warm you, my dear," she said when she gave it to her, "always keep you warm like my affection. Never lose it or sell it. My
heart is inside it!"

You know how sentimental people can be! Jane Betts was, in her

230

nature, something of a cynic, and her marriage with the red-faced colonel made her in after life yet more cynical, but those months of friendship with May Beringer touched, for a moment, her truest, sincerest affection. She did not know it, but she was never again to care for any one so deeply as she did for that ugly, awkward, lanky old woman.

So, did this chunk of amber enshrine both their affections. It was shaped square like a little block of wood, and this block was surmounted with a carved red amber dragon. It had in it the most lovely lights and colours, that flashed and trembled from the deepest Venetian red to the fairest honey gold.

When the shimmer of the fire or the light of the lamp caught it, it did indeed seem to be stirring with the fire of its own heart. The dragon raised its head, his eyes shot flame.

For May Beringer it was simply the heart of her life. There, enshrined in that lovely thing, was all the happiness of her days. So long as that remained to her she could not, as dear Jane had said, be altogether cold and chill.

Pip settled into the new room very easily. He had his cushion in the corner near the fire; he gave his mistress one look to see whether she really intended that it was here that they were going to live, and then when he saw that that was so, behaved as though he had never known any other home.

May Beringer knew not a single soul in Polchester. Never before in her life had she been in a place where she knew nobody. She missed the kind landlady of St. Lennan very badly, but guarded herself against talking to strangers, being warned by her experience with the silver-haired gentleman.

But she liked the town greatly. It reminded her of Exeter, and yet there were not associations with dear Jane at every step. She was soon a familiar figure up and down the High Street and at the cathedral services. She was remarkably straight-backed and tall for her years, and people called her "the old Grenadier."

There was something comic about her, with her sallow face, her hooked nose, her old-fashioned garments, and the fox terrier trotting at her side. People always noticed her and wondered who she was. A little cracked, they thought she must be.

"Grenadier" was in fact the very last thing to call her. I said in my first account of her that she had always been frightened of everything; now, with her old age, her fears had accumulated upon her. Alone in this strange town, with no friend in the world, it was natural enough that she should know fear. There is a fear that comes upon lonely old people that is like no other fear. It is a fear bred of loneliness—the sight and sound of all these hurrying multitudes pressing in upon you, hurrying past you, looking with hard, careless eyes into yours. You are near the end of your days, you have lived all your life upon the earth, and this is what it has come to, that there is not a living soul who needs you nor thinks of you. Death is approaching, and there will be no one to be with you at the last. It were surely better that you had never been born.

In May Beringer's case there was this to be added, that soon—in six months' time or so—she would have no money. Unless she obtained some work what would happen to her? Work! As she looked at the crowds that passed her in the High Street and the Market-place she did not know how she would ever begin to ask for work. Had she been a peasant there would be things that she would have learnt to do. Like Mrs. Bloxam, she might have gone out charring. But because she was born a lady she could do nothing. Nothing.

Mrs. Bloxam was her one comfort. That kindly woman, after the first day or two and her natural reaction against a "messy dog"—when she had observed too that Pip, the animal, was not a bad dog at all, very clean in his habits and devoted to his mistress—decided that the poor old maid needed her services quite as badly as did the other two old women—more, indeed, because Mrs. Amorest had a quiet, assured courage of her own, and Mrs. Payne, although she was "that queer you never would believe unless you saw her," nevertheless had her own private sources of satisfaction. No, "that poor old Miss Beringer" needed her the most.

Mrs. Bloxam spent more than her fair share of time in that house, as her husband was for ever telling her. She had plenty of other work to be busy over, and more paying work too, but her "old ladies" were her chiefest charge. "Poor old sillies," she called them—"living all alone top of that shaking old house—shouldn't like——" she half-apologised to her husband. He when sober admired her and when drunk abused her, whatever she did, so that his opinion was of no very great value.

But her furrowed crimson face, her large round features, her char-woman straw hat stuck askew on one side of her head, her queer hoarse laugh as though she had a tankard of ale in front of her mouth, her way of standing, her thick legs spread, her head back, her hands on her ample hips—all these things were soon jewels beyond price to May Beringer, who, in no time at all, was telling her everything about her life even to the intimacies of her friendship with dear Jane.

At this point she always cried a little, and even Mrs. Bloxam rubbed one eye with the back of her hand, that was of the texture of alligator skin.

"To see that poor old dear sitting up in bed with her grey hair all about her face, with her old green muffler round her throat—poor worm!—you can't but pity her."

"You'm too soft-'earted—that's what's the matter with you, Jennifer," said Mr. Bloxam, sober for the moment. But Mrs. Bloxam was no angel, and to see her in one of her tempers was to be reminded of the Homeric ages. But May Beringer saw her at her best—for the time being, at any rate.

Chapter 4: Red Amber

It was not until the second Sunday after her arrival in Pontippy Square that May Beringer met Mrs. Amorest and Mrs. Payne.

It was a cold Sunday morning. From her bed May Beringer could see the sun like a red orange above the grey roofs of the houses. The houses were threaded with white frost, the smoke rose against the grey sky a greyer shadow, and the limbs of the one tree were silver-lined.

Did she move her head the sun appeared also to move and to rock in friendly greeting, and because the glass of the window was rough and coarse-grained the sun swelled as though with sudden ribaldry and then ran thin and tight like a drawn string.

It was warm in bed and cosy and faintly the bells could be heard. Two sparrows came hopping to the window and then a robin. Very soon her breakfast would come in and she could give them something. She had told Mrs. Bloxam that she would always have a boiled egg on Sunday as an extra to the toast and potted meat that was her customary fare.

At the thought of the egg she smiled and sat up in bed, bending over to the chair for her green sweater; she tied the arms of this tightly round her neck, allowing the body of it to fall over her breast, then she looked for the piece of amber and saw that it was there secure although scarcely visible in the dim light. Then she looked through the window again and saw the faintest thread of pale blue break the grey. So, it would be a fine day. A fine clear frosty Sunday! Could anything be nicer?

A moment later Pip was at the door welcoming Mrs. Bloxam, who arrived carrying pressed against her mountainous bosom a tray, and her black bonnet with black bugles (her Sunday wear) was pushed to the back of her head and her face was all smiles.

"Now, here's a nice Sunday sirprise, my dear," she shouted (she always shouted at her old ladies although they were none of them deaf). "There's that kind woman giving you one of her sausages this morning."

"What woman?" asked Miss Beringer.

"Why, to be sure, Mrs. Hamorest of course. I'd 'ardly been in 'er room two minutes when she says, 'Mrs. Bloxam,' she says, 'there's a sausage more than I can manage,' she says. 'I've been wondering whether Miss Bellringer' (Mrs. Bloxam's perversions were always of kindly intention) 'would like one,' she says. 'Of course, I 'aven't exactly called on 'er, but we're all friends in this 'ouse,' she says, 'or I'm sure we ought to be. You just ask 'er, Mrs. Bloxam. I know Mrs. Payne don't care for sausages,' she says; 'it's just waste giving them to 'er.' 'Why, mum,' I says to 'er, 'Miss Bellringer looks just the sort of lady to relish a sausage, and it's a friendly feeling in you, mum,' I says, 'and if Sunday isn't a day to be friendly on, where *will* we all be?' I says. Poor worm! and 'er looking so pretty sitting up in bed with 'er kind thoughts and 'er snow-white 'air and 'er pretty little ways. So, I just brought it along, miss, feelin' sure you'd relish it, and I've cooked it to a turn in Mrs. Hamorest's frying-pan—you just wait, my pretty, your turn's coming. Almost 'uman, miss, isn't 'e? More 'uman than some, I'm thinking."

During this time Mrs. Bloxam was arranging Miss Beringer's bed, patting and pushing the pillows, smoothing the sheets, and setting the tray so that it sat evenly over Miss Beringer's lap. When that lady saw the tea, the egg, the buttered toast, the crisp and bursting sausage, her pale face flushed. Not a bad beginning to a pleasant Sunday. And she must go in and thank Mrs. Amorest. She was longing for a friend. She ached to love somebody again. Mrs. Bloxam entertained her with gossip, giving her detailed horrors out of the *Sunday News* with infinite relish and gusto, lit the fire, tidied the room, took away the tray again, and departed.

Then May Beringer sank back into slumber again, the easy slumber of the old, and lying there, the green muffler yet tied about her neck, so pale she was and still that it might have been death that held her.

The clock ticked on, the dog also slept, there was not a sound in

234

the house. Then when it was nearly two o'clock, a coal fell out of the dying fire and crashed upon the grate, Pip woke and barked, up Miss Beringer started thinking the house on fire. She looked at the clock, and seeing how late it was, was soon out of bed. She washed in water icy cold, put on the warmest underclothing she had, and that was not warm enough. But she had been given by the landlady at St. Lennan a grey knitted woollen waistcoat, and this was a great comfort to her now. Her best clothes were her dark red jacket and skirt. The skirt was short both for the period and her age, but they were not yet faded and they were warm. She stared at herself in the little looking-glass over the wash-hand stand and was pleased. She looked young for her age, she thought. She was strong and healthy. It was not so absurd that she should find work as governess and companion.

For a moment her fears left her. She was brave and optimistic and happy. Full of this spirit she went out, Pip closely at her heel, crossed the passage, and knocked on Mrs. Amorest's door.

"Come in," said a little faint voice, and, entering, she was at once charmed—charmed with the neatness and tidiness of the room, some red-brown chrysanthemums in a thin silver vase, the old rose-coloured chairs, the blue and silver scene beyond the window, the orange fire faint like paper beneath the winter sun that flooded the place, and then the little woman with her snow-white hair, her beautiful hands, and the smile that shone in her eyes as, turning, she saw her visitor.

"It must be Miss Beringer," she said, coming forward.

"Yes, it is," said May Beringer, her long body trembling with inter-est and excitement. "I had to come in and just thank you for being so generous, as I am sure indeed you have been, to a perfect stranger and one whom you've never seen in your life before and have no reason at all to be kind to."

Miss Beringer always said everything twice or three times. It seemed to make her statement more definite.

"You *will* sit down, won't you?" Mrs. Amorest asked, drawing one of the armchairs near to the fire. "Because we are such very near neighbours we must know one another a little."

"I'm sure that's very kind of you," said May Beringer breathlessly. "I sound as though I'd been running up a whole flight of stairs, don't I? but I haven't really. It's only my nervousness. I'm always shy at meet-ing any one for the first time. I've always been so ever since a child, and indeed I can't remember a time when I wasn't nervous. As quite a little girl I was as shy as anything."

"You mustn't be shy with me," said Mrs. Amorest gently. "I'm a very unalarming person. What a delightful dog!"

"Yes, isn't he? I've always been partial to dogs. I've had dogs as companions for years and years. In fact, I'm never without a dog. His name's Pip!"

"Pip! What a nice name! Come here, Pip! Come and make friends."

Pip came, seeing that his mistress wished him to do so, but no one was very real to him save his mistress. However, he licked Mrs. Amorest's hand and then lay down, his head on his paws, waiting until his mistress should wish to move.

The two ladies considered one another. While talking amiably they were taking in one another's points. Each was thinking the other really old and pitying a little, but each needed a friend.

It was nevertheless very soon evident that May Beringer would be clay in the hands of Mrs. Amorest, and when that old lady realised that it was so there came into her heart not contempt (she felt contempt for no human being) but a little sigh, perhaps of regret. What she wanted was someone stronger than herself, someone on whose opinion she could rely, someone who would give her true and wise advice. It was very soon evident that May Beringer would be no projector of wise advice!

They talked a little, keeping their own confidences, and soon a silence fell. It was then that Mrs. Amorest said, "Now, I wonder. I had been thinking of going to the cathedral service this afternoon. Would you care to come too?"

As soon as she said it she wished that she had not, for reasons that were, for her, weak and snobbish. Poor Miss Beringer would attract attention walking into the cathedral: her face was odd, her clothes were odd, and Mrs. Amorest was sure that her walk would be odd. Mrs. Amorest, absolutely courageous though she was, hated to attract attention by any eccentricity. She hoped that Miss Beringer would decline, but at once, when she saw the light in Miss Beringer's eyes and heard the happiness in her voice as she said, "Thank you. I'll most certainly come. I'll go with you with pleasure," she was glad that she had suggested it. She thought to herself, "Poor old thing, she must be terribly lonely," and at that very same moment May Beringer was thinking to *herself*, "Poor old thing, I'm sure she's as lonely as anything. It must be wonderful to have someone to go with."

So, they went very happily together, slowly down the stairs because the stairs were dark although it was early afternoon, and then slowly through the streets because it was a cold and frosty afternoon. That at any rate was the reason that they gave to one another. The real reason was that their limbs were not so strong nor so active as they had been.

They still did not give one another any confidences, May Beringer having in her mind always the old man with the silvery hair, and Mrs. Amorest because, in spite of her recent rashness with Agatha Payne, she was very good at keeping her own counsel.

Nevertheless, by the time that they had reached the high cathedral door they were very good friends: May Beringer because she wanted someone to love willy-nilly, and Mrs. Amorest because she was touched by May Beringer's apparent helplessness. Within the quiet of the cathedral they were happy indeed. They sat in the back of the nave unnoticed by anybody, and although the seats might have been more comfortable (and why, indeed, are they not more comfortable?) they were very glad to sit down and rest.

Mrs. Amorest knew the cathedral by heart. She liked always to have the same place in the nave, almost the place where she was now sitting; thence she could see to her right framed between two pillars the window that had the pictures of the boy Christ, Christ with His mother, Christ playing with the boys by the river-side, Christ in the workshop, and the others.

She loved the colours, mistily purple and green and olive, but she loved it also for its subject, thinking of her own son, as she loved to do, when he had been small and helpless and divinely in need of her. Those days seemed to her but of yesterday, and closing her eyes she could see the bright blue Glebeshire skies and the sharp jagged teeth of the rocks, the valley running to the very lap of the sand, the white cottage set like a determined foot on the brow of the patient hill; Ambrose working at his poetry in the upstairs room with the slanting roof, and Brand in the garden crawling across the tiny plot of green to pull the cat's tail. . . .

All that she would see, and much more, as the organ wandered from pillar to pillar as though it were searching for her, and suddenly the clergyman's voice rose cutting the dimness and calling her to her prayers. She was never so near to her son as in that church, and while she stayed, her eyes closed, a hand seemed to be laid upon her brow and a voice to whisper to her that all was well with her and that she must be at peace.

She did not fear; she feared nor man nor woman nor life nor death—only God. But today instinctively as she sat there she realised that the woman next to her was compact of fear. She did not know how she had realised it, but this was true, and once again, as in her room, a little tremor of irritation shook her. She did not care for helpless people. Never in her life had she done so. She admired nothing so much as independence and courage, and perhaps that was the one lesson that life still had to teach her—tenderness for the weak. There was nothing she had admired so much in her son as his independence. She admired it also in old Agatha Payne.

But here was a woman who would, she foresaw, in no time at all, be depending upon her, wanting her advice, her assistance, her authority. Poor old thing! Mrs. Amorest, as they rose together to listen to the anthem, felt kindly indeed, and, because the anthem was Wesley's "Wilderness," her whole maternal being rose up in poor Miss Beringer's service. So much can familiar music do!

Miss Beringer, for her part, was not thinking overmuch of her companion. She was thinking of the comfort that it was to sit down, but the seats were hard, and there was a nice cosy light over everything—pretty place—pretty place—sleepy, sleepy—strangely sleepy . . . and then jerked awake to hear, far far away, the reading of the First Lesson.

No, she did not consider Mrs. Amorest very deeply, save that she wanted to love her. She wanted to love somebody, quickly, immediately, somebody of her own class with whom she could go for walks, and somebody, too, whom one could depend upon, somebody who would find work for her and advise her, and also somebody who would allow her to have her own way when she wanted it.

This old lady seemed really what she needed—old, of course, poor old dear, but then that was so pleasant for Miss Beringer to be of use to someone who needed her.

"The Wilderness and the Solitary Place . . ." sang the choir. At once May Beringer saw the long white stretch of the St. Lennan sands, the gulls wheeling with discordant cries through the grey air:

The Wilderness and the Solitary Place
Shall be glad—glad—glad—

Her legs were aching. Just below the knee there was a strange grinding pain. She looked about her to see whether anyone were sitting down. No one immediately close to her, and Mrs. Amorest as straight as a stick, her little head up like a bird's—a stick and a bird! A stick and a bird!

"The Wilderness and the Solitary Place." Truly the pain that had crept up now into her knees was too bad to be borne. She sat down. Mrs. Amorest did not turn her head, but May Beringer would like to have whispered, "It is not because I am truly tired, but I have today a pain in my knee. I can stand as well as you, but today I have a pain. Any one might have it."

And then she fell asleep, quite suddenly, and dreamt of Jane Betts. The general murmur of prayer which seemed to her in her dream to be the rustle of mice in the straw—she was about to call out to Jane "Take care, dear! Look out for the mice!"—aroused her. She slipped down upon her knees. They hurt her badly, and the wooden prayer-stool cut into her very bone. She could not think of her prayers because of the pain, but vaguely behind the pain ran the mice scampering about in her head. Afraid of what? Of the cat perhaps. A large dark cat with green eyes. She shuddered, and fear came down upon her like a large grasping hand, and she was glad that she could feel Mrs. Amorest's shoulder against her.

They walked home through the velvet-frosted dark. The dark, studded with stars and lights on the hills like the eyes of innumerable animals watching. Not cats, because they were not green, but tigers and lions, lions and tigers.

She explained this to Mrs. Amorest. They were walking very slowly because they were both extremely tired, but they would not mention this.

"They are like the eyes of lions and tigers," May Beringer said.

But Mrs. Amorest was thinking of the money that her cousin was going to leave her, and she did not hear. One thousand pounds! One thousand pounds! What might she not do? She and Brand together....

"Yes," she said, "don't they sing beautifully? Especially that boy.... There's something about a boy's voice that always makes me want to cry. Silly, of course. . ."

Poor old thing! She was deaf then as well as old! Poor old thing! When May Beringer spoke next, she shouted, but still Mrs. Amorest's mind was distant, and they arrived in Pontippy Square in silence, two very very weary old women.

Slowly, slowly they mounted the stairs, stopping on every landing for breath; and it was as though when they stood there they were listening for someone or something. They could hear only the beating of their hearts.

Arrived on their own floor May Beringer, breathless, gasped, "I always make a cup of tea about this time. I wonder whether you would come and drink it with me?"

Mrs. Amorest said that she would be delighted. "A minute to take my hat off."

When, later, she came into May Beringer's room she exclaimed with pleasure, "What nice things you have!" May Beringer's heart went out, bursting with love, to the dear old thing looking so charming there in the middle of the floor, with her neat little figure, her beautiful hair, her sparkling eyes. Here *was* someone to love indeed!

Mrs. Amorest admired everything,—the blue carpet, the round mahogany table, the four mahogany chairs, the armchairs, the bookcase, the pictures after Cuyp,—especially the bookcase.

"I do love reading, don't you, Miss Beringer? What have you got here? Mrs. Henry Wood! She writes *good* stories, I think. And those volumes of *Good Words*. I shall ask you to lend me one someday. And Sir Walter Scott. My husband always used to say that Sir Walter Scott had the true romantic spirit, although a little old-fashioned of course. But then my husband was more modern than I was. As of course he would be, being a writer. He wrote plays and poetry and was very well known in his time. Very well-known indeed. Ah! I see you have Tennyson. Don't you love *The Idylls of the King*? I do. That one about Guinevere is such a beautiful tale, I think, but sad, of course. Terribly sad. But then they did wrong, poor things, and it was right that they should be punished. Still, I can never help but be sorry for them a little. Tennyson was such a *noble* poet, I think. Perhaps a little *too* noble sometimes. Don't you think people can be *too* noble, Miss Beringer, just now and again?"

Mrs. Amorest's eyes twinkled as she straightened herself after looking at the bookcase. That was what her husband used to call "her wicked, sarcastic side"—the side of her that he had never understood, so that she had been forced to drive it under during their married life, but even now, after all these years, it would on occasion break out.

She moved around admiring everything, while May Beringer saw to the kettle. She saw then the piece of red amber. She stopped where she was, lost in wonder.

"Oh dear! What a beautiful thing!"

"Yes," said May Beringer, her voice awed and reverent, "that was given me by my dearest friend."

"How wonderful! I really never have seen anything so beautiful. May I pick it up for a moment?"

"Certainly. Do look at it." May Beringer's voice shook with pride.

When Mrs. Amorest had it in her hand she was pleased indeed. She loved beautiful things, but beautiful things were always so remote, behind shop windows, in museums or picture-galleries, always ticketed and catalogued, and above your head a notice that said "Don't touch."

When her hands closed about this and she felt its coldness and its strength, when she held it up to the light and saw the shaft of gold strike through to its very heart, when she saw the liquid bubbles of rich ruby red that danced in the cleft of thick, honey-coloured, misted fibre, when she saw the dragon with his flaming head and gold-flashing claws, when she felt its sturdiness and independence and form, she could only say and exclaim, as she replaced it reverently on the mantelpiece:

"You *are* fortunate to have it! It lights up all the room."

May Beringer *was* pleased! To praise her red amber was to praise her Jane Betts, and to bring straight back there into the room all that warm friendship and love, all those happy days. The kettle was boiling. The biscuits were spread upon the blue plate, the bread and butter was cut. They sat down happily to the round mahogany table.

"I have had a strange pain in my knee today," said May Beringer. "I think it must be the frost. I wonder whether the frost can have given me a pain in my knee. I really never have anything the matter with me. As a rule, there's nothing the matter with me at all."

"Well," said Mrs. Amorest, "I don't wonder. This sudden cold weather can give anyone anything. Now have you any Elliman's? Because I've always found that rubbing in a little Elliman's last thing at night is quite wonderful. Now if you haven't any I'd be only too glad——"

There was a knock on the door. Both ladies were startled. "Come in," said Miss Beringer.

The door slowly opened, then there was an interval during which nothing happened save that Pip drew back towards his mistress, growling. Then Mrs. Payne came forward. To Miss Beringer, unprepared for her, she must have been amazing enough. She was wearing her old red wrapper and her crimson shoes. Through her hair was stuck the black comb with the glass diamonds. Her shapeless body, her large heavy bosom, her high colour—one of the raggle-taggle gipsies indeed, hemispheres apart from the two Englishwomen who sat there looking at her.

She had been going to speak, her mouth had opened, a smile had been preparing, but at the instant of entering she had been transfixed, even as Lot's wife on looking back to the accursed cities of the Plains. She stared, her eyes, large and black and piercing, were held as though by the glory of the Lord; she put her hand up to her breast and, breathing deeply, seeing neither of the women in front of her nor anything in the room save the mantelpiece and its contents, gazed.

It had been unusual enough for her to leave her room. The cause had been the enthralling excitement of Mrs. Amorest's money. For days now she had considered it, and with every day and with every hour of every day the thing had grown more dominating.

If that old woman was going to be left one thousand pounds a year she would have some of it—a lot of it, half of it, more than half of it. The old woman was without a friend in the world, nor would she have a relation when her cousin died—you could not count that son of hers who, sure enough, had abandoned her for ever.

No; all that Agatha Payne had to do was to increase her influence, to make the old woman fond of her. Already she was fond of her; that was proved by the many occasions on which she came to visit her, but Agatha Payne must make her more fond of her. She must be very friendly and agreeable and neighbourly. . . . All day she had been forcing herself to be neighbourly, but her laziness was difficult to subdue. It was a cold day, although the sun was shining, and bed was very agreeable. As you went on through life, bed became more and more agreeable. But at last, around four in the afternoon, Agatha Payne had forced herself out slowly; as she washed and lazily put on a few clothes her brain crept round and round the thought of Lucy Amorest's money like a cat around a bird's cage.

She thought neither easily nor readily. Did she begin to think deeply, that pain bound itself about her head. She would sit before the old red tablecloth letting the cards slip through her fingers—knave of diamonds, four of hearts, queen of clubs, seven of hearts, three of clubs—and the fish would come swimming out of the green tank and would circle lazily about her head. Always she saw Lucy Amorest's money, like a fish larger than all the others and with dazzling scales of gold swimming just in front of her. She would put out her hand to touch it, but with a swerve of its tail it would be away, out of her reach, just above her head.

At last she became active enough to determine on a visit. She would go and see Lucy Amorest. So, with a flick of her eye sending the fish back into the tank again and leaving the cards loose on the table under the guardianship of Miranda, she opened the door, shuf-

242

fled across the hall, and knocked.

There was no answer from Mrs. Amorest's room. She knocked again. Still no answer. Where could the old woman be? She opened the door and looked in. No one there. She closed it and stood, licking her finger, considering. She would not be out, it was late now and dark. Ah, the other old lady, the new tenant! And suddenly the fear struck her that perhaps this new tenant, this Miss Bellringer or whatever Mrs. Bloxam said her name was, might also have her designs on Lucy Amorest's money.

Lucy Amorest had told her—why then should she not also tell Miss Bellringer? Agatha Payne's face grew angry and troubled. Let them just try, those two! She'd show them! Already it seemed to her that she had a right to Lucy Amorest's money, to part of it at any rate. Let anyone come in and deprive her of what was truly hers and she would show them!

It was with the sudden determination that they were at this very moment plotting together in there that she moved towards the third door farther down the passage (the one that had until lately concealed the life, hopes, and last torments of old red-faced Mr. Hopper, dead of double pneumonia) and knocked. Someone said "Come in," and she entered. It was immediately after that that the critical moment of her life came to her. She had been expecting to see nothing but two old women gossiping together; rather than that she saw, straight before her, as though it had been placed there for her especial glory, the heart and centre of all the colour of the world. The lamplight, the leaping fire illumined it. Ruby and crimson and amber, blood red and honey gold, threaded with flame and clouded with smoky bronze, the pedestal and the dragon came to her. From that instant of their mutual greeting they were one. Far back, deep set in her gipsy ancestry, she had been arrayed as a queen and colour of flame and fire and running splendour had been her rightful dower.

Now she clutched her soiled wrapper about her breasts and lusted for possession as never in her lazy, sensuous, imaginative life she had lusted before.

Mrs. Amorest, looking upwards, felt something strange in her gaze. It was strange that she should be here at all. But she did the honours. "Miss Beringer," she said, "this is Mrs. Payne who lives with us on this floor."

Agatha Payne came forward. Miss Beringer awkwardly rose, and, as she always did when she was nervous, giggled. Agatha Payne spoke in her deep thick voice:

"I am glad to meet you."

"You'll have some tea, won't you?" said Miss Beringer. "I'll fetch another cup. You must want some tea, I'm sure. I'll get a cup in a moment." She went to the cupboard and Agatha Payne settled down into the vacant chair, her eyes still on the mantelpiece.

"We've been to the cathedral," said Mrs. Amorest amiably, "and we've enjoyed it so much. They had that anthem about the Wilderness that I always like. A boy sang so well. Have you been out, Mrs. Payne?"

"No, I have not." Mrs. Payne smiled and did her best to look amiable. "Now don't you go out overtiring yourself. It would never do for you to be knocked up. We can't have you ill."

"Oh, really," said Mrs. Amorest, laughing, "I am very well indeed. I never was better. I did feel a little bit tired when I first came in, but I'm quite rested now. Miss Beringer's tea has done me a world of good."

Miss Beringer had brought another cup and Mrs. Payne had her tea. Her chair was too small for her. She billowed around it. Her eyes never left the mantelpiece.

"That's a beautiful thing you have there," she said at last.

"Oh, my piece of amber," said Miss Beringer nervously. "Yes, that's my piece of amber, my most precious possession. It was given me years ago by my dearest friend. I'm so glad you like it."

"I do like it," said Mrs. Payne, breathing deeply and staring at it so fixedly that you might think that she hoped to draw it to her, magnet-wise. "I do like it."

"I'm so glad you do," said Miss Beringer. "It's been much admired. Everyone likes it. They say I could get a great deal of money for it if I wished to sell it. It's worth a lot of money, I believe."

"Do you think you would sell it if you were offered a large sum?" asked Agatha Payne.

"Oh, dear no!" said Miss Beringer. "Nothing would induce me. It was a present from my dearest friend. The greatest friend of my life gave it to me. I would never sell it. Nothing would induce me."

Agatha Payne slowly rose. Her knees were trembling with excitement. "May I look at it closer?" she asked.

"Why, certainly," said Miss Beringer. "Please do."

Agatha Payne went close to the mantelpiece.

"May I have it in my hands a moment?" she asked.

"Yes, certainly," said May Beringer.

She took it, held it in both hands and stood there brooding over it, exactly as though she had been an old gipsy vagrant telling fortunes.

The cool texture of it, so different from its warm burning colour, stole through into the secret places of her heart. She felt, as she held it, that it was hers, that it had always been hers for ever and for ever and for ever.

She put it back, very tenderly, and her lips moved as though she had been bidding it a momentary farewell. Slowly she came back to the other two women. She sat down again and finished her tea. They talked a little, Pip slept, snapping at imaginary flies in his dreams. A silence fell and the old ladies sat, staring in front of them, lost also in their dreams.

Then Agatha Payne departed. She turned for a moment at the door and looked back at the mantelpiece.

When she was gone Miss Beringer broke out:

"Oh, I don't like her at all! Mrs. Amorest, do you like her? Don't you think there's something queer? There's something very odd about her indeed!"

Mrs. Amorest said, "Poor old thing! She lives so much alone. She's old and all by herself. We ought to be kind to her."

"Oh, I don't know," said Miss Beringer in great agitation, "I don't think I can be kind to her. I don't like her at all, I really don't. Did you see the queer way she looked at me?"

"She always looks a little strange," said Mrs. Amorest. "She has those big black eyes."

"It wasn't only those eyes," said Miss Beringer. "No, it certainly wasn't only those eyes. I'm sure she's going to do me a mischief. I know she is. And did you see the way she held my piece of amber? Just as though it was hers. I'm sure she'll steal it from me."

"Dear Miss Beringer," said Mrs. Amorest, "please don't disturb yourself. Mrs. Payne is a good woman. I know she is. I've known her for a long time. There's nothing to be afraid of."

"Oh, I don't know, I'm sure," said Miss Beringer. "I'm sure I don't know. It's very kind of you to say so, but I'm sure I don't know. I've always been afraid of something all my life. It seems to be my destiny. It's my fate to have something to be afraid of. I'm sure I don't like being under the same roof with her. She'll do something to me in my sleep."

Mrs. Amorest consoled her as best she could, but in her heart was a little scorn for this silly, frightened woman, and a foreboding that she herself would have a tiresome time with such a companion. She said goodnight kindly and, moved by her own good heart, bent forward and kissed the other's withered cheek.

"Don't you worry, dear," she said. "Have a good sleep and you'll find you won't be thinking of it in the morning."

But Miss Beringer did think of it. After Mrs. Amorest's departure she went to her door and locked it. Then she called Pip to her and sat with the dog straddled upon her lap, staring wide-eyed into the fading fire and every once and again giving a little shiver.

CHAPTER 5: CHRISTMAS EVE—POLCHESTER WINTER PIECE

It was a seasonable Christmas that year. Enough snow fell, then enough frost came, and then the sun shone. If it did not shine, at least it rode a circle of crimson fire through the heavens and, before the frost but after the slime of preparatory fogs, fragments of its fire splashed the High Street and spread in pools across the Precincts floor.

As I have intimated in other chronicles, Polchester of the old days was an enclosed town. The Riviera was unknown to it and the Garden of Allah a dream with Omar. Though London might call to the richer citizens on one occasion or another, at Christmas time every one stayed at home and, more wonderful yet to our modern disillusion, enjoyed family parties with Christmas trees, plum puddings, stockings, and the waif invited into the hall. It is not true, however, that the weather was any more romantic then than it is today; there were just as many rainy and muggy and foggy and dirty and dismal skies, and Glebeshire, warmer than any other part of the British Isles, has never had an intimate acquaintance with crisp and shining snow. About once in twenty years there are snowfalls, frosts, and blue skies, and how happy then everyone is and how eagerly everyone hands down the year to an envious posterity!

This was such a year, and ten days before Christmas the frost came and held, the powdered snow remained jewelled and resplendent, the sun looked down from a sky as delicately blue as an egg-shell and laughed to see the fun. And fun there was!

Magnet's toy-shop in the Market Cloisters had a Father Christmas, a true and veritable Father Christmas to be seen with two crimson cheeks and long snow-white beard any afternoon between two and four. Jeremy Cole so beheld him, and his sisters Mary and Helen, and the Dean's son Ernest, and the Fisher girls, and little Tommy Chawner. He did not say much, but he moved between the dolls and the trains, the balls and the soldiers, as only Santa Claus could move, with an authority, a benignity, a ripe wisdom that no impostor could have been clever enough to feign!

Everyone did their best. In the Market-place there was a Punch and Judy with a thick-set jolly-faced man in charge, and he might have been that very same Garrick, friend of Maradick, whose history has been elsewhere narrated. I don't say he was, and I don't say he wasn't. Half-way up the High Street, Gummridge's the stationers had a whole Christmas tree in their window. Here was a stumbling-block to the whole High Street traffic. It was quite impossible to get any child—any perambulator baby indeed—past that window. It was a tree frosted, coloured, and shining, hung about with every glittering bauble, shaped to a perfect pinnacle of exquisite symmetry.

But best of all was the window of Hunt & Griffin, the General Store, for here, for the first time in Polchester history, was a whole front window given over to pageantry, to none other than the scene in the life of Cinderella when, despondent beside the fire, she is amazed by the sudden apparition of her peaked-hatted Godmother. There is the fire and there Cinderella, there the pots and pans, the brick floor, and the huge kitchen rafters, there the Godmother, and there beyond the snow-lined window-pane the vision of the gold coach and the snow-white ponies. So great was the confusion outside this window that had this occurred in these traffic-haunted times the show must have been forbidden, but in those lucky days nobody minded, nobody cared. Let the children have a good time, Christmas comes but once a year, and even Mrs. Sampson, although her neuralgia was at its height, could not but admit that the window made a happy display.

The town rang during those days with laughter. Propter Hill outside the town had just enough snow on it to allow of tobogganing, and Pol Fields, having been flooded, gave for a whole wonderful fortnight the most marvellous skating. The town rang with laughter and the ringing of bells. The cathedral let itself go and burst into perpetual peals of merriment to the great annoyance of late sleepers, dyspeptics, and ruminating essayists. There was fun everywhere, apples and oranges in the Market-place, and carols up and down the streets after dark.

It was the best Christmas that Polchester had known for many a day past or would know for many a day to come.

Mrs. Amorest was one who had always enjoyed a seasonable Christmas. To her as to every old person Christmas was filled with sad memories, but she had a wonderful gift of enjoying fun at the moment of its occurrence, and being aware that she was so enjoying it, and because the fun in her life had been neither frequent nor extravagant very small occurrences amused and excited her.

This was the happiest Christmas known to her for many a day.

Struggle as she might not to think of the money coming to her, she could not keep it out of her consciousness. She told herself again and again (and when she was alone in her room she repeated the words aloud sometimes) that she must not place too strong a reliance on her cousin's promise. "He may have altered his mind the next moment. It's silly to believe him." Nevertheless, the solemnity of his words, the caress of his hand as it rested on her head—these things were difficult to dismiss.

And the happiness that came from the promise was also difficult to dismiss. She was naturally happy. Give her the least excuse and she must be happy. Although she believed that God did not intend that human beings should be very happy because they were in this world for the training of their souls, and souls were better trained by sorrow than by joy, nevertheless an imp of happiness would continue to jump in her heart and stir her little world with his discordant cries of joy. Joy at what? A kindly action, a splash of sun across the street, a barrel-organ round the corner, a stained-glass window, an apple, and a piece of cheese. She *could* not keep down her spirits as, being a penniless, lonely old widow of over seventy, she should.

And, this Christmas, she lost completely her self-control. She adored above everything else in the world the spending of money, perhaps for the very reason that she never had very much to spend. She had never been able to believe that statement often written in the papers that millionaires did not know what to do with their money. Did not know! Why, she could spend a million pounds quite easily at Gummridge's alone! But there! The newspapers were never to be trusted. She liked greatly to be given things, but still better was it herself to make presents. The excitement of giving someone something he or she wanted was intense, to watch the opening of the parcel, to see the stare of pleasure and surprise, to hear the exclamation, to feel the affection flowing out—was there any luxury in life like it?

And it was a luxury that, of late, she had been compelled to deny herself. Last Christmas she had given Agatha Payne half a dozen pocket-handkerchiefs, Mrs. Bloxam a piece of ribbon, and her cousin a pocket-book. Worst sorrow of all, it was impossible to send Brand anything. No use to throw parcels out into the void. The best she could do was to write two letters, one a month in advance, and this she sent to the only address she had, something in California, and then one on Christmas Eve, such as she had always written to him at Christmas time. This she also sent out to California, but she wrote it because for a moment it brought him closer to her—she felt, with his photograph up there in front of her, as though she had him with her in the room. These were all but poor substitutes for reality, and, cheat ourselves as we may, our subconscious selves refuse to be deceived. Mrs. Amorest knew nothing about her subconscious self, but she did know that after last Christmas she had a miserable sense of inadequacy and frustrated purpose. She had made nobody happy.

Even Mrs. Bloxam had disappeared into the intimacies of her family to emerge two days later with a black eye and a bruised cheek. This year she would fling her cap over the mill. She had prospects. She did not face them finally, those prospects, did not take them, hold them in front of her, look them in the eyes and say to them as one always ought to do to prospects, "Now, are you sound and healthy? Have you got heart and lungs and legs and arms and a good stiff back?" No, she merely reported on them—she heard that they were good and healthy and promised very well indeed! Then she went ahead.

The plan came to her in the middle of the night, or rather in one of those early morning hours when the first cock crows and the hidden despair raises its abominable head. Lying there in the early morning she drove her despairs away and considered Miss Beringer. Poor Miss Beringer! What a frightened, nervous, trembling creature she was! She would like to do something for her! She would like well to give her a happy Christmas! And Agatha Payne, too. It was then that the idea came to her.

At first, she was frightened of it. It would demand energy and persistence. And *had* she money enough? Money in the future would not do. She examined her purse and found that she had sufficient did she use part of next quarter's rent. She trembled at that, but she was sure that kind Mr. Agnew, when he knew of the promise that her cousin had made to her, would not hesitate to advance her. . . .

She trembled. Her heart warned her. Her cheeks were flushed and she had a guilty air. But she held to her purpose, and once she had begun she did not look back. Once she had begun she *could* not look back. She moved, during those frosty coloured days, about the town, the very spirit of adventure. She found that she must go quietly. The excitement tired her, and sometimes she would, in a moment, feel so weary that she *could* not get to the top of the High Street, and on one occasion when she was at the top she could not go down again and had to take refuge in the shop of Mr. Bennett, the grand bookseller. There she sat, greatly alarmed, on a chair in the very middle of the shop with busts of Byron and Walter Scott looking down on her and a grand smell of Russia leather and old vellum in her nostrils, and the complete works of George Eliot at her elbow.

Old Mr. Bennett was very kind to her although she told him at once that she was not there to buy anything, and who should come in at that very moment but Archdeacon Brandon himself, magnificent, handsome, superb, ordering somebody "on the Psalms" with the air of a king and a conqueror. She looked around her with the hope of seeing some of her husband's plays, and when she did not would have liked to ask Mr. Bennett whether he kept them in stock, but her courage failed her and she could only thank him very much and slip out of the shop as quietly as possible. Fortunately, she did not hear the archdeacon's question: "And who was that shabby little woman?" He asked out of all kindness, feeling it his duty as the father of the flock to keep his eye upon all the inhabitants of the town.

She tried to keep her head about her purchases. She found, as many another has found before and after her, that the best things were always the most expensive. And then when it came to the central purchase of all, to the core, the heart, the kernel, the pinnacle, the *pièce de résistance*, the *raison d'être*, and any other foreign phrase that you prefer, she found that *here* expense was inevitable. Try as you would, it must cost more than you had supposed.

Of course she only wanted a small one, but even the small ones. . . . And then at the last, two days before Christmas, she found in the Market-place, in a corner behind the old woman under the green umbrella, the very thing, a darling, a perfect specimen, a miracle, and, when she enquired of the nice round-faced man whose possession it was, she found that it was only . . . well, less than the experience of the last two days had led her to believe possible, although more, a good deal more, than she had originally intended. She bought it and ordered that it should be sent to her room, blushing a little in spite of herself as she named the address. She gave her name very carefully, begging him to be watchful that it should not be sent to any other room by mistake, and he promised her, saying that he would himself bring it.

He did in fact arrive with it when she was there, and she liked him very much, holding him in conversation for quite a while, and then giving him an orange for the baby. After that she guarded her room like a dragoness and would not allow May Beringer, who was already forming a too constant habit of "dropping in," to cross her threshold.

Christmas Eve arrived, and Mrs. Amorest, awaking to the inspiring voice of Mrs. Bloxam, was delighted when she discovered how fine and clear it was; no wind, the smoke rising from the chimneys elephant grey against the blue, the thin rind of frost, the sparrows already chattering at her window for their crumbs.

After her little mid-day meal, she sat down to the table, found her paper and envelopes, and wrote to Brand.

Her letter was as follows:

My dearest, darling Boy—I must write to you as I always do, although I sadly fear that it will be a long time before you get this letter. The one that I wrote to you a month ago may reach you before Christmas, and I hope it will. This I am writing because it seems as though I am talking to you, and I don't wish to allow Christmas to pass by without having a word with my dear boy. Perhaps you have been writing to me and still to the old address. I told them in Cheltenham to forward anything on, but they are so stupid at the post office, although, as a matter of fact, I always think it wonderful, considering the sort of postmen one sees walking about, that they don't lose more letters than they do—quite boys some of them are, and they none of them have very intelligent faces, although I daresay they are good men.

Well, dearest boy, I try to imagine to myself the kind of Christmas you are having, but it is really difficult for me, because you told me in the last letter I had from you that it was quite hot at Christmas time. That seems to me very strange and not very nice, I think. Of course, it is often warm here for Christmas. Both last year and the year before that we had rain and muggy weather, but this year it is delightful, with a hard frost and the sun shining, cold and seasonable. It's so pleasant for the children and more healthy for everybody, I am sure.

I am very well in health. That cough I had when I wrote to you last has quite gone away and I am sure it's those lozenges that I found at Cubitt's (he's our best chemist here in the High Street). If only I could hear that you are quite well and will come home soon for a visit I would be quite happy. You know, dear boy, I am an old woman now and can't expect to live for ever, so that I do hope you'll be able to come home soon. It's very nice here and I'm very comfortable. There's something else I'd like to tell you about, but I suppose that I must not just yet because it isn't quite settled. I think of you so much and pray for you night and morning. At this time of the year when God came down to earth and took upon Him our flesh and was a little baby in a manger, I think we should all make Him feel how thankful we are. I know that He is looking after you and so I don't worry about you. At least I know that you are warm. You used to be so careless about your underclothing when you were a little boy. My dearest boy, you are always in my thoughts.—

Your loving

Mother

She sat for a long time after she had written the letter with his photograph in front of her. She thought of him in all the ways that she had known him—as a baby at her breast, as a small boy in his first trousers, as a boy going to his first day-school and forgetting her so quickly in the new excitements of other boys and games and masters, as all right and proper boys must do, of course. And then, as he grew, her interest in the strange new personality that developed, as flower from the bud—a personality that was so strange because it was like neither herself nor his father, somebody quite new. And then his growing independence, his chafing at the literary and artistic interests of his father, his desire for the open-air life and complete independence. Then her own strange sympathy with him; and although she loved him so dearly she understood that he should want to get away and be free.

She had felt it herself in her married life, and she realised that he *was* her own son, not by right of the quiet and domestic character that was most obvious in her, but by right of that secret independence and sharpness of judgement that her married life had subdued in her. He left her and at intervals returned to her. She had been a woman of forty when she had borne him, and he had been only twenty-seven when she had last seen him, still a boy although so strong and independent! She looked at the photograph until she seemed to draw him out of the frame and he came to her and put his arms round her and teased her in the old laughing way that he had always had. But she was not simply a sentimental woman; she was in fact scornful of emotion that led to nothing, and so she put the photograph back upon the mantelpiece, put on her bonnet and her coat, and, because it was already three o'clock and would soon be dusk, hurried off to take her present to her cousin.

This year she was giving him a picture, a photogravure in a nice black frame of Holman Hunt's "Carpenter's Shop." She had not been quite lately to visit him lest she should seem to be reminding him of his promise. She had not heard how his health was, but she hoped that this bright weather had helped him, and that he would perhaps see her. Nevertheless, as she crossed the bridge and climbed the hill a little chilling wind, whence she knew not, breathed upon her heart. Rising out of the dark purple-hued river appeared the figure of Agatha Payne.

She saw, quite unexpectedly, reasons for May Beringer's terrors. There *was* something alarming about Agatha, something not quite normal and healthy, something odd and twisted. It came, perhaps, because the poor old thing lived so much alone, but Mrs. Amorest gave a little shiver and thought to herself that she would move from that house in the spring to somewhere brighter and more companionable. She could not drive the company of Agatha from her mind. All up the hill it kept pace with her, and then, in another flash of memory, she saw a picture of her childhood, something that had not come to her for many a year. It was a picture that used to hang in the dining-room, of a witch weaving her spells in a dark and lonely wood. Before her was a large iron pot into which she flung toads and snakes and strange purple-tinted leaves. From the cauldron came a blue thick smoke. It was true that the witch did not physically resemble Agatha. She was old and skinny, with a back bent double and long groping fingers, but there was something . . . something. . . .

And then, pausing for breath before she entered her cousin's gate, she smiled at her folly. Her practical mind drove her fancies like mist into the frosty air.

The house, always ugly and forbidding, seemed simply not to belong to the fresh and wonderful day. The woods that fringed the hill were marvellous in their mystery, the fragments of the river that gleamed among the brown folds of the sloping fields glittered like shreds of broken glass faintly amethyst, the powdered frost shone and twinkled in the sharp and friendly air, but the house was untouched by this beauty; aloof and hostile it seemed to deride and despise any spirit that could wish goodwill to men and friendship to all the world. To Mrs. Amorest especially, as she approached it, it seemed to say: "You aren't truly so sentimental as to believe that the human race is loving and kind. Rid yourself of your illusions. You should be ashamed of yourself at your age that you have any."

As she rang the bell and heard it clang defiantly through the house she felt again a dim and unhappy foreboding. She always disliked her meeting with the housekeeper. She felt that that woman despised and patronised her, and now today she wished that she might encounter no one who raised hostility in her heart. But one could only pass to her cousin over the housekeeper's body. There was no other way for it.

The woman herself opened the door and was more forbidding than she had ever been. Mrs. Amorest suspected that in some way she had learnt about her cousin's promise. Always before there had been a tacit recognition, however reluctant, that Mrs. Amorest had some right there. Today she blocked the doorway with her peevish ill-natured body and showed no sign at all of moving. Mrs. Amorest felt a sudden, almost affectionate, pity for her gift. It had cost, as it seemed to her, a large sum, but in the eyes of this woman it would be simply another wheedling attempt on her part to exhort more money from her cousin. She summoned her courage and smiled her friendliest smile.

"Good afternoon. How is my cousin today?"

"Not at all well, I'm afraid."

"Oh dear, I am sorry to hear that. I thought that this fine weather might have done him some good."

There was no answer to this, so after a little pause Mrs. Amorest, feeling the chill of the afternoon air, said:

"Of course, it *is* cold, isn't it, but I thought that, being in bed, he might not notice it. Has the doctor been today?"

"Yes, the doctor has been."

Well, she might ask me into the hall, thought Mrs. Amorest. "Could I see him for a moment, do you think?"

"I'm afraid not, Mrs. Amorest. It was the doctor's orders that he was not to be disturbed."

"Not for a moment? I really would not bother him. Just to wish him a happy Christmas."

"I'm afraid not. Those were the doctor's orders."

"Would you not ask him whether he would not see me for a moment?"

"I'm sorry, but he is not to be disturbed by anybody."

There was a pause, and then Mrs. Amorest said cheerfully: "Oh, well, I'm sure that's quite right if the doctor says so. I only wanted to wish him a happy Christmas. I have a little gift." She produced it from under her arm. "I have written a little note in case I should not be able to see him. Would you kindly give it to him?"

"Certainly."

She took the parcel, looking neither at it nor at Mrs. Amorest, but forward into the brown and naked garden with a frown of determination as though she were forewarning some plant that was whispering hopefully about the spring that she was not going to stand any of that sort of nonsense.

There was another little pause, then Mrs. Amorest said: "Would you most kindly wish him a very happy Christmas for me? Of course, I know that it can't be a *very* happy Christmas for him as ill as he is, but I always think it makes a difference if one knows that people are thinking of one, don't you?"

"I will certainly tell him."

"And I hope you'll have a happy Christmas too," said Mrs. Amorest, trembling with the cold, and wishing altogether in spite of her better feelings that the woman should herself know what it was to be kept out of a warm house on a cold day.

"Thank you very much, Mrs. Amorest. I wish you the same, I'm sure."

That was all. There was nothing more to be done. The door closed with a horrible final clang, and in some strange flash of vision she knew that she was never to enter that house again.

She walked down the hill, and, in spite of all her courage, forebodings now crowded upon her. It was true that it was not her cousin's fault that he had not seen her. He had not known that she was there. But surely, she had been foolish to build upon his idle word! And that woman. She had designs. She certainly had designs. She had looked at Mrs. Amorest with a hostility that could mean only one thing. And a sick man was so helpless, the worse his sickness the weaker he was. . . . As she crossed the bridge over the Pol it seemed to her that in another moment her courage would desert her. Because if that money did not come to her!

She summoned all her pluck, standing for a moment on the bridge and watching the river take on its evening colour, softly purple under the dark shadow of the rising hills.

Then, thinking of the evening that was coming and the fun that it would be, she smiled. Things always turned out better than you expected. The stars that were now breaking into the sky above her head were the eyes of God. She was watched over and cared for and protected. She had no need to fear.

The town as she passed up through the High Street was bubbling with merriment and gaiety. The shops blazed with lights; the street was crowded; everyone was laughing and happy, hurrying along loaded with parcels, stopping to speak, it seemed, to anyone who was near that they might wish them good luck. This was the world that Mrs. Amorest loved. Why might it not always be like this? She stopped at the Cinderella window. How pretty and touching! She turned round to a stout man beside her and said, "Isn't it pretty?"

"Indeed, it is, mum," he answered her, smiling. "My little girl wants to take it home. Don't you, Pansy?" and a diminutive child squeaked out "Yes."

"What a pretty little girl!" said Mrs. Amorest.

"Thank you, mum," answered the fat man. "A merry Christmas, I'm sure."

"And the same to you," said Mrs. Amorest.

The rest of the way home seemed easy.

Arrived in her room, she set about the development of her plan. She had asked Agatha Payne and May Beringer to come and visit her at eight o'clock. She had two hours for her preparations. The time flashed by and in a moment, it was a quarter to eight. She hurriedly put on her silk dress, hung around her neck her thin gold chain with the locket that held Brand's portrait, brushed her lovely white hair, put on her lace cap fresh and crisp from the laundry, then her stiff white cuffs. Finished. Completed. She sat down to survey her work. A smile played about her lips. It was the most beautiful thing that she had ever seen in her life.

At five minutes past eight there was a knock on her door, and then another knock. Agatha Payne and May Beringer entered. They stood bewildered on the threshold.

It was indeed a pretty sight. The curtains were drawn and the far end of the room was duskily shadowed, but at the fireplace end stood—the tree!

And what a tree! Of just the right size for the room, it had a shape and symmetry that surely no other tree in all Christmasdom could equal. It tapered gradually with exquisite shape and form to a point that quivered and flickered like a green flame. On the flame sturdily triumphed Father Christmas, diminutive in body, but alive in his smile, his stolidity, his gallant colour. It was the colour that entranced the eye. Mrs. Amorest had worked with the soul of an artist. She had not overburdened the slender branches. The thin chains of frosted silver that hung from bough to bough seemed of themselves to dance in patterned rhythm. Balls of fire, emerald and ruby, amethyst and crystal, shone in the light of the candles. And at every place colour blended with colour. The tree was always the tree. The light that flashed from its boughs was not foreign to it, but seemed to be, integrally, part of its life and history. It had been placed on a long and broad looking-glass, into which it looked down as though into a lake of crystal water. The candles seemed to be the voices of the tree; it was vocal in its pleasure, its sense of fun at its own splendour, its grand surprise that after all it had come off so well.

In proportion, in blending of colour, in grandeur of spirit, it was the finest tree in England that night. On either side of the tree were two tables spread with white cloths. On one table were some parcels beautifully tied with coloured ribbons, and on the other sandwiches, a plum-cake with white icing, some saffron buns, and a dish of sweets and chocolates.

The two ladies stood amazed. So pretty was the room with its soft pink colours, its light dim, save for the aureole of golden splendour shed by the tree, so utterly unexpected the display, that words would not come; only at last May Beringer cried, "Oh dear! Dear me! Dear me!"

Both ladies had dressed in their party best; May in her orange silk, that suited her, I fear, not too well, and Agatha in her dark purple, a dress of a fashion now forgotten, too small for her, but that neverthe-less with her black hair finely brushed, her dark eyes flashing, gave her the air of older days, the air that had made Mr. Payne, thirty-five years ago, call her his "Gipsy Queen."

"Oh, I do hope you won't both think me too silly," said Mrs. Amorest, coming forward, "but I simply had to do something this Christmas. We've just done nothing the last two Christmases and it did seem too bad. Don't you think so? I do hope you don't mind?"

"Mind?" said May Beringer, coming towards the tree and gazing at it with her mouth open like a schoolgirl. "Why, Mrs. Amorest, it's lovely! It's the loveliest thing! Why, I can't speak. I can't, indeed. Words won't come. I can't say anything at all."

Agatha Payne was moved more deeply still. The colour possessed her as colour always possessed her, coming towards her like a living breathing person, holding out its arms to her, whispering to her, "You and I! We are the only ones here who understand. I have been waiting for you, and you alone."

Indeed, it seemed to her that the tree belonged to her and was hers absolutely. The two other women vanished from her consciousness; she could see only the pale golden flame of the candles, so steady, so pure, so dignified, the balls of amethyst and ruby and crystal as they swung and turned and gleamed so slightly and yet always with a secret life and purpose of their own.

And the deep green of the tree, richly velvet under the light of the candles! She stood absorbed, entranced, waves of sensuous pleasure running through her body.

So silent were they both that after a minute had passed Mrs. Amorest was alarmed.

"I'm so glad you like it," she said almost timidly. "Shan't we sit down and look at it? I like to think of all the other trees there are tonight in everybody's homes and the children dancing round them and the presents——"

She broke off because a longing for Brand came to her so urgently that it was all she could do not to call out his name. For a moment it seemed to her foolish humbug, sham, and ridiculous sentiment, that the three of them, old, forgotten, not wanted by anybody, should indulge in this display. But looking up at the tree she was comforted. Anything so beautiful had its own purpose. She had made a beautiful thing. She felt the joy of the creator in her handiwork.

They sat in a row looking at the tree. May Beringer was, all in a moment, voluble. She had so much to tell them,—of the trees that she had known, the trees that she had had in her own house, the trees that she and Jane Betts had decorated together, the Christmas festivities that they had had in Exeter (you would think to hear her that Exeter was the centre of all the splendour and gaiety of the world). Oh! she talked and laughed and was so wildly excited that she nearly cried.

Agatha Payne said very little. She only stared and stared at the tree.

The next part of the entertainment arrived. Mrs. Amorest picked up the parcels in their lovely white paper and coloured ribbon and, blushing a little (shell pink faintly colouring the ivory of her cheeks), said:

"These are little tiny things that I got. You mustn't laugh at me, please, for getting them. I think the chief part of a present is that it should be wrapped up in paper, don't you? But I hope you'll like them."

And they did like them. At least May Beringer liked hers. She had a case with three pairs of scissors and a book in a purple cover, *The Light of Asia*, by Sir Edwin Arnold. Agatha Payne said little about hers—only "Thank you, Lucy," in a deep hoarse-throated murmur. She had a box of coloured cottons and a purple blotter. She could not take her eyes away from the tree.

Then they cut the cake and ate the sandwiches, and Mrs. Amorest made tea and listened happily, cosily to May Beringer's reminiscences.

How happy it was with the blazing tree, the dim room, the bells pealing beyond the window, the crackling fire!

Each old lady forgot the other. They were lost in their own world of remembered and recaptured life,—past joys, past sorrows, past desires, past regrets. The clock ticked on, the candles burnt with steady flame, the bells rang out.

Gradually Lucy Amorest closed her eyes. She heard May Beringer's voice from a vast distance. Then her own faintly replying, "How curious! Indeed . . . In . . . deed."

Her head sank upon her breast. May Beringer also, bathed in the warmth of the room, comforted with tea and happiness, closed her eyes. Her head nodded—once and twice and thrice. She pulled herself up. Stared sharply at Mrs. Amorest. Saw two Mrs. Amorests, then three. Her head fell. She also slept.

Only Agatha Payne, her dark eyes fixed, sat, without moving, staring at the tree.

Chapter 6: Agatha Secretly . . .

On the following evening Agatha Payne entered Mrs. Amorest's room and asked her whether she would light the tree again. She did so, but the candles were now very low. They flickered up in wild and despairing flares. One caught a branch and must at once be extinguished. The two ladies sat there watching the death of the tree. It was Christmas night and very silent. The ladies said very little to one another, and at last Agatha Payne with a husky "Goodnight" vanished.

Agatha's soul was like a house of many stories. In youth she had lived in the top story, attic in shape but with a truly fine view from the windows. Here there had been light, air, and fine prospects. Then as the years passed she moved down on to the middle floor, where she was exercised about the furniture of the bedroom and held elegant receptions in the drawing-room. After the middle years she moved definitely on to the ground floor and lived during a great part of her time in the dining-room nibbling at the crystallised cherries, squeezing the pears on their china dish, and slipping into her mouth the chocolate almonds. There was no view from the dining-room windows.

But the first time she stumbled down over the dark stone steps into the cellars was one day after her husband's death, when her sister-in-law came to visit her. She hated her sister-in-law because her sister-in-law was afraid of her. She hated and despised her, so she pushed her down the cellar steps in front of her, made her scream, showed her the dank, dark place, and hauled her up again. For herself, she saw that there were things in the cellar that interested her—rows of dusty wine-bottles, spiders' webs, and broken furniture. She came to live down there almost entirely. Of course, here there was no view at all.

This was her own house and nobody else lived in it at all, but in the house in Pontippy Square there were several other lodgers.

Living deep in her own cellar with her fish and her coloured cards, she had not been until now aware of the life beyond her. Lucy Amorest a shade, and behind that shadow others yet more shadowy.

She was vaguely conscious of desires, but deep down in her cellar she had grown unaccustomed to the full light. She was uncertain of the division between reality and unreality. Nor did she greatly care.

Old people, when they are happy and contented, are the spectators of life. They sit and watch with smiles on their faces, and hands happily folded. But let them feel that they have not had enough out of life, that life has treated them ill, that there is still time to snatch a valuable or two, and they will plunge into the *mêlée*, cap awry, hair disordered, and will, as likely as not, make a pretty scene of terror and dismay before Death with his bony fingers leads them out of the battle.

Agatha Payne had for many a day now been a spectator only of her own emotions and atmosphere; now in a flash the thin bony body of May Beringer and her piece of red amber were in front of her, tugging at her, dragging her out of her lethargy and idleness, possessing all that was left of her imagination and lustful desires.

It was after that Christmas Eve and the lighting of the tree that the whole forces of her spirit began once again to move. She thirsted for a continuation of that pleasure that was so sharp in its apprehension that it was a lust. She wanted something; she must have it; she must have that piece of red amber. She must have it not only because she wished that her eyes should be able to rest on it whenever they desired to do so, but also because she wished that it should be hers, hers body and soul; she wanted that response from it that you only get when you are master. She wished that when she put her hands about its cold smooth surface she could feel that its heart was beating at her touch, and that it knew that it belonged to her and to her alone.

She must have it, and she would get it, because Mrs. Amorest (who was coming into money and would be very rich) would buy it for her from May Beringer.

And if May Beringer would not sell it? Here began the second impulse of her excitement. She had, at the first view, not disliked the woman. She had had no very active feelings concerning her. Then she had perceived that the woman was afraid of her.

As the rabbit is to the snake, as the sparrow is to the hawk, as the mouse is to the cat, so was timidity to Agatha Payne. She was not, take her life from first to last, a cruel woman. She had, in the first periods of it, done kindly actions. She could admire, she understood loyalty, she remembered brave deeds. But did anyone cringe to her, did she detect fear in the eyes raised to her, then a savage satisfaction warmed her heart and the stir of persecution crept into her eyes. Even then she did not actually intend cruelty. She felt a scorn for any coward, and when, added to the scorn, there was irritation, it was natural enough that it should be sharp and contemptuous. After that curiosity had led her forward. Was anybody so true a coward as that? Could their fear lead them to such subterfuges? If she did this, would their action be that? Of what stuff *could* they be made?

That was in her younger days. For a number of years now she had not moved sufficiently into the outer world to encounter new personalities—neither Mrs. Amorest nor Mrs. Bloxam feared her.

She was also moving in her cellar ever deeper and deeper into the dusk. It was hard for her to see now because of the shadows. Her curiosity was less active than her desire to satisfy her thirsts and hungers. When she lusted for the red amber it was because she wished to draw it into herself. She sat like a spider lazily in the centre of a web that had grown up around her rather than been actually created by her. She would draw May Beringer into the centre of it and eat her up did she not let her have that piece of red amber.

But she bore May Beringer no ill-will. She only lazily despised her.

Then as the days passed her consciousness was aroused more actively and she began to hate her. She hated her for the noise that her slippers made, for the way that she sniffed and would not use her handkerchief, but especially for her nervous "Bye-bye" with which she always ended their meetings.

"Bye-bye," "Bye-bye," "Bye-bye," bleating like a sheep. And what a thing for a lady to say, and, if say it she must, why not bravely and with spirit instead of that timid, unctuous eagerness?

Agatha, back in her room after a visit, would stand looking at her fish, at Miranda, and the cards, would stamp her foot and mutter "Bye-bye—Bye-bye. Bye-bye. Idiot!"

She hated, too, May Beringer's dog, as crawling and sycophantic as its mistress. She stood glowering at it, casting spells over it, wishing it evil; and the dog knew standing there, with its head down, shivering, giving her once and again a supplicating glance.

So, during these wet, muggy January days she made it her habit to pay May Beringer visits. She went because the red amber irresistibly drew her. She must see it every day, and if possible twice a day. And soon she went because she wished to see that terrified glance flash into May Beringer's eyes. She liked to see it there. It should be there permanently before she had done with her.

Old Mrs. Payne was looking, Mrs. Bloxam declared, ten years younger.

On the other hand, she did not forget Lucy Amorest; or perhaps, to speak truly, Lucy Amorest's money. She was vague about Mrs. Amorest's money as she was about everything in the outside world. Someone must die before it became Mrs. Amorest's, but somebody would die very soon. She had only to look at the cards, to allow them to trickle through her fingers, to rattle on to the table, to perceive clearly how soon somebody would die. . . .

And then there was the old woman with more money than she could use.

She would appear at Mrs. Amorest's door, tall and shapeless and silent. Staring. It was generally in the early dusk of the winter afternoon, and often in these days the rain tickled the window-panes and rustled about the coals. Mrs. Amorest would be reading her book. She would look up and see the tall old woman there.

She was not afraid of Mrs. Payne, but since she had realised May Beringer's alarm she had been aware of a sort of uncertainty, a discomfort, a hesitation. She felt now a purpose in Agatha Payne's visits. The woman was after something. But what? There was nothing that Mrs. Amorest had that *could* attract her. And yet there she was, wanting something.

She wished, too, to be friendly. When Mrs. Amorest looked up she saw her leaning against the post of the door, smiling in a grim, strange way.

"Come and sit down, dear," Mrs. Amorest would say, laying her book on the table, and in her lumping, clumsy fashion Agatha Payne would shift to a chair and overflow into it. On a certain January afternoon of storm and rain, it seemed that she had made up her mind to something. She stared with her motionless black eyes for some while before speaking, then at last she broke out:

"How's your cousin, Lucy?"

Mrs. Amorest, startled, raised her snow-white head. "My cousin?"

"Yes. The one who's dying and leaving you his money."

"Oh, Agatha, I don't know whether he's really leaving me his money. I oughtn't to have said anything about it."

"Nonsense," Agatha's voice rumbled out. "Why shouldn't you say something? If he promised it to you, he promised it to you."

"But he didn't promise it. He was only being kind for the moment. And I've never seen him since. I am afraid that he is very ill indeed. I do wish that I could see him. He has a housekeeper who doesn't like me, I'm afraid."

"Oh, doesn't she?" Agatha's eyes stared. "Why doesn't she?"

"I don't know. I don't think I like her either."

"But he did promise it to you?"

"Yes."

"He said that when he died———?"

Mrs. Amorest broke in: "Agatha, don't you think there's something rather dreadful in our talking about money like this, when we're both so old? You know we're both over seventy, and although we don't talk of it often, nor think of it either perhaps, yet some time one must remember that one can only have a few more years to live. Aren't you ever afraid of death, Agatha?"

Agatha Payne raised her head as though she were trying to see more distinctly through the dusk of a darkening room.

"We can have twenty years yet," she said hoarsely. "You're strong and I'm strong. Mrs. Bloxam had a little girl who died when she was five. What's the good of thinking about it?"

"We ought to think of it, I'm sure," said Mrs. Amorest vigorously. "Not in an unwholesome way, of course, but as though we were going from one country into another. And we must give an account of ourselves. God will know all, and if it were not for His infinite mercy our danger would be great indeed. His love—I like to think of His love."

There was a long silence between them. The coals clicked in the grate. The rain stroked the windows. At last Agatha Payne said, "What would you do with the money, Lucy, if you did get it?"

"Do with it?" Mrs. Amorest started. She had been dreaming. "I should find my boy and make him comfortable."

"Oh, your boy!" Mrs. Payne snorted. "Would you lend me some of it?"

"Lend you some? Why, of course."

Mrs. Payne smiled. "You're a good creature, Lucy. But I'd do the same for you. Have you seen Miss Beringer's fine coloured piece on the mantelpiece?"

"That pretty thing! Yes, I told her how greatly I admired it."

"I don't know what an old woman like her is doing with it. She can't appreciate it."

"She likes it," said Mrs. Amorest, "because her greatest friend gave it to her, and that's a very good reason."

Agatha Payne got up. She yawned. Then she shuffled to the door. She seemed already to have forgotten her companion. She went without speaking.

But that night she asked May Beringer to come in and drink a cup of tea with her. May Beringer came, although dearly would she have liked to refuse.

For one thing, she hated old Mrs. Payne's room. It smelt to her "graveyardy." She was sure that the windows were never opened. For another, Pip would not pass that threshold. Not that Mrs. Payne wanted him to do so; she hated the dog, and quite frankly said so. But the dog would not have gone had all the bones and biscuits from the dogs' Paradise been held in front of his nose. His terror of Mrs. Payne was something curious to witness and dreadfully distressing to his mistress, who had never seen him like that with anyone before. Long before the old woman's tall figure appeared in the doorway he knew that she was coming. He would raise his head. His eyes would sharpen, his gaze would be fixed on the door. When she entered he would crawl under the chair. His spirit would be broken by her presence.

All this did not cause May Beringer herself to like the lady the better. But she was in any case a weak creature, and when she was afraid, she was pitiful.

We are so largely the playthings of Fate in our fears. To one, fear of the dark, to another of physical pain, to a third of public ridicule, to a fourth of poverty, to a fifth of loneliness—for all of us our own particular creature lurks in ambush. Nor is it our choice of place or creature.

There was nothing in the world that May Beringer did not fear, but behind all her terrors there was a strange determined obstinacy. As a girl at school it had been discovered by other girls that you could terrify, torture, have all the fun of your life by resolved and calculated persecution, and then, in a moment when you least expected it, up would come this obstinacy, this martyr determination. Often enough some tiny thing called it forth. She would yield with shrieks of terror to demand after demand, and then at the last, over a pin, a cloud in the sky, a falling leaf, she would stand up and act Joan the Martyr to the end of time.

It depends, after all, on what you have in your eye. For one it is a seat in the House of Parliament, for another a lop-eared rabbit, for another a ship at sea, for another a shadow on a green field, for another quails in aspic, for few the welcoming light in a friend's eye, for fewer yet the resting of God's hand upon the shoulder . . . for May Beringer it was the memory of Jane Betts.

Here her brain moved curiously, because in some odd way she connected Agatha Payne with Jane. Because she never analysed anything she did not track this down, but dimly in her distressed mind it came to this, that Agatha Payne wanted to take Jane away from her. But that was absurd, because Agatha scarcely knew that Jane had ever existed. And yet there it was. That was the way that May felt about it.

She realised that Agatha Payne was paying her visits twice daily, and that there was some reason for these. She did not as yet connect them with the piece of red amber.

She had been twice to Mrs. Payne's room and against her will. She had felt quite faint there, as though someone were trying to strangle her. She had hated the gloom, the half-light, the green picture with the fish.

She never knew what to say to Mrs. Payne. She trickled a conversation on ordinary occasions, but here words deserted her. She always felt at her worst here and overwhelmed with apprehension. Apprehension of everything, but especially of being without any money at all, quite alone in the world, dying of starvation, forgotten, in the room in Pontippy Square. Sitting in Mrs. Payne's room she would see this vision and twist her bony hands together on her lap, struggling with the agony of it.

She could not think why this old woman asked her to come when she disliked her as she did. Disliked her! There was never any question of that; the malevolent look that she caught sometimes in Mrs. Payne's eye was witness enough.

Tonight Mrs. Payne showed more plainly than ever she had done before her intentions. She brewed the tea, very strong and dark, laid out the two plates with the sweet biscuits, and then, sitting up at the table and letting the cards fall through her fingers, said:

"I don't want to be impertinent, Miss Beringer, but do tell me of your plans."

"Oh, I don't know," said May Beringer, cracking and uncracking her fingers, "I really don't know. It's so difficult to say, isn't it? How can one truly know? I hope to find some work very shortly."

"What kind of work?" asked Mrs. Payne.

"Companion to some lady, perhaps. Some old lady, you know, who can't look after herself. Someone too old to really care for herself."

"These old women," thought Agatha Payne. "Strange creatures. Never realise they are old. Lucy Amorest just the same. Think they'll go on for ever." She looked at May Beringer in her faded green dress and cheap string of coral beads, with her untidy hair and large nose, and was, at that glance, so strangely irritated that two of the fish came out of the tank and swam slowly, lazily about the room. She would like to do that silly old woman a mischief, apart altogether from the piece of red amber. Yes, she would. She would like to put her rough strong hands about that skinny neck and squeeze it. Oh, she would! She offered May Beringer another sweet biscuit and said, kicking her heel in the air:

"But those jobs are rather hard to find, you know—and you're not as strong as you were."

May Beringer, at the bare mention of the words, felt a shoot of pain through her limbs, and said:

"No, that's quite true. But I'm very hale and hearty still. Still quite strong. If the work were not too arduous. . . ."

"Would you sell that piece of red amber you have, if things went badly?"

"Oh no. I shouldn't like to sell that. I shall never sell it. It was given to me by my best friend. My best friend gave it to me."

"But if you had to sell it. . . ."

"I would rather starve. I would indeed. I would rather die of hunger."

"It is certainly a beautiful piece."

"Yes, isn't it? But it is because my great friend gave it me that I value it. If she hadn't given it me I shouldn't value it so much."

"No. I daresay not. You lived in Exeter, didn't you, in your youth?"

"Yes." May Beringer sighed as though she were relieved at being in safety again. "I was very fond of Exeter."

"I wouldn't like to live in Exeter," said Agatha vigorously; "too sleepy."

"Oh, it wasn't sleepy in my time, I assure you," said May Beringer. "Not sleepy at all. No indeed. There was so much going on. All sorts of things were always happening."

"Really," said Agatha ironically, "I wouldn't have thought it. What kind of things?"

"Oh, I don't know," said May Beringer vaguely. "Meeting one's friends and concerts, and in the summer, we had picnics——"

"Picnics!" said Agatha scornfully.

"Yes, beautiful picnics they were too. We used to have the moors so close to us and on a fine day——"

She had a strange sense while they were talking all about nothing that she would fall asleep were she not careful. Her head was already nodding. It was because Agatha Payne's eyes were fixed upon her so persistently. The room went round and round. Then Agatha said something that woke her very sufficiently. "Do you know when you're going to die?"

May Beringer's eyes stared.

"To die? Oh no!"

"Do you want to know?"

"No, I don't. I don't want to think about it."

"Ah, you're a coward." Agatha was slipping the cards swiftly through her fingers, so that they were like live things.

"No, I'm not." May Beringer was close to tears. "But I don't want to think of it. It's not a thing you want to think of."

"Why not? It's coming some time. That's certain. It's better for many. Take yourself now. If your money gives out and you don't get a job, what are you going to do?"

"I don't want to think of it. Indeed, I don't."

"But you ought to think of it. You ought to make provision. Who will you leave your things to?"

"My things?"

"Yes. Your odds and ends. That piece of amber, for instance."

"I hadn't thought of it." Poor May Beringer. All those forebodings that so resolutely she kept away from her were now crowding in.

"Haven't you made a will?" Agatha asked, rattling her cards like pistols.

"No. It didn't seem worthwhile."

"Well, I should make a will at once. You never know what will happen."

There was a little pause, then Agatha said again:

"You'd better know when you're going to die. Try the cards. They'll tell you."

"Oh no." May Beringer shrank back in her chair. "I shouldn't like that at all. I shouldn't approve of that. I don't think we're meant to know."

"Oh yes, we are." Agatha's black eyes never left May Beringer's face. "Here, draw your chair up to the table. I'll show you."

"I'd really rather not, thank you. I have rather a headache. If you'll excuse me——"

"Nonsense. It will interest you. Come and have a look. You've never seen cards done the way I do them."

"I'd really rather not. . . . ."

"Come along now."

In another moment May Beringer was sitting up, straight and stiff, beside the table. Opposite her, propped up against the wall, Miranda with unblinking eyes watched them.

Agatha Payne dealt out the cards. They lay in rows of six on the cloth.

"Nothing there," she said, swept them up, shuffled, and dealt again.

May Beringer stared with agonised intensity.

"There they are. Six of clubs. Queen of clubs, four of diamonds. Ah! This is you! Just as I thought. Eight of spades. . . ."

"Why am I the eight of spades?" May Beringer asked.

"It isn't you who are the eight of spades. It is the combination with the other cards. You're in danger——"

"In danger?" May echoed feebly.

"Yes. They show it quite distinctly. I'll deal some more. Four of hearts. Five of diamonds. Knave of clubs—yes, there you are—don't you see? Ten of spades—the ten with the knave of clubs and five of diamonds. You're threatened by something very serious indeed."

"Oh dear," said May Beringer, drawing back from the table as though she were afraid that she would contaminate herself by touching the cards. "This isn't right. Really it isn't. I think I'll go to bed if you don't mind."

Agatha put her hand on her arm. "Wait a minute. Let's see some more. We're just coming to the exciting part." She made a little pile of cards, a dozen on top of one another. Then she dealt another row of six.

"There you are," she said, as the eight of spades appeared. "Isn't it extraordinary? You're in luck tonight. They are coming out well. Now let's see."

She took a card—the king of clubs—from the pile, then another—the three of spades—yet another—the six of spades. "All black," she said, stroking her lip. "That settles it."

"Settles what?" asked May Beringer.

"According to the cards you have about a month to live. Of course, there may be nothing in it. Still, it's an odd thing."

"It's wicked!" May Beringer cried, trembling all over as she rose from the table. "It's absolutely wicked. You should not do such things, Mrs. Payne! They aren't right. They are against religion."

Mrs. Payne grimly smiled. "I haven't much use for religion, if you ask me," she said. "You should make your will, you should indeed."

But May Beringer had, on occasion, courage. She pulled herself together, drew herself up, and said with great dignity:

"Goodnight, Mrs. Payne—and thank you for a very pleasant evening."

But in her own room, when her door was closed, she caught Pip to her breast, and, holding him tightly, burst into a flood of agitated tears.

Chapter 7: Death of Hopes

On the 3rd of February, in the morning, Lucy Amorest's cousin died. She had made in January two attempts to see him but had been no more successful than on her Christmas visit.

She had been, herself, needing all the courage that she could muster. She had not been very well. She had caught a cold in this wintry weather, and then there was the house. What exactly was the matter with the house she could not be sure, but six months ago it had been tolerable; now she disliked it so actively that soon she must leave it even, if needs must, for the highways and hedges. At the thought of the highways and hedges she smiled. She had an odd sense of humour, all her own, something detached and cynical and ironic.

Ironic about herself. She would chuckle sometimes without a moment's notice in the middle of her undressing or lying awake at chilly morning hours or reading the *Standard*, and the chuckle meant that she was seeing herself from the outside as something very ludicrous— ludicrous in its own importance about itself, in its little assumptions of dignity and eagerness and desire. When she saw herself in that way she lost all her anxieties and perturbations of spirit. So unimportant was she in the general scheme of things that it was absurd indeed to see how the little creature worried and fussed. Fuss and worry! worry and fuss! Everyone at it, everyone trying to get their money's worth, and the one thing that mattered—the love of God—scarcely entering their heads.

On such detached occasions she felt a human intimate relationship with Jesus Christ. That He had a sense of humour she well knew; if He had not, He would never be able to endure the eternal conceit and self-absorption of human beings. It was because He could laugh a little, seeing with His tenderness and understanding what children these humans were, that He could be so patient. She would never be so patient—and sometimes she was exasperated so keenly with herself that she could shake herself. During this month of January, she felt just this half-ironical, half-kindly exasperation about herself. She *could* not put the thought of this money out of her head, and she *could* not feel a proper patience with May Beringer, and she *could* not have the kindly feelings that she ought to have towards old Agatha Payne.

Moreover, she had dreadful dark suspicions that she was a good deal of a snob. She didn't want to spend the rest of her days with women like May Beringer and Agatha Payne. She liked good talk and laughter and fun. No one enjoyed a really *silly* time more than she did. It was too bad that she must always have her laugh to herself. Never mind, when the money came she would go——She pulled herself up. There she was again. Counting her chickens. She was ashamed of herself.

She caught her cold on her second visit to her cousin's house. It was a biting windy day, and once more the housekeeper talked to her in the doorway and refused to step aside. Horrible woman! Mrs. Amorest indulged in a nice, warm, consoling, comforting luxury of dislike on the way home. She could not abide the woman, and she was glad that she could not. She would like to give her a piece of her mind, and then she chuckled again because she was always such a failure at giving people pieces of her mind. She could never remain indignant for more than two minutes together. It never seemed worthwhile; she saw the ludicrous side of bad temper so quickly. Her husband used to say that it was very irritating of her. It was never worthwhile to lose one's temper with her.

She would never have heard of her cousin's death had it not been for her visit to the grocer's. Mrs. Conduit, the kind wife of the grocer, told her. He had died that morning in his sleep and was to be buried on Thursday—service at St. John's—in the May Lane Cemetery.

The news threw her into a terrible agitation. She did not now think of the money, but only of the way that he had stroked her hair, falling asleep. Poor Cousin Francis! He had looked at her so kindly on that last visit. He had meant always to be kind, but it had been so wretched and gloomy for him in that large ugly house, always ill, always suffering. She shed tears in her room, sitting in front of the tiny fire thinking of him.

There was another thought waiting for her, but she kept it back. Her own loneliness. Her last relation was gone. She had no relations now and no friends in the whole world, save only her boy. The last of the family was gone. There were others perhaps somewhere, but she had long lost sight of them and they of her. The world was a large place to be alone in, but she prevented that thought from reaching her, keeping it behind her. Nevertheless, it was there with her in the room. She could not drive it out. She did not sleep at all that night, lying there during the hours that crept one by one to her bedside, nodded at her and stole off again. She read her Bible and her Prayer Book, but she could not bring them close to her. The house with its silent mutterings was all alive around her. Strange doors closed and opened, steps were on the stair, walls whispered. Her candle guttered, flamed upwards, died, and she had not another. Her room was very cold, and the dawn would never come. Mrs. Bloxam found her wide-eyed and shivering at eight o'clock.

Nevertheless, with the morning her spirit returned. Francis was happier now in Paradise, away from that unfriendly dwelling-place and his sufferings over. She liked to think of him in Paradise, his surprise at what he found there, his wide-eyed astonishment at the kindliness and the fun, the laughter and the flowers.

He would be young again, and instead of the grasping and acidulated Greenacre there would be St. Michael and all the angels. He would be no longer naked and alone. He would worry no more about his money, he would have finer things to think about. He would not be suspicious and imagine that people were making a fuss of him simply for what they could get out of him.

He would be learning, too, the beauties of service. He would be doing things for others. The angels would soon be setting him to jobs that would be new for him indeed. He would not like them at first. He would feel that he was wasting his time, and then, as happiness came flooding in, he would see that that was the only way *to* be happy. When he saw that, what a change it would make in him! He simply would not be the same man.

She amused herself with these thoughts and saw it all so truly that any unhappiness she might have had about his fate left her—he was far better off than he had ever been.

271

The next thing was—what should she do about the funeral? Go, of course, although no card had been sent her; no word even of his death had yet come to her. She did not mind that. They were too busy to think of her. But—what should she wear? She had a black dress, but it was so shabby, so faded that it would never do. Her grey silk was all that she had, and that would seem too gay at a funeral. But there was a black silk scarf given her many years ago by a friend; and her bonnet of dark purple; and her black gloves.

She would like to send some flowers, but the thought that this might seem ostentatious and pushing restrained her. She bought on the Thursday morning a bunch of early snowdrops and thought that she would have an opportunity of putting them on the grave.

Thursday was a lovely day, one of those February days that come in Glebeshire and seem to promise an immediate bountiful spring. The sky was clear-washed to a blue that was almost white; clouds, fragments of faintest lawn, floated so lightly that they seemed to be blown, as in a children's game, from place to place. The woods that fringed the hills were shadowed the most delicate rose, and behind the shadows were softly dark, like velvet. The air was clear and still, so that the shouts of children and the barking of dogs and the rattle of wheels could be distinctly heard.

She found the walk up to St. John's a climb. This was a dark stuffy church with heavy green windows, stony-faced cherubs, and a shining cold floor. She slipped in at the back, unnoticed. She was surprised at the number of people present. She had thought of him always as a lonely man with no friends, but the church was quite full. There was a subdued murmur of voices and much moving of heads to see who was who.

At first, she knew no one, and then she saw Mr. Neilson, her banker, and then Mr. Agnew, the kind little solicitor, with his bald shiny head and broad resolute back. In spite of herself, at the sight of him, her heart beat. He, in all probability, knew the contents of Cousin Francis's will, and he seemed to her for the moment to be the arbiter of all the fates and destinies of the world.

Then she saw Miss Greenacre, darkened with a thick black veil, come slowly up the aisle. The coffin was in front of the altar covered with flowers. The organ began to play and the choir filed in. The sun seemed to blow in gusts through the green windows and to run in patterns up and down the floor. It was very cold and smelt as though the church were always closed.

She could not attend to the service. Her confidence about Cousin Francis's happiness was gone. It was so lonely for him. She could not drive from her consciousness the feeling that it was he who was there in that coffin. She knew, of course, that it was not so. It was only the worthless clay; but the chilliness and the green light and all the casual black heads of the indifferent people depressed her so that soon she was crying between the fingers of her worn black gloves. A stout man next her pushed and heaved as though he were wishing for release, and the organ went on wailing like a peevish child.

Outside, when they started to walk to the cemetery, it was better. Although they moved slowly they were soon in the lanes above Orange Street, and here it was very beautiful. The trees were bare, but you could feel their happiness at the consciousness of the strong sap that was pouring through their veins. The sky was as clear as egg-shell china, and once and again there was a break in the hedge showing fields as fresh as watered silk. How incongruous that black, slow, silent procession! The carriages crawled reluctantly; in subdued voices the mourners spoke. Lucy Amorest walked nearly at the last. No one had addressed a word to her that day.

When they turned into the cemetery they were on the hillside, and all the valley of the Pol lay below them. On the side of the hill opposite to them was the grim stone house, a speck in the distance, that had been Cousin Francis's home. It looked so unimportant now beside the gay shining beauty of the town that sprawled on the hillside, and over all the cathedral sailed, in the clear light, away, away, away, so lightly set that it seemed that another tug of the wind would release it and send it flying to heaven.

They crowded about the open grave. The clergyman, thin and peaked, his surplice blowing in the breeze, said the last words. The coffin was lowered. Words were indistinct, and human beings unimportant. Mrs. Amorest could not see the grave; she caught fragments of the white surplice, and, clutching in her glove the snowdrops, felt that she had not courage to step forward and throw them down on to the coffin. No one regarded her. She was as though she had never existed. They did not know that he had stroked her hair and said that she was better than all the others. Well, it did not matter. He knew and she knew. He was aware now that she had tried to see him and had been prevented. There was now an understanding between them as there had never been when he was alive. Miss Greenacre was of no further importance; she could not come between them anymore.

She walked back very slowly as the afternoon light gathered in, but she was not unhappy. She was very glad that she had been able to go, and she gave the snowdrops to a little street child who stared at her with wide-open eyes, too deeply astonished to thank her.

Four days later she received this letter from the little bald-headed solicitor:

> Dear Mrs. Amorest—I wonder whether you will be passing one morning and could look in and see me for a moment. I have something that I should like to discuss with you if you have time to give me.—I beg to remain, yours sincerely,
>
> John H. Agnew.

Time to give him! The letter shook in her hand. Time to give him! The crisis of all her life had come. The breakfast things on the table were dim, the rose-coloured furniture, the shadowed, misty air. Only, through the haze, looking up, she saw distinctly Agatha Payne in the doorway staring at her.

It was so obvious that important news had come to her that she did not attempt to disguise it. But faintly behind her agitation she felt an anger that had been piling up in her breast for days at the way that Agatha Payne had now of coming into her room uninvited and unheralded. Whether the woman made a pretence of knocking or no she could not tell but look up and there she would be in her old dirty purple gown leaning against the wall. She had apparently now a great purpose of showing herself friendly, but active friendliness did not come easily from her. What was the old woman about? This morning she was direct enough. She said at once, coming to the table and pointing with her thick, shapeless finger:

"You've had a letter about the money?"

Then, as Mrs. Amorest said nothing, she went on in her thick, guttural voice, "I know he died nearly a week ago. You went to the funeral. So, you needn't try to hide it from me."

"Hide it from you," Lucy Amorest said, looking up. "I wasn't trying to do that. Why should I?"

Indeed, her excitement was so great that she did not, at the moment, mind Agatha Payne knowing anything she pleased. Nevertheless, she would not have her coming into the room like that without so much as a knock.

"Would you mind, dear," she said, smiling, but speaking with firmness, "knocking before you come in? It is pleasanter, don't you think, for both of us?"

But Agatha Payne had not heard. She had one hand pressed to her bosom and with the other she was still pointing.

"What does he say in the letter? Does he say that you've got the money?"

"He says I'm to go and see him," Mrs. Amorest answered. "It may not be about the money at all."

"Of course, it is. What else should he want to see you about? Aren't you in luck? Well, I never! Whatever will you do with it all?"

Then, after a little pause, she added, "When are you going to see him?"

"I shall go this morning, I think. I may as well."

"I should think you'd better. I couldn't wait a minute if it was me." She stared at Mrs. Amorest as though she would devour her. She slowly sucked her fingers, one after another. Then she withdrew to the door.

"I shall like to know," she said, "what he says to you."

"Oh, I daresay," answered Mrs. Amorest brightly, "that it won't be anything at all."

But in her heart, she knew that, were that so, she would suffer great disappointment. Her knees trembled as she felt her way down the dark old stairs of the house. Her heart thumped as though it would hammer her body to pieces. All the scene was dark before her.

Mr. Agnew the solicitor lived in Hampden Street near the Marketplace and to the left of Orange Street. It was a dark, poky little street, but it debouched on to a twist of the Pol which, in the unexpected way that it had, sauntered into the city and then hurried out to the hills and fields again. Mr. Agnew's number was nine, and his office was on the third floor. At the bottom of the stairs she rested. Did her heart not beat less wildly she thought that she would never reach the top. It was amazing that ordinary life should push so tumultuously around her. A boy passed the door, whistling. A man with a cart cried out that he had vegetables to sell. The cathedral bells began to ring. A donkey hee-hawed, a child cried, and the sun flickered in pools about the stairs. All this as though nothing tremendous were happening to her at all. She laughed at herself then and the laugh helped her forward. How absurd of her to imagine that her affairs mattered to anybody! After all these years even that simple lesson was not yet learnt.

She climbed the stairs and knocked on the door that had "Agnew & Pace, Solicitors," upon its glass.

"Come in," said someone.

She went in, and a young boy wearing a bright blue tie, a large horseshoe pin, and a very confident air asked her what she wanted.

"Mr. Agnew wrote to me," she said timidly, "and asked me to come and see him."

"Would you mind giving me your name, ma'am?" said the bright young man.

"Mrs. Amorest is my name."

"I'll tell Mr. Agnew. He's engaged at the moment. Would you take a seat, please?"

Mrs. Amorest sat down, but it was terribly hard to wait. To be so near and yet to be kept without information. The room was so cold and so hard, with a map of England on one shining wall and a photograph of Polchester Cathedral on the other, and the young man working so earnestly at the table. All so quiet that the clock on the mantelpiece seemed the only live thing there.

At last the bell rang, and the young man said very politely, "Will you go in now, ma'am, if you please?"

For a horrible moment she was afraid lest her knees should refuse to support her. She did tremble for an instant when she stood, then bravely she moved forward. She was reassured when she saw the kindly smiling face of Mr. Agnew. He surely could have nothing but good news for her when he smiled at her like that. He came forward to meet her, shook her by the hand, set out a chair for her. He was a short stumpy man with a broad back. His broad back and round, shining bald head were the two features that, on every occasion, freshly astonished Mrs. Amorest.

"Well, that is good of you," he said in his warm friendly voice— but his words were always a little measured, as though he had to pay for each one and was determined not to be extravagant. "I do hope that it has been no trouble for you to come in and see me?"

"No trouble, thank you," said Mrs. Amorest, trembling in spite of herself.

"Really, the weather is very pleasant," he went on, rubbing his hands cheerfully together. "Very pleasant, indeed."

"Yes," said Mrs. Amorest, smiling faintly.

"And one's always taken in afresh," he went on. "That's the curious thing. Always believes spring's arriving, although of course it can't be so early in the year. And then back the frost comes and all the buds are nipped and the flowers ruined."

276

"Yes. It is strange," Mrs. Amorest admitted.

"What I say is," went on Mr. Agnew, smiling broadly and showing two splendid rows of white teeth, "that the climate's changing. To my mind there can be no doubt of it—no doubt at all. Permanently, I mean. They say it's the icebergs—and I shouldn't wonder. Tricky things, icebergs. Ever been to America, Mrs. Amorest?"

"No, never."

"Well, I remember a voyage I took over there to see about some client's affairs—when was it? Let me see, in '82, I think—or was it '83? Never mind. . . . Whenever it was, we got into the thick of those beastly things. Pretty they were. Green like glass. But dangerous! My word! The Captain didn't have his clothes off for three days and nights. Lucky we were to come through as we did."

"You must have been alarmed," said Mrs. Amorest.

"Yes, we were. Icebergs and fogs. Those are the things you have to look out for at sea. All the same we had a good captain. That's the principal thing. Queer place, America. Well, well . . ."

He stood there smiling, rubbing his hands together, and Mrs. Amorest sat in her chair, also smiling and rubbing *her* hands together. In spite of herself she felt faint. She could not see the room clearly and she was very cold.

"I do really hope it's been no trouble to you coming to see me."

"Oh, none at all, Mr. Agnew."

"Well, that's good. That's fine. Let me see—where were we? Oh yes! Quite so. Quite so."

He stood over his table fingering papers. He picked them up and put them down. "Oh yes!" He drew himself up and looked towards her. "What I asked you to come and see me about, Mrs. Amorest, was just this. Your cousin Francis Bulling's death was very sad. Very sad, indeed. But he'd been ailing for a long time. You were not at the funeral, I think?"

"I was there."

"Oh, you were! Indeed! I call that wonderful of you, such a climb as it is up to that cemetery. A terrible business for catching a cold, a funeral, especially in the winter-time. I would hardly have expected you to be present. I always say that one funeral means a dozen." He looked up, smiling broadly. "But I'm glad you're none the worse. I am, indeed."

She waited, her hands folded on her lap.

"Where were we? Oh yes, it was about his will that I asked you to drop in. The fact is that he's left you something expressly by name."

"That was very good of him," said Mrs. Amorest.

"Yes, he was a good-natured man, Francis Bulling, at heart. He didn't like to show his feelings. That's a British trait to hide our feelings. Most of us are the same that way, and I must say I think it's a pity. Many of us are not given credit for the feelings we have got. Now the French are supposed to be all feeling, but I assure you that at heart I'd back an Englishman every time. Very superficial, the French."

"Yes," said Mrs. Amorest.

"Now to come to the point. I'll read you what he says—'To my cousin, Lucy Amorest, I would wish to leave some personal possession of mine that she may choose, that she may keep it and remember me by it.' There you are. That's exactly what the will says. He's done the same to several others, his housekeeper Miss Greenacre and one or two more. It shows that he had more feeling than appeared at first sight."

Mrs. Amorest said nothing.

"The executors selected a few things, and to save you trouble I have one or two here in the office. If none of them struck you as very inviting, then you might like to go up to the house and choose something there. But they seemed to me very serviceable—very serviceable, indeed. There's an especially fine ink-pot and . . . but you shall see for yourself."

He rang his bell. The smart boy appeared in the doorway.

"Just bring in those things of Mr. Bulling's, Charlie. They are in that farther cupboard. Carefully now. Carefully. We don't want anything broken."

Charlie reappeared, his arms loaded. He placed the things, very reverently, on the table in front of Mr. Agnew. There was a large and very heavy inkstand, a blue leather writing-case, an ivory paper-knife with a silver handle, a small silver match-box, and a glass paperweight stamped with red and blue flowers.

"Now, Mrs. Amorest," said Mr. Agnew cheerfully, "here they are. And do tell us quite honestly if none of these strike your fancy. There are plenty of other things up at the house, but I thought we might save you the trouble of a journey. The point after all is to have something to remember him by—something you'll have on the table in front of you."

"I think," said Mrs. Amorest quietly, "I should like the match-box."

"Would you, indeed?" said Mr. Agnew heartily. "Well, I must say that seems to me a very wise choice. I agree with you. It's small—takes up very little room, and it's altogether a handsome affair. Francis Bulling used it himself thousands of times, I've no doubt at all." He rang the bell again.

"Charlie, just wrap this up in paper for Mrs. Amorest, will you? She'll take it along with her."

There was silence while Charlie wrapped up the match-box. Mrs. Amorest said nothing, but sat there, without moving, her hands folded. Mr. Agnew was uncomfortable. He did not know why. He, who was never at a loss, had nothing to say. He had expected that the old lady would be pleased that her cousin should have remembered her. But she was always quiet; never showed what she was feeling. Nice old lady. One of the old kind that were getting rarer. Like the climate, people were changing. Every one levelling up. He couldn't say that he liked it. Much harder to get good clerks now than it used to be. Ah, there was Charlie with the parcel.

"That's right. That's right. Sure you've got everything? Mind you come in and see me if there's ever anything I can do for you. Only too delighted. Good-day. That's the door. Then down three flights. Do hope it hasn't tired you."

After she was gone he stood at his window looking out upon the sun-dappled Pol, the shining field, the houses with their red-brown flanks rejoicing in the unexpected warmth. She was old. Hard on one to be as alone in the world as that at her age. Nice old lady, too. He felt the bulging muscle of his arm, smiled, and went to his work.

CHAPTER 8: MAY BERINGER TRIES TO ESCAPE

Deep down in her cellar Agatha Payne was working. She was working with an energy, an enthusiasm, a fidelity to her new ambition that she had not known for years. She had now a purpose. She saw, glittering through the thick and misted cellar light, the sheen and splendour of the most beautiful treasure of the world—*her* treasure, her gold and ruby amber, hers, always hers, stolen from her by that long, thin, ridiculous old maid whom she could frighten by a whisper, terrify with a chuckle.

She liked so to terrify. It gave her hot and sensuous pleasure when she saw the cheeks of that foolish old woman blanch; her heart beat thick when she saw tears tremble on those red-rimmed weak eyelids. Ah! she would make them fall before she had done!

And so, her two pleasures went arm in arm together! She could lead them both by the hand—her lust for power and her lust for that piece of liquid ruby, that stout-set, bold, and scornful dragon standing so firmly on his amber pedestal.

279

She was awake as she had not been for years. All her energies were active. No more lazy lying in her old chair tossing her scarlet slipper in the air, no more crumbling of nougat out of its paper packet, no more half-dreamy watching the silver-finned fish as they sailed with gaping jaws about the room. She had work to do, and work that must not wait.

The first thing that must be ascertained was the time when old Lucy Amorest would receive her money. Everything depended on that. Once the old fool was in command of it, very little further effort would be needed. She would ask for a loan of twenty, thirty, fifty, a hundred pounds. The old thing would not refuse it; she was a foolish old woman always wanting to give something away.

There was a trouble, then, that that long stick of a Beringer would not wish to sell. A present from a friend, she had said—her dearest friend. She could soon be frightened into changing her mind. The time would come when she would promise anything in order to be free. To be free of what? Of terror and dismay. That she and her wretched dog might go to sleep at nights without a sudden waking. There was only a thin wall between the one room and the other. So much could be done with a thin wall at midnight!

But she did not, as yet, plan anything very terrible. Only a little fun, entering into it with something of the spirit with which one boy bullies another, even with a sort of good humour. But she must have the red amber. It was hers, had been hers long before the Beringer woman had seen it. Centuries ago her fingers had closed around its firm cold sides, felt its beating strength, watched the light slip and coil and unfurl about its heart. It had been hers since the beginning of time, and It knew it.

Her impatience on the morning after Mrs. Amorest's visit to her solicitor was urgent. She could not keep quiet but was dressed before Mrs. Bloxam came in with her breakfast.

"Poor Mrs. Hamorest!" said Mrs. Bloxam. "She's 'ad a bad night. Couldn't sleep a wink, she tells me." Then she looked at Mrs. Payne with mild surprise: "You're up early, ma'am."

Although she was not naturally very sharp, her interest in the old ladies quickened her observation, and afterwards, when events forced her to look back, she recorded to interested friends her distinct impression that "things had been going on. She looked different, all sharp like, and as though she was listenin' for something. She was a queer one, that old Mrs. Payne. Not quite right in 'er 'ead, a long way back, if you ask me."

Mrs. Payne indeed was very sharp this morning, and it was not long before she was fumbling with the handle of Mrs. Amorest's door. On entering, she suffered quite a shock of surprise at that old lady's appearance. She was not given to thinking of others, especially when, as now, she was herself driven by one dominating desire, but even her almost crazy egotism was pierced by the forlorn, sick appearance that Mrs. Amorest presented.

She had not been expecting a visitor, and she sat listlessly at her table, her hands in front of her, her eyes fixed on some distant point.

She had always, when Mrs. Payne had seen her, presented a brave front to the world, and something deeply hidden in Mrs. Payne's better part had subconsciously admired that. She was not, however, now moved to any kindness or pity. Her only thought was of the money.

"Good morning," she said huskily.

Mrs. Amorest looked up, and, seeing her, passed her hand over her eyes as though she would drive from them some unwanted vision.

"Good morning, Agatha," she said gently.

"I came in," Agatha said huskily, moving towards the table, "to ask you about the money. Is it all right?"

"The money?"

"Yes—the money your cousin left you."

"I was wrong about that. He hasn't left me any money."

"He hasn't——?"

"No. He didn't do what he said he would. I was silly to believe in it."

"He's left you nothing?"

"Something of his to remember him by. I chose a little thing of his—his match-box."

"And that's all?"

"Yes. Why should he? I was only his cousin. It was very kind of him to think of me."

"Then he cheated you."

"Oh, no. I cheated myself. It was only one day he was feeling kindly. I happened to be there. He would have said it to anyone else who was kind to him."

"I say he cheated you." Agatha Payne's voice was hoarse with anger. "He said he'd give it to you. He made a solemn promise. May he rot in hell, I say."

Mrs. Amorest was frightened. She had known for a long time that the woman was queer, but there was something about that tall, fat, shapeless figure standing now right over her, something in those staring black eyes and that deep reverberating voice that filled her with a new alarm. The woman was mad. Mrs. Amorest wanted to be alone. What had anyone else to do with her affairs? She must think things out. She was face to face with the sharpest crisis of her life. But it was her crisis. No one else had anything to do with it. Why should it be of importance to Agatha Payne whether she had her money or no? She felt, too, in the last fierce words that the woman had used, some sudden obtrusion from another world of experience that had not been, and never could be, her own. She had called her Agatha and had been called by her Lucy, but she had been always aware that there could be no real contact between them. And now she seemed to see, in a flash of revelation, that Agatha Payne's past had been worlds away from her most esoteric imagination. There were twists of a life that was as strange to her as the manners and customs of the natives of Central Africa.

"It's kind of you to be interested, Agatha," she said; "but there's nothing more to be said about it. It was only an idea that I had that he might leave me something. I shouldn't have spoken to you about it."

"No, you should not." The other woman turned savagely upon her. "Making me believe things that were not true. It's wicked—a wicked shame. And you'll pay for it. No one's deceived me yet and not paid for it. You just wait."

She threw up her head as though she would spit upon her, then half-lurched, half-stumbled from the room. Back in her own place she cursed and swore like the old gipsy that she was. That mild, milk-faced old woman had taken her in, pretending this and pretending that. Just to make herself more important. She had always known that no money was coming to her. Talked like that to amuse herself. Amuse herself! She'd amuse her before she was finished with her! Her knees were trembling and she flopped into her chair. The fish came out of the tank and swam, circling about her head. Miranda, like some familiar spirit, sat and watched her, her beady eyes fixed in some sort of grim satisfaction upon her plight. The sharp pain constricted about her head, binding it ever and ever more tightly. Then, slowly, it withdrew. Thoughts moved clearly and steadily once more through the air that was now cooler and the light that was now stronger.

Mrs. Amorest faded into dim background. But more powerfully than ever before the piece of red amber shone before her eyes. What is this lust of possession, this ache and longing for the absolute power of dominion? Napoleon moving towards Moscow, Philip II. stretching his fingers over the Netherlands, the vineyard of Naboth, Marie Antoinette and her fatal necklace, Piemente and the box of moidores, Agatha Payne and her piece of red amber—the soul alone knoweth its secret tyrannies.

She sat there all day until evening.

She sprawled back in her chair and saw it gleaming there on her mantelpiece in front of her. Surely it was there! She knew now its every shade and glitter and trembling light. Well, if there was to be no money there was the other way. The Beringer woman should give it to her whether she wanted or no—yes, if she must wring that scraggy old neck to get it.

She got up at last and made herself some cocoa, then moved out towards May Beringer's room.

She stayed outside the door and gave two knocks, one loud and abrupt, the other soft, an echo of the first. While she stood there, a smile was on her lips. That will make her jump. *That* will make her jump. She's frightened now. She knows it's me. And her dog is frightened. He knows too. He's under the bed. On her side of the door she fancied that she could hear the other woman's frightened breathing, sharp and hurried. She's standing there with her head on one side, waiting. She hopes I'll go away. She's praying that I will.

Then she knocked again, loudly.

"Come in," said the whisper of a voice.

She pushed open the door and went in with jollity, laughing. "Well, Miss Beringer, and how are you finding yourself? I thought I'd pay you a little call. I've just drunk my cup of cocoa, and half an hour's talk with you before going to bed will do me good."

She moved across the room as though she owned it and pulling out the roomiest chair plumped down in it. She sat in her accustomed attitude, one knee over the other. Her eyes were fixed on the red amber that now was in shadow and glowed a smouldering ruby. That was the pedestal; the dragon stood translucent gold.

May Beringer, untidy, confused, stood like an owl bewildered by unexpected light. Her hand was at her thin bony breast.

"I'm not so well, thank you," she said. She looked indeed today infinitely old and worn. "I haven't been sleeping too well." She broke then, with a kind of hurried speech as though she had but little time, into a most eager appeal. "Mrs. Payne, tell me—why are you persecuting me like this? Why do you come to my room? Why did you knock on my wall last night? I haven't done anything to harm you. I haven't hurt you in any way. I never saw you before I came here. I never interfered with you. I know it's silly of me to go on like this, but I haven't been sleeping——" she broke off. She had been struggling with her tears. They came now trickling through her hands that she pressed to her face. She collapsed on to a chair and sat there, her head forward.

Mrs. Payne said nothing. The dog appeared from under the bed. After hesitating a moment, he came forward slowly and pressed himself, all huddled up, against his mistress's foot. She looked up and went on slowly, jabbing a rather dirty handkerchief against her nose:

"I know it's silly of me to go on like this. It's foolish of me and weak, I know. But I'm really not well. If I don't get my sleep my health always suffers. You must excuse me. I'm not so young as I used to be. I've been feeling much older this winter. But won't you leave me alone? I've done you no harm."

Agatha Payne was savouring an exquisite and delicious pleasure as she watched her. It was not a pleasure of cruelty nor of passion, but rather of power, and also of a deep consciousness of sensation. She almost liked May Beringer as she sat there snivelling; a very little more, and she could have gone and put her arms around her and comforted her. But she had not known many sensations in the last year or two— only her cards and her food and her cup of cocoa.

She was happy now as she had not been for many a day.

At last she spoke in her strange bass voice, deep like a man's.

"You are imagining things," she said. "You are ill. The cards said you were going to be."

"That's it," May Beringer broke out. "Why did you show them to me? What made you? I know I'm silly if you put things into my head. I always was as a girl. I've been like that ever since I was a child. I'm not going to die. I'm not going to die. I'm not going to die!"

Her voice was almost a scream.

"The cards said so," Agatha Payne answered slowly. "I didn't make them come as they did."

Miss Beringer turned and looked at the other woman with a considering gaze as though she were seeing her for the first time. "Why do you hate me? I've never done you any harm. You came here. I didn't ask you to come."

"I came because I wanted to be kind to you, because I thought you were lonely."

"I'm not lonely," May Beringer broke out desperately. "I'm not at all. I don't want anybody. I can get on by myself."

"I like you," said Agatha Payne, smiling. "I like to be with you. I enjoy our little talks. Perhaps I'm the lonely one."

"No, you're not," said May Beringer excitedly. "You're not lonely at all. But you want to tease me and frighten me. And you want something else. You want my piece of amber."

Mrs. Payne said nothing.

"That's what you want. You can't deny it. But you won't have it, however much you want it. I'll put the police after you if you take it. I'll have you put in prison. Yes, I will. I'll have you put in prison."

She was in a state of terrible excitement.

"Who says that I want it?" said Agatha Payne quietly. "You have strange ideas in your head. You are ill. You should see a doctor."

May Beringer made a great effort at control. She sat, staring in front of her, as though she were summoning all her forces to her aid. At last more quietly she said:

"Yes, I am ill—at least not well. My back is very painful." Then she added with real dignity: "I think we can't be friends. We are too unlike one another. I am an old woman now, and it's too late to change myself. And I'm easily frightened. Perhaps at nothing. I don't know. But I do ask you not to come and visit me anymore."

"When you're ill," said Mrs. Payne, "in bed and can't move, you'll want somebody. You'll be glad to see me, perhaps."

"I'm not going to be ill. Do you hear? I'm not going to be ill. I know you want me to be ill. You're wishing me to be ill now. But I won't be ill. You want me to die, and then you can have the piece of amber; but I'm not going to die. It's only my back. That will be better tomorrow, and I'm going to sleep even though you do knock on the wall."

"Knock on the wall!" repeated Agatha Payne scornfully. "Who says I knock on the wall?"

"You do! You know you do!" May Beringer cried, rising to her feet. She pointed to the door. "I don't want you in here. You are not to come again. It's my room. I can have whom I like. I forbid you to come any more."

Agatha Payne nodded her head. "I shall come when I like," she said. "You can't stop me." Then she added slowly: "But if you'll give me that piece of amber I won't come any more."

May Beringer snatched it from the mantelpiece as though she feared that it would vanish from before her face. "Nobody shall have it," she said. "It's the only thing I've got."

Agatha Payne rose slowly and went to the door. "We'll see," she said. "We'll see."

There was no knocking on the wall that night, and May Beringer fell into a strange, heavy, confused sleep in which dreams were for ever forming a tapestry of illusion near her, showing her their sombre and kindling colour but always distant and indistinct. The piece of amber was there, and Jane Betts and Pip, and behind these a dark lowering sense of danger.

She did not wake when Mrs. Bloxam brought her her tea, and it was mid-day when that kind woman finally roused her with a shake on the shoulder, telling her that the sun was shining and that she had brought her a fresh cup, not wishing to disturb her earlier, she seemed so "proper drowsy."

She awoke with a great start, sitting up in bed with a consciousness that something terrible had happened to her. What was it? Ah, of course she knew. She must escape from here. Dreadful danger was hanging over her head. She must be away.... But how? when? where? While Mrs. Bloxam was scattering about the room, making things a little brighter and more comfortable, she was endeavouring to compose her brain. She sat up in bed, her hands to her head. Her brain worked so slowly now. She could not see clearly. Things would not hang together. But one fact was plain. She must leave this house, and at once. She could not be another night under the same roof with that terrible wicked woman. And she must escape secretly.

No one must know. Otherwise that woman would find out where she had gone and would follow her. She must return to St. Lennan, the place that she ought never to have left, to her old friend with whom she had lodged for so long. She would find work there. There must be something that she could do, even though it were only to sweep the floor. Were her back not so painful there were many things that she could do. She seemed filled with energy under the impulse of her terror. If only she might escape from this house never to see its walls again! She was now in a fever of agitation. She seemed to be in a moment practical and far-seeing. When did the trains go to St. Lennan? The day was moving on. The afternoons at this time of the year were very short. She must be away before dusk. She was out of bed and moving rapidly about the room, a strange figure, with her long sloping body, her loosened grey hair, moving restlessly from spot to spot in her grey flannel nightdress and her old bedroom slippers.

"Why, miss, whatever is the matter?" Mrs. Bloxam asked, realising her agitation.

"Mrs. Bloxam," Miss Beringer said, catching the other's stout arm, "have you got such a thing as a time-table about you?"

"About me, miss?" said Mrs. Bloxam, slapping her dirty apron. "No, miss, I can't say as I 'ave."

"Do you think you could get one for me?"

"A time-table, miss?" Mrs. Bloxam was all eyes. "Why, you'll catch your death o' cold wandering about like that, miss. 'Ere, let me get you your woolly waistcoat. A time-table? Well, I'm sure I don't know. A local, miss?"

"Yes. A Glebeshire one."

"Well, I'm sure I don't know. Mrs. Carstairs next door might 'ave one."

"Do go and see. Won't you? Please. Do go and see whether you can get one. A Glebeshire one. All the trains in Glebeshire. It's so important. At once. Now. Please. Please."

"At once, miss? And your fire ain't lit and you 'aven't drunk a drop of your tea."

"Oh, never mind about that. Please don't bother about that. If you'd only go at once."

"Well, I'm sure. Why? Are you going away, miss?"

"Yes, I am. I must. I'm not well here. I must go away at once. And, Mrs. Bloxam, I'll pay you your wages up to the end of the week. I'm so sorry to leave you. You've been so kind to me. But I have to go away—at once. Without losing a minute."

"Well, miss, I'm sure——It don't matter about the bit of wages, but going out on an afternoon like this, and you as delicate as you are—I shouldn't like——"

"It's all right. It is, really. It's perfectly all right. I'm going to friends."

"But whatever will you do about your things? You can't take them all with you sudden-like."

"I'll send for them. I'll give you an address to send them to. But please, please get me a time-table. And don't say a word to anybody. Not a word. I do beg you not to say a word to anybody."

Miss Beringer had been pouring all this forth in an agitated whisper, looking at every instant towards the door as though expecting it to open and reveal the hated figure.

Mrs. Bloxam patted her on the shoulder. "There, there. Don't you worry. I'll get you the time-table."

After she was gone May Beringer dressed, pulling on her clothes as though she had but a moment to escape, and talking, as was her habit, in the same agitated whisper to Pip, who followed her every movement with nervous, anxious eyes.

"We mustn't stay, Pip. We mustn't, indeed. She'll do us some harm if we do. She'll do us both harm. You know you're as afraid of her as I am. She hates us both, Pip, and she wants to steal our things. She's a bad woman, Pip. She'd be a thief if she could. She's a bad, wicked woman. But she's not going to get what she wants. We'll get out of her way and go back to our friends, who'll be so glad to see us, and you'll be able to have exercise as you ought to and run on the sands again. You'll like that, won't you, Pip—and we won't be frightened any more. If only my back didn't hurt, Pip, we could have such a good time. Perhaps it will be better when we are beside the sea again. The sea air always did us good, didn't it, Pip?"

When Mrs. Bloxam returned, May Beringer was wearing her hat and was quite ready to go out.

"Have you got it, Mrs. Bloxam?" she asked in a whisper.

"Yes, miss, I've got it. It's an old one. Last November. But I daresay the trains are the same."

"I expect they are." She clutched at the little green flimsy timetable and began eagerly to turn the pages.

"Here we are." She read down the page. "Yes, there's a train at 3.30. There are very few trains. I mustn't miss that one. It seems to be the last. Three-thirty, and it's now quarter past two. That will do very nicely."

"What will you be doing about your bag, miss? You can't carry it all that way by yourself."

"Oh no, Mrs. Bloxam. I shall only take this small bag, and I'll catch the omnibus at the corner of Malpas Street. That will be quite easy. And now, Mrs. Bloxam, I do beg of you not to say a word to anybody—in any case not today. Will you promise me that?"

"Yes, miss, I promise."

"And I'll write to you from where I'm going, so that you can send the other things on. And here's your money."

She opened her old faded green purse and counted out the money. Then followed a very touching little scene, Mrs. Bloxam begging her to keep it until she could afford to pay her, or at least until the end of her journey, but May Beringer was firm. Mrs. Bloxam must be paid. They then shook hands.

"I'm sure, miss, I wish you every kind of good fortune," Mrs. Bloxam said.

"Thank you, Mrs. Bloxam, you've been a very kind friend."

Left alone she paused and listened, her hard, ugly, black, straw hat a little askew on her head, Pip's chain in her hand. There was no sound. No one was moving through the house. The woman had left her alone for that time at least.

She had pushed things into her shabby black handbag helter-skelter, then feverishly pressed its gaping lips together and insisted on their closing. With the same excitement she affixed the chain to Pip's collar while he stood by, little shivers of excitement shuddering along his body. Then very softly she opened the door, peered out, saw nobody, and on tiptoe started down the stairs.

Arrived in the Square, the sun round and orange above the crooked roofs, she looked for a moment back at the house, grim and grey above her, the windows blind-eyed in its ancient corpse-like body. Oh! might she never see it again! That was her prayer. Never, never! She would like to have said goodbye to Mrs. Amorest, who had been kind to her, but she would write to her from St. Lennan when, safe and secure, she could snap her fingers at her recent terrors. She heard the cathedral clock ringing out the hour, and in a panic scurried down the Square dragging Pip after her. The bag was heavy, her back seemed to have a red-hot needle thrust through its spine, but the thought of her escape heartened her to the forgetting of all ills. She stood at the corner of Malpas Street breathing heavily, waiting for the omnibus. A new alarm beset her. Perhaps they did not allow dogs in omnibuses? Whatever then should she do? She had not money for a cab. There would not be time to walk. Tears filled her eyes, and, as though he realised that he was the cause of the trouble, Pip gazed up at her with beseeching gaze.

The omnibus came lolloping up, and she was glad to see that there were but two passengers inside it, and the conductor was a fresh-faced kindly-looking young man.

"Oh, I do hope you don't mind a dog," she panted at him. "It's only as far as the station."

"Well, it's not strictly allowed," he said, trying to look severely at her, but pulling the string to send the omnibus farther in its journey; "but it's for the other passengers to say. If they object——"

"I do hope that you don't object," said Miss Beringer, jerked down on to her seat (they were now crossing the cobbles of the Market-place); "I am only going as far as the station, and he's a very well-behaved little dog. You can see how well-behaved he is."

The two passengers were a stout man with a red face, who simply nodded his head in a dignified manner but said nothing, and a young woman with a face like an apple and a hearty smile. She said that she liked dogs, and that her husband had several, and that he was a dear little fellow, and he reminded her of a dog that her father had had once who had also been a dear little fellow and had been run over by a butcher's cart, which was the worst of keeping pets because something dreadful always happened to them, watch them as you might.

The friendliness of the omnibus cheered Miss Beringer considerably, and with every jerk she was taking a farther step from the enemy. It was the hour before the winter dusk, and all the town was bathed in a yellow opalescent shadow. Houses and doors and windows were transfigured. As the omnibus climbed the hill to the station, the hills and fields beyond Seatown came into view, swimming in golden air. The river flashed like a bar of music heard unexpectedly. The houses darkened even as they passed them.

"We're a long way over the shortest day," said the amiable young woman, "but it doesn't seem to make much difference."

Up on the hill where the station was, there was a blowing hearty air. The station platform was exposed, and you could see from it low levels of green fields, a wood now purple dark, and a cottage silver in the early dusk. There was no one about. She sank down on to the hard platform seat, gathering Pip into her skirt. Every bone in her body was aching, and she seemed to have so many bones—more than the average number, she was sure. She would not buy her ticket for a moment; there was plenty of time. She liked to look across to the quiet fields and the masts of trees black and silver against the orange sky. So peaceful and so quiet after the last days and nights. It was past three o'clock, but there was plenty of time. There was no movement about the station.

A train against a side platform whistled and jolted away. A porter passed, looked at her for a moment, and then walked on.

She sat in a sort of blissful dream. The thought of returning to St. Lennan was wonderful to her. Indeed, she should never have left it. The fear that she might not be able to earn her living seemed to disturb her no longer. She had not, in any case, she suspected, very long to live. This afternoon, tired out, bathed in the fading sunshine, the pains in her back and at her heart gradually receding, she did not seem to care. If she had not long to live at least she would die then among friends, with Pip and her bit of amber and the long seashore and the rumble of the waves.. . . .

She sank into a kind of doze, her head nodding forward on her breast, then woke with a start. What if she should have missed her train? She hastened up, dragging Pip after her. She hurried into the ticket office and, fumbling in her purse, said sharply through the little window:

"A third single to St. Lennan and a dog ticket, please."

There was a pause, and then a very abstracted voice answered her: "Where did you say, madam?"

"St. Lennan, please—and a dog ticket."

The abstracted voice answered her, "No train to St. Lennan today. Last left ten minutes ago—3.5."

She had not heard. His words meant nothing.

"Third single to St. Lennan, please," she repeated.

A bearded, spectacled face appeared then at the window.

"No further train to St. Lennan today, madam. Last went ten minutes ago—3.5."

Fear surged down upon her. "Oh, but there must be. I looked at the time-table. It said 3.30. Truly it did."

"Changed 1st of January. There *was* a 3.30. Changed to 3.5."

Terror had her by the throat. She stammered.

"Sorry, madam. No further trains to St. Lennan today."

The bearded face withdrew.

She turned round. A porter was passing. She stopped him. "Oh, porter, please, surely it can't be true. There *must* be a train to St. Lennan at 3.30."

He was a kindly man. He smiled at her genially. "Sorry, mum, changed 1st of January."

"Oh, what shall I do? What shall I do? It's dreadfully important I get there today. What *can* I do?"

"Well, mum, you could . . . let me see." He consulted the page of train times on the board. "Difficult place to get at, St. Lennan. You could take the 6 o'clock to Pentecost and catch the St. Borlase 4.30. No. You couldn't neither. That 'ud be too late. You could . . . I'm blowed if I see what you can do today, mum. There's the 6.30 tomorrow morning."

The 6.30 tomorrow morning! The 6.30 tomorrow morning! What could she do? Sit in the station all day and all night? She had not money for an hotel. She had no friends. No one. The only thing was to go back.

She stood looking out on to the station square now quite deserted. Through the silence a summons as it were of fate came to her.

She bowed her head, and slowly, Pip close to her side, she crossed the square.

CHAPTER 9: THE SENSE OF DANGER

Mrs. Amorest had recognised, as she walked up the High Street after leaving Mr. Agnew's office, that the hardest crisis of her life had come upon her. She met it almost as an old friend because she had been for so long expecting it. Like many other brave and spirited women, it had always been the little things in life that had shown her weaknesses—to the big crises she had always risen as the swimmer braces himself for the crest of the green-towering wave. During the walk home, she was dazed. Though she might have suspected the actual splendour of the annual thousand pounds, she had not in her heart doubted but that there would be a hundred or two—and a hundred or two would make all the difference.

And now there was nothing save a silver match-box!

Back in her own room, she seemed to be standing, precipitately, on the edge of a dark and bottomless oubliette. What lay down there? How deep was the fall? She realised with a flash of surprise that for years now she had expected that "one day her cousin would do something for her." Although she had never uttered the thought in outspoken words, she had always, when funds were creeping so low as to be almost invisible, known that at any rate there was Cousin Francis. Now there was Cousin Francis no longer.

It was fit and proper punishment for her. She recognised that. The thought hurt her now that her visits to her cousin had been frequent only because she "had expectations." But she was no sentimentalist. She did not allow herself the luxury of self-chastisement without justification. She had gone to see him because she was fond of him, because she was sorry for him, and because he was the only relation left to her in the world save Brand. The only relation! She could not have believed that his death—when she had seen him so seldom—would make her now so lonely. She wondered at her own loneliness. Why had she, when she was by nature gregarious, loving her fellow beings, made no real friends in the town? It was, she supposed, her pride, her dislike of revealing her poverty, her hesitation at being unable to return hospitality. But what would she give to have a true friend near her now!

After her conversation with Agatha Payne her courage for a moment failed her. She felt old and worn and desolate, and all that day she must clench her teeth and refuse to look either to the right or to the left. Beasts in the jungle on either side of her! Then, next morning at breakfast time, a marvellous thing occurred.

"There's a letter for you, mum," said Mrs. Bloxam, coming in with her hat askew and her accustomed air of bustling energy; "and that poor Miss Bellringer is terrible bad this morning. Suffering something cruel—and all because she would go to the station yesterday, against my advising her too!—there! and I shouldn't 'ave said nothing about it."

Mrs. Amorest took the letter and trembled through all her body. She did not hear Mrs. Bloxam's voice nor see the room nor the rain-driven day beyond the window pane. The letter was from her son.

The envelope was covered with stamps, addresses, inks blue and red and green, and that strangely mysterious and yet intimate handwriting conveying the information "not known here. Try Chester Street——"

She gazed at the envelope for a long time and, swimming up from beneath deep waters, murmured to her companion, "It's from my son, Mrs. Bloxam. At last, after two years."

Mrs. Bloxam paused, her arms *akimbo*. Her cheeks were suffused with generous pleasure.

"Is it really, mum? Well I never!"

At last, after gazing at the envelope for a long time, she had the courage to tear it apart. It was not a very long letter, but she caught it up and kissed it, then held it against her cheek.

The address was "Monterey, California," and then the date! She looked at it again and again to make certain that she was correct, pushing her reading spectacles up and down her nose. At last she said, "You look at that, Mrs. Bloxam. I make it out January 4, 1895. And this is February 1896. It must be wrong. The letter can't have been a whole year coming."

She would not allow the letter out of her hand, so Mrs. Bloxam leaned over her and studied it very carefully.

"I'm not a great 'and at reading, mum, if the truth be known, but that is certingly a 5——"

"A whole year!" Mrs. Amorest repeated. "Where can the letter have been?"

She read it then, and it was as follows:

Dear old Lady—I can't pretend to have been much of a letter-writer during the last year, and I'm ashamed of myself. The truth is that I'd made an oath to myself not to let you know anything until I'd brought a deal off here. What I wanted to do was to make my pile, turn up unexpectedly in Cheltenham, give you the fright of your young life, and then make you a duchess, as you ought to be—but I've had the worst of bad luck over and over again. Tantalising isn't the word for it. If things hadn't at times gone so astonishingly well I'd have given it up and come home to England long ago, but I've so nearly brought it off once or twice that I can't make up my mind to leave it. I was on to a wonderful thing, three months ago, and then what did I do but tumble down with diphtheria here in San Francisco, and another fellow got the chance.

I'm all right now, and there's some land prospecting down South, near a little place, Los Angeles (get out the map and look for it), that promises fine. Hold on for a while yet and I'll astonish you still one fine morning. I don't like to be beaten. I'm enclosing a photo I've had taken here. You'd hardly recognise your promising son, would you? I'm fit as anything now, and it maybe it won't be long before you see me.

I was pleased to see from your last letter that you are keeping well and are happy. The address on your paper is Polchester. Don't know the place, but gather you are still living in Cheltenham. Isn't Polchester the place where there are some cousins of ours? Perhaps you're staying with them. You don't say. Glad you're stopping on at Cheltenham, where you've got plenty of company. Don't be lonely, old lady.

So long for the present, and look out for me any day.—Your loving son,

Brand.

She sighed deeply as she finished it. Then she read it all through clearly.

"You see, Mrs. Bloxam," she said, as though that lady had read the letter, "I didn't want him to think I'd left Cheltenham. It might have fussed him. And I was thinking then I might return there at any time. I left them this address in the post office there. I don't know wherever this letter can have been." She spelt out the envelope again. "It's because he's written the address so badly. Careless boy. 'Try Chippenham.

Not known here.' I should think not. It must have been lying in the post office for months. Isn't that too bad?"

Then she gazed and gazed at the photograph. She would, of course, have known him anywhere. But how he had filled out! How he had broadened and thickened and strengthened! He looked well. He was the handsomest man on earth.

"He may come any minute, Mrs. Bloxam. I knew he hadn't forgotten me, whatever they might say. He's coming back a rich man."

"Is he indeed, mum?" said Mrs. Bloxam. "And here's your tea, mum, and it'll all get cold if you don't drink it."

She lay back bathed in a luxury of happiness. She could think at first of nothing but her joy in being in touch with him once again. She lay there smiling, lost in happy dreams.

But when she had dressed, new thoughts came to her. That letter had been written a year ago. He had had diphtheria. What might not have happened in the intervening year? A whole year, and there had not been a line from him! That sense of fear she had had ever since her meeting with Mr. Agnew—a sense that some danger was tracking her and was drawing like a furtive but determined animal ever nearer and nearer—came close to her now. She was to be tantalised with the letter. It was to be a sign to her that she was never to see him again—his last farewell letter to her!

"What is the matter with me now?" she said to herself. "I was never like this before. Something new has come into this house. I never doubted but that he was coming back to me, and now, when I have his letter, at last after so long waiting, it seems to tell me I shall never see him again." She gazed and gazed at the photograph. "Oh, God! Give him back to me!" she prayed. "I don't think I can go on alone much longer. I'm so tired of being alone. Give him back to me!" and then, struggling against her stronger, more rebellious spirit, added, "Thy will be done."

Mrs. Bloxam came in very greatly disturbed. "There's that poor Miss Bellringer," she said, "crying something pitiful. She says she's frightened of something. Mrs. Payne 'as been in and upset 'er. She says it's 'er 'eart, and 'er back's 'urting something shameful. Poor worm! She's not long for this world, if you're asking my opinion."

Mrs. Amorest was not herself feeling her strongest. All the excitement of the last two days and the lack of sleep had made her, as she used chaffingly to confess to her friends, "a little weak in the knee." But the sight of Mrs. Bloxam's good-natured face so truly disturbed touched her deeply. She went at once, crossing the passage, into May Beringer's room.

Entering, she was aware sharply once more of a sense of danger. She was not an imaginative woman nor one given to nervous fears; she had pluck and courage fortified by utter belief in powers that could put all the battalions of evil to ignominious flight, but she was weary and unstrung. She stopped on the threshold. Her eyes went instinctively, as though they were guided, to the mantelpiece. The red amber was not there. She looked then at the bed. Miss Beringer, propped with pillows, was sitting up, her woollen waistcoat tied by the sleeves around her thin and bony neck. Her long, flushed face was yellow and drawn. One arm was thrown over the dog, which, lying full length on the bed, was crouched close to her side; in the other she held the red amber.

Mrs. Bloxam, standing beside the bed, was uttering consoling words and offering some beef-tea on the little battered black-japanned tray. The fire was not lit. The room was very cold and dark. "Now do, my dear," Mrs. Bloxam was saying, "drink this nice beef-tea. You'll feel a different woman when you've drunk it. I'll take the dog for a run."

"No," said Miss Beringer, holding the dog closer to her. "You've taken him out once this morning, thank you. I don't wish him to go again. Thank you very much." She drank the beef-tea as though she were thinking of something else.

"Well, if you don't mind me saying so, miss," continued Mrs. Bloxam, "it really isn't 'ealthy to 'ave that dog on the bed with you. It isn't really, miss. Not that it isn't a clean little dog, but dogs is dogs."

"No, thank you, Mrs. Bloxam."

"And 'ere's Mrs. Hamorest come to cheer you up. Why, bless you, you'll be right as tuppence tomorrow, you see if you ain't. Don't you let yourself get down'earted. Keep up your spirits. The sun will be shining tomorrer mornin'."

"Thank you, Mrs. Bloxam, I'm sure it will," answered Miss Beringer patiently.

"Is there anything else I can do for you while I'm at it? I'll just be getting Bloxam's dinner and I'll be back in a jiffy."

"Thank you, Mrs. Bloxam. There's nothing else I want, thank you."

Mrs. Bloxam departed. Mrs. Amorest came then and, drawing a chair, sat down beside the bed.

"Do you mind my coming in for a little?" she asked. "You needn't talk if you don't want to. I always think a little company's pleasant when you are not feeling well."

"But I do want to talk," May Beringer said. She put the piece of amber on the bed beside her and caught Mrs. Amorest's hand. "Do you mind my holding your hand? Do say if you mind."

"Why, of course not," Mrs. Amorest said gently. "Now tell me what's the matter. Don't you think you ought to see a doctor?"

"A doctor can't do anything." Her hand shook in Mrs. Amorest's grasp. "It's that woman next door who's killing me."

"What woman? Mrs. Payne?"

"Yes." May Beringer's voice sank to a whisper. "Speak softly. She can hear what we say."

"But of course, she can't," Mrs. Amorest reassured her. "There's a thick wall between."

"No, but she can. Walls are nothing to her. It's fate. She's going to finish me. She made me miss that train yesterday."

"What train?"

"I was going away and I got to the station and I missed the train. She knew I'd come back."

But this was not at all the kind of talk with which Mrs. Amorest's clear, cool brain could have patience. "Now that's really nonsense," she said, smiling and patting May Beringer's hand; "you're ill or you wouldn't have ideas like that in your head. You've had ideas about Mrs. Payne since the first moment you saw her. Of course, Mrs. Payne is a little odd. She's not quite like other women, but she doesn't mean any harm. Why, I've lived in this house for months and months with her, and she's never done any one any harm."

"That's because," May Beringer whispered feverishly, "you haven't got anything that she wants."

"What do you mean?" asked Mrs. Amorest, feeling in spite of herself the darkness of the room and a kind of foggy chill that seemed to hang like a mist about the bed.

"It's my piece of amber she wants," May Beringer went on, "and she's not going to have it. Never, never, never! Not if I die to prevent her."

Mrs. Amorest leaned forward and stroked her friend's forehead. "Dear Miss Beringer, you mustn't imagine things like that. Truly, it's only because you're not well. Now let me arrange your pillows and make you more comfortable."

May Beringer began to cry, a weak helpless sobbing. "You don't understand," she said, as the tears trickled down her cheeks. "You think it's absurd because you don't know how people can want things. You're good, and you wouldn't take anything that belongs to somebody else. But she's bad, and she isn't right in her head either. She was in here and said if I gave it her she would leave me alone."

"She was in here? When was that?"

"The night before last. That's why I meant to go away. She frightened me so! Oh! you don't know how frightening she can be when she looks at you with her black eyebrows and smiles. She is going to kill me if she can't get it!"

Mrs. Amorest looked about the room, her small lined face wrinkled with surprise. "She said that? That she would leave you alone if you gave her that piece of amber?"

"Yes, she did indeed. She's quite crazy to have it. She says it belonged to her before it belonged to me—as though dear Jane didn't give it to me after buying it herself from Mr. Faithorner in Exeter."

"Then she must be mad—mad, and wicked too." Mrs. Amorest was trembling with indignation. "Why, that's as bad as being a thief!"

"She *is* a thief," said May Beringer. "She'd take it at once if I were alone in the house. But she knows that Mrs. Bloxam and you know it's mine. She *is* a thief."

"I can't understand it," Lucy Amorest went on, "anyone wanting anything like that. Of course I like to have nice things, but I wouldn't *take* anybody's. . . . Why, it's truly wicked! And that's only a bit of stone or something. It isn't as though it were alive. What is it made of really?"

"I don't know," said May Beringer, looking at it tenderly as it lay there on the counterpane. "I think the Chinese find it on the seashore or something. But I'm not certain about its not being alive. You will think me very silly, Mrs. Amorest, but I'm an old woman and have lived a long time, and I sometimes think that things are more alive than people. When you've put a lot of feeling into something, don't you give it a sort of life? It may be grateful, you know, for your being so fond of it.

"Of course, that's very fanciful, and perhaps it isn't very religious, but one gets queer fancies when one's old. Jane (she was my dear friend, you know) said when she gave it me that it had some of her heart in it, and I think perhaps it has. I know that wicked woman can kill me first before she gets it from me."

She was trembling all over, and Lucy Amorest, touched with pity, put her arm about the thin bony body.

"Now you're not going to feel frightened any more. I'm here, and I won't let her touch you. I'm going to speak to her and give her a piece of my mind."

"Oh no, you mustn't do that." May Beringer sat straight up in bed. "You don't know what she will do to you. You mustn't, indeed you mustn't."

Lucy Amorest smiled.

"She can't hurt me, dear. There is Someone will protect us both, stronger than Agatha Payne. Now how do you feel in general? Is your back hurting you?"

"It isn't my back so much as my heart. Put your hand here and just feel how it jumps." Mrs. Amorest placed her hand against May Beringer's breast and felt the strange irregular beat—it seemed to jump like an animal imprisoned and then altogether to die away.

"Well, I think you ought to see a doctor," she said, nodding her head decisively. "I know a very nice one, let me tell him to come in this afternoon."

But May Beringer shook her head vigorously.

"No, no," she said; "I had a doctor once in Exeter and he said I must wear spectacles, and so I did for two years, and there wasn't anything the matter with my eyes at all. I don't believe doctors know a thing more than we do ourselves. They are all humbugs, if you ask me."

She was energetic; there was some colour now in her cheeks; Lucy Amorest's visit had done her good.

"I must leave you now for a little. I'll come back in the afternoon."

"Oh, you will, won't you?" May Beringer's eyes were beseeching. "You are so good to me. I'm sure I don't know why."

"Nonsense." Lucy Amorest bent down and kissed her. "You sleep for a little and you'll feel ever so much better."

"I don't want to sleep. I have such dreams."

"You won't this time. You try and see."

She went back to her room and thought it out. Her principal feeling was one of anger and indignation with Agatha Payne. She had never heard anything so wicked and so cruel. To frighten and bully that poor old thing simply because she wanted that toy!

The fact that May Beringer had really been to the station and tried to escape by the train brought it all home to her most vividly. Never would she have embarked on such an adventure had she not been most truly frightened—frightened by that wicked old woman!

Lucy Amorest ate her frugal luncheon, then knocked on Agatha Payne's door. There was no answer, so she waited for a little, then knocked again. Now there was some sound from within, and she entered.

The atmosphere was so close that she stayed for a moment by the door. A very large fire was burning. The room was exceedingly hot. Agatha Payne was sitting at the table playing cards. She gazed intensely. She did not look up. Her lips moved. She sat hunched, her dress pulled up to her knees. Her hands, holding a card, hung hovering over the table. Mrs. Amorest was frightened. For some unaccountable reason she wanted to turn and go straight back to her room again. She had never been frightened in Mrs. Payne's room before. It was perhaps the heat and absence of any air.

"Excuse me, Agatha," she said, "I want to speak to you a moment."

Mrs. Payne did not look up. She bent forward, touching the cards as they lay on the table. This angered Mrs. Amorest. She forgot her fear. She came forward, close to the table.

"Excuse me," she said again, "but I *must* speak to you. It is something of importance."

Mrs. Payne laid the card in her hand carefully on the table, then looked up.

"What is it?" she asked.

How strange she looks! Mrs. Amorest thought. Her large black eyes, dull like pools of ink, were expressionless. Her big heavy body was lurched together as though with a slight push it would tumble forward and lie, like a heap of clothes, on the floor. She had the air of someone who had been drinking.

"I have been seeing Miss Beringer," Mrs. Amorest said. "She is very ill—very seriously ill."

"What have I to do with her?" asked Mrs. Payne. Her body was galvanised into energy. She turned round in her chair and her eyes filled with a strange brooding expectancy; life had struck there as light strikes a pool.

"You have this to do with her," said Mrs. Amorest indignantly, "that you have been in there and something you have said to her has frightened her. She is easily frightened, and her heart is bad. You must leave her alone or I will have a doctor here who will make you."

"Indeed!" said Agatha Payne, looking at the little woman with a deep and slow contempt. "Who says that I have frightened her?"

"She says so herself. She has an idea in her head that you want to steal something of hers. I can't believe that of you, but sick women have strange fancies. She has done you no harm. Why won't you leave her alone?"

"Leave her alone!" Mrs. Payne laughed. "The silly old fool! Silly old fools both of you. A pair of sentimental old women. You with your precious boy and she with her dog!" She turned contemptuously back to her cards.

Mrs. Amorest flushed angrily.

"You leave my son alone," she answered. "And you leave Miss Beringer alone too. From what she tells me, you're no better than a thief."

"Thief, is it?" said Agatha Payne, looking at the cards. "Now you leave me alone, Lucy Amorest, and mind your own business, or it will be the worse for you."

"It *is* my own business!" Mrs. Amorest answered. "The woman is sick and has no one to care for her. If you go near her room again I'll—I'll call for the police!"

"You will, will you?" Mrs. Payne laughed. "And what have the police to do with it? You'd look fine and silly with the police coming in. You'd have them arrest me, I suppose? And for what? For going into that idiot's room to see whether she wanted anything! That's all I get for my kindness!"

She got up slowly from the table and moved over to the fire. Her thick heavy body seemed to tower over the rest of the room.

"Now, look here, Lucy Amorest," she said, "you mind your own business. I've stood you long enough—poking your nose in here where you are not wanted. I've not interfered with you, have I? Well then, leave me to myself."

"You may say what you like to me," Mrs. Amorest answered. "I'm not afraid of you, but that poor woman's life is in danger. Give her another fright and with her heart as it is anything can happen, and then you will be a murderess as well as a thief . . . !"

She paused, her breast heaving with indignation.

Agatha Payne seemed to quieten. She stared beyond Mrs. Amorest to the far spaces of the room. "She is so bad as that, is she?" she said gruffly. "Well—what does it matter? You are sentimental, Lucy, as always. She is old; she is sick; she is penniless. We are all old and sick and penniless. Three old, sick, penniless women. Do you know that? There are other old women, thousands of them, who have homes and friends and money. Perhaps they are happier than us, perhaps they are not. Perhaps, although they have all those things, there are others who are waiting for them to die, waiting for their places. They are tiresome; they have memories only of a time that others do not know. They admire things that all the others think absurd. With old age it is always the same. After seventy the sooner you go the better. With everyone it is so, but with us! How sentimental to pretend that we should live! We are not happy; we make no one else happy. This old woman in the next room, she is always complaining and crying and suffering. It would be a kindness if I were to go now, put my hand around her neck and choke her. You believe in another life where she will be happy and play on a harp, and yet you hinder her from going there. It is your sentiment. But in the end, you are more cruel than I."

"You speak like that," said Lucy Amorest, "and yet, although you are old like her, you would give everything to have something of hers, a piece of coloured stone that is nothing—nothing at all."

"Speak of what you understand," Agatha answered almost amiably. "What do you know of lust or desire for anything? You have never felt passion with your milk-and-water religion and your sentimentality. If I were to know that I had only half an hour more to live, I would want the sensation of owning that beautiful thing. Beauty! You don't know the meaning of the word."

She slumped down into the rocking-chair and with her back to Mrs. Amorest rocked there, kicking her shoe in the air.

To that broad back bulging between the bars of the chair, Lucy delivered her last words: "You must leave her alone. Whether I am sentimental or not, I will see to that." Then she left the room.

She felt the cool, even chilly air of the passage refreshing after that close heat. She would not think of herself. There was something in that woman's words that had struck deep into her heart, but that she kept away from her. She was tired, worn out. She went into her room and, lying down, slept. It was evening when she woke. Her room was dark. She stared about her at first, not remembering where she was. Then recollecting, she started up, blaming herself that she had neglected that poor woman. She lit her candles, brushed her hair and washed her face. She took a story of Grace Aguilar's from the shelf, then hurried into the other room.

May Beringer was lying down, the piece of amber in her hand, Pip beside her. The room was cold and had a faint thin light.

"Oh, I am so sorry," Mrs. Amorest cried, "I have been so long away. How are you now? Better?"

"I tried to get up but my back hurt so," Miss Beringer's tearful voice answered her. "I thought you were never coming."

Soon Mrs. Amorest had made the room bright again. The fire was lit. The candles shone. The kettle boiled and there was a hot cup of tea. But May Beringer's face did not change. She seemed for ever to be listening for something. She drank the tea, suffered her pillows to be shaken and her sheets smoothed.

Then Mrs. Amorest sat down beside the bed. "Now," she said, "that's better. I have brought a book I thought you might like. Such a pretty story. Do you like to be read to?"

"Yes," said May Beringer.

"Shall I read a little of it?"

"Yes, please. You don't hear anything, do you?"

"Hear anything? No, of course not. Now I'll begin. Are you quite comfortable?"

"Yes, thank you."

"Chapter one. . . ."

CHAPTER 10: DEATH OF MAY BERINGER

The firelight made patterns on the wall. Lucy Amorest's voice rose and fell. May Beringer lay without moving, staring in front of her.

The words began to swim before the reader's eyes. The print in patterns of grey and black and ivory thickened like swarms of flies across the light. The head nodded. The book crashed to the floor.

"Oh! I beg your pardon," Mrs. Amorest cried. "Reading aloud always after a time makes me sleepy. And I expect that it is making you sleepy too. You've had enough of it, I'm sure."

May Beringer did not reply. She was striving to be brave enough to utter certain words. What she wanted to say was: "Please, Mrs. Amorest, don't leave me tonight. I'm sure you could make yourself comfortable with the armchair and the other chair. I will never forget it if you stay. Only for tonight. Please, please don't leave me alone."

That was what she wanted to say. For the last hour she had not been listening to the words that were read but had been forming these words in her brain. "Oh, please, Mrs. Amorest . . ."

But she had not the courage to utter them. She was frightened about this, as she was frightened about everything else in her life. She had detected in Mrs. Amorest something, not precisely hard, but rather restrained and critical. Mrs. Amorest would think May Beringer a fool for her fears, and although she did not mind that she should be thought a fool could she only get her way, the immediate moment when she would make her suggestion and then see that look in Mrs. Amorest's eyes was too difficult for her. She rehearsed the words to herself again and again but the pushing them from silence into sound was too difficult for her.

And yet that awful moment when she should be left alone with all the long night in front of her was terrible for her too. Every way there was fear. That woman was waiting for her on the other side of the wall. She could see her standing there, listening, waiting until Mrs. Amorest should be gone. Oh! if only Mrs. Amorest would, herself, propose that she should stay.

She read on and on until May Beringer could have screamed from irritation. It wasn't that silly book that she wanted to hear, but rather those blessed words, "Wouldn't you like me to stay here tonight? I could make myself quite comfortable on that chair ..." The book fell to the floor; the moment of departure had arrived.

Mrs. Amorest rose from her chair and gave a little yawn. "Why, how late it is! I've been reading a long time. Don't you think that's a very pretty story?"

"Yes."

"I like the way she writes, don't you?"

"Yes, I do."

"We'll have some more tomorrow. I've quite forgotten how the story goes. It must be a long long time since I read it."

And May Beringer was saying, "Oh, do say you'll stop with me. Stop with me at least until I have fallen asleep." She struggled to have the courage to force out the words:

"Don't you think ... ?"

"What is it, dear?"

"... you could make up the fire a little before you go?"

"Why, of course I will."

Mrs. Amorest made up the fire, patted the pillows a little, then kissed May Beringer. "Now are you sure you are comfortable? Your heart isn't troubling you so much, is it?"

"No, oh no!" She put out her hand and drew Mrs. Amorest to the bed.

"Do stay with me a moment longer. I don't want you to go."

"Why, of course I will, dear."

"You don't think me foolish, do you?"

"Of course not."

"I am foolish and frightened. A silly old woman. But you've been so kind to me. There's one thing I'd like you to do."

"What is it, dear?"

"Would you mind, before you go, saying a prayer, a prayer about the dangers of the night and being kept safe?"

Mrs. Amorest nodded her head. "I know," she said. She knelt down beside the bed and closed her eyes. Still holding May Beringer's hand, she prayed:

"Dear Lord Jesus, we are Thy children and Thou knowest what is best for us. We pray Thee now when the night comes down over our heads and there is darkness everywhere that Thy might may be ever before our eyes, and that whether we are waking or sleeping we may know no fear. The powers of darkness are obedient to Thy command. Our trust is in Thee, and because Thou lovest Thy Children Thou wilt give them nothing that can do them harm. So, trusting, we fall asleep in Thy arms, dear Jesus. Amen."

"What a nice prayer," May Beringer said with a sigh. "I have never heard it before."

"Yes, it is a nice one," said Mrs. Amorest. "Our nurse used to say it to us when we were children."

"Where did you live when you were a child?" asked May Beringer, holding Mrs. Amorest's hand very tightly.

"We lived in the Lake District," said Mrs. Amorest, smiling. "Near Keswick."

"Were you happy as a child?"

"Very happy. My father was a clergyman. We had very little money, but we didn't want much. There were three of us and we lived all day on the hills. We used to walk for ever and ever. We knew all the hills and all the lakes. Scawfell and Great Gable and Cat Bells and Crummock and Buttermere and St. John's Vale and Wastdale Head and Grasmere." She said the names over slowly, tasting them on her tongue. "And I have never been back there. If I could once more see Thirlmere from Helvellyn——" She broke off, laughing. "I forget I'm an old woman. I couldn't climb even Helvellyn now. I've loved Glebeshire and Cornwall and Devonshire since, but not as I loved those hills."

"Doesn't it always rain up there?" May Beringer asked. "I've heard it does." And behind these words the others were following: "Oh, please stay here with me tonight! Please stay here with me tonight." But she could not force them. They would not come.

"No, of course it does not. That's only the silly nonsense that people talk. There is a lot of rain in all parts of England, but we used to love when we were children to see the storms come up over the hills, hiding them, and then breaking like paper and letting the light come through. And the Lake—Derwentwater—you should see the colour run over it like someone dancing. I wrote poetry about it when I was a girl, and then I married a poet, which was better than writing poetry."

May Beringer stared desperately about her. Was there nothing that would put it into Mrs. Amorest's head to stay?

"Well," said Mrs. Amorest, gently withdrawing her hand, "I must go now. You must have a long sleep and then you'll see how much better you'll be in the morning."

"Won't you stay a little?"

"No. You must go to sleep now." She bent down and kissed her. "Go to sleep and have beautiful dreams."

"Oh, please stay a little while." But Mrs. Amorest was gone.

Mrs. Amorest was gone, and in the silence that followed her departure there came a new sound that May had never heard in that house before. It was the dripping of a tap. It must be out there on the landing. How clearly it came through the closed door. Like someone counting time. One, two, three, four—then a pause—then several drips together. Like an old man querulously complaining, and then in the steady drip, drip again something stern and remorseless. Someone counting as though he said, "Now when I've reached thirty . . . ."

May began to count. She counted to ten, and after that so many came together that she could count no longer. She would never sleep with that horrible thing at her door. The fantastic idea came to her— and one's ideas are fantastic when one is sick and has been lying in bed with so many idle thoughts hovering about one—that that horrible woman had started the noise. It would be like her. There would be other noises also in the house that would be of her agency. Oh! I must escape from this! I must! I will go into Mrs. Amorest's room and never mind if she thinks me a fool. I will tell her that I must stay with her, that I won't be alone. . . . . .

She moved, got half out of bed; but her head was swimming. The room danced round and round her. Pip climbed off the bed, gave her one beseeching look, and crawled away out of sight.

That frightened her. He had been so strange during these last two days, as though he also was sick, nervous, and frightened, refusing his food. Even Mrs. Bloxam had noticed it.

She sank back upon the pillows again, and thence weakly cried,

"Pip! Pip! Come back. Come here. Good dog! Good dog!" But Pip did not reappear.

A curious lethargy slipped upon her. It was as though something had seized her limbs and she would never be able to move again. She was almost asleep and fancied through her half-closed eyes that figures moved dimly about the room. She was in her childhood once more; all the family were round her with their noise and their selfishness and their jokes, in which, for some reason, she was never able to share. There was Gertrude, her eldest sister, with her large fishy eyes, her thin frizzled hair; always trying to marry somebody. May hated Gertrude and Gertrude hated May. Gertrude was for ever putting her in her place, telling her not to do this, not to go there, not to be such a silly. May could hear her voice very plainly, that shrill high voice saying, "Don't be such a silly, May. Isn't May a silly?"

And she was a silly—for ever doing the wrong thing. Had Gertrude been kind to her and shown her how to do things it would have been different. If Gertrude had been kind to her as Jane Betts (afterwards) was, what a bright happy woman May would have become. But they were always laughing at her, so that, although May was in any case a clumsy and awkward girl, she was yet more clumsy and awkward. Well, Gertrude was dead now. Dead. May had beaten her there. But was she dead? Was she not standing there by the fireplace in just that lilac-coloured dress she used to wear, with just that same affected smile? And there was Rupert, fat and red-faced.

How anxious Rupert had been about his figure! But it was difficult because he loved food, and he would starve himself for a week and then break down and eat more than ever. But he had been kind to her when he remembered, only he did not remember very often. He was kind to her, but he despised her. May tried all things to make him despise her less. She wanted someone to be proud of her. Someone. Any one. Their stupid ignorant governesses. Miss Marchmont. Miss LeFevre. Miss Albany. May remembered them all although it was so long ago. But it was not so long ago after all. It was only the other day. Was not that Miss Marchmont there now, standing in the corner near the door?

Miss Marchmont was the thin bony one with the flat bit on the end of her nose which somebody said was like the portraits of Rembrandt, so that after that they always called her "Miss Rembrandt," and didn't she hate it! Surely it was only yesterday that Miss Marchmont had been seen coming into the house at five in the morning and had been compelled to leave that very day! How excited they had all been and how curious!

What had she been doing that she should stay out all night? The girls had talked among themselves, and even May had been admitted into the family councils. The boys had known more than the girls did, and hinted at what they knew but wouldn't tell . . . And there was May's mother—there just beyond the railings of the bed. How May had adored her, and how she had longed to be adored in return! But it was always the other girls who were petted and praised and shown off in company. May had done things that she was sure her mother would like, and her mother would have liked them too had only Gertrude or Clara or Isabella done them, but because it was May . . .

Her mother had not been happy. May saw that now. She had found her once crying in her bedroom and had longed to put her arm around her and console her, but she had not known how to do it nor what to say. She had failed in that, as she had failed in everything else in her life. The shadows moved and moved again. The fire leapt and fell. May slept. She dreamed. She was hurrying along a windy road. It was night, and on one side of her was a dark wood. She was frightened, of course, and she knew that when she came to a cross-roads someone would be there waiting for her. Someone terrible. She did not want to go on. She tried to stop, but the wind drove her along.

Had she more courage she would run into the wood and hide there, but no, she must go on faster and faster. The cross-roads were there and standing clearly to be seen in the pale light was someone waiting for her. She was flung onwards crying for mercy. She tried to turn back, and then as she saw the hands stretched out to grasp her she woke. She lay, the sweat on her forehead, her body trembling, her heart running and jumping and missing, and missing and jumping and running. She could see quite clearly. There were no longer any shadows in the room. She heard, so plainly that it seemed that it must be with her now beside her bed, the running tap. One, two, three, four. . . . She lay, trying to remember Mrs. Amorest's prayer. "Lord Jesus, Lord Jesus, Lord Jesus," she repeated.

She closed her eyes, but a sound forced her to open them again. She cried, "Who's there?" The handle of the door was turning. Very carefully and quietly, closing the door behind her, Agatha Payne came in.

"Good evening, Miss Beringer," she said. "I came in to see whether you wanted anything."

"I want nothing." With a great effort, breaking the restraint that held her, she turned and lay with her face towards the wall.

Agatha Payne sat down on the chair beside the bed. "But I want us to have a little talk. If you are sleepy, I can wait. I am not at all sleepy myself."

May neither answered nor moved. A long silence followed, and for May it was filled with an agonising determination not to show her fear. She would not move; she would not speak. She was biting her lips, her hands were fiercely clenched, one holding tightly the red amber. That woman might kill her, but she would not move. Then her heart ceased to beat. It ceased absolutely. She began to suffocate. Someone seemed to be pushing her up to the wall so that her face was pressed against the faded wall-paper. She could not endure her suffering and she turned in the bed.

That woman was sitting quietly on the chair. She was wearing a loose wrapper of a dirty yellow; one end of the wrapper had slipped off her shoulder, revealing it of a curious copper brown colour, and part of her breast. She sat leaning forward a little, staring at the counterpane.

On seeing Miss Beringer turn she asked, smiling:

"Why do you complain about me?"

"I haven't complained."

"Yes. To Mrs. Amorest. She came into my room and was very insulting. I'm sure I've been very kind to you. There are not many who would bother about a miserable sick old woman like yourself."

"Oh, go away. Please, please go away!" May Beringer whispered.

"Go away? Oh no! I am very comfortable here. I shall stay for half an hour or an hour, or perhaps two. Perhaps all night."

"I know. You have come to steal my amber from me."

"Steal? Oh no—certainly not. I have come to make you more comfortable. To smooth your pillows!"

She leant over the bed.

May Beringer gave a little cry half-strangled by her fear and shuddered to the wall. "Don't touch me! Don't touch me! I'll scream. I'll rouse everybody. Don't touch me!"

Agatha Payne, holding her wrapper about her brown neck with one hand, leaned over her. Her hair, raven black in the firelight, had loosened and some of it hung untidily about her face.

"Your screams won't be heard. There's only old Lucy Amorest. She's fast asleep by this time, and there's the passage between. Besides, you can't scream. You're too frightened. Try and see. But I have not come to hurt you. Only to spend an hour or two. You go to sleep. I shan't touch you. What do you think I am, a murderess?"

"Yes, you would murder me to have my amber."

"Murder! That's a nasty word. Why don't you take things more quietly? See! I'm sitting down. I'm kind enough if you know how to deal with me, but when you tremble like that it gives me pleasure. Can't you understand? The more you tremble the more I like to tease you. I lift my hand, and see!—you shake all over!"

"Can't you see that I'm sick?" May Beringer whispered. "I'm not young any more. My heart's bad, and my back. It's true that you frighten me. Everything always has. You did from the first moment I saw you."

"Well, well," said Agatha Payne, moving her hand slowly up and down the counterpane. "Fancy that! I wonder why. Of course, I'm not very handsome, and sometimes I think I'm not quite right in the head. I've had a good deal to try me at times. But you shouldn't tempt me. I'd have been quiet enough if you hadn't shaken and quivered at the mere sight of me. That would excite anybody."

She looked at her, huddled up beneath the clothes, crouching as though fearing a blow. "You're a miserable old woman, aren't you? We aren't much, the three of us up here at the top of this house. Birds of a feather!

"But at least Lucy Amorest's got some spirit. You haven't the spirit of a flea. Why, if I were to drag you out of your bed, strip you naked, and beat you round the room, you wouldn't object."

"That's what you want," said May Beringer, panting. "You want my piece of amber. You'll have to kill me to get it."

Agatha Payne shrugged her shoulders. "I'll have it someday, never you fear. Now, why don't you give it me quietly? It's only a toy when all's said. Or suppose we share it? I have it a month and you have it a month. Let's look at it."

"No, no, no!"

"All right, then. I can wait."

She sat in silence for a little and then she went on: "What do you cling to life for? You're sick and always in pain. You've got no money. You haven't a friend in the world. I've at least got my passions, and Lucy Amorest's got her pluck. But you! You'll be happier dead—far happier."

May Beringer began to cry. "You're cruel to me—dreadfully cruel. What have I ever done to you? You are the cruellest woman I have ever known. Tomorrow morning I'll have you turned out of the house. I'll tell them all what you are doing to me."

"And what am I doing, pray? Having a little chat. Looking after you a little. Crying? What do you do that for? Don't you know it excites me? Crying? I've never cried in my life, not when my lover left me because he was tired of me. You've never had a lover, not with that face of yours. But I had—plenty once. I was handsome, and I didn't care what I did. You! You snivelling old scarecrow! It would be a fine sort of man that would make love to *you*!"

May Beringer sat up, a strange sight with the tears drying on her cheeks and her grey hair hanging about her face. She kept her hands beneath the sheets.

"I beg you to leave me just for tonight," she said. "You can do what you like in the morning—I won't tell anyone—but for tonight . . ."

"Yes," said Agatha Payne, "give me that piece of amber and I'll go."

"No. Never. Jane gave it me."

"Very well, then. I'll wait a little. I don't care. I can sit up all night if need be."

She gave a little shiver. "It's cold in here. You've let the fire almost out. I'll have a blaze in a minute."

She went over to the fire, shovelled on the coal from the scuttle, found a piece of newspaper which she held up, going down on her knees. The room was for a moment dark, then a golden light sprang up behind the newspaper, there was a roaring chuckle and the fire was ablaze. Agatha stayed there on her knees before the glow.

She liked the heat, she knelt there, her hands spread out fan-wise. The fire, brilliant now and leaping, changed the room. Great shadows were thrown on the walls—Agatha's hand was gigantic like a flat moving fish. The only candle was near its end and leapt also as though it were emulating the fire, throwing its own shadows in silly rivalry. Agatha knelt without speaking, and in the silence, May Beringer heard very clearly the dripping, drunken voice of the tap: "One . . . two . . . five . . . I sh . . . hate . . . I . . . shall . . . get . . . it . . . for being . . . late one—two—three—four . . ."

She had her idea. While that woman had her back toward her she would slip from the bed, run across the passage, and escape into Mrs. Amorest's room. It was as though she were attempting the most dangerous feat of her life. She half rose, drew her knees together, slid to the other side of the bed, had her feet on the floor.

Instantly Agatha Payne turned. "Hullo! What are you about?"

May Beringer stayed frozen, her body limply attached to the bed.

311

She had even now her chance. The door was not far. Once in the passage she could at least cry out so that Mrs. Amorest would wake and hear her. But she could not move. For one thing her legs were trembling so pitifully that they would not support her body and she was almost slipping to the floor. She could only gaze miserably upon that woman, still kneeling but turning her great shapeless body towards her, the blazing fire giving her black hair a glittering sheen.

"I was going for a moment," May Beringer whispered, "into the passage."

"No, I think not." Agatha Payne slowly rose, looking steadily at her. "If you want anything I can get it for you." Then her expression changed. "Ah! So, you have it in your hand. I wondered where it was."

May Beringer put the hand that clutched the amber behind her back. "Ah! let me go! Please let me go!" she whispered.

"I should think not." She took a step towards her. "You'll catch your death all naked. You get back into bed. I'm mistress here now. You want looking after, I can see." She made another slow lurching step towards her. May Beringer could not take her eyes from that face, nor that shining hair, nor that shapeless body. She crept back into bed and crouched there, her grey hair now all about her eyes, staring through her hair, the bed-clothes huddled about her.

Agatha Payne came over and sat down in the chair once more.

"So that's what you were up to, was it? Escaping into the passage ill as you are. I can see you're not safe to be left. A nice report I must give to the doctor tomorrow when I've let you wander all over the house."

May could only stare and stare; her breathing came in pants. Her body gave little jerks from time to time as though it were trying to shake from itself some dreadful weight. Her face was of a grey ivory shadow. Only her eyes, terrified, peered out like someone staring into the dark.

The candle gave a leap and went out.

"So, you're holding it there under the bedclothes, are you?" Agatha Payne went on. "That's a childish thing. Like a schoolgirl. Give it me for a moment. I'll return it to you."

"No," came a small dry voice as though from an infinite distance, "I won't."

"Oh, you won't, won't you?" Agatha sucked her finger reflectively. "Perhaps I shall have to make you. In spite of my affection for you, I don't think I *can* sit here all night. You'd much better give it me and have done with it. You'll have to tell them in the morning that you've given it me, or I'll come in tomorrow night too—and the night after that and the night after that until you *do* give it me. What a fuss to make about a little thing! I'm a determined woman. I always have my way in the end. You'd much better give it me and go to sleep quietly."

The voice came again dry and distant, "Jane gave it me."

"Oh, she did, did she? You've told me that before. You haven't seen your Jane for years, and I'm sure she's forgotten all about you long ago. Do you know that when you're dead there's not a single soul will be sorry? That's a nice thought, isn't it? But I don't want to be unkind. If you weren't such a poor miserable creature I wouldn't bother with you, but you excite me. I like to see you cry. I like to see you tremble. Now, you'd better give it me or I shall have to take it."

The voice came again, "I won't. Jane gave it me."

"Now, come on. Give it up." Agatha leant over the bed. May Beringer with a little strangled cry moved towards the wall.

Agatha Payne moved her hand, and, quite gently, touched May Beringer's shoulder. "I'm not going to hurt you, but I'm going to have that piece of amber—just because I said I would. Come now."

Great shivers shook May Beringer's body. Two tears welled into her eyes and then slowly trickled on to her dry cheeks.

"Come, give it me."

Still gently she shook the other's shoulder. Then something moved in her, some sudden passion or fury. She leaned right over the bed, her wrapper slipping, her hair loose and wild.

"You silly fool, don't aggravate me. I *shall* hurt you if you don't take care. Give it up now. Give it up." May Beringer was pressed against the wall but her head was turned, staring up into Agatha's.

"Are you going to let me have it? I shan't ask you again." There was no reply, only a long-drawn heaving sigh.

Agatha Payne stretched her arm across the other's body, reached down below the clothes, and pulled at the hand. May Beringer drew herself up over the pillow against the iron bars of the bed. Her body shook. Her lips were drawn back. Between her set teeth came little shuddering sobs.

"Now, then, don't be a fool any longer. You see I mean what I say." Their faces now were almost touching. Agatha's hand pulled at the clenched fist. She felt the cool of the amber. With a rough, strong movement she pushed up May Beringer's arm.

At the same moment it was as though some sudden shock galvanised May's body. She rose straight up against the wall, stiffly like a rod, her eyes staring out over the fire-shadowed room. A convulsive movement shuddered through her. She whispered, "Oh, Jesus! Jesus!" then with a sigh collapsed against Agatha·Payne's bare breast.

The hand was still tightly clenched. Agatha took the amber, then, drawing back, saw the body slide under the bedclothes huddled in a heap, but the head, with staring eyes, rested on the pillow.

May Beringer was dead. There was no doubt of it.

Agatha drew back, holding the amber in one hand, folding the wrapper over her with the other.

"I didn't mean that!" she whispered huskily. "I didn't mean that!" There was a sound at her feet. The dog crept from under the bed and looked up at her. She looked down on him, then stood stroking the amber with her hand. She went back to the bed, smoothed the counterpane. The body lay now as though it were asleep, only the eyes were wide. She stood thinking. She went to the mantelpiece, placed the amber upon it, then very quietly stole from the room.

Chapter 11: Mrs. Amorest Shows Courage

It was of course Mrs. Bloxam who in the morning first learnt of poor Miss Beringer's death. She came tumbling into Mrs. Amorest's room: "Oh, mum! Poor Miss Bellringer! It's 'appened just as I thought. Lyin' as though she'd just dropped off in 'er sleep, pore worm, and nobody by 'er. A peaceful death that's certain—pore dear lady."

Mrs. Amorest, wakened from sleep, was at first unaware of the facts behind Mrs. Bloxam's cries. Then she put on her red flannel dressing-gown and hastened with Mrs. Bloxam into the other room.

"I closed 'er eyes, mum. They were starin' open. Pore lamb. She wasn't 'appy and she was a lonely soul. I daresay it's best for 'er that she's gone."

Mrs. Bloxam then standing there in her shabby black hat shed tears. Miss Beringer had, after all, two true mourners.

"I wish now," said Mrs. Amorest, looking down at the poor, tired, worn face, "that I had stayed here last night. I think that she wished me to. When I'd gone to my room I nearly came back. There was something in her eyes that seemed to ask me. At least it was a peaceful way to die, in her sleep, without pain."

Then she saw the dog crouching at the foot of the bed. "Oh, Pip! Poor Pip! What will he do now without his mistress?"

She went up and stroked him. He shivered beneath her hand, looked at her with miserable eyes, but did not move.

Mrs. Amorest looked about the room. "There is that piece of amber on the mantelpiece that she was so fond of. She had it in her hand when I left her. She must have got out of bed to put it up there."

They stood together in silence. At last Mrs. Amorest said, "We must lock the door and send for a doctor. There might have to be an inquest——"

Mrs. Bloxam looked frightened. "Oh lor', mum. And me give evidence?"

"It might be, when there's a sudden death like this. Do you know a good doctor near here?"

"Yes, mum. Dr. Bluett. A very nice gentleman."

"You'd better get him at once, Mrs. Bloxam."

"Yes, mum, I will."

They locked Miss Beringer in. Pip refused to leave the room and he was locked in also.

Back in her own place Mrs. Amorest hurriedly dressed, and as she dressed she blamed herself. She had been hard on poor May Beringer. Had she shown her more sympathy she would have made her happier. Her scorn for weakness and sentimentality in others was her fault, her grievous fault, and all her life it had been so. She could look back over the many years and see occasion after occasion when she had been hard and stern. So, she thought. She had been selfish too, filled with alarm about her own little unimportant affairs when this poor woman had been lonely and longing for affection.

But when she was dressed and stood looking from her window at the grey roofs, the creamy sky flecked with shreds of blue, there stole upon her, in spite of herself, a strong apprehension. She was alone now in this house with old Agatha Payne. So sharp was this realisation that she had the impulse to pack her bag instantly and go somewhere else. But where? She would find nowhere else so cheap, and in a boarding-house or lodging-house her liberty and freedom would be threatened, her privacy spied upon, her poverty laughed at. With this came realisation number two—that at this moment she had not a friend in all the world, and that were she to drop down dead as May Beringer had done, with the exception of Mrs. Bloxam's ready tear not a sigh would be breathed, nor a heart show pity.

The sight of May Beringer's pinched white face stranded there, like a derelict boat, on that desolate shore—the picture of that room with its shabby furniture, the grey ashes of the fire, the chill of the air, these things drove at her very heart. She would need her pluck today, must stiffen her back, hold up her head as she had never done in all her life before.

The doctor arrived, and after five minutes in May Beringer's room he paid a visit on Mrs. Amorest. He was a little round fat man, pale, and bald like a billiard ball, neat in a grey suit, a little pompous but kindly.

"Excuse me, madam, but your name is Mrs. Amorest, I think, and you are a tenant in this same building."

Mrs. Amorest said that she was and asked him to sit down. He seemed to like the gentle little lady, was surprised, perhaps, to find such a lady in such a place.

"You were a friend, I think, of the lady who has just died?"

Mrs. Amorest said that she was; not a close friend, Miss Beringer had only recently taken the room.

"Quite so. Quite. And I understand that she was in bed all yesterday. You were with her in the evening?"

"I was," said Mrs. Amorest.

"Did she complain of anything?"

"Yes, of her back and of her heart. She had complained of these to me before."

"Oh yes. Quite so. Had she any trouble, anything to disturb her in any way?"

Mrs. Amorest hesitated. "She was a very nervous woman, easily frightened. She was worried about her money affairs, I think, and her health."

"Exactly. Thank you very much. That's what I supposed."

He got up and made a stiff ceremonial bow, but he smiled and looked kindly.

"Will there have to be an inquest?" Mrs. Amorest asked.

"Well, there may be," Dr. Bluett answered. "It seems a clear case of heart failure. She had been seriously ill for a long time. The slightest worry would be bad for her. She might have dropped down dead any moment in the last ten years, I should say. Had she any relations or friends who ought to be told?"

"Really, I don't think there was anyone," Mrs. Amorest said. She had a strange feeling that she would like to keep this little billiard ball of a man for a while in her room. He was so friendly. It might be only his professional attitude, of course, but she thought not. She thought that if they pulled their chairs up in front of the fire and had a chat they would become good friends. Strange how long it was since she had had any one to pull up a chair with!

"No one at all?"

"I don't think so. She had one great friend, but she has not heard from her for many years."

"Poor woman. A lonely life." Dr. Bluett gave a little sigh that was as though he were blowing very faintly on a penny whistle. "No one ever came and saw her?"

"I think nobody."

"Dear me. How lonely she must have been." He looked at Mrs. Amorest then as though he were about to say something more personal, but he checked himself.

"Anyone else live up at the top here?"

"Yes, there's a Mrs. Payne—a widow."

"Was she a friend of Miss Beringer's?"

"Not really. They met once or twice, I think."

"Well, I may have to disturb her. I don't know. I may not have to bother you again. Good morning."

Mrs. Amorest longed to say, "Oh, do bother me again! Come and see me. I'll give you tea. You don't know what a kindness you'd be doing," but of course she said nothing of the kind.

He bowed beautifully at the door and rolled away down the stairs. When he was gone the silence of the house was insupportable. She did not know what terrors and dismays might not surround her. She would go and buy poor May Beringer some flowers.

As she left the house she fancied that its forbidding dark windows leered after her. She was not given to "dreams and symbols," but she had come to hate the place and felt that it also hated her.

When she arrived in the busy part of the town it was gay enough. The sun was shining and the High Street bustling with people. There was Canon Bentinck-Major talking on the very edge of the curb to that pretty girl, Joan, daughter of Archdeacon Brandon. Mrs. Amorest adored to see pretty young things with plenty of health about them. What she always said was that she could not understand why the Old Lady in the Shoe should be bothered. She only wished that she'd had her chance! Then there was Canon Ryle, the precentor, smiling and polite to whomsoever. Mrs. Amorest would have liked a smile from him. She admired so greatly the way that he sang the services in the cathedral, but of course he did not know her so of course he could not smile! Then here was Mrs. Combermere with her dogs and walking-stick and mauve hat with a bright red feather. Now she was greeting the Precentor, and it seemed for a moment that they changed sexes, so masculine and downright was Mrs. Combermere, so smiling and attentive was Canon Ryle!

And then (by this time Mrs. Amorest was almost at the bottom of the High Street), who should turn up the hill from the river but the great Archdeacon Brandon himself! Oh, but Mrs. Amorest did admire him! Some said that he was vain and imperious, but Mrs. Amorest did not think so. She felt that when you were as large and as handsome and as commanding as that, you had a right to be a little vain! He moved with such vitality, such energy, as though he knew just what he intended to do at every step and no one should stop him! She admired him most as he passed from his stall to the Lectern to read the Lesson. How beautiful then he was with his head up, his shoulders back like a general leading his forces into battle! Mrs. Amorest was not senti-mental about men, she knew their faults as well as another, but about Archdeacon Brandon she permitted herself some indulgence.

She liked a man to *be* a man, and whatever else Archdeacon Bran-don might be, no one could deny him his masculinity!

She had thought that she would buy the flowers from the gnarled old woman in the market: thither she went. But she had not realised that it was Market Day. The Square was filled with pigs and sheep, dogs and cows. Stout farmers were standing importantly in groups; the booths were all set out with their wares; women were crying their goods, boys shouting, horses neighing. She had not been for many a day in such a regardless multitude, and she stood bewildered with people pushing her on every side, the sun dazzling her eyes. All the world was so gay, and there behind her was that silent house with May Beringer lying dead in it and half-crazy old Agatha Payne mumbling over her fire.

She had a queer impulse to cry like a little girl lost and terrified. She felt again what she had been feeling so often of late—but now with overwhelming force—that nobody wanted her. No one in the High Street had smiled at or recognised her, and now they were jos-tling and disregarding her as though she were not alive at all! What would happen to her if her few investments descended even lower than they had already gone? She simply would not be able to live at all. She would starve slowly up there in that horrible house and nobody would know and nobody would care. What happened to old ladies when they had no money and no friends? No one cared about old ladies. They cared about old women of the other class. There were homes for them and clubs for them, and societies, and people came and visited them and brought them food and warm clothing. The alms-houses nowadays were comfortable and friendly, and all the old women gossiped over the fire. But old ladies were not supposed to go into alms-houses; it was not thought that they needed them.

And old ladies were forced to maintain certain appearances. They were expected to look like ladies, to wear nice clothes, and if they did not people laughed at them and thought them odd. The very last thing that Mrs. Amorest wanted was pity or charity, but she did want friends and someone—any one—to care whether she lived or died.

If Mr. Bloxam deceased and Mrs. Bloxam in the course of time grew old there would be no appearances for her to keep up, and people would visit her and her own cronies would come and sit by her fire and gossip. She thought, desolately, standing there, of Brand; but that letter from him had been posted a year ago. For the first time in her history she admitted to herself that he might be dead. It was probable indeed that he was. Why did no one ever think of ladies who were poor and lonely and ill? Everyone else in the world was thought of, from the natives in the centre of Africa to the slum children in Seatown. It was true, as Agatha Payne had said, that old people were tiresome and in the way. It was men like Archdeacon Brandon and pretty girls like his daughter Joan whom the world wanted!

This was bad for Lucy Amorest, unlike her in every way. She bit her lips to keep the tears back, and then when a stout farmer knocked past her anger took the place of tears. How rude they were! She refused to be ill-treated by any of them. She was not dead yet, although they might think so. She found her way to the old flower-woman and spent the last penny in her pocket on a large bunch of daffodils. They cheered her a little. They were bright and gay and cheerful and, most certainly, no respecter of persons. To them the rich and the poor, the young and the old, were all alike.

She despised herself, as she went up the High Street again, for her mood of pusillanimity and cowardice, and, as was her way, spoke to herself inside herself: "Now, Lucy Amorest, you're every bit as good as anybody here. If they look down on you, you look down on them. The game isn't over yet, and there's a good time coming." The daffodils promised her at least that spring was coming, and she was always happy in the spring. As she looked at the blue sky and felt the breeze on her cheek she felt for a moment that she was back again on her beloved northern hills, climbing Cat Bells to turn and see Derwentwater like a silver platter at her feet, looking down upon Thirlmere from Helvellyn, seeing the wind blow the reeds like music on Rydal.

Nevertheless, she must positively beat herself back to Pontippy Square. It was as though something was warning her; never had she found it so hard to cross the cobbles of the Square and pass on up that cold, deserted pavement. No life in any house. The windows dead and deserted. Silence absolute.

She climbed the stairs, hating her cowardice, went to her room and took off her hat, then, with the daffodils in her hand, crossed to May Beringer's door. She unlocked it. The room was cold and bleak. She knelt down beside the bed and tried to pray but, to her horror, no prayer would come.

The house—the stairs, the walls, the grey-faced windows—seemed to push in between her and her prayer. She could not realise God at all; she could not think of May save as motionless there, passing to corruption with her closed eyes and yellow face. She could think of no prayer at all. She began, "Our Father," and could not remember the words.

She opened her eyes and stared about the room. She thought that May Beringer's left eye opened, winked at her and solemnly closed again. The daffodils that she had laid on the bed looked already faded and dead. There was around her nothing but death and decay.

She got on her feet and stared about her, feeling that in another moment she would surrender to some horrible blasphemy or impiety.

"Dear Jesus Christ," she said aloud, "do not leave me."

Something moved and she gave a little cry. It was the dog. He came to her, crouched against her dress and looked beseechingly up at her. The relief at his company was so great that she knelt down there on the floor, took him into her arms, and pressed his head against her breast. He did not move except that faintly he licked her hand. He seemed very feeble, and now when she moved towards the door, carrying him, he did not protest.

With a sigh of relief, she was back in her room. The late morning sun was pouring in, shining on the rose-coloured furniture, the silver match-box, Brand's photograph. She looked about her with pleasure. The air was different here; shabby old room as it was, it was her own place, filled with her own personality. It knew her—it had witnessed her hopes and fears and disappointments. It recognised that she had tried to brighten it and give it colour and life. It was grateful. She poked up the fire, put a cushion in front of it, and laid Pip there. Then she poured half the milk out of the bottle into a deep saucer, crumbled up biscuit into it and tried to persuade him to eat. But he would not touch it. Little convulsive shudderings passed over his body. Once and again he raised his head and stared at the door in acute apprehension. Mrs. Amorest had the strange fancy as she looked at him that he was oddly like his departed mistress. The look in his eyes was the same. She had seen just that half-hypnotised stare of alarm in May Beringer's eyes. He would not touch the biscuit and milk, feebly wagged his tail as though he appreciated her kindness, licked her hand again, but would touch nothing. Yet he had not eaten anything since the preceding evening and must be very hungry.

She took her George Herbert and sat down near the fire and tried to be caught into the poems that she so dearly loved. But just as before she could not pray, so now she could not attend to the poetry. She continued to look at the door, and when the dog raised his head and gazed in terrified fashion at the door she also was compelled to look. The conviction slowly came to her that the dog had been witness of something dreadful. He was frightened in reminiscence as well as in anticipation. He had the look in his eyes that she had seen once or twice with human beings, once in the face of a little child who was terrified of her mother, once in a woman who had a drunken husband. What had happened last night?

Had May Beringer woken before she died and realised that death was upon her? Had she tried to call for assistance? Why had she placed the amber piece on the mantelpiece? Had her heart attack come upon her while she was out of bed? No, she had been lying peacefully there. There was no sign of any physical distress. But how Lucy wished now that she had stayed there all night. She knew—she saw it all now so clearly—that May Beringer had longed for her to stay, had not had courage to ask her. Had she felt a little more sympathy, shown a little more understanding, she would have offered to remain and May Beringer would not, perhaps, have died. She blamed herself bitterly and vowed that, for whatever years of life might remain to her, she would never be scornful of others' weaknesses nor hard in her judgements.

There was something very humiliating to her in the thought that after all these years she had not learnt human charity. She heard the cathedral clock dimly strike one, and to change her thoughts she prepared her frugal meal. She sat at the table drinking her tea and eating her bread and cheese. She took from the bookshelf an old faded volume of the *Cornhill*. It was one that contained Anthony Trollope's

Small House at Allington with the Millais pictures, and as she turned the pages she felt comfortable. The old illustrations with the quaint dresses, the leisurely, happy life, Lily Dale, who knew only the stress of choosing between two lovers, the slow, long afternoons, the quiet evenings, brought back her own youth, happy days, multitudes of friends, eager anticipation of glorious life; all that past seems in retrospect so safe and secure that one wonders why one did not realise its blessings more fully.

She fell asleep in her chair with the volume on her knees; she woke with a start to find the sun low, sinking behind the chimney-pots, and Agatha Payne in the room.

"Agatha!" she cried, starting up, the volume dropping to the floor. "I never heard you come in."

Agatha Payne said nothing. She stood looking out of the window.

"What is it? Do you want anything?"

She slowly turned round. "Why didn't you tell me that May Beringer was dead?" she asked.

Lucy Amorest answered, "Why should I have bothered you? There was nothing more to be done. We had the doctor. She died quietly in her sleep."

"I knew," said Agatha, coming up to the fire. "There was no need to tell me."

"You knew?"

"Yes. She came and told me herself."

Mrs. Amorest said, "What do you mean—she told you?"

"She came this morning and told me. She's never going to leave me again. She's given me the amber, though. She says she doesn't want it anymore."

Terror seized Mrs. Amorest. She felt nothing save an urgent passionate desire to escape. She had had enough. She could endure no more.

"Oh, don't tell me!" she cried. "You don't know what you're saying. She's dead. She's gone."

"She hasn't gone," Agatha replied slowly and quietly. "She's here in this house. I killed her body but I haven't got rid of her. She is never going to leave me anymore. She says so."

"You killed her?" Mrs. Amorest's voice was a low whisper of horror.

"Yes. I went in last evening and killed her. I didn't mean to, but I frightened her and she died. However, it doesn't matter now, except that I don't want to be left alone with her. She might do me some harm."

Mrs. Amorest rose from her chair and faced her. "Stop that! I won't have it. You don't know what you're saying. You're mad. You don't know what you're saying."

"I know very well what I'm saying. It's true. She came to me this morning as I was sitting in my chair. She stood as close to me as I'm standing to you. She said that I could have the amber and that she would never leave me. But I won't be alone with her. I won't. There's her dog. He knows what I did."

Mrs. Amorest said, "You're ill, Agatha. You must get out of this house and I must too. You don't know what you're saying. Go and lie down in your room. You'll sleep, and when you wake these fancies will have gone."

Agatha moved back to the window. "You're a fool, Lucy. You always were. It's true what I'm telling you. And what's the good of my leaving this house? She'll come with me, I tell you. If I died she'd be with me just the same. But she won't come while you're there. You can keep her away. Well, I've tried you. I'll go now, but I'll come back."

She moved slowly, with her old lurching movement, out of the room.

Is it madness? Is it delusion? Where does this thing begin and end? The transition is so slight and when you are weary, hungry, old, lonely you are fitting prey for any wandering spirit. Agatha Payne—May Beringer's death—these things were real. Real, too, the isolation and the fear. Lucy Amorest had never before in all her life known what fear truly was. She knew it now. She knew it so that it held her where she was; she stood where Agatha Payne had left her as though a spell had been woven about her. Her head was up. She was listening. A tap was dripping in the hall. One—two—three—four and then a number together. She had not known that there *was* a tap in the hall, but now it was the only voice in all that listening, waiting world. Agatha Payne was mad, crazy, off her head. Was she imagining that she had gone into May Beringer's room or had she in reality been there? Had some horrible scene occurred? Poor May Beringer! Oh, poor May Beringer! But if the woman had been there she had not taken the amber. Perhaps it was she who had placed it on the mantelpiece. She had been afraid, it might be, that she would be accused of theft or violence. Had she been sane enough to fear that?

Lucy Amorest's knees were trembling. She sat down upon the bed, leaning forward, her hands clasped, holding herself together. Must she spend another night alone in that place with that woman? But where to go? To a hotel? To Mrs. Bloxam? She shrank from that. There was cowardice in it and especially it seemed to her, in some odd way, that she would be deserting May Beringer all alone there in that chill room. Moreover, she felt that she had no strength.

The room was so dark now and the fire so low that she could see nothing, but it needed an immense determination to move to the table and light the candles. When she had lit them, they seemed to illuminate the room only in patches. By the door there it was quite dark. It appeared to her now that it must be another woman who must dare to move to the fire, place coal on it, draw her chair to it, find a book. That was what she *should* do, but she was paralysed, standing in the circle of candle-light, listening and counting mechanically to herself the drippings of the tap in the hall. Poor May Beringer! Had she also heard that tap, lying there in bed and counting? Lucy had despised May's fears, but now she herself had fears as terrible.

She had forgotten the dog. He stirred. He raised his head, then let it fall. That released her from her spell. She went forward and knelt down beside the cushion. She put her arms around him. She heard him sigh, a ghost of a little sigh. He shivered, then lay still.

She knelt for some time with him thus in her arms, then some suspicion flew to her brain. She stroked his head, felt his heart. There was no beat there. He was dead.

She laid him down and drew desperately to her feet. He had died of terror. She knew it as clearly as though in his distress he had whispered it to her before his going. Panic came then crowding in upon her. She could not, she must not stay in this house another moment. She moved, stumbling across the room, found a small handbag in the corner by the chest of drawers, began to pull out handkerchiefs—anything that her hands touched—and to press them into the bag, and at every moment she paused listening. Panic grew upon her. She was afraid to stand in the dark and moved over to the candle-light. The sight of the dog lying so limply and desolately there moved her to an agony of distress. She knelt down by him again, stroking him, speaking to him, doing she knew not what. "Oh, Pip! I can't bear it. I'm frightened, Pip. I must get away and I don't know where to go. I'm so frightened. I'm so frightened! I can't think. I don't know what I'm to do, I'm all alone and Agatha's coming back."

She ran to the door thinking that she would lock it. There was no key. She remembered, as though it had been a hundred years ago, that it had not fitted and had been sent to be mended. She ran back to the fire again. She stood, squeezing her hands together, saying over and over again: "I don't know where to go! I must get away! I don't know where to go!"

The door opened. She cried out, "No! No! You can't come in! You can't come in!"

She saw a great figure that seemed to tower to the ceiling. She heard a strange voice. The figure moved forward, and at that, as though at last her endurance had snapped and she could bear no more, she put out her hands as though to shield her face and sank to the floor.

Chapter 12: The House is Abandoned

The man moved forward into the light. He looked about him in puzzled fashion.

"Is anyone here?" Then, as there was no answer, to himself aloud, "There's not a soul about, but the candles are burning——"

He looked over the table and saw the old lady crumpled up on the floor. With a step he was across to her, had her in his arms, was stroking her forehead and crying, "Mother! Mother! It's Brand! Mother! Mother! Old lady——"

He gazed about him distractedly, then heard the dripping of the tap clear through the door that he had left open behind him. In another moment he had a cup in his hand, was in the passage, had filled it and returned.

He picked her up and laid her gently on the bed, took out his handkerchief and damped her forehead, stroking her tiny hands with his big ones, whispering to her.

She stirred; opened her eyes for a moment and closed them again. He heard her murmur something. Then she felt the strong warm pressure of his arms about her, resisted a little, then, still without opening her eyes, settled back against his chest with a little sigh of contentment.

There was something very boyish in the look of distress and anxiety and love that he bent upon her. He was impulsive and forgetful, warm-hearted and generous, but living for the immediate hour, unsubtle, knowing nothing of analysis of character, loyal, quickly angry, nothing mean nor small nor jealous. A little of this you might have guessed from his broad, ugly, good-natured face, his large loose body, the kindliness of his eyes, and something proud in his gaze as he looked down upon her.

He would do anything for her now that he had her in his arms, but that did not mean that he had not gone on, carelessly, happily, without worrying in any way about her for three years or more.

She opened her eyes again and, very slowly, realisation crept into her heart. She started away from him saying confusedly, "What . . . ? Who . . . ? Where am I?" The familiar things about the room first assured her, then she saw the body of the dog. "Oh! I remember. Someone came in!"

She looked up at him, his large, brown, rather chubby face, the eyes startlingly blue, the hair receding, but fair and thick—she broke into the full triumph of her discovery:

"It's Brand! It's Brand! It's Brand!"

She began to laugh hysterically, buried her head in his rough tweed waistcoat, her hand feeling blindly about his neck, then pulled his head down to hers, kissing his eyes, his mouth, his cheeks, his ears, his forehead again and again, running her fingers through his hair.

"It's Brand! It's Brand! It's Brand!"

"That's better!" He caught her in a great hug, lifting her right off the bed. Almost he might have done it with one hand as though she had been a little grey sparrow. "That's more like it! I frightened you coming in. It was a silly thing to do, now I come to think of it, but like most of the things I do, the thinking came afterwards when it was too late. Now, old lady, let's have a look at you. What have you been doing to yourself? You've vanished to nothing at all."

But she could pay no attention to his questions, she could only say over and over, "It's Brand! It's Brand! It's my son! It's my son!"

"But here," he remonstrated at last, laughing, "we've got to begin to be sensible. What on earth are you doing here anyway? What are you doing in this miserable room, and you look half starved?"

But she could pay no attention to his questions. She gazed into his face as though she were quite crazy, her mouth open, her eyes wide-staring, her hands moving ceaselessly about his body, his hair, his face, his shoulders, his chest, his hands, her fingers touching and holding, withdrawing and clutching again as though she would never be sure of this new reality. And he, looking at her, discovered something of what he had done in leaving her for so long without any word. A passion of love caught him. He put his arms around her, held her close, whispering, "Darling Mother! Darling Mother! I've been a bad neglectful son, but I've got you for keeps now. We will never be separated again."

So, they stayed for a while, but Mrs. Amorest was no melting sentimentalist. She drew away from him at last and looking up at him with

326

the old sarcastic smile that he had known so well as a small boy, and
had been afraid of, too, said to him quite sharply, "And so at last you've
had time to think of your mother? I fancy you're just dropping in for
five minutes on your journey somewhere or another. Well, we must
be thankful for small mercies, I suppose." This opened the second stage
of their proceedings.

"Now, Mother," Brand said, raising his long heavy body from the
little creaking bed, "it's about time we began our bit of talk. You come
along to this chair. . . . Why, what's the dog?" And then more quickly,
"The dog's dead."

"Yes," she said, "he died ten minutes before you came in. That's one
thing that had been upsetting me. It's been an awful day." She gave a
little shudder. "If you hadn't come——"

"Poor little beggar! Was he your dog, Mother? Had you had him
a long time? Look here, we'll put him over there by the window." He
picked up both the dog and the cushion and took them to the end
of the room.

He settled his mother in the armchair, tried one of the other chairs
for himself and found it impossibly small, pulled a pillow finally off the
bed and settled himself on the floor at her feet.

"Now," he said, looking up at her. (Strange how quickly an old
familiar action can override the years; the touch of her fingers upon
his hair slew twenty years at one blow.) "We've got to talk seriously,
Madame. And, first, I suppose you would like to know why I came
here, frightening you to death without a word beforehand."

"Indeed, I would," she said. "I remember when you were a child
of five telling you that you never thought of others. It's true now as
it was then."

"What a thing to tell a poor child!" he answered. "But scold me. I
deserve it. I deserve it horribly." His voice fell to a graver note: "I've
been a cad, Mother, in this—a perfect cad. But you'll understand it perhaps a little bit better—although there's nothing to excuse it, mind—
when I tell you that I have been picturing you comfortably at Cheltenham with your friends and that little house with the garden you told
me about, and old Mr. Somebody the parson, and young Mr. Somebody Else the banker. I thought you were having no end of a time."

"So, I have been," she murmured, "having no end of a time."

"I haven't had a letter from you there for the last ever so long. It's
true that the last I had was from this town, but I fancied you were
here on a visit to your cousin or somebody. Then I myself was always

expecting to come home. Did you ever get a letter I wrote from San Francisco just about a year ago?"

"Yes, I got it. It was delayed a little, but I got it."

"That was before I went down to Los Angeles. I'd had the world's worst luck before that. Things were always on the point of coming right and just didn't, and then that illness in San Francisco topped everything. I ought to have been home a year and a half ago. Anyway, down to Los Angeles I went, and the luck turned as I hoped it would, right bang in my direction, has stayed there ever since, and looks like staying!"

"What were you working at, dear?"

"Oil and land are the things there. Of course, my little exploits are pretty small at present, but if the place develops, as it seems to me it's bound to, I stand to net a mighty pile. Anyway, I've made enough, buying and selling, in the last six months, to settle you comfortably for the rest of your days, old lady."

"It never occurred to you, I suppose," she asked, "that a letter or a telegram to say that you were coming would have been natural and decent?"

"To tell you the truth, Mother," he burst out, kicking out his long legs towards the fire, "I was all excited with the idea of bursting in upon you. You see, I saw you all set and cosy at Cheltenham, having the vicar in to tea. Many and many a time I pictured it to myself, you sitting there, all cosy, with the curtains drawn and the kettle humming and the cakes and bread and butter on the table and the vicar telling you how good his last sermon was. . . . Oh, you know! And me bursting in upon you like a bomb! Why! I meant to give you the fright of your life—but I didn't think it would be like this. Whatever's been happening? Where's your money gone? You had plenty last time you wrote to me?"

"Plenty!" she smiled rather scornfully into the fire. "That's not exactly the word I'd use. I don't suppose you ever gave a very great deal of thought to the amount—you were never much for details. Don't ask me what has happened to it all. Everything just went down and down. That's all I know. That's all I ever could understand from Mr. Agnew. He used to try and explain technical things to me. I know some of it had to do with railways, but the trains always seemed to me to be full whenever I went near a railway station. But stocks and shares are beyond me, and I've a kind of idea they know I don't like them by the way they run away from me."

He was serious enough by this time. Behind her light tone he was beginning to suspect something of what these last months had been to her.

"How long have you been here?" he asked her sharply. "In this house? These rooms? I'm so late as I am because I missed the train in London. We got into Southampton early this morning. I went off to London the quickest possible, got some money and came on to Cheltenham. I wasn't there half an hour. The post office told me where you were. They had forwarded a letter, they told me, only a week or so ago. I was lucky enough to catch the train on—and here I am! But how long have you been in these horrible rooms? Tell me."

"Oh, I don't know," she answered, smiling. "Long enough to want to get out of them!"

"Get out of them!" he cried, springing to his feet in a fury. "You shan't stay in them another hour! By God, you shan't."

That was so like him she thought, looking up at him lovingly, and a little sarcastically too. To leave her for so long without inquiry and then to be in a passion of rage at facts to which he had himself contributed. No imagination. He never had had any, and that was strange when his father had had so much. Not like his father at all, with his square thick-set head, his ugly nose, his loose, big-limbed body. She adored him so, as she looked at him, that her hands moved with a little flutter of desire. Then they rested quietly on her lap, and, rather drily, she said:

"And suppose I don't want to move within the next hour? I suppose you've been ordering about people in America to such an extent that you think you can do the same to me. But you've never ordered your mother about yet, and it's not likely that you'll begin now; although I'm seventy and more, I'm not in my grave yet."

How quickly they were recovering their old relations! He found himself already beginning to defer to her, to fear, ever so slightly but nevertheless sufficiently, the accuracy of her sarcasm, and to adore in her, as he had always adored, her independence and courage. It had not been with him, at all, out of sight and out of mind, but it *was* easier for him to realise things and people when they were directly there in front of him. He was realising the old lady more strongly with every moment that passed and beginning already to wonder how it was that he had managed, for so long, to get on without her.

He was walking about the room looking at the furniture, asking questions:

"But tell me, Mother—you haven't really told me a thing—what made you choose this place? Is there anyone else living here? Was that *your* dog? I must know everything."

"You must, must you? I shall tell you only as much as is good for you. As a matter of fact, there were three of us up at the top here—two other old ladies beside myself, but poor Miss Beringer died last night of heart failure. And that's her dog."

Brand whistled. "Died, did she? That can't have made things any more cheerful." He looked down at the dog. "Poor beggar—missed his mistress."

"Yes." Lucy Amorest's lip quivered. "Poor May. Oh! I wish she'd lived just for a little while, and now that you're back, you and I. . . ." The tears filled her eyes. She turned from him, bending her head in her arm in a passion of sobbing. At once he was with her. His arms were around her. He held her close to him. "Why, Mother, what's the matter? Here, old lady, bear up. It's all right now. The trouble's all over. We are going to have the most glorious time. It's all right. It's all right."

"I know . . . I know," she sobbed. "But May. . . . It was my fault. . . . She died of fright, and I might have stayed with her . . . and if you hadn't come I too . . . I was so lonely, and Agatha Payne coming in like that and the money going and no one caring. . . . Oh, Brand, if you hadn't come!"

"I know. I know. I've been a beast, a cad, a brute. I'm so selfish I deserve shooting. I'll never forgive myself for this. The trouble with me is that I never can realise anything unless I see it, but I've learnt a lesson. . . ."

She pulled away from him, smiling, wiping her eyes. "You'll be just the same a month hence—you know you will. But I gave birth to you, so I suppose I'm responsible for you in a kind of a way. I'm not going to think of these last months ever again. Although I am seventy-one I am going to begin life all over again."

"Indeed, you are!" he cried. "And you're going to begin it by leaving this house within the next half-hour. We'll go to the best hotel in Polchester tonight, and tomorrow London!"

"And the first thing I do when I get to the hotel," she told him, "will be to order a hot-water bottle. I wouldn't like to tell you how I've longed for one all this winter. You can have a hot bath when Mrs. Bloxam comes and lights the heater and all the rest of it, but every night! I should think not!"

"Mrs. Bloxam? Who's she?" Brand asked.

And of all the miraculous and stupendous surprises who should come in at that moment but Mrs. Bloxam herself!

"Oh, mum," she said, pausing in the doorway and becoming accustomed to the candle-light after the deep dark of the stairway, "I couldn't 'elp coming to see 'ow you was getting on. I was just giving Bloxam 'is tea when I said to 'im, 'Bloxam,' I said, 'I'm not 'alf comfortable in my mind about that poor Mrs. Hamorest with Miss Bellringer dead beside 'er only a yard or two away'; and I put on my shawl and come right acrost. If it would make you easier, mum——"

Then she saw a man. "Why, Lord bless us!" she cried. "'Oo's that?"

"Come in, Mrs. Bloxam, and meet my son. He's come all the way from America to look after me!"

"Why, what do you make of that!" cried Mrs. Bloxam.

"Brand, this is Mrs. Bloxam, who's been kinder to me than anyone else in the world. If it hadn't been for her I don't believe you'd have found your mother alive at all."

Brand gave Mrs. Bloxam so warm a greeting that she was more confused than she had been for many a day. She spoke breathlessly, with deep sighs intermingled, as though she had been running for a mile. "Why, to think of that, and all the way from America; and I always knew 'e was coming, didn't I, mum? When you was losing 'eart I always thought different. 'Why, mum,' I said, 'of course 'e's coming! Do you think a fine upstanding young man like that is goin' to leave 'is very own mother without a word?'—with your mother thinking all matter of dreadful things that you was dead and buried and what all. And only this very evening there was a stranger in Bloxam's tea, which I pointed out to 'im as certain to mean something good. Well, glory be to God! and all the way from America, and you're looking fine and 'ealthy, sir, if I may say so, and the very spitting image of your mother too."

All this was very pleasant, and happiness reigned.

"There's a thing you can do for us, Mrs. Bloxam," Brand said, "and that is get us a cab in about twenty minutes. My mother isn't going to stay in this horrible house another night."

"I'm sure you're right, sir," Mrs. Bloxam said, pulling herself up a little. "But as to 'orrible, I'm not so sure. I've looked after all my ladies to the best of my strength, and it's been none so easy neither with Bloxam uncertain in 'is 'abits and three children, which the youngest, Flossie, is always catching one thing and another, poor worm. I'm sure I've done my best and all them stairs to climb, and two corpses within a six month. Of course, it ain't like a 'otel, and you couldn't expect it to be with one of these old-fashioned 'ouses, and the water 'aving to be 'eated every time there's a bath, which takes hours and hours. All the same, I'm sorry not to 'ave given satisfaction, and me workin' morning and night as you may say, seein' that Bloxam is often not in of a night till three in the mornin'——"

Mrs. Amorest put her arm around Mrs. Bloxam and kissed her on her crimson cheek. "You've been an angel to me, Mrs. Bloxam. My son meant that the house isn't very bright and cheerful, and you know yourself you've often said so."

Happiness was restored. Mrs. Bloxam departed to discover a cab.

"And now—what am I to take and what am I to leave?" Mrs. Amorest cried, looking about the room.

"You're to take nothing but what you'll want for the night and for a few days in London," Brand answered. "We'll have the other things sent on."

"And the silver match-box," said Mrs. Amorest.

"Hullo! who gave you that?"

"My cousin. He left it me in his will."

"Is that all he left you? Stingy beggar!"

"Oh no, Brand. There was no reason why he should leave me anything."

When she had placed her few things in her bag she knew that there was something further that she must do. She must go in and say goodbye to Agatha Payne. How she shrank from it! That other world! She had abandoned it for ever—oh, surely for ever? To return, even for a moment, filled her with dismay. But go she must.

"Wait here for me, Brand," she said, "I must go across the passage and say goodbye to my neighbour." She looked at him with longing:

"You won't be gone while I'm away, will you?"

He hugged her and kissed her. "I won't move," he assured her.

"I don't trust you," she answered, nodding her head at him. "If I don't keep you in sight you may be in America."

She knocked on Agatha Payne's door and entered.

Within it was as though some spell had been removed. Always in that room with its close air, obscurity and old green picture, she had been conscious of discomfort and apprehension. Now because all was at last well with her, and she had passed back again into her own natural kingdom of light and air and happiness, she saw only an old woman rocking herself before a fading fire, a shabby tablecloth scattered with dirty playing-cards, a guttering candle.

But something had happened to Mrs. Payne. As she turned at the sound of the opening door Lucy Amorest could see that she was ill, her cheeks flabby and grey, her eyes wandering and excited. Something of her own fear was returning. Oh, thank God! thank God! that so soon she was escaping.

"Agatha," she said gently, "I've come to say goodbye."

Agatha Payne continued to rock herself as though she had not heard.

"I've come to say goodbye."

"Goodbye? Where are you going?"

"My son's come. Brand. And you said he wouldn't." (She could not keep back that tiny triumph.) "You see I was right after all. He came this evening. We are leaving in a quarter of an hour."

"Don't bother me with your nonsense," Agatha said. "I'll believe in your son when I see him."

"No, but it's true," Lucy Amorest persisted. "He's in my room now. We are going to a hotel for tonight and to London tomorrow."

But the other woman was pursuing her own thoughts.

"Lucy," she said, "come here."

Mrs. Amorest went close to her. Agatha Payne laid a hand on her arm. "Listen! Do you hear anything?"

Lucy listened. "No, nothing," she said.

"Don't you hear anyone knocking on the wall?"

"No."

"But you must. Listen again. Do you hear now?"

"No, I don't."

"But it's quite clear. There! Now you can hear it. She's mocking me because I did it to her. She'll be at it all night."

"It's the tap you hear, Agatha—the tap in the passage!"

"You were always a fool." She gripped Mrs. Amorest's arm more tightly. "Now you can hear it. One—two—one—two. . . . I'll beat her at that. I'll beat her."

She lurched to her feet and, leaning forward, knocked on her wall three or four times, pausing between the strokes. She looked round, a grim triumph on her sullen face. "Ah! Now she's stopped! That will keep her quiet for a bit."

Lucy Amorest moved away. "Agatha, there isn't anyone. Truly there isn't. You're imagining it." She had a passionate desire now to leave the room. Brand, all the life he brought with him, was receding. He was less real. Agatha Payne was real, and they did not belong to the same worlds, Brand and she. "Agatha, listen. You must listen. I'm going away—now, at once. I must go away."

Agatha Payne turned upon her. "Going away? Oh no, you're not. What! leave me in this house all alone with that Beringer woman! Oh no! You don't! You try it, that's all!"

"But I am. I must. My boy's here."

Agatha moved to the door and set her back to it.

"You don't leave this house—not while I'm alive in it."

Mrs. Amorest felt panic, as she had felt it earlier in the afternoon, slip over her. Where was Brand? Oh, why had she left him? If she called to him he would not hear. What should she do? And she was worn out with the troubles and the joys of that day. No strength was left in her.

"I must go. Please, Agatha. My boy's waiting."

"Your boy!" Agatha Payne answered scornfully. "That's a trick. I know you, Lucy Amorest. You were always a little liar."

"No, but it's true. Come with me into my room and see. You'll feel better in my room. It's staying in here all day by yourself that's so bad for you. Come with me and meet him."

"I won't come," she answered sulkily. "And you'll stay here. We'll stay here all night, the two of us, and when *she* comes she'll have two to deal with."

"But it isn't true, Agatha. She can't touch you. She's dead. She is indeed."

"Dead! I know better than that! You're a little liar, Lucy Amorest. That's what you are!"

"No. Come with me into her room. You can see. Say a prayer with me beside her bed. You won't be frightened any more after that. Come with me."

Her fear had left her. Its place was taken by pity. Something in Agatha Payne's eyes—something lost, wandering, hopelessly lonely—touched her very heart.

She went to her and kissed her.

Agatha Payne moved from the door. "You can go if you like," she said. "I don't want you. You can't help me. She'd never be afraid of you, you feeble little thing!"

"Tell me some way I can help you, something I can do."

"I don't want your help." She went back to her rocking-chair and sat down. "You can't help me! It's between *us*—and I'll beat her yet!"

334

She sat there, rocking, staring at the fire. She did not look round again, and so Lucy Amorest left her.

Brand was waiting. "The cab's here!" he cried. "Everything's ready. Now, old lady, step out and the sooner we leave *this* place behind us the better!"

Mrs. Bloxam was downstairs, the cab was waiting. Something that Brand placed in Mrs. Bloxam's hand at parting gave her exceeding joy. She shed a number of her happy and facile tears.

The old cab stumbled off across the cobbles. Brand put his arm about his mother and drew her close to him. She had, for a moment, a vision of the house, dead, with blind eyes, and in that upstairs room a woman alone, waiting and listening—no sound anywhere but the dripping of the tap in the hall.

Then her own joy wrapt the rest of the world away from her.

"Oh dear," she murmured, sighing with contented peace. "Is it right, do you think, to be so happy?"

LEONAUR

ALSO FROM LEONAUR

AVAILABLE IN SOFTCOVER OR HARDCOVER WITH DUST JACKET

MR MUKERJI'S GHOSTS *by S. Mukerji*—Supernatural tales from the British Raj period by India's Ghost story collector.

KIPLINGS GHOSTS *by Rudyard Kipling*—Twelve stories of Ghosts, Hauntings, Curses, Werewolves & Magic.

THE COLLECTED SUPERNATURAL AND WEIRD FICTION OF WASHINGTON IRVING: VOLUME 1 *by Washington Irving*—Including one novel 'A History of New York', and nine short stories of the Strange and Unusual.

THE COLLECTED SUPERNATURAL AND WEIRD FICTION OF WASHINGTON IRVING: VOLUME 2 *by Washington Irving*—Including three novelettes 'The Legend of the Sleepy Hollow', 'Dolph Heyliger', 'The Adventure of the Black Fisherman' and thirty-two short stories of the Strange and Unusual.

THE COLLECTED SUPERNATURAL AND WEIRD FICTION OF JOHN KENDRICK BANGS: VOLUME 1 *by John Kendrick Bangs*—Including one novel 'Toppleton's Client or A Spirit in Exile', and ten short stories of the Strange and Unusual.

THE COLLECTED SUPERNATURAL AND WEIRD FICTION OF JOHN KENDRICK BANGS: VOLUME 2 *by John Kendrick Bangs*—Including four novellas 'A House-Boat on the Styx', 'The Pursuit of the House-Boat', 'The Enchanted Typewriter' and 'Mr. Munchausen' of the Strange and Unusual.

THE COLLECTED SUPERNATURAL AND WEIRD FICTION OF JOHN KENDRICK BANGS: VOLUME 3 *by John Kendrick Bangs*—Including twor novellas 'Olympian Nights', 'Roger Camerden: A Strange Story', and ten short stories of the Strange and Unusual.

THE COLLECTED SUPERNATURAL AND WEIRD FICTION OF MARY SHELLEY: VOLUME 1 *by Mary Shelley*—Including one novel 'Frankenstein or the Modern Prometheus', and fourteen short stories of the Strange and Unusual.

THE COLLECTED SUPERNATURAL AND WEIRD FICTION OF MARY SHELLEY: VOLUME 2 *by Mary Shelley*—Including one novel 'The Last Man', and three short stories of the Strange and Unusual.

THE COLLECTED SUPERNATURAL AND WEIRD FICTION OF AMELIA B. EDWARDS *by Amelia B. Edwards*—Contains two novelettes 'Monsieur Maurice', and 'The Discovery of the Treasure Isles', one ballad 'A Legend of Boisguilbert' and seventeen short stories to cill the blood.

LEONAUR

ALSO FROM LEONAUR
AVAILABLE IN SOFTCOVER OR HARDCOVER WITH DUST JACKET

THE COMPLETE FOUR JUST MEN: VOLUME 2 *by Edgar Wallace—The Law of the Four Just Men & The Three Just Men*—disillusioned with a world where the wicked and the abusers of power perpetually go unpunished, the Just Men set about to rectify matters according to their own standards, and retribution is dispensed on swift and deadly wings.

THE COMPLETE RAFFLES: 1 *by E. W. Hornung—The Amateur Cracksman & The Black Mask*—By turns urbane gentleman about town and accomplished cricketer, life is just too ordinary for Raffles and that sets him on a series of adventures that have long been treasured as a real antidote to the 'white knights' who are the usual heroes of the crime fiction of this period.

THE COMPLETE RAFFLES: 2 *by E. W. Hornung—A Thief in the Night & Mr Justice Raffles*—By turns urbane gentleman about town and accomplished cricketer, life is just too ordinary for Raffles and that sets him on a series of adventures that have long been treasured as a real antidote to the 'white knights' who are the usual heroes of the crime fiction of this period.

THE COLLECTED SUPERNATURAL AND WEIRD FICTION OF WILKIE COLLINS: VOLUME 1 *by Wilkie Collins*—Contains one novel 'The Haunted Hotel', one novella 'Mad Monkton', three novelettes 'Mr Percy and the Prophet', 'The Biter Bit' and 'The Dead Alive' and eight short stories to chill the blood.

THE COLLECTED SUPERNATURAL AND WEIRD FICTION OF WILKIE COLLINS: VOLUME 2 *by Wilkie Collins*—Contains one novel 'The Two Destinies', three novellas 'The Frozen deep', 'Sister Rose' and 'The Yellow Mask' and two short stories to chill the blood.

THE COLLECTED SUPERNATURAL AND WEIRD FICTION OF WILKIE COLLINS: VOLUME 3 *by Wilkie Collins*—Contains one novel 'Dead Secret,' two novelettes 'Mrs Zant and the Ghost' and 'The Nun's Story of Gabriel's Marriage' and five short stories to chill the blood.

FUNNY BONES *selected by Dorothy Scarborough*—An Anthology of Humorous Ghost Stories.

MONTEZUMA'S CASTLE AND OTHER WEIRD TALES *by Charles B. Cory*—Cory has written a superb collection of eighteen ghostly and weird stories to chill and thrill the avid enthusiast of supernatural fiction.

SUPERNATURAL BUCHAN *by John Buchan*—Stories of Ancient Spirits, Uncanny Places & Strange Creatures.

LEONAUR

ALSO FROM LEONAUR
AVAILABLE IN SOFTCOVER OR HARDCOVER WITH DUST JACKET

THE COLLECTED SCIENCE FICTION AND FANTASY OF STANLEY G. WEINBAUM 1—INTERPLANETARY ODYSSEYS by Stanley G. Weinbaum—Classic Tales of Interplanetary Adventure Including: A Martian Odyssey, its Sequel Valley of Dreams, the Complete 'Ham' Hammond Stories and Others.

THE COLLECTED SCIENCE FICTION AND FANTASY OF STANLEY G. WEINBAUM 2—OTHER EARTHS by Stanley G. Weinbaum—Classic Futuristic Tales Including: *Dawn of Flame* & its Sequel The Black Flame, plus The Revolution of 1960 & Others.

THE COLLECTED SCIENCE FICTION AND FANTASY OF STANLEY G. WEINBAUM 3—STRANGE GENIUS by Stanley G. Weinbaum—Classic Tales of the Human Mind at Work Including the Complete Novel The New Adam, the 'van Manderpootz' Stories and Others.

THE COLLECTED SCIENCE FICTION AND FANTASY OF STANLEY G. WEINBAUM 4—THE BLACK HEART by Stanley G. Weinbaum—Classic Strange Tales Including: the Complete Novel The Dark Other, Plus Proteus Island and Others.

THE COLLECTED SCIENCE FICTION & FANTASY OF JACK LONDON 1—BEFORE ADAM & OTHER STORIES by Jack London—included in this Volume Before Adam The Scarlet Plague A Relic of the Pliocene When the World Was Young The Red One Planchette A Thousand Deaths Goliah A Curious Fragment The Rejuvenation of Major Rathbone.

THE COLLECTED SCIENCE FICTION & FANTASY OF JACK LONDON 2—THE IRON HEEL & OTHER STORIES by Jack London—included in this Volume The Iron Heel The Enemy of All the World The Shadow and the Flash The Strength of the Strong The Unparalleled Invasion The Dream of Debs.

THE COLLECTED SCIENCE FICTION & FANTASY OF JACK LONDON 3—THE STAR ROVER & OTHER STORIES by Jack London—included in this Volume The Star Rover The Minions of Midas The Eternity of Forms The Man With the Gash.

THE CRETAN TEAT by Brian Aldiss—The Cretan Teat is a wry and comic novel that interweaves its own fiction with an inner fiction about the discovery of a Byzantine painting of the Mother of the Blessed Virgin Mary suckling the infant Jesus and a fake ikon that becomes an instrument of Nemesis.